I0817876

A Rum Truck

By Mike Avitabile

Printed in the United States by Lumberloft Press

ISBN 978-1-7345497-1-3

www.mikeavitabile.com

www.lumberloftpress.com

For CK

This book would not have been possible without you…

or your endless need for naps

One

"I've always had a thing for rum."

She looked at me with a pair of 'whatever' eyes, like I was nothing and she was something better. I wanted to just walk away. To spit on her shoes. Give her the finger. Run her over with a scooter. Stick pins into a voodoo doll. Anything. I wanted to do anything other than be there talking to her. But there I was. Doing that. I couldn't pull myself away.

"I've always had a thing for boring, pedestrian conversation," she replied.

Then came the eyes again. I was thinking about a red scooter. Blue would have been alright, too. Just not yellow. No thank you. But if I had to, I could run her down in a yellow Vespa and later explain the color choice to whoever saw it happen. They would understand.

"Pedestrian?" I asked.

For a moment, I thought she was reading my mind and she knew about the scooter fantasy that I was having.

"What?"

I couldn't blame her for asking me to repeat myself. The music was pounding so loudly that it was almost impossible to hear my voice.

"I said…'pedestrians?' What do they have to do with rum?"

Yeah. Change the subject. Nice. It was also an honest question. I don't know a lot of words. I thought pedestrian meant, you know, *pedestrian*.

She didn't say anything and just shook her head. Her hands were bracing her body as we sat on a bench, and she propped herself up slightly and then rested again before speaking. She had rings on every single one of her fingers. What a bitch.

"Pedestrian. It means dull. Or, in this case, purposeless. Or pathetic. Or pointless. *Ped-es-tri-an*."

It was a parade of P words. I felt like I was in an episode of *Dawson's Creek* or a Woody Allen movie. I had never heard anyone sound so smug in real life.

"Ah."

I slugged back the rest of my drink. She looked me in the eyes and waited for me to continue. So I did.

"That's a shitty thing to have a thing for, huh?"

"You're telling me."

"Yeah."

I stood up with every intention of leaving her alone on that bench. She looked up at me with a completely ridiculous and out-of-the-blue sense of longing, like she suddenly gave a shit about me. And then she held out her plastic cup.

"Get me a refill, pretty please?"

Instinctively, I reached for my wallet. Not to pull it out, but just to reassure myself that I still had it and that it would be full of money when I went back to the bar…kind of like how you look at your wrist when someone asks you the time, even if you're not wearing a watch.

"You bet."

I started around the corner of the bench and toward the liquor bottles lined up across the wall.

"I'm having a gin with blah blah blah," she said.

I was out of earshot and glad of it. Girls on spring break are fucking awful.

I was in a club. Cesar Club, they called it. Because that was its name. It sits in the bass-thumping heart of an all-inclusive beachside resort in the city of Puerto Vallarta. That's in Mexico, in case you don't have access to a map. I have no clue what night of the week it was, but it was March, and that meant that there were probably hundreds or thousands of drunk college kids stumbling around. They all had only two things in their sunburned heads: sex and booze. Same goes for me.

Cesar Club wasn't really much of a club. The bar was poorly stocked, and the bartenders were poorly skilled. Fantastic combination, really. The bartenders all ran around like those firecrackers that whiz off in a bunch of different directions when they burst. They scrambled everywhere behind the counter, they were annoyingly loud, and they were mostly pointless. They never seemed to be helping any specific person, but they were never idle or available. It was a fucking time trap, and it's a wonder that any drinks were served at all.

In fact, there was just one guy who was doing any bit of anything behind that bar. He looked very excited, like he had a secret erection or an ice pack under each armpit. Or maybe both. He was sweating from his brow and his nose so hard that he flicked drops of sweat from his face every time he jerked around. You had to pull your cup as far away as you could from his side of the bar when he was turned around, otherwise you might end up with some extra salt in your margarita. No bueno.

If the fire code limited the club to a hundred people, then there were at least two hundred in there at the moment, not counting the staff. The bouncers at the door were less interested in their jobs than anyone I had met the entire week. And that is quite a tall statement, but I stand behind it. I actually think that one of them was asleep on his stool when we got there. He just sat there and didn't move while another guy took our cover.

I leaned on the bar like I had been trained to do by watching people in the countless commercials and TV shows and movies and billboards and other bars that I had been in. I didn't bother to take my money out of my wallet and wave it around in my hand like a pour-me-a-drink-flag. I had already learned that one of the firecrackers would take it, smile, tilt his ear toward me, nod at my request, and then never come back. I was too thirsty to be charitable. And by that, I mean that I wasn't drunk enough to return to that bitch sitting on the bench just yet.

I turned my head and looked over my shoulder to see if she was still there. A fat guy was blocking my view. Dammit.

"Wachoo want for thee girl?"

The only useful bartender had finally made it over to me.

"I'll have a Private Reserve and coke. And…"

"Yeah, rum and coke. I know, señor. Wachoo want for thee girl?"

He nodded beyond my shoulder and I looked back. I started to wonder how this bartender could have such a good memory. It was impressive. But then again, that was his job. Also, the probability was strong that I was going to be buying a drink for a girl. And even if I wasn't, he probably knew that there was a chance that I would buy that drink even if there was no girl to bring it back to. I wouldn't want to look stupid. This guy had it all calculated.

"A gin and something."

"Yoooooou got it, señor!"

He hurried off and started pouring the drinks. I didn't pay attention to the gin thing. I didn't even care what he made. He could have lined the cup with sawdust…it was all the same to me. It was something else. But once he set up my drink, I watched like an eagle over a river full of trout. Or some shit like that. The bottle of rum tipped up and began to glug-glug-

glug out of the spout and through the stacked shapes of ice. His finger was on the soda trigger, but he held it steady. Glug-glug…glug…glug-glug-glug… My eyebrows raised in anticipation. Glug-glug. Glug-glug. His finger slid slightly down the button, but he still didn't press it in. Glug-glug-glug. My eyes were bugging out of my head.

And then, when the cup was practically full of rum and ice, he hit the soda button for what couldn't have amounted to more than a half of a second. A sliver of lime was twisted and dropped in, and my rum and coke came sliding across the bar and into my hand. The thing had the color of a swimming pool mixed with a glass of iced tea. I licked my lips and slapped down some bills on the bar. Almost reluctantly, I grabbed the gin drink too, and I turned my body around toward the rest of the club. Over my shoulder I yelled a *thank you*, and although I wasn't looking, I knew he was already working on his next drink. That guy was a soldier of the beverage industry, and he deserved a medal of honor. Or at least a day off.

The music dipped down for a rare second before the opening beats of one of the more popular Backstreet Boys songs began charging down my ears. Fuck. Locals hit the small, wooden dance floor as if the song was the newest hit. Maybe it was, to them. It was almost surprising to see any locals there at all. But then again, we weren't in Cancún. I waded through the sea of churning bodies, past the stationary fat man, and I headed toward the bench where my gin drinker should have been sitting. And she wasn't.

In her place was a row of ugly girls, and at the end of the line was my buddy, Booker. Booker and I had come down to Mexico together. Although neither of us was actually in college, we were the right age, so we pretended that we were students and we fit in just fine. His story was that he was a mechanical engineering student at Pepperdine, and mine was that I was pre-med at UCLA. We had gone to high school together and were now members of the same fraternity, just at different schools. Beta Beta Beta, if anybody asked.

These girls were a sobering sight. I clutched my rum and coke like I was afraid that one of them would take it away from me. Booker was always pulling weird shit like this. As if he just liked to test my limits, he would sometimes show up with the most horrendous looking girl and then act as if he was totally serious about trying to get with her. This time, his arm was swung around a particularly wretched looking beast. She had flabby, pale arms and a tight, neon shirt that hugged her lumpy torso in all the wrong ways.

"Hey there, big man. What's happening here?"

Booker looked at me with all of the intent of a guy who didn't want to burst out laughing, but he just couldn't hold it together. He hunched over and threw his free hand up to catch his face as he cackled into it. The girl to his left just sat there, unflinchingly cool, despite the fact that there was nothing cool about her or the situation. Or her ugly friends. Or my friend, for that matter.

"Blake," he muttered as he swallowed down his laughs, "I'd like you to meet Vanessa."

He pointed to the one closest to him.

"This is Shayna."

She was the one beside Vanessa.

"Mandy?"

He gestured to the next one down the line, to which she nodded.

"And that's Carla."

She was the last one, and she was the one closest to me. Carla was probably the ugliest of them all. Lucky me. I had to turn my attention back to Booker or I was going to have to walk away. All of these girls were ugly. Just ugly. There wasn't even one that I could imagine wanting to see in daylight.

"That's great, Booker. Great. So what happened to the girl I was sitting with here a minute ago? Did this one sit on her?"

I motioned my head to the one closest to me. The ugly girls all immediately took notice of my extra drink and stared at it like a pack of circling vultures, as if I might offer it to one of them. Apparently my comment didn't faze them.

Booker's answer was exactly what I had expected it to be. He looked out at the dance floor like a captain on the bow of his ship, his right hand extended over his brow to block out the strobe lights that beamed down from the ceiling. I didn't even need to hear the words come out of his mouth. I pulled the drink to my lips and tried to gulp it all down as fast as I could. The four beasts stared up at me, and one of them let out an intentionally loud sigh. I really wasn't in the mood. Halfway finished, I tipped the cup back and let the drink roll away from my mouth.

"Sigh all you want, you're not getting a free drink from me. Or any guy in this bar."

Booker stood up almost on cue, knowing that this was no longer a safe place to be. I tilted the drink back and socked away the rest. I slapped the cup down on the railing behind the bench – that poor bench, buckling beneath those behemoths – and I spun on my heels in the direction of the bar again. Booker followed behind me and made no gesture to the girls whatsoever. He trotted alongside me, laughing.

"What was that, man?"

"Dude, those girls were *disgusting*. Let me ask *you*. What was that?"

Booker smiled and reached for his wallet as we approached the bar.

"That was obviously my fantasy. Four ugly bitches in a foreign country."

He leaned up against the bar and held his cash out in his hand. So naïve.

"Nice fantasy. Sorry to ruin it for you."

I leaned in and pulled his wad of money from his fingers, though he didn't let it slip without a good tug.

"What the shit, man? I want another drink! You're not cutting me off because of that."

He tried to swipe his money back, but I pulled it toward my chest, and he whiffed.

"Those firecrackers will take your money right from your hand and never make you a drink," I explained.

He nodded slowly. I could see him trying to think of what to do next.

"That guy with the round face is the only one here who could make a drink to save his life. I'll get him."

"Think that situation comes up often?" he asked.

"What situation?"

"Making a drink to save his life. Think he has to face that situation often?"

"Shut up, man. You know what I meant."

Booker smiled.

"Yeah, of course. You meant that he oftentimes is held at gunpoint while making a drink and that he doesn't collapse under the pressure. I get it, I get it. I was just asking, that's all."

"Shut up."

The round-faced man came over and took Booker's drink order. Rum and coke. I yelled to the bartender to make two, and he nodded with his back turned to us.

"So he's hanging off of a cliff, right? And a man is holding on to his arm with a tight grip. But the man is thirsty."

I gave Booker my best deadpan stare. I wanted to laugh, but I also needed to pretend like I wasn't amused.

"And the guy who is going to save him is like, *'Hey, I really could use a drink right now. Trade you for your life.'* And you're saying that he is the only guy behind the bar who could pull it off?"

"That's exactly, *exactly*, what I'm saying. You fucking asshole."

Booker kept smiling. When our drinks came, he took a sip of mine before giving it to me.

"You're welcome."

"Thanks, buddy."

Smoky fog began to billow in from the rafters, paired with the familiar sound of a fog machine doing its work. It's a hollow, quiet hairdryer sound that really isn't replicated in any other mechanical item that I can think of. The pink, blue, and yellow strobing streams of light began to filter and dampen through the haze. The fat man was still standing in the same place, and I started to wonder if he had moved all night. Maybe it just wasn't worth his effort. Maybe standing still netted the same outcome as moving around, but without the annoyance of actually having to move. He might have had it right the whole time. And there I was, judging his laziness when in fact, he was just being efficient. A small, benevolent part of me wanted to walk up to him and start a conversation. The rest of me decided that gulping down my drink would make for a better evening.

"There are so many nasty looking girls here," Booker observed.

"Some of them aren't *that* bad looking. They just look like sluts."

"I guess we could wrap it up twice if we had to."

"Don't talk about putting condoms on like it's a group activity. *We* aren't wrapping up anything."

"You'd put a condom on for me if I needed you to though."

"What the fuck? No, I wouldn't."

"To save your life?" He started laughing.

"To save my own life, sure. Not to save yours. You can catch whatever the fuck you catch. I'm not putting a condom on you."

"A second condom."

"Oh yeah. Not gay. It's already in one condom, so it's not still a dick."

"Exactly."

"Let me know when that situation comes up, and you can see what I do to help you out."

There were girls everywhere. Even though most of them were ignoring us, we were still determining which ones we'd have sex with and which ones we wouldn't. This is how most guys that I know play their cards. We are always assuming that there's a chance. I call it penile optimism. You hope for the best, you prepare for the best, you act shocked when it doesn't happen, and then you shrug it off and keep trying.

We weren't exactly the best looking brothers from Beta Beta Beta. Keep in mind that we were its only two members. Booker hadn't shaved for a few weeks. My face, while hairless, was sunburned beyond socially acceptable levels. From drinking all week, our guts were bloated and puffy, and our club clothes were now going on their third consecutive night out.

We smelled. But to our benefit, everything in Cesar Club smelled. So there was really no way of knowing what our specific odors were until we were outside. If we got to that point and we were with anyone else, we were most of the way there. Girls don't leave clubs with crusty dudes like us unless they're so fucked up that they can't think straight. And if they're that, then we're probably in luck. I know that makes me sound a little bit like a rapist, but I promise that I am not.

Booker and I took turns visiting old Round Face at the bar until some of the shitty songs that the DJ was playing started to sound like they were worth dancing to. The drinks were so cheap that it was hard not to go back. Even if you factor in the lost cash for every time that Round Face wasn't able to serve us and one of the other bartenders took our money until he became available, it was a cheap night out. There wasn't even a cover charge. Now, I know that just a few moments ago, I mentioned the guy at the door who took our cover. And now I'm saying there wasn't even a cover charge.

I get it. Very confusing. All I can say is, you shouldn't be questioning my legitimacy here. That's a terrible way to start this relationship, and we have a long story ahead of us. How about you trust me and question something else instead? Like Mexico, for example. Ninety percent of that country is a scam, and you're doubting the guy who is just trying to tell you a story? Come on. If you don't believe me, that's not my problem. It probably means you have intimacy issues. You should get that checked out.

Theoretically, there was a cover charge for anyone not actually staying in a room at the resort. But since the bouncers didn't give a shit about anything but sitting there on their asses, we had never been asked to fork up whatever the cost was – *except* for that night. See? Legitimate explanation. In fact, the lack of cover was most of the reason we traveled to this specific resort and the shitty club in the first place. The ones near our hotel just wanted to rip us off. Cesar Club, on the other hand, was only interested in ripping itself off. I can only imagine it has since been shut down.

"You have a goal tonight?" I asked Booker at some point.

"Yeah. To get laid."

"I meant a drink goal."

"No. My goal is to get laid."

"I want to have fifteen drinks. I think I'm on twelve now. I can make it."

"I want to get laid."

"Yes, I heard that."

"How do you even remember how many drinks you have?"

It was a good question, but he already knew the answer. I had been doing this for a while. I could get somewhat preoccupied with numbers. He usually didn't give me a hard time about it, though he probably should have. It was a little O.C.D. and a little lame, but I couldn't help it.

Some people keep beer caps or straws or napkins rolled up in their pockets. Others keep some change in their pocket for each drink, and they count it all later. Others don't try to count at all because they are just looking to get drunk and that's that. Some ask their friends to count. Some don't even drink. I just kept count in my head. I would probably have a much better time if I just didn't care, but I don't know how to do that.

Booker made his way back to the bar for his next drink. Mine was still half full. I shook my head when he looked to me for another round. He came back with one anyway, so I double fisted for a little while. And that's when they came over. There were three of them.

They were fucking hot. And not in the conventional, spring-break-college-chick way. They didn't have wet t-shirts or blonde hair or any of that shit. They were just regular brown-haired girls with tight little bodies all wrapped up in regular, brown-haired girl clothes. And that was fucking hot to me.

Because all night, you can sit in a club filled with these testosterone-juiced college guys, and you see them pick off one girl after another after another. And it can get you in a down place after a while. But when a group of hot girls strolls up to you, even if they're not as hot as some of the other girls, the fact that they come up to *you*...that right there makes them the hottest ones around. It's all about perspective, to me. And if you don't think that way, you're just going to be pissed off at the testosterone freaks who steal away all of your girls. And that's no way to spend a vacation.

They looked drunk, and I'm sure we did too. The cutest one came over to me and put her hand on my shoulder like she was a mentoring father or a basketball coach.

"What are you drinking?"

Great opening line. I already liked her.

"Private Reserve. What's your name? And what's in your cup?"

"Meghan. Rum and coke."

"What kind of rum?" I asked.

"I don't know."

"You should get Private Reserve. It's *by far* the best one here."

She flashed a pretty, white smile at my face.

"Wanna buy me one?"

I looked over at Round Face behind the counter, and I nodded without looking back at her. I stepped back to the altar. With a drink in each hand, I leaned up against the bar and waited for him to come over. I gulped away at the emptier of the two cups with the hope that I could drop it to the floor before he saw me. Just as I was slugging down the last mouthful, he tilted his head up to me and a small, curved smile spread across the right side of his mouth. He had a look on his face like, *already?* I nodded. He spoke to me in a smooth, quiet voice.

"For the lady, señor?"

If I hadn't known any better, I would have thought that he was concerned by the way he gently asked me, almost wincing as each word slipped out of his beach ball face. Like he knew how fucked up I was just by looking at me. Like anyone wouldn't know that by looking at me. My face was probably drooping and hanging like the jowls of a bulldog.

"Si. El Rum y El Coke. Si?

"Yoooooou got it, amigo!"

His hesitation wore off almost instantly. Before I could fish out the bills from my wallet, the drink was ready and in my hand, smelling so sweet and sticky that I wanted to lap it all up right there and forget about the girl whose name I already couldn't remember. I turned around half expecting her and her hot friends to be gone. But they were still there. Jackpot.

I strolled back to the group, trying to look cool without looking like I was trying. I probably didn't pull it off. Booker had his arm around one of the girls, his drink in that same hand. He was smiling, but it was a fake smile. I could see that behind his grin, he was trying to think of a clever way to maneuver the drink to his other hand. He wanted a sip, and it was awkwardly stuck on the other side of the girl's face. I handed the rum and coke to my girl and forced myself back into the conversation.

"So are you guys staying here?"

They all turned and looked at me, but none of them spoke.

"We already went over this while you were gone," Booker answered.

"I wasn't asking you. I was asking these nice ladies."

I smiled at them, and they gave me pity smiles back.

"Yes," my girl said. "We've been here since Sunday."

"We went over that while you were gone too," Booker added.

"Thanks for the recap. Why don't you have some of your drink?"

He looked at me and shook his head. He looked like he wanted to tell me to fuck off, but he restrained himself.

"I'm fine."

"Yeah. You look fine."

"I am."

The girl he was wrapped around started telling some boring ass story that no one seemed interested in. I don't even know if she was interested in telling it. Everyone was drunk. It didn't really matter. I wasn't paying attention anyway. All I could do was watch Booker eyeing his drink. It was too amusing to ignore. The girl kept on yapping, and he kept staring at his hand, like he couldn't just take his arm off of her to take a sip of his drink. The fog machine was chugging again, and I could hear it hissing as it released its clouds into the air. The haze that wrapped around us is all that I can really remember until we went outside. I don't remember how Booker got his arm back.

These girls just wouldn't leave us alone. And although we didn't want them to, it's hard to understand why they wouldn't have just moved on. We weren't anything special. We were also a guy short, which left one of the girls on her own. Fog kept pumping into the room, and there was a moment where it started to make me feel uncomfortable. I was afraid we were all going to suffocate. Why did there need to be so much fog anyway? Were the people there *really* that ugly?

My girl just couldn't get enough of me. She laughed at everything I said. She kept touching my arm, wrapping her hands around my neck, running them through my hair, touching my face, touching my lips.

Somebody made the suggestion that we leave, and no one disagreed. My penis started to get excited.

Round Face gave me a thumbs up when he saw me and Booker staggering toward the door. I made a mental note to give him a fat tip the next night. He took care of me all night, and I wanted to return the favor. We got out to the sidewalk where the mating dance continued.

"Which one of these towers are you guys staying in?" Booker asked.

"We went over this while you were gone," I replied.

"We did?"

"No. That was a joke."

My girl laughed, almost too loudly. It wasn't that funny.

"We're in that one," she said, pointing in the general direction of all three towers behind us.

"How tall are they?" I asked.

The girls all looked at each other and started to think harder than they really should have. What a stupid question. I don't know why I asked it.

"Probably a few hundred feet," my girl replied.

"I meant how many floors. Actually, I take it back. I don't care."

"We're on the eighteenth floor," she added.

"Yeah? Should we go up there?"

"Uh huh," she slurred.

Booker's girl stepped in, as girls do.

"Meghan, are you sure? We have to wake up early tomorrow."

"No, we don't."

"Yeah. No, you don't," I added.

The girl didn't smile or laugh.

"We *said* we were going to wake up early tomorrow."

"*No,* we didn't."

Booker jumped in.

"How about we walk you up there, and if you don't want to hang out by the time we get there, we'll just leave. How about that?"

"You can leave," I said to Booker, unhappy with his compromise. "Why do I have to leave?"

"You can't leave a place you aren't," he replied.

"A place I'm not?"

"Come on. How about we.... Wait. Where'd your friend go?"

We had been sparring long enough for us to lose track of the third girl that neither of us were interested in. She was somewhere farther down the sidewalk, walking toward a group of three Mexicans. *Shit*, I thought. This chick was going to start some conversation with these guys and ruin our whole chance. My whole chance and Booker's chance too. The damned third girl. Why weren't we paying attention to her? *Shit*, I thought again.

The guys that she was walking toward were in the middle of an argument. They didn't even see her approaching. One of the guys appeared to be trying to make a delivery to the club, but it was definitely after hours. The other two guys looked like they were telling him to leave. The other two were wearing uniforms, so I assumed they were associated with the resort in some way. The girl just stood there listening to the three men arguing in Spanish. I don't think she understood any of it, but maybe she did. I don't know. They disregarded her until there was a natural break in the discussion, and then they all turned to her and tried to find out what she wanted.

As it always goes in Mexico, they were absolutely courteous and polite to her, even in the midst of their argument. There is always the chance that she could spend less money if she felt at all uncomfortable. That consequence is never good for a Mexican in Mexico. On the resort, that is.

Booker's girl, now looking somewhat disinterested in him, began to head toward her friend as some sort of protective gesture. My girl stayed with me, her arm wrapped around my side and her hip pressed against mine. My chances of hooking up with her felt like they were diminishing with each second that passed. I wanted to grab her and run behind the club and pull our shorts down to our ankles and just go at it. She seemed like she was up for it. I didn't want to hinge my chances of getting laid on the volatility of some other girl that Booker couldn't close.

"You're gonna lose the girl," I warned him.

"She has a boyfriend," my girl stated.

"Come on. Really?"

"Yeah. But he's not here."

"We'll pretend you didn't say that."

Booker just stood there staring at the two girls as they tried talking with the group of three Mexicans. Women. Always with the talking. The conversation continued on, and on, and on, and fucking on and on. The argument appeared to be shelved for a bit now that two attractive girls were there. After a few minutes had passed, my girl loosened her grip on my waist. *Shit,* I thought. The window had closed. Now she was curious what her friends were up to, and her interest in me was waning. One of the Mexicans in a uniform put his arm around Booker's girl and gave her a sideways hug. His arm hovered on her shoulder afterward, hesitant to leave and slyly remaining in contact with her.

"She has a boyfriend," Booker muttered, shaking his head.

My girl let go of me entirely and looked at me with her sweet eyes.

"I'm gonna go see what my friends are doing, okay?"

That was it. My chance was gone. I gritted my teeth.

"Yeah. It's fine."

She smiled.

"Be back in a minute."

Yeah, right. She started to walk away. I looked at her ass, swaying from side to side in her white shorts. I imagined running up to her and grabbing her by the arm and swinging her around, passionately begging her to run off to the beach with me. She would give me a look of disgust and then continue on walking toward her friends. I knew there was no chance at that point. Booker looked at me helplessly and said nothing.

"Dude…that fucking fifth wheel. She fucked it up. She fucked it up!"

I was almost what you would call livid. Booker just looked at me and sadly shook his head slowly from side to side.

"Wanna go back inside? There are lots of girls in there."

He nodded his head toward the thumping club, and I just imagined the disappointment of Round Face as I came back inside, stag.

"No. I wanted *that* girl…"

I turned my head back to the group to find the ass that I was just staring at. She was cuddled up next to her friend, and the six of them were laughing and having a good old time, like they had known each other for years. Ugh. If we had one more friend, that could have still been us. Stupid fifth wheel.

"Well, let's just wait here. I'm sure they'll come back."

We both knew that wasn't true. The longer we stood there, the longer we looked like total saps. It had been almost five minutes at that point, since Booker's girl had wandered away. They weren't coming back, and we both knew it. Yet we continued to stand there.

That's when I saw it.

There are those quintessential moments in life, those undistilled, sweet, and utterly satisfying moments when everything in your mind just redirects toward one thing. The rest of the world ceases to exist. Nothing else is there, and nothing else matters. Those moments are as close to perfection as you'll ever get.

I forgot all about the girls, the Mexicans, my dick, the bar in the club, Round Face, my dick, and everything else. I forgot about Booker, even. And my dick. If this were a movie, the music in the background would start to get really echoey, and every sound would drown out except for a solo trumpet, and even that would be echoey too. You would start to hear my heartbeat, and the picture would slow down. That's the movie way of saying what I just said. It's a completely focused and dedicated moment. With a trumpet.

About thirty feet away from me was a short, box-like truck. It had a two-door cab and a cargo box in the back, shaped just like a U-Haul but without the logos. From where we were standing on the sidewalk, I estimated that it was about ten to twelve feet long. I tapped Booker on the arm and turned him with ease toward the magnificent-looking vehicle. He gasped out loud.

I had never seen a truck like this before. But I had dreamed of it, I think. It was stunningly beautiful.

It was not a U-Haul. Painted on its side was the proud and gorgeous logo of Mexico's finest rum. It was the same rum that Booker and I had been binging on for the entire week. When we weren't ordering it at the bar, we were slugging back sips from the bottle as we lay out by the beach. Private Reserve. It was not a shockingly original name, but the taste was just fantastic, and it made up for any shortcomings that its marketing team had made when naming it. And now, this glorious truck sat on its four wheels in front of us, no doubt stocked in full with cases upon cases of our liquid gold.

Gears turned in my drunk head. The Mexican who wasn't wearing a uniform was the driver, that much was obvious. He must have been late with his delivery, and now the two men working for the resort had a problem with him. Or, they had a problem before our girls strolled their way. Then the problem got put on hold. Booker and I were staring at the truck in silent awe. I eyed the driver's hands. They were empty.

"Booker…" I said quietly, as if the volume of my voice mattered at all.

No one would have been able to hear us with the thumping of the club to our backs.

"Yeah?"

I watched the driver as he circled around the group in a quick run. He looked like he was acting out a part of some story. Everyone laughed, and then he did it again.

"I don't think he has his keys on him."

He looked at me and raised his eyebrows, and then he looked back at the truck. It was so beautiful, it was hard not to stare.

"How can you tell?"

"I didn't hear them jingling when he ran just now."

"Oh, now you have superhuman hearing?"

"Yes. Yes, I do."

"Okay. He doesn't have his keys. So what?"

I looked directly at him.

"Let's take that truck."

He turned abruptly away from staring at it and looked me in the eyes. He was so drunk, even I could tell. And I was really drunk too.

"Take it?"

I nodded.

"How? Like, carry it?"

"No. Not carry it. What the fuck is wrong with you?"

He looked at me as if he had no clue how one would take a vehicle.

"I think the driver left the keys in the ignition," I said.

He rolled his head back to the truck and then back again to me.

"You want to take it?"

"Yeah. It's *full* of rum."

"You think so?"

"Fuck, of course it is. That needs to be ours. *Something* tonight needs to be ours."

I glanced back at the girls and at the Mexicans. They were so preoccupied with whatever story the driver was telling, no one would have noticed if I was shot dead on the sidewalk by a rifle held by Bigfoot. I had on my serious face, and Booker knew not to mess with it. He just had to decide whether or not to approve. His decision was fast.

"Okay."

The club walls pulsed angrily behind us. I gave Booker a slight shove, and we started walking slowly into the street. I looked at the girls a few times, wondering if they'd notice us. A part of me was hoping that they would. Maybe they'd come back over, and then I'd eventually get laid that night. But they didn't look. So we walked across the cobblestone driveway of the resort. The truck was parked alongside an island at the center of the circular entrance. The logo looked simply beautiful. As we got closer to it, I started to smile.

Booker and I both headed for the driver's door. Although it may have seemed to someone who was watching — and hopefully no one was — that we were about to argue for the driver's spot, we weren't. I always drove for the two of us, whether we were drunk or sober. He was just trying to make himself seem less conspicuous, as the passenger door was facing the club, the driver, and practically everyone else. The driver's door was facing nothing but a small row of shrubs and plants. We crept alongside the truck and had a moment of contemplation as I peered inside and saw the keys dangling from the ignition.

"Are you sure you want to do this?"

I looked at Booker. He looked insulted, as if we had been planning this for years, since we were kids.

"Of course I want to do this. I want this as much as you do."

He was obviously wasted, so I decided to not provoke him to talk anymore. I opened the door slowly to avoid any noticeable creaking, and I ushered him inside as I kept watch. He slid stealthily across the bench and flattened his body against the seat, diagonal and out of sight of anyone on the other side of the truck. I winced as I made my next move, fully drunk yet also aware that I was about to enter a don't-look-back type of situation. I gasped a deep breath and hopped into the cab, pulling the door behind me but not shutting it to avoid making a loud noise. The keys tapped against my leg. Booker and I looked at each other.

Here we are, I thought. Sitting inside of a truck full of rum, in Mexico. It was one or two o'clock in the morning, and we had no business being behind the wheel of a vehicle, let alone one that we did not own. And especially not one full of alcohol. But, oh man, it seemed *so* right.

I gripped my fingers on the keys as Booker lay still. I stepped down softly onto the emergency brake to release it. I didn't dare to look at the group on the sidewalk. It was now or never. Seize or be seized. Drive or be driven over. Rum or no rum.

I chose rum. I turned the keys, and the engine roared to life. I didn't see any of this, but I imagined the driver realizing what was happening and jolting toward his truck in slow motion. The girls looking startled. The resort workers seeming befuddled. The bouncer at the club awakening from his nap. The slow-motion run across the cobblestone, his ankles shifting to the left and right at each awkwardly shaped rock.

Booker's hands tensed as I shifted the column down to drive. My foot slammed onto the gas, and the truck lurched out of stillness and hurled down the bumpy driveway. Ahead of us I could see the gated entrance to the resort. It was the type of gate that has an arm, the kind you see at a parking garage. Stopping would mean surrender, so I stepped further onto the pedal and blasted ahead. The arm snapped at the base and flew to the side of the truck, the wheels rolling over it like it was a twig. I glanced back in the side view mirror to see the driver running frantically down the driveway as I turned sharply right and onto the main road. I flooded the engine with gas as I stepped down fully onto the pedal. The truck rumbled down the street, echoing through the trees on either side. Booker slid upright and stared frantically ahead, as if we were in police pursuit.

"Calm down, man," I said reassuringly. "There's no chance in hell anyone is going to catch up with us. It's two in the morning and the driver is on foot. Way, way back there."

He looked over at me nervously. I knew I had to calm him down, so I shouted out as loud as I could, hoping to relieve some of the tension.

"Wooooooooooo-weeeeeeeeeeeeeeee! Owwwwwwwwwwwww!"

"Ouuuuuuuu-wwwwwwwwwwwwwweeeeeee!" he yelled back.

Apparently that had helped. We took turns yelping into the sticky night air as we sped down the road, completely unaware of where we were going or what we were doing. Rows of palm trees lined the road, their trunks painted white, as were most trees in the area.

I had asked a taxi driver once why they painted them, and he said it was to help drunk drivers from hitting them at night. Then he said it was to stop a bug from eating the tree. Then he said something about the Chicago Bulls and Michael Jordan. So I don't know.

We watched them pass, and I was glad that they were painted white. I was drunk as hell and didn't want to wreck our new rum truck before we even had a chance to enjoy it. We turned onto a state highway. Booker's hands relaxed as he propped himself against the seat and stared out the window.

"Where are we going?" he asked.

I didn't say anything. He looked over at me and laughed, and it made me start to laugh too.

Two

I've always had a thing for rum. Okay, maybe not *always* always. But at least for a while now. It almost runs in the family, to an extent. My first memories of it reach back to when I was just a little kid, maybe four or five years old.

My dad would come home and go through the usual routine that one goes through after a day of work. He'd change out of his clothes, he'd eat dinner, that kind of stuff. The final step in this routine involved a cabinet in the kitchen near the dishwasher. It was a cabinet that my brother and I weren't supposed to go in. It was the one with the booze. He would reach down and pull out a clear bottle with a clear liquid. It looked like water, and I used to wonder why anyone would keep water in a bottle when you could get it from the sink. It seemed like a waste of a bottle to me.

He would pull out a short glass from another cabinet. He used the same short glasses we used for orange juice on Saturday for breakfast. My brother used them for the milk he poured when he ate his cookies while we watched cartoons before bed. I didn't do the milk and cookies thing.

I didn't like milk in my cereal either. I liked to keep my wet and dry worlds separate. Nevertheless, it was one of those glasses. They were short tumblers with diamond shapes etched into the sides, made of green glass. They were thick, but not so thick that you wanted to try dropping them to see if they wouldn't break. They'd break.

He would reach into the freezer and pull out a tray of ice cubes. Every night, it was the same thing. Pull the ice cube bucket out about halfway from where it sat the rest of the day. Turn the ice cube tray upside-down over the opening of the bucket. Twist. Listen to the cubes crash into the bucket below. Push the bucket back into place and close the freezer door. Fill the tray at the sink, open the freezer door, place the tray back where it sat. Pull out three ice cubes from the bucket and drop them into the green glass. And then close the freezer door.

He would take out a bottle of Coca-Cola from the fridge. Regular Coke. Not Diet Coke, not New Coke, not Cherry Coke, not whatever the fuck kinds of Coke are out there today. It was the one with the red label. The real thing, as it was called back then. He would gently spin open the screw cap to the clear bottle and place the cap upside-down on the counter, and then he would do the same thing for the Coke cap. He would pour about one-third of the way up the glass with the clear stuff, stop, and then pour a splash extra. The rest of the glass would be filled with Coke. He left about a half of an inch from the top of the glass so that he could swish his drink around. He loved to swish the drink around.

If there was anything that my dad loved, it was the sound of ice rattling around in a short glass as he twirled it in motion. You couldn't give him a straw. No way. The ice would stir the drink just fine. All he needed was the ice and his hand. There was nothing better. Straws were for women.

It's only a matter of time before the things that you see become the things that you grow to feel comforted by. Had my father given up drinking, I'd have been sure there was something wrong with the world. Had the clear bottle been replaced by a dark one, I'd have been worried.

But none of this ever happened, and so after a few years of this routine being burned into my own daily routine, I stopped my Dad to ask him what the hell was going on. At this point, I thought that the Coke was too sweet for him and that he had added his special water to weaken it a bit. That was my hypothesis. He didn't always do this. It was just at night or when he and my mom had their friends over. It didn't make much sense, but that was my best guess.

I had some footie pajamas on. They were red with white plastic pads at the bottom and a zipper that ran from crotch to chest. I was a kid. That's what we wore back then.

"Dad?"

He looked over at me from his chair and away from a rerun of *M.A.S.H.* He swished his drink around and then turned back to the TV.

"Yeah?"

"Can I have some of your soda?"

He swished it around again. When he stirred it counter-clockwise, it meant that he was comfortable, he was relaxed, and he was leaning toward happy. Clockwise meant that he was thinking. I have no idea how I picked up on this.

Clockwise was the direction at the moment. I winced.

"This soda is for Daddy only."

No, it wasn't.

"I had that same soda on Sunday. When we were playing in the pool and Mom said I was thirsty looking and I said I wasn't thirsty and she said well why are you drinking the pool water and I said…"

"Blake."

I had a tendency to run on and on.

"You did not have this kind of soda. Trust me."

"It was from the same bottle. I saw Mom pour it."

He stirred clockwise.

"Let me ask you something."

I sat up and crossed my legs so that my feet were beneath my thighs. They called it Indian-style back then. I don't know what they call it now.

"Did Mom pour anything else into your cup?"

I shook my head.

He started stirring counter-clockwise. I noticed, and he noticed me noticing. I noticed him noticing me noticing him, but it stopped there.

"Come here."

I got up and walked over to where he sat. *M.A.S.H.* continued to play on the screen behind me, and neither of us paid any attention.

"You've seen me make my drink before. You know that we don't have the same soda. You know that I put something extra in it."

"Yeah, but…"

"No. You know that. So why do you want some of my soda when you can have some of your own?"

I want to know what yours tastes like. Yours has water sometimes, and I want to know why. Does it taste better?"

He smiled and stopped stirring his drink.

"Alright then. Here you go."

He lowered his hand from the armrest of his chair and placed the short glass into my two hands. I felt wrong already. I wasn't supposed to be drinking out of a cup without a lid on it in the family room. I could spill. I usually did spill.

"Go ahead," he said. "Take a sip."

I quickly pulled the glass up to my lips and swallowed a small mouthful.

"Ahh! What's wrong with it?!" I blurted out.

My dad took the glass back from me before I spilled it everywhere, and he took a long pull himself. His moustache was wet, and he licked it to gather the drops of his drink that hadn't made it all the way into his mouth. He smiled and gulped down the drink. I was confused.

"My water doesn't taste very good, does it?"

He kept smiling. I tried to think of the right answer. If I said no, then he would be right. And I wanted to show him that maybe I knew what I was talking about, probably because I was already turning into a little punk kid and I wanted to be right about something.

"I liked it."

He was surprised.

"You what?"

"I thought it was good. Can I have some more?"

He looked into the kitchen where my mom was washing the dishes.

"Sure."

I took the glass back from him and took another gulp. It tasted horrible. But as my dad smiled, I knew that I wasn't exactly supposed to like it, but that he thought it was cool that I did. So I held back my grimace, and I smiled too.

"You like that, huh?"

"Yeah. Yeah, I do. It's different. Why does the water taste so different?"

"Because it's not water, Blake."

"What is it?"

He looked into the kitchen again before leaning closer to me and speaking quietly.

"Rum."

"Rum?"

"Rum."

"Rum."

"Yes. Rum."

"Will I get in trouble if I drink rum without you?"

It was a loaded question, and I didn't even know it. My dad answered immediately.

"Yes. But if you ever want some more, ask me. Don't ask mom, just ask me. And if you're being good, you can have some."

"Really?"

He looked into the kitchen again.

"Yeah. Now go on back to the couch so we can watch *M.A.S.H.*"

"Okay!"

Even at night, the air didn't get any less sticky here, any less suffocating. We were, after all, within the tropics. A part of me thought that the humidity would taper off even just the slightest bit at night. Maybe a percentage point or two. But it didn't. It just lingered and soaked into your skin. You could almost imagine that somewhere deep in the forest, there was a pile of earth that was just *steaming* – it was so full and ripe with moisture, and it was humidifying the entire plate of land that we were inhabiting like a sick child's room. Never at night did I want air conditioning more.

Never was I further from receiving it.

Booker sat with his head halfway out the window, the gusts of air billowing open his cheeks as it slammed through his mouth and to the back of his throat. The truck bounced along on the uneven road and he just stared out into the black abyss of the night, the white painted trees sliding by through the thick sea of the air around us. Often checking the fuel gauge for fear of having to make a stop, I reassured myself that we had over a half of a tank left before we had to find a gas station. Just like checking a watch, I had developed the annoying habit of checking and re-checking and re-checking the gauges of the dashboard, many times over in the same minute. I looked at the small green numbers on the dash again. It was 4:32 in the morning.

Booker sputtered, and I imagined him catching a fat bug in the back of his throat. He leaned back in toward the middle of the truck, his face still peering out toward the trees alongside us.

"What time is it, man?"

I checked the clock out of habit. Goddammit.

"4:32."

"Damn. That's later than we were up last night."

"Mmm. It is. It really is."

I didn't know what else there was to say to that. Booker stared out the window like an obsessed hunter checking for prey. Unless his prey was one of those painted trees, he appeared to be out of luck. The forest beyond us was still, not even shifting slightly from a breeze or the velocity of the truck passing by. Just rows upon rows of tropical rods, their leaves too tired and swollen with liquid to bother budging and the wind too lazy and thick with moisture to bother blowing. We were the only moving object in any direction, as far as I could tell. We zoomed down the narrow, poorly lit roadway with vague intention.

You've got to understand the situation that we were experiencing in its full entirety. Vague intention is probably an understatement. We were fucking clueless.

At this point, I had been behind the wheel for a good two or three hours. It was still dark, but soon the sun would begin to rise. I decided that there was no worry of a police pursuit. We had already crossed state lines from Jalisco into Nayarit and on through into Sinaloa. I doubted that the country had a level of coordination that would give them the chance of finding one speeding, stolen truck in the middle of the night. It was upon realizing this that I came to the understanding of what we had actually done. I tapped Booker on the shoulder to see if he was still awake, and he was. My voice sounded hesitant as it left my mouth. I made an adjustment to try to sound more assured.

"You realize…what we did…right?"

He turned around and faced me. I pulled my eyes from the road to meet him for a moment. I turned back before he spoke.

"I'm right here with you, man. I realize it. We're in a stolen truck. It's alright, you know? It's okay."

I felt that way too, but I was afraid he wasn't grasping the situation in its entirety. It was more than just the truck.

"This truck has cargo. So there's more than just a vehicular crime here. It's got some worth to it."

He nodded.

"Yeah, I know. That's why we took it, right?"

"Pretty much," I agreed, and I rubbed my jaw. "So, you realize that we don't have anything else, right?"

He looked puzzled.

"What else would be in here? The soda? A tray of ice cubes?"

He laughed, and I smiled.

"No, I mean, like, we don't have any of our luggage."

His smile slowly faded.

"We left all of our shit back in our hotel room. And you know we can't go back now."

"Fuck. I didn't even *think* of that! How did I not think of that?"

"I didn't either. We were wasted."

We still were, at that point, so the past tense reference was really in vain.

"We can't go back, huh?"

I shook my head.

"Because we can't bring this truck anywhere near P.V., right?"

I nodded as though I had sage wisdom, though I was just agreeing with the obvious. He threw his hands up and shrugged.

"Oh well!"

"You're okay with not having any of your stuff?"

He thought about it, and I did too, both of us going through mental checklists of what we had brought for the trip. For me, I knew that I had packed light. A few shirts and some shorts, one book, a notebook, and some toiletries. I didn't even bring my good razor. I looked over at Booker. I realized that he wasn't as fortunate, with the expression he had on his face.

"I brought a few things I'd like to have kept. But...with all of this rum we've got in here," he proclaimed as he slammed his hand on the back wall of the cab, "I'm sure I'll forget whatever it was that I brought. It's all just materialism, right?"

It was something like that, so I said yes.

We cruised past a sign that indicated we were entering the city of Mazatlán. I imagined all of the girls lying in their beds, drunk from their own spring breaks, the same scene we had just left but in a different city. I felt tempted to stop off and take a nap. It was already past five in the morning. My mouth was dry and parched, and my eyes were burning. I knew that it'd be a bad idea, so I wiped it from my head. Checking the gas gauge, though, I knew that we had to fill up. I still had a whole hell of a lot of pesos, and I didn't see any other use for them. So after we had passed through what seemed like the center of the city, we veered off the highway at a Pemex station and discretely filled the tank.

Luckily, I guessed correctly as to which side the tank was on so that we didn't draw any extra attention turning the truck around at the pump. As two white guys driving a cargo truck, we knew that we weren't exactly inconspicuous. Booker ran into the station and bought a few things to snack on and hurried back to the cab before I had even finished filling up. We took off like ghosts and left no remnant or memory behind. Or at least we hoped as much. One never knows, I suppose.

With a full tank of gas, Booker and I knew that we had to make a decision. Nothing epic. It was more of the practical kind. A few kilometers ahead of us, it appeared as though our path would split along two different highways. 20 and 15. Both seemed as though they were going to continue going north, and while we had no reason to think this, we decided it'd be best to just shoot for it and see which one prevailed. I chose 20, and Booker chose 15. Booker won, so we headed slightly west at the highway split.

Who knows. I've looked back at maps since then, and I can't seem to find a highway 20 in that area of Mexico at all. Maybe they changed the names. There seems to be a 15D there now. Or maybe I was so hazy from all of the booze and sun and lack of sleep that I got it all completely wrong in my head. It doesn't matter.

For all we could have guessed, 15 might have led right into the ocean. The road opened up and rolled on ahead of us, miles and miles of nothing spectacular. I got lost in a mental daze for a while. When I snapped out of it, the sun was just beginning to crest over the hills to our east, and the little green clock on the dash read that it was 6:15. We had been driving for about four hours. And by we, I mean I. Even though we had filled up less than fifty miles prior, I checked the gas gauge constantly. The needle remained near the F. All these little cities that you'd never hear about in your entire life of living on this planet, they all whizzed by us as the day heated up with the rising sun. We were somewhere near La Cruz when I realized that the jungle had more or less disappeared. We were entering rows and rows of farms, all meticulously laid out and strung alongside the highway on either side. We weren't too sure if 15 had been the right choice, but it kept going north, so we didn't question our judgment.

"Those bitches..." Booker muttered unexpectedly after miles and miles of mutual silence.

"What bitches?"

I looked out my window and then out his. I didn't see anyone or anything even resembling a human, let alone a bitch.

"Those bitches last night. They totally ditched us for those Mexican assholes. And we were *so* close to nailing them. You were *so close*. Right?"

"I was close," I admitted. "But you were pretty far off."

He looked hurt, but I didn't care. It was the truth.

"The reason they wandered away from us was because you couldn't seal the deal. Which is fine. I mean, after all, you said it yourself. They were bitches."

"They were."

"So it wasn't your fault, necessarily."

Not satisfied, I had to dig him a little deeper just to let him feel like an ass.

"But if it was anyone's fault in this truck, it wasn't mine. So I've got to blame you."

His head slumped a little and he stared forward at the dry nothingness ahead of us. A bird flew overhead and shit on the hood of the truck. We both saw it and raised our eyebrows.

"Nice shot."

"I know," he replied.

"You still feeling drunk at all?" I asked him. It was an honest question considering how much we had drank and the fact that neither of us had a chance to sleep it off.

"No. You?"

"Nah. My buzz went away around the time that you swallowed that bug."

He jumped up, almost hitting his head on the roof.

"You saw that? Oh man! That was nasty!"

"Yeah. Not that that was a buzz kill or anything, but it was just around then when I realized that I wasn't even drunk anymore. Which is good, considering I'm driving a *stolen* truck full of rum. Not exactly the kind of thing I want to get pulled over doing."

"Not in Mexico."

"No, not anywhere."

Shitty little villages passed us on either side. I wondered to myself how human beings could live like that.

"So, fearless leader…" Booker said to me, full of sarcasm. "What is the plan here?"

"Plan?"

"Yeah, plan. Like what the hell are we going to do with this truck and all of this rum? The plan."

"The plan? What do you mean plan? You're seeing it right now, man. Here it is. Unfolding before you. The highway, the country of Mexico. This is my plan. I have no plan. Do you think I wrote up a fucking itinerary?"

"Easy…"

"Well, I mean, what do you want me to say?"

"Jesus, dude. Chill out. I'm just asking what you think we're going to do with this. We can't just drive forever, is all."

I sat there and didn't say anything for a bit.

"Well, why not? Why can't we drive forever?"

I didn't mean forever, but he took it literally, and I knew it before he even started speaking.

"Not like *forever* forever, but I mean, what's stopping us from driving this all the way on up to the U.S.? This highway has got to make its way up there eventually, right?"

Booker looked at me like I was crazy.

"You're suggesting that we drive this truck, this stolen truck that's full of rum, all the way up and back to L.A.?"

He said it like there was another plan that I could have had in mind.

"Booker, look at what's around you. Look!"

He just looked at me. He never listened.

"What are we supposed to do if we don't keep driving? Buy a fucking house? Get a mortgage from a Mexican bank and start our own lettuce patch? We *have* to keep driving, you meat sack! There's nothing else we can do."

"That's your plan?"

He was just trying to push my buttons. It worked.

"YES – that IS my PLAN! What the fuck do you mean? I'm driving this truck all the way up this stupid fucking highway, and we're going back home with it. What else are we supposed to do? We're like six hours north of Puerto Vallarta. That's like the distance from L.A. to San Francisco. You've done that drive. That's a long way! What the hell else are we supposed to do? Turn around and get arrested and get our assholes stuffed in a Mexican jail for the rest of our lives?"

"I'd rather start a lettuce patch with you."

I looked at him with my eyes on fire, and he continued.

"The B&B Lettuce Patch. It'd be nice."

"Fuck you," I spit at the windshield.

He started laughing.

"I'm just saying that your plan is stupid. I know that we have to keep driving now, but it's a busted up plan."

"Oh yeah, genius? Tell me why that is. Tell me a better plan!"

I was still pissed even though I knew that he was just ribbing me.

"Ah. I don't have a better plan. See, this wasn't my idea in the first place. This was all you."

"Point the finger, nice."

"It was, dude. But anyway, it's irrelevant. My point here is that we can't drive this truck all the way up, even if you wanted to."

I looked at him as if he had some supreme knowledge that he was holding out from me.

"Why?"

"It's a stolen truck, you idiot. It's full of rum."

"I know that. I know that."

"How are we supposed to cross the border with a stolen truck full of booze? How the hell is *that* going to work?"

I had no time to think before the word came out of my mouth.

"Shit!"

He looked incredulous.

"You mean you didn't realize this? You thought you could just drive this beast over the border and no one would stop us or think it was a little odd? With the big fucking Private Reserve logo all tatted up on the side of this thing? Really?"

"Shit!"

"You have got to be kidding me," he said as he slammed his hand down against his knee.

"No. No. I'm not. I didn't even think of that. Not at all. Goddammit, not one bit. Fuck! Shit!"

He sat there for a while with his hand on his knee, looking out of place and a bit stunned. I just kept driving, though my speed had dipped down to about 80 km/h, whatever the fuck that was. My body had become tentative and unsure of what to do next as the gears in my mind turned and turned, their teeth not gripping on each other. Another shitty little village passed by us, and I tried to figure out which of us was the first B in the B&B Lettuce Patch. It was probably him. It was his idea.

Three

"I've always had a thing for rum."

We were sitting on a wooden bench that looked older than time. I was taking small, short breaths, trying to keep the dust out of my mouth. The air had a horrible taste to it. I didn't realize that air could have a taste until then. The birds that were flying around looked like little blimps. They pushed along so slowly.

The bench was at another Pemex station somewhere near a city called Obregón. If you never make it to Obregón, your life can still be complete. Not that it's not a nice city. I only have this one experience, so what do I know? It probably could have been worse. To me it felt like a small version of Bakersfield. Just a bunch of dust and tired-looking people and shitty looking cars. And sun. Oh yeah, there's sun. Booker and I were sitting there, each with a sandwich in our hands. The bread was already crusty from the relentless sun despite the fact that we had just taken off the cellophane wrappers. They tasted almost as bad as the air, but we were hungry and we didn't have options.

We had made it so far north that it no longer looked like the Mexico that I was used to. It looked like the Old West, or at least how the Old West looked in movies. All along the way, there were dingy shacks dotting the roads. Some of them had four walls, some just had three. Some had roofs, some decided they didn't need roofs. Most of them had graffiti on at least one wall. All of them had a layer of dust that you could see from a distance. There was not much else to look at other than those sad little shacks. We would joke that we wanted to see tumbleweed roll by to confirm how desolate and shitty it really was, and then tumbleweed would roll by to confirm how desolate and shitty it really was.

By the time we got to Obregón, my expectations were so low that I was impressed that some of the intersections in the town had stoplights. Stoplights require electricity. Electricity requires a power grid. Most of the buildings had windows in their window holes. This town was on to something. I could feel it.

"You say that a lot. What do you even mean by that?"

I had forgotten what I was saying. I was just staring off into nothing, musing about the dust.

"Huh?"

"That you've always had a thing for rum."

He picked out a withered tomato from his sandwich and flopped it onto the ground.

"What's that even supposed to mean? Why do you say that?"

"Oh, I don't know. I just meant that I've always liked it. It's always been something that has had a certain effect on me. More so than any other type of booze, or drugs, or anything like that. I've just always had a thing for rum. So it's kind of shitty that we have a whole fucking truck of it and that we probably can't even do anything with it. It's not even kind of shitty. It's really shitty. Like this sandwich."

I took another bite anyway.

"These sandwiches are awful," Booker replied, his mouth full of his.

We both frowned as we swallowed our next bites. I shifted my weight forward, and the bench creaked beneath me. Whoever had built this bench had a real sense of humor. It was a rickety, piece of shit bench in the middle of a dry, dust-filled square of land. It was next to a parking lot. There were no trees and no shade from a building or a nearby mountain range or anything.

Nothing. Just a solitary bench in the middle of nothing. Just dust and rocks and beyond that, a few cars and some pavement. A real comedian had laid the plans for this one. And yet there we were, using it to its fullest. The fullest a bench can be used for is sitting, as far as I am aware. Our truck cab was somehow even hotter and less tolerable than sitting directly in the sun. The rum was probably at a rolling boil, the bottles jittering in their cases from the pressure.

There was a moment, about three hours earlier, when Booker and I realized that we didn't even know what was in the cargo area. We had been driving for so long with that don't-look-back mentality, and we had never stopped to take a look at what we were hauling. We had just assumed that there was something inside. I don't remember which one of us brought it up, but as soon as the idea was out there, we had to pull over and look. It was around nine in the morning. We stopped at a Pemex. Always fucking Pemex.

We faced a moment of embarrassing failure. The two of us were miles upon miles away from our luggage and from the airport where we were supposed to board a plane in a couple of days. We were staring at the sliding back door to a stolen truck that might have been completely empty. I was cringing and shaking my head.

"What if there's nothing in here?" Booker asked.

"Don't fucking say that. Don't."

"It would be pretty funny though."

"Fuck you. It would *not* be funny. It would be terrible!"

"Terribly funny."

"Don't, man. Just don't."

I was jingling around the keys, trying to figure out which one opened the goddamned lock.

"Did you hear anything moving around while we were driving?"

"Don't."

"I didn't. I mean, that doesn't mean anything…but I didn't hear anything."

I found the right key and slid it in. I purposely did not look at Booker at all. I didn't want to see his face. It felt too cliché. I didn't want to remember the look of someone who had stolen an empty truck. I flung the door open.

"Oh, thank fucking God holy shit that is a *lot* of boxes!"

We started counting. Or at least I did. There were forty-three cases, to be exact, with twelve bottles in each. I was so excited, I nearly shit my pants. Booker had to hold in a yelp of excitement. We probably looked like the two happiest truck drivers in the world if anyone were to have seen us. Some of the boxes were on their side, and some looked like they had slid from the front to the back at least a few times. That was probably my fault, but I didn't care. I was just happy that the truck wasn't empty.

Meanwhile, in Obregón, I had forgotten what happiness was. I think my sandwich was about to set on fire in my hands.

"We should have gotten more to drink," I said.

I had bought a bottle of water, but I drank it in one go.

"But we have plenty to drink!"

"Not that. I don't want rum right now."

"Ladies and gentlemen!" Booker announced. "There is a first time for everything!"

"I think the sun is getting to me. Let's just get back on the road."

I threw what was left of that abomination of a sandwich onto the ground and headed back to the truck, checking the lock on the back as though I was now very concerned about the safety of this cargo – like I was a real truck driver or something.

Booker climbed into the cab, sucking the tips of his fingers and wiping them down the front of his shorts. We were pretty dirty, and we smelled like it too. Luckily, our days of competing in beauty pageants were far in the past.

I had gotten a little bit of information out of one of the gas station attendants along the way. He told me that Highway 15 would lead right up into Arizona. Not realizing at the time that a big fucking body of water called the Sea of Cortez was effectively preventing us from crossing over into Baja California and up toward L.A., I assumed that he had just made a mistake and he hadn't actually meant Arizona. Somehow, I forgot that Baja even existed, and I assumed that the ocean that we occasionally saw to our left was the full Pacific. It was irrelevant at the time anyway. We decided to keep heading north and figure it out later.

"This highway fucking sucks," I mumbled under my breath.

Booker laughed.

"Hey. Don't say that. It has feelings, and it can probably hear you."

"Sorry, highway."

"Say it like you mean it, Blake."

"Fuck you, highway."

"That's not very nice."

"Look at this thing. It looks like they haven't paved it since it was first built. And it's twisting and turning all over the place even though there's nothing for it to go around. Who the fuck invented this highway?"

"I don't think people invent highways."

"It's horrible."

"I like how it doesn't even bother with a barrier between us and the oncoming traffic."

"It's probably to make it easier for people who have to live here to commit suicide."

"Wow."

"That's what I would do."

"Maybe I should be driving?"

"This is hell," I said.

"Do you think the rum is losing some of the alcohol by being in the back of the hot truck all day?"

"Don't even fucking start with that. I'm sure it's fine."

"Are you?"

I looked over at him and shook my head. Sometimes I think he just liked getting under my skin. He was pretty good at it.

We were nearly at the point of delirium. We wondered aloud what our actual plan was, as if there was an invisible third passenger who hadn't revealed the blueprints yet, just sitting there and waiting for us to ask. *Exactly how are we were going to make it across the border? And why? Hello? Is anybody there? We're idiots, and we have a problem. Please send your thoughts and prayers and maybe some ice cubes. Thanks.*

The B & B Lettuce Patch began to sound more and more appealing. But the thought of that lettuce eventually ending up on one of those shitty Obregón sandwiches shut the idea right out of my head. The road was relentless. Why wouldn't it just fucking quit? I wanted to be back in L.A. more than I would have ever imagined.

We passed by signs for places that didn't even sound real. Noche Buena. That means *good night.* La Bandera. That means *the flag.* Palma. That means *palm.* Hacienda La Poza. That means *House of Poza*, whatever the fuck that is. Who named these shitholes? We rolled through Hermosillo at around three o'clock in the afternoon and had to stop off to fuel up again. Another goddamned Pemex. I tried to sign up for a rewards card, but they didn't have one. The highway just straight up ended there, and it picked up after we crossed through the city. What a trap. If it wasn't for a few mostly hidden signs that we spotted, we might have just been stuck there.

When we were filling up the tank, I asked the attendant at the station how far we were from the border. He may have been the oldest working man in the entire world. He was at least a hundred and fifty years old.

"Nogales, tres horas," he said.

Then he died.

Booker and I had already deduced that Nogales was some sort of border crossing point. There had been signs and pamphlets stapled to the telephone poles that we saw, offering van rides to the city for a fixed fare. I had never heard of Nogales, so I assumed it was on the Mexico side of the fence. But that was just a guess. Three hours didn't sound too bad, especially after driving for what had already been almost thirteen. What's another three? We wouldn't even have to fill up again!

We grabbed some more snacks and hit the road, weaving through the city until we found our way back to Highway 15 or 15D or whatever the fuck it was. It was a poor son-of-a-bitch of a road. I began to imagine little eyes peeking out from the tar, squinting as we rolled over them and hoping that we'd pull off and leave it alone. Eyes that whispered, *"Help me!"* and then got run over by the two tons of our rum truck as we kept on going. Poor, ugly highway.

"Three hours, man," I reassuringly said as we gained speed and the road opened up.

Booker's head was slumped against his hand, propped up against the door frame. His hand tilted up and down to force a nod from his head.

"That's not bad. Three hours. We're almost there."

He picked his head up with a defeated sense of weakness.

"Almost where?" he sighed.

"Nogales."

Duh.

"And where the fuck is Nogales, Blake? What the fuck is a fucking Nogales? Huh?"

I hadn't really thought about it. Officially, that is. I had unofficially contemplated and assumed that it was a border crossing town. But now, with a finite distance between us, and that distance getting shorter with each passing moment, I realized that the vagueness of an assumption had a very good chance of causing us some real headache if it didn't pan out as expected.

"A border crossing town?" I asked, pathetically.

"You sound pretty sure."

He waited for a response for only a second before continuing.

"I mean, we've all heard of Nogales in geography class. Nogales…the border crossing town. Right, dude?"

"You don't have to be an ass. I got your point as soon as you asked me the first time. I don't know what it is or where it goes."

"So why are we going there?"

The tone of his voice had risen a bit. It was the kind of tone that you have when your nostrils are flaring. That kind of angry voice that you have when you're starting to get pissed off but you don't want to show it.

"Because we have nowhere else to go. You know this, alright? This is a tired subject. We are idiots. We have a stolen truck, we have five hundred bottles of rum, and we have no idea what to do with it."

"So why fucking Nogales, man?"

He spoke like his balls were wrapped around each other in a Boy Scout knot. I didn't have time to even think before I blurted out my response.

"Why fucking not, *man*? Why the fuck not?!"

He slumped his head against his hand again and tilted it up and down in the nod fashion.

"Touché."

The heat from the sun and from our heads made the truck cab feel like it was a hundred and sixty degrees, even with the windows down. The highway eyes winced as we plowed them over, each one of them begging for mercy. Nogales was still another two hundred and fifty kilometers away, and they knew it as well as I did. But this truck wasn't going to stop now. It wasn't going to stop in stupid fucking Nogales either, wherever that even was. This truck was going to keep on rolling, baby. And nobody involved had even the slightest clue what that actually meant.

Four

I've always had a thing for rum. Back in high school, when all of my friends were trying to score beers for the weekend parties and for pre-gaming before the school dances and whatever bullshit we were celebrating, I was always the guy with the special request. *A bottle of rum, please.* I said it so often, it may as well have been the opening line to my senior yearbook write-up. Maybe not with the word *please* in there. I wasn't that polite. To me, beers were for pussies. And besides, they got you too full to really get properly drunk. Even back then, I was more concerned with potency than ease of acquisition. I had *priorities*.

It helped that I had an older brother who would pick me up a bottle or two of whatever I asked for if he was heading out to the store. He lived at home while I was in high school, so I didn't need to fuck around with the hassle of fake I.D.s and the risk of getting caught and all of that garbage. I had a source. He wasn't that cool, and sometimes he would deny me for no particular reason. But he was a source, nevertheless. I never told anyone where I got it from either, because I knew (like anybody knew) that once there was a source, everybody was going to want in on it. I kept it quiet. And in return, my silence paid out dividends. Of rum. It was a decent compromise, even though it didn't make me too popular. But that was alright. I had *priorities*.

Priorities. Sometimes they shift due to changing circumstances. In a cozy, southern California upbringing, your priority as a teenager is whatever the hell you want it to be. Rum, in my case. As a guy taking a stolen truck on a fifteen-hour drive through western Mexico, your priorities are a little different. Scenery is a priority. It helps keep you sane. Wind from the window – that's to keep you cool. Caffeine, of course, because there's just jack shit to look at, and your co-pilot isn't really contributing in any positive way. Hand leaning on face, face staring out windshield, windshield staring at lumpy, beat-down roadway, roadway staring ahead toward nothing. Or Nogales. Whichever seems more appealing or will get you there faster. That's the real priority.

I wanted to pull over and pop open a bottle from the cases in the back and take a siesta on the side of the road. The heat was tapering a bit, and if it wasn't for the lack of ice and coke and glasses and limes and basically everything except the rum, I'd have probably suggested it to Booker. And there we would be for the next few days on a rum bender. It didn't sound too bad, really. It certainly sounded better than sitting on our asses in the goddamned truck.

But it was probably better that we kept on going. Mexico back then wasn't as dangerous as it later became, but it still wasn't a place you wanted to find yourself stranded and unable to get away from. Besides, we were nearing what seemed like the end of this god-awful trip, and to stop just short of the finish line would be ridiculous. It was around half-past four in the afternoon. As we were passing through places called Santa Eva, Benjamin Hill, and Santa Ana, Booker came up with what sounded like a pretty good idea.

"Do they still barter here?"

Okay. Maybe it didn't sound like a good idea right off the bat, but it had the potential that we desperately needed.

"What do you mean?" I asked.

"Barter. Do they still trade for things here, in Mexico, instead of using a full currency and pay-type situation."

"How the hell would I know?"

"Because you're the expert on Mexico, Mr. Nogales," he spat back, almost without a breath between our two sentences.

"Ha. But really, they might. I don't know? I'm sure there are farmers out there who have stuff, and they trade them to other farmers for their stuff. And drug dealers and shit like that. But I would imagine that they're pretty much using cash to buy things."

"Exclusively?"

"No, probably not exclusively. They have credit cards and checks like we do."

"Right."

"But I'd guess they use cash a lot. What are you getting at?"

"Think. Think about what we have and the problem we have with it."

He leaned forward, sat upright, and started shifting his shoulders around in his sockets. He was clearly sore from sitting for nearly a day straight. My shoulders were killing me too, as was my tailbone. Man was not meant to drive a truck through the night instead of sleeping. It's unnatural, and my ass hurt like hell. Booker continued a moment later.

"We have all of this rum, and there's no way that we can cross into the U.S. with a cargo truck full of it, right? So I was thinking…what's stopping us from trying to barter this shit away to some locals? Like for things, like food or clothes or drugs…"

"Yeah, because crossing the border with drugs will be easier than with what we have," I interjected.

"Okay, not drugs. But you know, there's all kinds of shit that we could get in exchange for this rum. I'm sure."

He had a good point.

"I'll one up you. What if we didn't trade the rum for things, but just sold them off instead? I bet we could fetch a hundred pesos a bottle and sell them out of the back of the truck in some shitty alley or right next to a liquor store or something. Ten bucks a bottle, five hundred bottles…"

"That'd be hella cash," Booker said.

He wasn't from northern California, but sometimes he would say "hella." I usually let him get away with it.

"That would be *hella* cash?"

"Fuck you. I tried. Do you think we could sell that many bottles though? I mean, how many bottles of rum do you think get sold around here per day? Probably not that many."

"Good point," I admitted. "But we don't have to sell them all in one day. Or in one place. There's no reason we can't just sell a few here and there and wander around until we get rid of them all. We'd obviously be making money out of it, so we could get a room somewhere and get some food and whatever."

"Yeah."

He paused. It made me think that he was going to give me the reason that it wouldn't work, the reason I wasn't thinking of. And he did.

"But you've got to remember that we need to be back in L.A. in like two or three days at the latest, or I won't have a job and your parents will realize that you're not actually going to school anymore."

It was like being Wile E. Coyote and realizing that your parachute was an anvil.

"Ah, shit. You're right. We really don't have that much time."

"Nope."

"Well, how the fuck are we going to sell five hundred bottles of rum that fast? I don't think we can."

"No, we can't. I think if we sold fifty, we'd be really lucky."

"Hella lucky," I added.

We both let out a sigh.

The truck rolled on, and soon we began to see signs for Nogales. But now it felt bittersweet. We didn't have anything of value. We just had a ticking clock on our hands. We had enough rum to last us a couple of years but no way to bring it back home with us. Our safest option would be to abandon all of it on the side of the road and call it a wash. But…fuck that.

Worse yet, we were sitting in a stolen truck. And although we were nearly half of a country away from where we had taken it, there was no telling what kind of shit we could get into if we sat idly in Mexico with hot wheels. One funny look, and we could get locked up in some shithole prison, never allowed a phone call for years.

I'd heard the stories. They don't have the same justice system that we have. We'd emerge a decade later with huge beards, torn assholes, and no idea who we used to be or what our lives were worth anymore. It was a grim alternative, and it was all for some rum that we hadn't even touched yet and maybe never would. Ironically, after all of that driving, I was now wishing we were further away so that we had more time to come up with a plan. Fuck.

The sun began to get lazy and fat as it sank lower toward the ground, a deep red beginning to spill out across the barren land around it. The few trees that we did pass now shined a dull, orange glow from their leaves. It was slowly and painfully nearing night, and we had no plan. With about fifty kilometers to go, we finally veered off of Highway 15 and headed north on 19 toward Nogales. A strange feeling began to come over me as I realized in my utter soberness that I had never heard of Nogales before this trip, and it was likely that it wasn't due south of California as we had originally thought. If it was, I probably would have heard of it, in the same way that Tijuana and Mexicali were places that I had heard of. Nogales wasn't ringing a bell. At best, it sounded like what the waiter would say at a Mexican restaurant when they were out of *gales*.

The conversation in the truck had turned into sporadic mutterings of, *"What are we gonna do?"* and, *"Ah, what the fuck..."* and, *"[Blank] kilometers, goddammit..."* We were two sailors up shit's creek without a paddle or a roll of toilet paper or a map of the creek or anything helpful at all. All we had were about five hundred useless bottles of rum.

We rolled into the first outskirts of town, and I started to feel a little optimistic.

"How bad can this really be?" I asked.

"How bad can what be?"

"This. Like being here in Nogales with all of this booze. We've got to be able to find *something* to do here tonight."

"Sure."

A cluster of unimpressive buildings started to appear, and I could feel my back almost leaping off of the seat. Nogales. I had never been so happy to arrive in a city that I knew nothing about. Booker pointed at a vacancy sign that buzzed in front of a shitty-looking motel. I swung the truck right and into the driveway. I parked in a spot around back on the other side of the structure and away from anyone that might be interested in a cargo truck with a rum logo on its side, just sitting at a motel for no apparent reason. Booker was rubbing his sides.

"This is probably a good place to at least take a real shit, don't you think? My gut is all bunched up. I feel like I haven't been to the bathroom in weeks."

"It was probably those shitty-ass sandwiches we had," I said with a laugh.

We both got out of the truck and went around to the back to make sure the lock hadn't bust open during the last leg of our trip. It hadn't. We wandered up to what appeared to be the check-in station. It was a small, dark room with an outward facing window, pretty much like the pay window at a gas station or the ticket counter outside of a theme park. My eyes burned, and I kept them focused downward as I slapped some money down on the counter and slid it under the gap in the glass window. I didn't want the clerk to think that I was strung out on some kind of drug, but I didn't want to seem suspicious either. I'm sure the motel saw a lot of fucked up things from time to time, so maybe I was worried over nothing.

Until I got out of the truck, I didn't even know that I wanted to get a room. There's something about being at your destination that releases a trigger in the mind, as if it is suddenly okay for your body to express its true feelings. I was sore. My knees buckled when I walked, and I felt the sweat between my toes. My ass hurt, my back hurt, my shoulders and my arms hurt, and my ears were burning. I hadn't felt any of this until we pulled up to the motel. It just came crashing out of the dam and flooded my body with all of these intense and terrible feelings. It was a sensory overload, but with really shitty sensations.

Booker looked no better. He sat on yet another bench while I dealt with the clerk and the payment. After I got the keys, we slowly hobbled back to the truck and each pulled out a bottle of Private Reserve, mine tucked under my arm and his grasped in his left hand. Room 14 had our name written all over it. Not literally. That would have been weird. I remember opening the door and breathing out a huge sigh. Booker tossed his bottle onto the bed and headed straight toward the bathroom without a word.

"You're already taking a shit?"

"Yes."

"Thanks for closing the door. I really want to hear you go."

"You're welcome."

I went over to the TV and turned it on. It was so old that it had knobs. I turned one of them a few times until I found something that wasn't static. The clicks were so dense that they sounded more like a clunk. Clunk clunk

clunk. A Mexican drama. I knew enough Spanish to understand slow conversation between seven-year-olds. It didn't take me long to realize that whatever I was watching was never going to make any sense to me. It was going way too fast. I tuned out and just stared ahead, waiting for my chance to hit the toilet.

Booker came out smirking. I had no real concept of time at that point, but in my memory it seemed like an efficiently fast shit. I swapped places with him and went in to do my business. I hate sitting on a warm toilet seat, but I didn't have the patience to let it cool off. It came out fast and hard and left me wishing I had a baby wipe or at least a stick to bite down on.

The sink was small and ugly. I was afraid to let the water touch my mouth, so I splashed handfuls onto my face with my lips curled in and away from whatever bacteria was floating around in there. The water felt amazingly refreshing against my face. It beaded up on my forehead from the oil that had been collecting on my skin all day. And from the day before. I didn't even bother to wipe my face. There was no towel anyway, so it didn't matter. When I stepped back into the room, Booker was lying on his back on the bed, snoring and fast asleep. His bottle of rum lay unopened and next to his ribcage.

I went over to the window and pulled the curtains shut. The room became surprisingly dark. Flopping down on the bed next to him, I closed my eyes and let the layers of stress peel away from my conscience. *Five, six, seven, eight.* Before I could even translate another word from the show that hummed out of that run down TV, I fell into a coma-like sleep.

I thought I was just going to take a nap, but that's the thing about naps. They are never just naps. They're sleep traps. Naps are like quicksand for the conscience. I lay down on that bed thinking that I'd be napping for a couple of hours, but the nap chose otherwise. That's the thing about naps, as I said. They control you. They don't even give you a chance to decide. Once you submit yourself to a nap, it's all over. Only the nap can decide whether you wake or not.

The blackout curtains didn't help either. They were thicker than any curtain that I had ever seen before. I don't know how the rod stayed attached to the wall. My body finally awoke my brain sometime in the late morning. My bladder was throbbing. I felt like I was in another world. I had no clue where I was, when it was, and for a few moments, who I was. When you wake up in a bed with another man and a bottle of rum rolling around between the two of you, it can make you question a few things. I walked into the bathroom reassuring myself that I was sexually interested in women.

My urethra screamed for the next ninety seconds. I don't know where it was all coming from. I peeked out of the bathroom, and Booker was still motionless on the bed in practically the same position as he was when he first lay down the day before. I decided to take a shower. There was a tiny bar of soap and no shampoo. It was better than nothing. When I was done, I stood in front of the mirror and drip dried onto the floor. I flexed my abdominal muscles and tightened my pecs, and I held in my breath to examine the different angles I could make with my body. None of them looked any good. They all looked like I had just been where I had just been, for as long as I had been there. Oh well. I wasn't trying to win a prize or anything.

When I stepped out of the bathroom, Booker was somewhat conscious. He was staring at the television with a blank, unhappy look on his face. It took him about fifteen seconds to clear his throat before he could get a sentence out.

"We either went out and had the best night last night, or we did nothing."

I nodded slowly and sadly. He took notice.

"So we did nothing."

He sat upright and started to rub his knees, as if he were a football player the day after a game.

"You passed out before I could even wipe my ass. And it was a fast shit."

He had a look of slight embarrassment, the kind that only I would notice. To anyone else, he would just look a bit angry.

"Well. Well, when did you pass out?"

I had some empathy, so I told him that it was right after he did. The look slowly drained from his face. He tempered the rubbing of his knees to a gentle caress as if he was petting a baby's head or a girl's ass.

I sat down next to him on the bed and stared ahead at the TV. Our generation had been conditioned to stare at this box for some sort of meaning, even when the language wasn't our own. It was the TV. It was a part of the day. I couldn't understand a goddamned thing anyone was saying. The words all sounded like you took a regular sentence and threw it into a food processor with a chili pepper. I think that might be racist, and I may want to remove it from this story one day. But for now, I will keep it in here. Somebody said something about an orange, but that's as much as I was able to understand. I looked over at Booker. He looked like he might fall back asleep, so I picked up the bottle between us and uncorked the top. I was hoping to inspire him to stay awake.

I wiped the bottle first, and then I pressed the rim to my lips and slugged back a warm shot.

"This is not as good as I remember it being," I said.

"That's a strong endorsement. I'll take one too."

I knew I was going to need it, so I took another shot and shook my head all around as I walked over to the window. The room was still very dark, but by now our eyes were so adjusted that it almost seemed about right. I knew that outside there was an explosion of light that just wanted to rip through the curtains and fry our eyes into puddles in their sockets. I pulled the curtains back so slowly that we almost had to pay the motel for another night.

"It is so bright out!" I yelled.

"*Whoa, whoa, whoa, Mex-i-cooo!*"

"Nicely done, JT."

The day was ready for us, and we were barely ready to be upright. Even with my shower, I felt like I could have slept another six or eight hours, no problem. My body was physically exhausted. Booker went to the bathroom. I struggled to pay attention to the television. There was a terrible glare shining off of the screen. It made it nearly impossible to see anything that was happening. I knew that if I closed the curtains, I might pass out again. I eventually gave up and lay back on the bed and stared at the ceiling. I took a few more shots until the throbbing feeling in my legs began to dull.

We got our shit together and wandered out of the room sometime before noon. The truck, thank God, was still parked in the same spot, the lock on the back securely fastened in place. Our treasure still tight. Our effort still worthwhile. We had no clue what the hell we were going to do with all of that rum, but at least we knew we still had the option to do something with it. I don't know what I would have done if our stolen rum was stolen from us. I might have lost it. Booker went to the front desk and gave them back the key.

The first time I turned the keys, the truck didn't start. It's funny how sometimes you don't even think of the things that could go wrong until they're right in front of you. If it hadn't started on the second turn, I might have just died on the spot. The coroner would rule it death by exasperation. That's assuming that this place actually had a coroner. From the look of everything around us, it seemed likely that most people who lived there died from the sheer hatred of their own lives. Their families probably just dragged their dead bodies behind a shed and hoped that nobody went looking.

We headed further into town. I think. It's hard to tell what was in and what was out. It all looked pretty similar. Some of the buildings that looked like businesses had saloon doors. That was pretty cool. Others had windows so old and thin that a fast mosquito might shatter through them. Some places had no doors at all. Because who the fuck needs doors.

For a while, the further we went along, the shittier the streets and stores became. Booker looked simply disgusted. He kept shaking his head. Each street we passed seemed somehow worse than the one before. The people creeping around in the searing sun had creases on their faces instead of wrinkles. All of their clothing was some shade of brown. It was as though Hell had indigestion and puked up this city, and then it didn't bother to clean it up.

It started to turn for the better as we got closer to the U.S. border. The people still looked the same, but the buildings started to look a little nicer. Like there was some sort of tourist momentum that they were trying to take advantage of. When Booker saw a parking meter, we decided it was okay to stop and try to find some food. If they cared enough to meter the parking, then there had to be something worth stopping for. Ever since those shitty sandwiches, we really hadn't made much of an attempt to eat. It was about time.

"Something tells me you're going to want to get Mexican food right now," Booker moaned.

He was right.

"Look at it like this, man. Any other kind of food around here, it's probably just for travelers, right? Or people who can afford more than the local cuisine."

"Cuisine?"

"Yeah, I'm fancy today. Cuisine. And if you lived around here, like you lived in Nogales, you'd probably be pretty bitter about these tourist assholes who come through and want to take pictures of your shithole town for who fucking knows what reason, right?"

"I don't think they get many tourists here. Look at this place."

"Whatever. Either way, they've got to be bitter. And if I was a bitter Nogalan, and that's probably not what they're called, but whatever. But if

I was bitter, I would shit and piss and fuck in their food before serving it to them. Wouldn't you?"

"What? No. What? What the hell is wrong with you?"

"Nothing. That's probably what they do."

"They *fuck* in the food? That seems…I don't know about that."

"Maybe just piss then. And shit."

"Fuck."

"Exactly. So I want local Mexican food because that's the only food I would trust around here. Besides, do you really think they're going to make a good pizza or burger anyway?"

"The pizza at the hotel in P.V. was pretty good."

"Does this look like the hotel in P.V.?"

I spread my arms around. A few people walking by started to look at me, so I put them back down.

"Close. It's pretty close."

"Right. So I'm sure their pizza would taste like shit. And that's probably because it actually had shit in it. Like shit-stuffed-crust pizza."

"Dude, honestly, what the hell is wrong with you?"

"I don't know. This place makes me hate humanity. I want to get the fuck out of here."

Five

I've always had a thing for rum. Not just in drinks either. Pretty much in any capacity I can get it. Rum raisin ice cream, hell yeah. Rum balls, are you kidding me? For sure. Problem is, I'm not much of a cook. And why should I be? I live at my parent's house, and my mom does that for me. And there are these things called restaurants and fast food drive-thru lanes and microwaveable burritos. Cooking seems like a skill that is better off for people who give a damn about what goes into their body.

That said, I do try to make myself a meal every now and then. Out of desperation. Or when I'm drunk. I came up with a recipe for rum-infused chicken breasts that you've got to try one day. Check it out.

Ingredients

1 lb. chicken breasts

½ cup of rum

Some salt

1 pan

First, put the pan on the burner. Then, turn the burner on. Place the chicken breasts onto the pan. Not on the handle of the pan, but in the actual middle of the pan. Once the pan begins to get hot, pour ¼ cup of rum into the pan and watch it begin to bubble. After a few minutes, flip the chicken breasts over. When the rum is almost evaporated, pour the other ¼ cup in the pan and watch it begin to bubble again. Isn't that cool? When the chicken is done, take it out of the pan and put it on a plate. Surprise! I didn't put plate on the ingredient list. I hope that just threw you for a loop. Lastly, sprinkle some salt on the chicken if you like salt. Then eat it.

That's my world famous recipe for Sautéed Rum Chicken with Optional Salt. It goes great with my newest creation, Rum Macaroni and Cheese from a Box. This one is even easier.

Ingredients

1 box of macaroni and cheese

Enough rum to replace the milk part in the recipe

First, read the instructions on the box of macaroni and cheese. Then, for every step where it tells you to use milk, use rum instead. When you're done, put it in a bowl or on a plate. Bam! Did that catch you off guard again? You are such a sucker. Take it over to a table and eat it, preferably alongside some Sautéed Rum Chicken with Optional Salt. Bon Appétit.

I was daydreaming about some of that fantastic chicken when Booker came by and slapped me in the balls. I didn't even see him approaching.

"What the fuck, dude?"

"Exactly."

"What do you mean *exactly*? You fucking asshole."

"Easy, man."

"That was a good hit though. Like you avoided my dick entirely and just hit my balls. You fucking asshole."

Booker smiled and nodded as he looked out toward the street.

"I figured out the solution to our problem. I've got it all lined up."

"What, what to do with all of this rum and how to get back home?"

"Yep. I've got the fix. We're gonna throw a party."

"A party. Here? With all of our friends, like Jose and Guadalupe and…"

"Wow. Way to be racist. Also, calm down. I'm not talking about making friends and having a good time and waking up the next morning and thinking that we've got to do it all again. I'm talking about a means to an end. A solution. To our rum problem. And that solution is a big ass party, right here. Sponsored in part by Private Reserve rum."

I stood up from whatever I was sitting on. I think it was a dusty, white rock – because that's all that Nogales had for chairs. I paced around a little bit. My foot was asleep.

"Hmm. A party. But where are we gonna have it? All we have is a truck."

"Right there."

Booker stretched out his arm and pointed across the street at this thing that looked like a tavern, or a place where you get raped as soon as you walk through the front door. Or a little bit of both.

"Oh, sweet. Did you steal that place too?"

"Whoa whoa whoa, let's not get this shit backwards, man. You stole the truck. Remember? I just sat in the passenger seat and watched you do it. Don't try to blame this on me."

"Whatever. Look at that place. It's a shithole."

"Well, yeah. Everything here is a shithole. That doesn't matter. What matters is that while you were sitting here staring off into the sun like a fucking mongoloid, I was over there talking to the owner who, surprisingly, speaks a good amount of English. And German too. Which was entirely unhelpful, but it's pretty random and I like that.

"Anyway, while you were sitting here, I negotiated a deal with that guy for us to use his place *and the alley in the back* to throw a big ass fiesta with all of our rum. We'll charge forty pesos a head for entrance and unlimited drinks. He'll supply the mixers and the cups and bathrooms and music. We supply the rum. And at the end of the night, we split the money fifty-fifty with him. I showed him how much rum we have, and he thinks we can go through most of it."

"How long was I sitting on this rock? You did all of this?"

"Hell yeah, I did, you robust mongoloid."

He looked triumphant and proud. And why not? He had pretty much solved our problem and found a way for us to get some money out of it. And have a party.

"Sometimes, Booker, you actually impress me. I'm liking the sound of this. Like...I think it'll actually work."

"Well, that's good. Because we don't really have an option at this point. I told that guy we were in for it, and he left right after to drive around and start telling everyone he knows to come on over tonight. I think we'll probably get chased and killed if we back out now."

"Excellent."

"It could be worse."

He was right. It could be way worse. Your life isn't that bad if you are in a non-negotiable contract to host a party and supply all of the booze that you stole, just to make some quick cash and get out of town. It could be way worse.

"What time does this all begin?"

"Diez."

He held out his hands and displayed all ten fingers as though I hadn't taken the same Spanish classes that he took. In fact, we had the same teacher for a few years. Her name was Ms. Pestana. That means eyelash.

"Damn, brother. Good job. Good job. I'm impressed."

We walked toward the truck and opened up the back to stare at our inventory: 514 bottles of rum. What a crazy thing. And somewhere down in Puerto Vallarta, there was a guy without a job or a truck or a sense of when to hit on a group of girls and when to let them stumble back to our room and let us play with their breasts. He probably had a wife and a few kids. Maybe a few wives, who knows. I don't know how the rules work in Mexico. And I sure as hell don't know how he was going to explain all of this to them. But, that's what you get for cockblocking. It never pays.

It was coming on five in the afternoon, and we had some time to kill, so we pulled a bottle from one of the cases and started on it. Within no time, we were already feeling it. The lack of food, the abundance of sun, and our sheer exhaustion made it quite the steep ramp.

We didn't have to wait until ten for people to start arriving. Apparently this guy who ran the rape tavern was really good at getting the word out. That, or there was just nothing to do in Nogales and this guy's place was the jam. Young people, old people, people with babies, men with canes and walkers. It was a trip to see who was showing up for this thing. There were maybe fifty or sixty people all shuffling around before we had even broken out the booze.

"Do you think we should charge them more than forty pesos?" I asked.

"Why? Forty seems fine."

"Well, look at how many people showed up for this price. Maybe we could squeeze a little more out of them. They're already here. What are they going to do? Leave?"

Booker gave me the stank eye.

"You're a greedy bastard."

"I just think they can afford a little more."

"You have no idea what they can afford. Who knows if they're even going to pay?"

"Oh, they better pay. Or we'll take the rum away. Why don't we ask the German guy what he thinks? He'll probably know if this price makes sense."

"No. And he's not German. He *speaks* some German."

"So we can't ask him because he's not German?"

"We can't ask him because we are making a pure profit from this, you dick. Forty is fine. Besides, I already agreed on it with him. So he already gave his opinion. It's forty."

"I wish you would have asked my opinion," I muttered.

"It's forty," he repeated.

We began carrying over cases of rum from the side road where we had parked. I walked quickly and scanned the road each time before opening the truck, paranoid that someone would see us. Booker thought I was overreacting. But for all I knew, these people could steal all of the rum, run away, and maybe even hijack the truck too. Nobody needed to know what we had going on. The last thing I wanted was to be stuck in this town without any wheels. We'd be as good as dead – which is not good, in case that phrase is confusing.

With hundreds of bottles behind his bar, the owner realized quite quickly that there was no point in him even using his shitty, little plastic cups. Everybody who walked in got a bottle of rum. Most people just sucked away at them without any mixer, chaser, or ice. Hot rum, straight out of a bottle. I had to admire them in a way. But it also made me occasionally shudder. How bad was it to live here if this was your version of a party?

Booker was strolling around, hitting on women and getting angry stares from their boyfriends and husbands. It was somewhat of a miracle that he didn't get us into a fight, or worse. The guy just did not understand boundaries. Or social cues. We were about as out of place as two guys in

Mexico could be, and he did not give a shit at all. But that was Booker. Always oblivious and usually lucky.

By eleven o'clock, I bet there were well over a hundred and fifty people there. I was too drunk to figure out how much money that meant we had, but I started to feel a bit stingy toward the barman who was getting half of our proceeds without actually living up to his end of the deal. Aside from the music and the place itself (which really only held about thirty people), with the rest of the crowd spilling out into the alley, he wasn't responsible for anything. No mixers, no cups, no nothing. Just music and an alley. We could have hosted this thing in the middle of the street and ran the truck radio at full blast.

Somebody shot a gun at midnight. When he heard it, Booker looked like he wanted to shit his pants. A part of me is willing to admit that I might have. I don't know if the bullet went into the sky, or into a man, or into a bottle of rum. I didn't see it. It caused a bit of a clamor for maybe twenty seconds or so, and then everybody just carried on. I assumed that meant it went into the sky, but you never know. People get killed in Mexico all the time. Maybe twenty seconds of turning heads is all you're gonna get when your ticket gets punched.

A little while later, I saw a girl giving a guy a blowjob while he leaned against the wall on the other side of the alley. I pulled Booker over to where I was standing so that he could see.

"Damn, man. Scandalous."

"They aren't even behind a fence or a dumpster or anything. They're just…out here."

"I don't think I could get hard in front of all of these people."

I agreed. The guy was standing a few feet away from everybody else. She was on her knees, just doing her thing. Every now and then she would stop and slug back some rum.

"Fuck! His dick must be on fire!"

"As much as I love the feeling of any part of a girl on my penis, I'm gonna have to pass on that. I don't want alcohol making its way up my urethra and who the hell knows where else. Fuck that."

"And fuck her for even making us even think about that. Jesus."

Later on, Booker told me that the couple started having sex. Just out there…in the alley, with everyone else around. I missed that part, and that was okay.

Sometime around two o'clock, I saw a girl catch on fire. That is not a metaphor or a play on words or anything like that. I think that someone had this smart idea to do body shots. But that wasn't enough. No. How about we set the alcohol on fire while doing it? Yeah. This chick, her shirt just burst into flames like she washed it in kerosene instead of Tide. She ripped it off like this had already happened earlier in the week and she knew exactly what to do.

She wasn't wearing a bra, or maybe it came off when she whipped off the shirt. Either way, her breasts were out in the open for the rest of the night. She had a decent rack and a few slight singes on her ribcage. No one tried the burning body shots after she caught on fire. That was good. At least they knew when to call something a failure and move on.

At half past three, Booker was simultaneously vomiting and shitting in a darker corner of the alley. I had a dog that did that once when he overate, but I had never seen a person get into that dilemma until that moment. It looked pretty rough. He later told me that he had completely soaked his shoes while doing that, though he didn't explain how. I didn't ask. I'm not sure which one I'd prefer having all over my feet. Probably the puke. Later on, he ended up tricking some guy into letting him borrow his shoes for a bit, and I think the poor hombre ended up leaving without them. I'm not sure how that happens, but it happens.

Mexico. Fuck.

As for me, I spent most of the night just wandering around trying to absorb the experience that was happening around me. It felt like a time of great gravity and importance even though I should have known better and realized that it wasn't. But I was drunk and feeling emotional, so it was very immense and meaningful in my mind.

This happens to me sometimes. I get drunk and introspective, and I try to take everything in like I have some newfound understanding and perspective that I need to exploit. Sometimes I take out my camera and shoot some video. The footage is always the same thing when I look at it the next day. A bunch of rolling panoramas of scenic views and some jittery shots of the crowd. I always end up deleting it.

The police are too busy making sure they don't get shot to break up parties in Nogales. We never had a visit from any type of authority of any kind. No fire marshal, police officer, paramedic, boy scout, trash collector, nothing. They let us do our thing for as long as our thing could last. I think it was around four in the morning when I started to get practical and I realized that there was no reason I couldn't escape the place with the entire stash of pesos and just get the fuck out. With Booker, of course.

The owner of the rape tavern was nowhere to be found, but he had stupidly left the cash box right behind the bar. For a place where crime was so high and cash was so seemingly scarce, I don't understand how this was his best decision. He must have either been really stupid, really fucked up, or a billionaire performing a social experiment. Those were the only options I could see. I think it was a mix of A and B.

I studied Booker, and he looked like a goddamned mess. He was leaning against the fence in the back, almost exactly where that blowjob went down a few hours earlier. He was staring up at the stars or whatever else he saw up in the sky. Since he had decided on the details of the party while I was staring off into the sky, I decided that it made just as much sense for me to make the decision to hit the cash box and grab everything I could while he was doing the same thing. I was going to do all of this first and *then* get him to follow me to the truck. I figured that to do this in reverse would have been a disaster. But sometimes, disasters are all that the world has in store for you.

Booker came stumbling over to me a few moments after I had crept behind the bar. My hands were on the cash box when I heard him shout at me.

"What are you doing in here?"

"Shut up. Nothing."

He looked down at the cash box.

"How much money did we make?"

"Dude, shut the fuck up! Just go back outside."

He lowered his voice a little, but it was still pretty loud.

"Why are you back here?"

"No reason," I said at the same level, and then I continued on in a whisper. "I'm taking the money and getting the fuck out of here. The guy just left it here."

"But he's still here," Booker said as he looked around the bar.

"I don't care. Fuck that guy."

I opened the cash box and started to grab as big of a pile as I could. There was more than I was expecting. It was too much for me to take on my own.

"Here," I said, shoving a handful of pesos into Booker's hand. "Stuff this in your pockets and head outside."

"What the fuck?"

"I'll follow right behind you. Actually…I'll wait a minute or two so it doesn't look too suspicious."

"This is so fucked, man. Why can't we just stay here?"

"Someone is going to find this money, and they're going to take it. He just left it here. So, I'm making sure that someone is us. Okay?"

I grabbed the rest of the money and stuffed it into my two front pockets.

"Go," I whispered.

He walked out through the crowd and into the alley, looking back at me once before he got outside. I shook my head until he looked away. He had no idea how to be discreet.

I waited a few minutes before I started to make my move. My pockets were stuffed pretty full, and it looked like I had some seriously thick quads. Once I was through the door and out in the alley, I passed a couple that was dancing. They were swaying slowly even though the music wasn't slow at all. The guy was holding a pistol in his hand, relaxed, hanging behind the girl's head. He was staring up into the stars. A true romantic.

Seeing that gun made my dick shrink about two inches into my body. Stuffed full of cash, I felt more uneasy than I had in a long time. I started looking around for Booker and didn't see him anywhere. I assumed that he had made it over to the truck, so I headed that way myself. I fumbled around in my right front pocket for my keys, realizing that like an idiot, I hadn't stopped to think about taking them out before jamming my pocket full of paper. A few bills fell out in the process, but I felt so rushed that I didn't stop to pick them up.

"Hey!" someone back in the alley yelled.

I immediately tensed up, hoping that he wasn't yelling at me. Then he yelled something else in Spanish. I don't know what he said, but it sounded angry. I didn't even think after that. I just started to run. I ran as fast as I could. I felt slowed down by all of the paper that was jamming against my legs, but I kept running. I heard footsteps and shouting behind me, and I didn't look back. There was a split in the path ahead of me. I ran left. It led straight to a dead end. *Fuck.*

I turned around and there were two guys approaching me, looking mad and excited at the same time. I felt my bowels start to push outward. I thought I was going to shit myself right there in that alley. *Fuck.*

One of the guys said something in Spanish, and he pointed to his shoes. Then he looked at the other guy, and he said it again. I heard the words *beso* and *zapatos*.

"Nah, no, no," I said.

The guy kept repeating it and looking at the other guy. He smiled and said it again.

Fuck.

I nodded eventually.

"Alright," I said.

I slowly walked a little closer toward them, trying to buy some time. I remember thinking, *Where the fuck is Booker? How the fuck did I run into a dead fucking end?* When I got within a couple of feet of the guy who was doing the talking, I started to lean down toward his shoes. *Fuck.*

Then I shoved him as hard as I could and started to run in the other direction and out of the alley. I was a pretty fast runner, and I knew that it was a better choice than doing whatever he was suggesting. Those guys were just going to kick my ass if I stayed there. I ran clear out of the alley and toward the main road. I didn't hear anything behind me at that point. When I started to get close enough to see the truck, I immediately ran toward it without any idea of what I was going to do. I couldn't leave without Booker, but I thought that maybe I could lock myself inside. I don't know. I just ran to the only thing of comfort that I saw.

Out of nowhere, some guy dove shoulder-first into my ribs and tackled me to the ground. It wasn't one of the guys from the alley. This guy came out of the front door of the bar. The guys from the alley caught up and held me up against the side of the truck. There was one guy on each of my arms. The guy who tackled me took a big swing and punched me right in the nose. And then the stomach. And then the face again. My head slammed back against the truck a few times. I know this because I heard the crashing sound against the metal.

After that, it was a big blur. I had no chance of fighting back. Those two guys from the alley had me squarely pinned against the truck. I took at least another few hits to the gut before I felt their grip loosen up. I looked up. From what I could tell, Booker was hobbling toward us with what looked like a vacuum cleaner in his hands, held high above his head.

"Get the fuck out of here!" he yelled, swinging the thing through the air.

I could barely see at first, but as my vision started to clear, it looked to me like he was limping. And he was definitely carrying a vacuum cleaner.

The guys who were pinning me against the truck started to back off. The one who was doing the punching turned toward Booker and started to look like he was about to take him on. Booker swung the vacuum around and let out a wild, primal scream. The guy backed away from us and stepped toward the guys from the alley.

"Get the fuck out of here!" Booker yelled again. "You motherfuckers! Get the fuck away!"

The Mexicans were yelling things back in Spanish that I definitely hadn't learned in Spanish class.

"Fuck you!" I yelled, trying to act tougher than I felt.

And then, before I realized that I had started the truck, it was turning onto the main road. I could barely see. My eyes were blurry, and I was blinking a lot from all of the dust that was kicked up and puffing into our faces. The windshield looked like a family of bugs had committed suicide on the glass.

"How can you see anything?" Booker asked.

"I can't. Not through the windshield."

I had my head partway out of the driver's side window. Safety first.

"How about through your eyes?"

"No. Not them either."

Booker sighed and rested his head against his hand, his arm propped up against the window.

"I can't believe that just happened. What the fuck happened?"

"I don't even know. I was trying to get away and I just…I ran down an alley that turned into a dead end. Those motherfuckers wanted me to kiss their shoes or something."

"What?"

"I don't know. I just shoved them and ran to the truck. Then that dude came out of nowhere and speared me into the ground."

"That was fucked up. I was off taking a piss when I heard a bunch of yelling, but I didn't really know what the hell was going on."

"Oh, that's where you were?"

"Yeah."

"Why were you limping? Were you limping?"

He laughed.

"Yeah. I twisted my ankle trying to run over and help you. I actually fell down too. I got a little scraped up."

"Poor baby."

I touched the back of my head and felt for a cut. It was throbbing. When I brought my hand back, my fingers had a shine of blood on them.

"Where did that vacuum come from?"

"Fucking Mexico," he replied. "I have no idea. It was just there."

"Well, shit. It saved our asses, I think."

I paused, and neither of us said anything for a bit. Then I continued.

"We have to get the fuck away from this town as soon as we can."

"No shit, man. And you need to get something to put on your cuts. You are bleeding out of both sides of your head."

I tried squirting some of the washer fluid onto the windshield, and I think that I heard the truck laugh. The wipers scraped back and forth and settled back into their slots, having done nothing but smear the mess a little more.

"Do you think it was worth the money?"

Booker sat up and looked somewhat excited. It made me a little excited.

"Oh yeah! I don't know. Maybe. I mean, probably? There were a ton of people there. I'm guessing that they all didn't pay, but I bet some of them did."

I looked down at my lap for a little bit – long enough to lose track of the road. I swerved when my eyes came back up, but it was just out of instinct.

"Look at my fucking pockets, Booker. Jesus!"

My legs looked like swollen sausages, like we had stuffed a replica Goodyear blimp up each leg. I was fat with money.

"Did we just loot the joint? Or whatever people say when they walk away with a lot of money that's not theirs?"

"I think we just made some fucking bank," Booker said.

"Yeah, or that. Did we just do that?"

"Let's count it."

"Later."

"Let's count it now. Come on."

He reached over and started to fish some of the bills out of my pocket. I stared ahead at the road, my head still halfway out the window.

"Not cool. Stop it!"

"Aww, is Blakey ticklish?"

"Yes, Blakey is ticklish. Blakey also doesn't want your hands in his pockets right now while he's driving this fucking truck and his head is throbbing from the goddamned beat down he just got."

"Blakey is a soldier, man. You took that beating like a pro."

"Booker…listen."

He stopped what he was doing but kept his hand somewhat in my pocket.

"Okay, first of all, either take the money out or get your hands off of my fucking leg. Don't just leave it there. Second…you don't think any of those guys would be following us for this, right?"

He moved his hand off of my leg and on to the seat.

"They might be."

"Should we hide the truck somewhere? Or just keep driving?"

"Definitely keep driving."

I shook my head, but not in disagreement. I think I do that a lot.

We rode along in the night, turning randomly down side streets and main streets, completely drunk and oblivious to where we were going. I started to smile a little bit even though my face felt like it had been run over with a steamroller.

"You are a crazy son of a bitch," Booker said.

Then he said something straight out of nowhere.

"And man…I love being a turtle."

I had to agree.

Six

"I've always had a thing for rum."

She looked at me and shook her head.

"That doesn't make it any better."

She had a face that didn't do her body any justice at all. She wore clothes that didn't really play it up either. It was only due to my general male desperation that I was able to discover what she had going on once you got past these diversions. That was a happy accident.

Her name was Harper. She was a friend of mine that sometimes let me sleep with her, unless she was in a bad mood or trying to date someone. At one point she had a little thing for me, but I was too caught up with the idea of not being in a relationship that it didn't ever go anywhere. Besides, I couldn't be with someone whose face I was embarrassed to have my friends look at.

Not that she was ugly. She wasn't. She was just very plain. She was a smoker, and her teeth were that slight shade of yellow that develops from too much nicotine or too much coffee. They were straight and of normal size and all of that, but they weren't the right color. Her eyes were nothing impressive – little brown dots underneath a very faint set of lashes, tucked under a very faint set of eyebrows. Her nose was nothing offensive, nor spectacular. Brown hair. Normal ears. Good jawline. Whatever else matters about a face, it was all there and normal. When you dissect her features one by one, she really wasn't all that bad. But when you put it all together, it was just too bland for me to get excited about. I never found myself staring at her directly. She was better off in the periphery.

Or in the bed. Underneath her usually forgettable clothes was a body that made me wonder if I was really that shallow after all. She never went to the gym, but she still had a tight little stomach. Her frame was small, maybe 5'1, and she packed a hell of a set. They had to be a C-cup, but they felt even bigger since she was so little. She had a tight, little ass and legs that gripped the sides of my hips like she wasn't gonna let me go. What a crazy little body. I learned a lot about what made me go when I was with her.

It was about two weeks after Booker and I got back from Mexico. I was lying in my bed. Harper was sitting up, looking out the window and into the yard. The air in my room was hazy with cigarette smoke, even with my window halfway open. Slants of light were peeking through the leaves and branches outside, casting patterns across the floor. Wisps of smoke curled around in the air. I stared at them longer than I had ever looked at the girl who was sitting right beside me. I don't know what she was looking at outside. Maybe the grass.

"So I still don't get how you guys managed to get out of that shitbox of a town and all the way back to L.A."

I had been telling her the story of my past few weeks, and I had conveniently arrived at the end of the party. What a coincidence.

"It was still a hell of a drive away. At the time, I didn't realize that Nogales was basically just south of Tucson…which is like eight hours away from here, at least. I was thinking we were really close to Tijuana, like we were just a town over."

"You didn't bother to look at a map or use your phone or anything?"

"Oh, hell no. Mexican data rates are ridiculous. That's why I didn't text you, remember?"

She looked at me suspiciously. I was lying, and she knew it. I ignored the look and kept talking.

"I did look at a map. I mean…I don't know. I wasn't thinking too much. I think I was in a perpetual state of intoxication the entire time. All I could think about was getting back home, which I knew was up."

I pointed up, in case she didn't know what I meant.

"So what happened after the party? Where did you guys sleep that night?"

"Oh, the truck."

"In the front or the back?"

"The front. But that's a good point. We probably could have lain in the back and stretched out a bit more. I was so cramped up. Especially sleeping behind the steering wheel. I really didn't have too many places to lean. It was probably the worst night of sleep I might have ever had."

"Luckily you guys were drunk."

"Thank God, right?"

"Thank God. So, you slept. And then what?"

"It really was pretty uneventful compared to the night before. And we barely slept anyway. I was too afraid that one of those guys was still chasing after us. So maybe we slept like an hour or something. And then when we woke up, we decided that with the money we pocketed from the party, we'd just buy a flight back to L.A. and be done with it. No more rum truck. No more rum even. Well, for a bit at least."

"So you just showed up at the airport with your jacked up face and bought a ticket with a bunch of Mexican pesos?"

"Well, no. We had decided that we'd be better off if we crossed the border and flew out of Tucson, once we realized how far away we were. Originally we were going to try to take a bus back to L.A., but it was just too far away. So we did end up crossing the border. On foot, actually. And then got a ride up to Tucson, to the airport. And the rest is logged in a C.I.A. database somewhere."

"Your face doesn't look too bad at least."

"Yeah. It was worse before. The swelling went down a lot. I still have a bump on the back of my head."

I still do, too.

"Oh yeah," she said, nodding as she ran her hand over it.

Throughout the entire story, she just kept staring out into the yard, like there was some magic show out there that only she could see. She turned around after my last comment and looked at me. I was lying on my back, my left hand resting against the lower part of my belly. From her angle, I probably had a bit of a double chin. She smiled half-heartedly and turned around to scout the location of her clothes. In my head, I hoped that if she found them, she'd just put them over her head but never down past her face.

"I think I'm gonna go. I've got some things to do."

It was such an empty comment, but I didn't have the courtesy to pretend like it was sincere. There was no bitterness between us, but there was no need to act as though there was anything more to it than what it was.

"Okay."

She started to put her clothes on, and my heart sank a little bit when she found the head hole in her shirt and I saw her hair pushing up through it. Oh well. She looked at me with a bit of a funny look, so I returned it.

"I wonder what my family would think if they knew I was sleeping with a car thief."

She smiled a little bit.

"Oh, don't worry about that."

I looked at her face for longer than I ever had. It really wasn't that bad.

"It's not like we *actually* sleep. Right?"

Her smile faded away, and she walked toward the door.

"And by the way, it was a truck, not a car!"

I was trying to add some levity, but she was just trying to leave. I heard the front door close. The muscles in my back relaxed as I reclined fully into my bed. I let out a fart. I had been holding it in the whole time.

The pattern of the light coming in through the trees had changed, and it was now climbing up onto my dresser along the far wall. I reached over and took a look at my phone. Nothing. I don't know who I was expecting, but whoever it was, they didn't try to find me.

I stared up at the ceiling and recounted our trip home from Nogales. I don't know why I lied to Harper. It's not like anything would change if I told her what we really did. She wouldn't care if I told her that we never got on a flight from Tucson. That we never even went up into Arizona. That we drove west along the northern edge of the Mexican border in that goddamned truck, sweating our asses off in the baking sun. That we stopped in Mexicali and found a hardware store that sold us enough paint to cover the Private Reserve logos and any trace of an indication that this might be a delivery truck. That we actually drove the damned thing through border control, shitting our pants the entire time. That we drove it all the way to L.A.

That it was parked in the parking lot of a strip mall only a few blocks away from my house. That it was probably a day or two away from getting towed to a junkyard. That I wasn't sure what the hell to do with it, but that I didn't want to get rid of it.

She wouldn't have cared about any of that, but for some reason, I didn't tell her.

I watched my sheets ruffle the slightest bit as a slight breeze blew through the window. How romantic. I picked up my phone and called

Booker. Romantic moments make me think of Booker. He didn't pick up because he was at work, but he text me back within a minute or two. His lunch break was in about an hour, so I was going to stop by and pay him a visit.

I wandered around my house a bit, not sure what to do with my spare time. I hadn't written in a while, since well before I left for Mexico, and I had no real intention of getting started anytime soon. Even though I missed it more than I missed anything else in my life, I couldn't bring myself back to starting again. Not that I was much of a writer. I really was shit. But it's what I wanted to do, so I did it.

That's how I lived back then. I just did whatever I wanted to do, or more accurately, I had the option to do whatever I wanted to do. Whether I did it or not was really inconsequential.

In high school, I pulled decent enough grades to get accepted to UCLA for undergrad. My parents were proud of me, and I was proud of myself too. I went for a quarter. Well, part of a quarter, but I liked to tell myself that I finished the whole eleven weeks and decided that it wasn't for me. What really happened was that I went for a few weeks, I didn't like it, and then I decided that my time would be better off spent doing something else. Anything else. I was living at home, and my parents were paying my tuition while I commuted to class. That was the deal. I didn't get the campus experience, but I also didn't get the crushing debt afterward. It was a fair compromise.

Except, I didn't hold up my end of the agreement. It was a short-sighted plan that I really can't justify anything about, but I decided to pretend that I was still enrolled in school in pursuit of a degree in film studies. In reality, I spent my days just writing and trying to build various little things here and there in my dad's shop in the backyard. That, and chasing girls. And drinking rum. That was about it though.

I had some decent Photoshop skills, so with that first quarter transcript that I did receive – the one that indicated that I had failed all of the courses

I was registered for – I was able to forge the remainder of my tenure at the University. My fake tenure, that is. Each quarter would roll by, and I would ask my parents for more money to pay for the tuition and the cost of the books and all of that crap. And they'd write me a check. And it would go straight into my checking account, where I'd slowly drain it until the next quarter began.

I was quite the fake student. Three years in a row of summer courses. I signed up for lots of labs because labs required extra fees and supplies, and that meant more money for me. At one point I almost fabricated my acceptance into a study-abroad program. The only thing that got in my way was my very temporary erection for a girl from the valley that I had met. She was not going to be able to find a way to spend the next spring in Rome with me. That three-week hard-on saved my parents quite a bit of money.

I sat down on the living room couch with a Tupperware half-filled with leftovers from last night's dinner. We had one of those coffee tables that could rise up on hinges and elevate to the proper eating height, if you were seated on the couch. My parents loved to use it. They were very proud of their transformable furniture piece. I never used it. I preferred to hunch over my food like a barbarian. If I wanted to sit properly, I'd be at the table. I figured it was better to not pretend that I was classier than I was. I was already pretending that I was well-educated. Well-mannered would have been too much of a stretch.

On days like this, the clock was my nemesis. It felt like it had been hours since Booker had last texted me. According to my phone, it had been thirteen minutes. I had a lot of time to kill, and I didn't know what to do with it. I started to think about our journey back from Mexico. It was one big, dusty blur. We escaped Nogales with a little bit short of four cases of rum, which was actually very impressive when you think about it. That party burned through almost forty cases of rum. That's not forty bottles. That's forty *cases*. Clearly, it wasn't all consumed on the spot. Somebody must have found the truck and raided us for a good deal of it, but what was interesting to me was that they didn't take it all.

No matter. We couldn't do anything with the remainder, whether it was four cases or four bottles or four truck loads. We had to get over the border, and it didn't seem like a good idea to be trucking along a suspicious amount of alcohol with us. We ended up trying to peddle the rum for cash in a few of the towns that we passed through. Nobody wanted to barter with us. There were a few people who accepted the rum for free, but even that was more difficult than I would have expected. The average Mexican is a very wary, shrewd negotiator. A free bottle of rum to them probably felt like standing underneath a big cartoon net, ready to drop on their heads and send them straight to jail. It was like giving away free condoms. Nobody trusted us.

I vowed to myself that I would never tell another soul about this. But since this is just writing, I can pass it off as artistic license. We actually had to ditch about two cases worth of rum before driving across the border. We couldn't find *anybody* to take it from us. Unbelievable. Had I not wanted to get the hell out of the country more badly than I'd wanted pretty much anything else in my life up until that point, I might have just found a tree to lie under and then leaned against it as I sipped through the bottles that we had left. Instead, we neatly placed two boxes up against a telephone pole, wished them farewell, and drove away. I never looked back. It was a disgrace.

I got off my ass and decided to walk to the butcher shop where Booker worked. Driving would have gotten me there in just a few minutes, but I had nothing else to do with my time. A walk wouldn't kill me, I hoped.

He was already sitting outside when I got there.

"What'd you fucking walk here?"

"Yeah."

"That bad, huh? You know you could always get a job, and work, like me. It wouldn't be that bad. You could make money, like a real person.

Pay bills, like a real person. All of those normal things you somehow don't have to worry about. You could worry about them too."

"Sounds stimulating. But I think I'd rather enjoy the free ride I'm on. What's on special today?"

"Tri-tip."

"How much?"

"$9.99 a pound."

"Shit. Is that good?"

"Hell yeah. Tri-tip is awesome. You've had it before…I made it that time we went out to your uncle's place."

"No, I know what tri-tip is, dude. I mean, is that a good price for it? $9.99 a pound seems like a lot of money for what pretty much tastes like thinly sliced steak."

"Don't even fucking start with me. Tri-tip is not just *thinly sliced steak*, okay? It's tri-tip. It's a real fucking thing."

Booker got very serious when it came to meat.

"Consider me educated."

"Asshole."

"Guess who I fucked today?"

"That butterface?"

I nodded without smiling or feeling good about myself.

"Why do you keep going back to her? Is it that good?"

"It's pretty good. It's better than this," I said, holding up my left hand.

I don't know who taught me how to masturbate, but I have always used my left hand even though I'm not a lefty. I don't know what's going on there. I just tell myself that it's okay to be different.

"I want to see what this chick looks like. She can't be that bad if you're always nailing her."

"She's pretty bad."

"Bad how?"

I looked around the parking lot like she might be there waiting to hear what I was about to say.

"She just isn't pretty. I don't know what else to say about it, really. She's not ugly. She's not repulsive or anything. She just isn't pretty enough for me to want anything serious with her."

Booker nodded.

He was wearing a white smock. It had light red streaks running down the sides of the sleeves and across the front bib. I never understood why anyone in the food industry thought it was a good idea to dress the people handling the things that could make them the dirtiest in the color that presented it the most. It'd be like laying down black carpeting in a birdcage.

"What time are you out of here today?"

"8:30."

"Want to come by after? I'm pretty fucking bored. Out of my mind, man."

"You know how to make a guy feel wanted."

"*You* know how to make a guy feel wanted."

Booker laughed. He started to walk back inside.

"Seeya at 8:40."

"Wait. What the fuck? I just got here. You're already going back in?"

It felt like the kind of scene in a TV show or a movie that I absolutely hated. I had come all the way to his shop just for a few lines of well-rehearsed dialogue, and then it was time for me to leave. Like people in the real world would ever go out of their way for such a brief encounter.

"I lied to you when I said that my break started in an hour. It was starting in a few minutes. I just wanted to be alone for a bit."

"What?"

He walked inside and ignored me. And there I was, sitting on the set of that movie, wondering what the fuck had just happened. Did I really just waste my time *walking* over there, just to talk about the girl I had nailed and what time we'd meet up later? I was starting to get upset when I realized that I literally had nothing else to do. I had wasted the previous hour daydreaming and waiting for the right time to head over.

At times like this, I wished that I had some great idea to write about. Or even more generally, something inspirational in my life. Something to put my effort toward. Something that made these empty, hollow fragments of time feel like they were a reprieve, not the main attraction of the day. I sat there on the wooden bench outside of that meat shop, and I felt the utter entirety of the weight of my life on my shoulders. It felt like a feather. And it made me sad as hell. I had nothing going on. At all. The highlight of my day was some meaningless sex with a girl whose face embarrassed me.

On the walk over, I had picked up a broken sprig from a plant that I couldn't find. It was lying helplessly on the sidewalk, and I felt the need to rescue it. From what, I don't really know. Being stepped on. A broom. A dog's raised leg. It didn't matter. It was a lonely, broken twig, no longer getting the water and nutrients and other shit that a plant needs to live. I walked along holding that branch, trying to extract some sort of metaphor from it. Was it my life? My future? My inability to form a relationship with anything other than someone I've known longer than I can even remember?

In the end, I came up with nothing. It turned out that it was just a twig after all. I still carried it with me to the meat shop. Booker looked at it a few times during our conversation, but he didn't say anything. He knew me well enough to know that this was something to just ignore. I'm not sure how he knew that, but he did. I left it on the table and walked home, half of the time worrying if I should have taken it with me.

When I got home, I decided to call the hotel that we had been staying at in Mexico before the rum truck took over the rest of our vacation. We had both left our suitcases there. On their own, they were probably worth at least a hundred dollars, let alone the contents within them. I didn't actually care about anything that I had traveled with. In fact, everything that I had packed for our spring break trip, I purposely packed with the idea that I may ruin it while I was there. But now that I was back, I figured it might be worth seeing what had happened to all of our things.

Calling the hotel was something that I had been avoiding. I have a hard time on the phone with people who can't understand me. It really frustrates me, to the point where I would just let them keep all of my things. But I had resigned to the fact that the suitcase that I had left behind was a nice one and I might actually want to get it back. It was April, and I was feeling the pinch of my dwindling checking account. Even though I was technically just starting a new quarter – and by that, I mean that I was pretending to be starting a new quarter – I had already spent a good deal of the tuition money that my father had given me. So rather than buy a new suitcase, I was going to try to get my old one back. And whatever other shit they had zipped inside.

Even just looking up the phone number was putting me on edge. I keyed it into my phone and stared at the numbers on my screen for a while before I actually pushed to connect. It took a while for it to start ringing.

"Hola y bienvenido a…"

"Hablas Ingles?"

I wasn't going to let her go on and on in Spanish when I had no clue what she was trying to say.

"Yes. Hello and welcome, sir. How are you today?"

"I am fine, thanks. I'm calling because, ha, I…"

"I'm sorry, sir, can you please hold one second? Sorry, thank you."

"Yep."

Hold music. Some shitty banjo with horns. What a stereotype.

"Hola. Hi, sir. I'm sorry about that."

"That's okay. So I am calling because I…I was a guest at the hotel a few weeks back. And I actually…myself and the person I was sharing the room with…we had to leave the country unexpectedly. We did not even have a chance to go back to our room to collect our belongings."

"Oh, no?"

"No. Yeah, it was very strange. I'm not sure what you would do in a scenario like this. Do you typically keep things that you find in a room, like a lost and found?"

"Oh, yes, yes. Yes we do. What is the thing you think you forgot?"

"Well, it's not just one thing. I had…all of my things were there. Everything I brought with me, except my wallet, thankfully. We left everything behind, and actually, we didn't even get to check out of the room."

"Oh! I think I heard about this, yes. You left all of your things in the room, yes?"

"Yes, that's right. You heard about this?"

"Why did you do that for?"

"Oh, well. It's actually a personal…it's a sad story. *Tristé*. I…when I was staying at your hotel, I received a call from the police in Los Angeles where I live, telling me that both of my parents had died in an accident. And that I had to come back to Los Angeles to identify the bodies. I'm their…I was their only son."

"An accident?"

"Yes, and…I'm sorry. Did you understand what I just told you? My parents have died. They died while I was staying with you. And I left all of my things behind."

"You left everything in your room, yes, yes. I heard about this, yes."

"I'm sorry. I'm…is there somebody else who might be able to help me? I am…I'm trying to see if I can get my suitcase and all of my things back, but I don't think you understand what I am saying. Is that right?"

"Oh, yes, yes. I understand, yes."

"Is there somebody else I can talk to who can help me with this?"

"You need help with the accident? Ehhh...you need help?"

"Jesus, no. I...is there somebody *else* there? Somebody who speaks more English? Who can help me? Talk to me? About my luggage?"

"Ahh. Yes, yes."

There was a long pause. I wasn't sure if she was going to get somebody else or if she thought the conversation had ended.

"Are you still there?"

"Yes, yes, sir. Hello. And welcome."

I hung up the phone and slumped against the back of the couch. Slightly racist thoughts went through my head. I was going to wait and call back in a few minutes and hopefully get somebody else on the other end of the phone. My second attempt failed. Same woman. On my third attempt, I just got stuck on hold for what felt like infinity. So I hung up. My fourth try, an hour or so later, I actually connected with someone who spoke better English. Or at the very least was willing to try to listen to me.

By the end of the conversation, she was so moved by my story that she offered to ship the luggage and whatever pieces they had identified as belonging to me, free of charge. She must have had some seniority there, being able to make a decision like that. Or maybe she had no clue what she was talking about either, and all of my shit was never going to make it back to me. All in all, I don't know if it was worth the effort, but I did feel a slight hint of happiness that I had at least tried. My day now consisted of two primary actions, not just one. Exhausted, I lay down and napped for a while.

Seven

I've always had a thing for rum. I went on a family vacation to St. Lucia once. Pretty island. Very nice people. Good weather and scenery. Great rum. Not the best in the world, from what I've determined, but well up there. The Caribbean is the place to be when it comes to rum, rum making, rum distilling, and whatever other rum-related activities there are to be done that I am not aware of at this time.

We stayed at a remote resort because that's what my parents thought would make for a nice vacation. It was about a mile and a half down a very bumpy, pothole-riddled dirt road that forked off of the main street. The main street was also made mostly of dirt and more potholes. Most of St. Lucia used the same building materials. There was no Home Depot or Loews. There was just dirt. It took us almost two hours to get from the airport to the hotel even though it was only something like twenty miles. I threw up in the van on the way there, and we had to pull over. It wasn't a great start to the trip. I felt somewhat bad about that.

My parents had planned very few things for our trip, and that was okay with me. We mostly sat by the beach and did what people in the Caribbean do. White people, that is.

We drank, we swam, we read, we ate, and we slept. It was nice, but it was fairly typical. Or *ped-es-tri-an.* I had done some research before we left, and I really wanted to go on a tour of a local rum distillery. My parents wanted to go too. We procrastinated throughout the week and made up reasons to put it off. There was a wine tasting event at the resort on Wednesday. Cleus, the sommelier, was hosting. We wanted to go to that. On Tuesday it was supposed to rain. On Thursday, we decided to take a water taxi to another resort where they had white sand shipped in from another island. That was a big draw. But when it was windy, the sand blew all over the place and nearly blinded anyone who wasn't wearing sunglasses. We saw a cave full of bats on the way back. We had to relax on Friday and do nothing because all of that white sand had made us tired.

So we had decided to take the rum tour on Saturday, the day before we were going to leave the island. Clearly it was our only free day. When we went to arrange for tickets on Friday afternoon, we learned that they did not give tours on weekends. The one thing I had really, *really* wanted to do, I had somehow avoided being able to do. Well done. I still haven't been on a rum distillery tour, but at least now I can say that I understand the transport function pretty well.

Booker had the day off, and we were going to the record store. I don't know why it was still called that. They didn't sell records, and they might not have ever sold records, for all I know. On top of that, I don't even know why we went there in the first place. It's somewhat hard to remember, but back then, people would sometimes still buy CDs. When they did, sometimes they bought them in a store. There was a very slight nostalgia to the idea of combing through rows of CD cases, but it wasn't enough to make me want to buy one. It wasn't even an appealing nostalgic event to experience. It was like going to a library. It isn't fun.

The Internet has made things so much easier and more efficient that it just seemed stupid to do anything other than search for something that you wanted online. The Internet is a crazy thing. We take it for granted, but it really is incredible. By the time this book is published, which may very well be never, the concepts that I describe in our journey may be out of touch. The Internet is to blame. Some of the events in my life that used to make sense don't make sense now.

Nevertheless, there we were at a record store, searching through rows of compact discs. Booker said it best.

"Scintillating."

"Isn't it?"

"It is. I mean, it literally is. This band is called *Scintillating*."

He was holding up an album with the word on the spine. On the front was a close up image of what looked like a chicken's eye. It looked upset.

"Oh. How appropriate."

"Right?"

I nodded in response.

The thing about Booker and I was that if we were together, we were alright. It really didn't matter what we were actually doing, as long as we had each other to play off of. We were very good at keeping each other company. We would argue. Drink. Rank girls we had slept with. Sort through CDs in a soon-to-be-shuttered record store. It didn't matter. As long as we were together, we were alright.

We crossed through the *S* section and made our way to *T*. Hopefully, in the future, the Internet hasn't changed the order of the English alphabet, and this still makes sense. In 2007, *T* came after *S*.

"Hey hey hey, what are you doing here?"

Booker was talking to a CD that was apparently out of place.

"You don't belong in the *T* section. Do ya? *Dooooo yaaaaa*?"

Flopping around in his hand was a paper case wrapped in plastic.

"Oh yeah? What is it?"

"*Juturna*."

"Fuck. I love that album."

"*Your face is light…*"

"*…and cocaine white…*"

An older woman (and by that, I mean someone maybe in her late thirties) was walking down the aisle next to us. She looked up, somewhat alarmed at our impromptu vocal arrangement. She walked away. She seemed annoyed.

"What the eff was her problem?"

"I don't know. Like singing in a RECORD STORE is that big of a DEAL."

I raised my voice so that maybe she could hear me, or at least that was my passive-aggressive intent. Booker jabbed me in the ribs with his elbow to hush me.

"They are so good live."

"They really are."

"Do you remember that time at the ICC Church?"

He laughed. Of course he remembered.

It was the middle of the summer, mid-July actually, and we had tickets to a show that started sometime around five or six at night, which was weird. It was on a Saturday too. Booker and I always got drunk before concerts. Before anything, really, but especially before concerts. In fact, to this day, there are only a handful of musical performances that I have ever seen fully sober. And most of them were probably on TV, or before I was fifteen. In this case, we had a drink or two before we started walking to the venue. It wasn't far from our friend's house where we were staying. We were in Boston. I don't remember why we were there and why our friend who we were visiting wasn't with us. I think maybe he was working that night. He didn't come with us to the show. I remember that much.

On our way there, we realized that since it was at a church, there wasn't going to be a bar or any drinks served there. Makes sense, of course, but we hadn't planned for that. We had a bit of a buzz going, so when we got there, we walked in and got our wristbands so we could come and go as we needed to. The first band was just finishing. Within a few minutes, we were left with nothing to do but stand there with a bunch of sweaty teenagers.

That sounded fun. So we decided to step out of the back of the church to wander around. We found our way to a liquor store and each picked up a bottle of coke and one of the little nips of rum. Or two each, I think. We asked for paper bags and then went outside to the curb, dumped about a half of the soda into the gutter, and poured in the rum. I think it was Bacardi. I would have protested, but they didn't have anything else. In the land of the blind, the one-eyed man is king.

A swish or two and a delicate opening of the cap to make sure we didn't explode the things all over ourselves, and we were all set. We had a pint or so of rum and coke for each of us. Since we couldn't go back into the church with our drinks, we went out back behind it and drank in the alley. The bands' vans were all parked along the back wall. The first band was already loading their gear into their van. It hadn't been more than ten minutes after they had struck their last chord. That's efficiency.

Booker and I sat against the brick wall of the adjacent building that formed the alley behind the church. We drank out of our paper bags like two hobos. A couple of guys from the band were throwing a football around while the others were still loading their gear in. Booker and I realized at the same time that we both had to take a piss. But with more than half of our drinks still left, we were stuck with only one real option. Going back into the church wasn't going to happen, and drinking them down really fast was detrimental to our already full bladders. So we did what logic told us to do.

We went back to the corner where the alley met the edge of the adjacent brick building, and we unzipped and let it all out.

The alley was on a slight hill, so each of us began to see our puddles turning into slowly traveling streams that ventured between our legs and out into the open space behind us. Once we finished, we started walking back to our seats against that wall, but then we realized that there was something interesting going on. Our urine streams were slowly racing each other. Booker and I began cheering them on, each of us looking back at the origin and hoping we had left enough there to fuel the stream to travel farther and farther along. This went on long enough that the guys throwing the football began to watch and cheer along with us. I don't remember who won, but I don't think I'll ever forget that race.

"I'm pretty sure I won," Booker proclaimed.

"Dude, we've already established that we don't remember who won. It wasn't even about that."

"That's what a loser would say."

"You're what a loser would say," I retorted.

He started to say something and then changed his course.

"Remember how good they were?"

We went to the show for the headlining band, but the singer had gone crazy and had to be sent to a mental hospital. So we were left with the next best act, a band that neither of us had seen and that we each had only heard a handful of times beforehand. We weren't sure what to expect.

"They were so fucking good. He is so crazy on stage. So into it…I don't think I have ever seen a more intense, involved performance by any one person."

"Yeah. I mean, I don't know. They were so good."

We sat there and daydreamed a while, Booker holding their first album in his hand.

"I think they played the whole thing that day."

"Well, yeah. They didn't have any other songs yet, remember?"

"That's true."

"We should go see them again."

"Yes."

"I wonder when they're coming around here next. Do you know?

I had to stop and think.

"I'm pretty sure whatever tour they're on now, it either doesn't come through L.A. or it already did."

I took out my phone and started to look it up.

"You can do that shit on your phone?"

"Yeah, dude," I said, sort of paying attention and not looking up. "You know that. I can do pretty much anything on this thing."

"I was thinking about getting one, but I mean...why bother, when you have one. You know?"

"Yeah, yeah. So yep, I was right. They were here just a couple of weeks ago. Now they're across the country again already."

"Shut up. You already looked that shit up? Jesus, man."

"Yep. The power of that thing, the Internet. Behold the power, Booker."

He was still holding on to the CD, and he started to shake it around a bit in his hand, looking like he was trying to get its lunch money to fall out of its pockets.

"We should go to some kind of show then. What else is coming up?"

I was still playing around on my phone.

"Brand New is on tour."

"*Love* Brand New. With who?"

"Kevin Devine."

"Alright, whatever. I *love* Brand New though. When?"

"Fuck, man. Yesterday."

"Are you kidding?" he yelled. "How did we miss both of them coming through here?"

"Avalon. Because we suck."

"Fuck!"

"Did you know that I still have that water bottle that Jesse Lacey threw into the crowd that time we saw them with Dashboard? It's gotta be a few years old now, at least."

"Who fucking cares?"

"They're playing in Vegas tonight," I added.

"Dammit. Where after that?"

"Tempe on Saturday."

"Where's Tempe?"

"It's like Phoenix, pretty much. Just outside of it."

"Alright. Saturday. Want to go?"

"Really?" I asked.

"Yeah. To Phoenix. Want to go?"

It was a straightforward question – and one that I've looked back and thought about so many times since then. There was an importance to it that I didn't understand. An importance that I couldn't possibly grasp at the time. I weighed the seemingly limited list of considerations in my head. I had no job, so there was no conflict there. My parents didn't pay attention to a damned thing I did, so that was going to be okay too. I didn't have a ton of money, but I also wasn't hurting too badly.

"Whose car would you want to take? Also, wait. What about your work? Don't you have to work?"

"I kind of don't want to work there anymore."

"Booker, you've been working there since you were sixteen. You can't just decide that because you want to go see a concert that you don't want to work there anymore."

"Yeah," he said, sadly. "I know. I just…I don't want to cut fucking meat for the rest of my life."

"Ah, here we go."

"What? I mean..."

"No, forget it. Forget I asked. I don't care. I don't. Not now."

I took a look at him, and he just looked sad. Dejected.

Shit.

"You'd really just not show up and drive to Phoenix to see a concert?"

"Yeah."

"You don't even know who else is playing."

"I don't care. It's Brand fucking New. It'll be worth it. As long as we're not late."

I laughed. We were always late to concerts. It was pretty bad. We had missed a number of bands that we had gone to see – that we had gone to multi-act shows just to see – only to not actually get to see them. This would be the quintessential definition of failure. Driving eight hours just to see some other shitty bands not be as good.

"Alright. I mean, I'm in. You know I don't have anything else to do."

He knew it.

"Nice."

"Who's driving?"

I didn't care who was actually going to drive, but rather, whose car was going to take us there. He shook the album around in his hand a bit while he mulled it over. Then he raised his eyebrows and his eyes got wide.

"How about we take the truck?"

I blurted out a laugh. But before I could reject it, he continued.

"Think about it for a second. It's what, an eight-hour drive each way? That's long. That's a lot of gas, and yeah, that'll be more expensive in the truck than in our cars."

"Yeah, exactly."

"But you're not thinking about the other costs."

"Oh, like the cost of the medical bills when I get my fucking ass kicked again?"

"That's not going to happen again. Come on."

"Easy for you to say. You're not the one who walked away with the bruised up face."

"Stop it. That was because *you* wanted to steal the money. That's karma, man. We already went over this. And that has nothing to do with this. In this situation, the truck actually *saves* us money."

"Oh yeah? How's that?"

"Okay. So, that's an eight hour drive. So we drive out there, we get there, and we get ready for the show. We get drunk. We watch the show, we drink after the show, and then...we drive back eight hours in one of our cars?"

"No. I mean, obviously not. But just because we drove that truck through all of fucking Mexico, and we were drunk almost the entire time and didn't get pulled over once, it doesn't mean it's our good luck charm and we can just hit the road in it when we're hammered and it'll be okay. Come on."

"Right, wow. Okay. That's not what I meant. I meant like, we are going to be drunk and we're going to be in Phoenix."

"*If* we go," I added.

"Right, *if*. Well *if* we go, and *if* we took the truck, we could just park it somewhere, bring a couple of blankets, and sleep in the back. Save ourselves the cost of a hotel, the risk of being fucked with if we're sleeping in the car...sorry, I mean, *if* we are sleeping in the car where the cops or whoever could see us. And at the end of the day, it'll probably cost less in extra gas than it would *if* we spent the night in a hotel."

"Fuck, man."

He smiled as though my words thus far were any encouragement at all.

"Think about it."

"I am. I am."

I laughed.

"Laughing is not thinking."

"Yeah. Okay, yeah. Wow. The truck?"

"The truck."

"Fucking truck," I said, and I laughed again.

"Fucking truck, dude."

And that was that. We were taking the truck to Phoenix to see Brand New. And although I had essentially buried myself into a lie of a life that I had no real plan or way of getting out of, something like this made me stop and remember how truly grateful I was to be living however the hell I wanted to be living. Not everyone gets to do this. Certainly not as long as I did.

We walked around the record store for a little while longer before heading back to my place. We stopped by the parking lot where the truck was parked, its windshield littered with fliers and tickets and splattered bugs. The paint job that we did was still holding strong, with no sign of the Private Reserve logo peeking through, no matter how hard we looked.

"Do you think we should wash it?" Booker asked.

I laughed. It was pretty damned dirty.

"Yeah, why not. She could use it."

I peered into the driver's side window and shook my head. It had been a couple of weeks since I had been inside, but nothing had changed.

And now, in a few days, we would be bound for Phoenix. Like the name itself, this trip would bring some well-needed change. A fiery rebirth for us all.

Eight

I've always had a thing for rum. I don't care much about the genre, but I do get a little sentimental over pirate movies. Even well-done commercials with pirates in them will get me. There's something about a boat, some barrels of rum, and the desperation that comes with being stranded at sea for so long. It makes me emotional. And not because I have any attachment to the ocean or sailing or any of that. It's only because I have such an attachment to rum. I find it undeniably romantic. I think that anything that is unknown is romantic, to some extent.

So when I was sitting on the couch in my living room with my hand down my pants, just playing around with my dick a little bit, I didn't mind that one of those *Pirates* movies was on TV. I was flopping it from one side to the other and then back again, feeling it grow a bit and then easing back until it relaxed. I had some John Mayer playing quietly in the background. I like John Mayer. I will stand behind that statement.

No one was home. No one is ever home.

It was a Friday. The Brand New show in Phoenix was the following day, and I was mentally preparing a list of the things that I wanted to bring with me. I don't know why I was over-thinking it. All I really needed was a sleeping bag and some booze, but my brain began to wander and think about the possibilities out there and what things I might want to bring should I encounter them. What if we met the band and they took us on the road with them as their friends? Or maybe a group of girls decided to come back to the truck with us and have an orgy in the back. What would I need to bring with me in order to accommodate these types of circumstances that I might encounter?

Lists are always a good thing. I can't shop in the grocery store without a list. I lose it. It nears the seriousness of a mental breakdown. Well, maybe not that extreme. But it feels pretty bad, like the walls of the world are falling down all around me and there's nothing I can do – not even finish my grocery shopping – before it all ends in a pile of dusty rubble with me buried at the bottom. That's how epic it gets when I forget my list. So I don't forget them anymore.

Booker, on the other hand, was probably going to entirely forget that we were even going to Phoenix. Sometimes I wondered why I picked such a dumbass to be my best friend. Or any of my friends, for that matter. They were all somewhat damaged in one way or another. Then again, I was too. Beggars can't be choosers.

I had once dated a girl who challenged me on the quality of my friends. It was a weird proposition to me. I was offended, but at the same time, I knew that she was somewhat justified in asking.

"Did you ever think about the fact that all of your friends are less intelligent than you?"

She was usually pretty blunt when she asked me questions.

"Not really," I said.

Nice answer, me.

"Not just less intelligent, but less capable, less charismatic, less interesting, less everything, pretty much."

I don't know why she had such a high opinion of me. Maybe I was giving her the goods in a satisfying manner. Sometimes that happened.

"Not really," I said again.

"Maybe it's some sort of insecurity you have, where you want to surround yourself with people that you know you are better than. So you don't feel bad about yourself."

"Hmm," I said.

I thought about it for a while, and I couldn't tell if it was accurate. It felt like it could be, just hearing her say it. But who doesn't like to feel like the man? Besides a woman, that is.

"I don't know. That could be true."

I thought about it for a while longer. We were driving somewhere, and it was raining. I was looking out the windshield and to the sides of the roads for answers.

It wasn't true, I figured out later. I didn't bother to tell her, because who cares what she thinks. We were very different people, she and I. She chose her friends with a certain precision and skill, associating herself with future investment bankers and lawyers and people who iron their clothes every morning. The kind of people with vocabularies that make you feel bad about the way you participate in a conversation. Her friendships were a conscious choice, like applying to a school or a job. She sought them out. I had never done that in my entire life. I still haven't.

The results of our two approaches were strikingly different, as you'd expect. She spent her time with the type of people that you would take with you to a formal dinner party. I spent my time with the type of people that would be serving the food.

But, come on. Who really picks their friends? There is something disingenuous about that in principle. I think that friends are the people that you connect with when you meet them, the people that you want to spend time with but without any agenda. I couldn't imagine seeking out a friend. My friends just kind of showed up at my doorstep, for better or worse. I have an extremely low bar for entry into this club. Do we get along? Okay, we can be friends.

And thus, Booker and I are friends. Because he's there, and we get along. We like to spend time together, and we have common interests. It's pretty easy. I can't imagine it any other way, but apparently, there are other ways. I wonder what those are like. I wonder if it's any better than what my life is like.

I doubt it. The best things in life are the ones that fall into your lap, not the ones that you pursue with laser-like focus. Or so I tell myself. My lazy, lazy self.

The day could not crawl by any slower if it tried to. It was possibly lazier than I am. I decided to take a nap on the couch. I lay on my back and stared up at the ceiling. The armrests were soft and cushion. Overall the thing made for a great place to sleep. When we had people visiting, I would usually offer to let whoever it was have my room if the guest room was already full. I'd take the couch. It wasn't because I was a generous guy. It was because the couch was that good. The only times I chose not to sleep there was when I remembered how shitty it was to be stuck in the middle of the living room after the first person in the house decided to wake up.

I napped on and off until it was dark out, and then I made myself some food. My parents didn't come home until much later. I don't know what they were up to. I texted Harper back and forth and toyed with the idea of having her come by. But I was too lazy to want to do anything to please her, so I played hard to get and ultimately just pissed her off.

I started to get nervous about the idea of taking the truck out on the road again. After the intoxication of the trip through Mexico had worn off, I was able to have a few moments of clarity where I realized how lucky we were that we never got pulled over. Re-introducing that possibility seemed like a bad idea, but I also knew that I didn't know enough about international law to understand what the risks were. Out of curiosity, I decided to do a little research online. I probably shouldn't have. It just freaked me out even more.

I went to bed with my window open, listening to sounds of the city as they mixed with the stuffed silence of my bedroom. It was a mash-up that no one would ever care about, but I listened for a while as though I might gain something from it. I didn't.

Saturday morning I woke up with purpose, or at least as much purpose as someone in my situation could have. I was excited. I was doing something for the day, which meant I had something to look forward to for a change. I made myself some scrambled eggs and ham for breakfast. I was almost finished when I felt a rumble in my gut that sent me to the bathroom. When I was done, I walked out smiling. I love starting the day by going to the bathroom.

I called Booker, and we arranged a time to meet up and head over to the truck. He came over a little after ten o'clock. This was about as early as we ever met up for anything. I felt like we were in the Boy Scouts and we were heading off on a camping trip. I wanted to find my canteen and compass to take with me. He walked in without knocking on the door.

"Yo."

He shut the door behind him and walked into the kitchen where I was standing. I was leaning over my plate, eating the last bit of my eggs.

"Hey, man. You're on time."

"Yup."

"I'm just about done. I have to brush my teeth and I'm good to go. You want something to drink?"

He pulled out a stool tucked under the ledge of the island counter and sat down.

"Are you gonna drive first then?"

"What? No, I didn't mean like a drink drink. I meant, do you want some orange juice or something like that."

"Oh."

He looked disappointed.

"Nah. That'll just make me have to take a piss. We've got a long drive."

"Yeah, we do. Why are we doing this again?"

"Why wouldn't we? I don't have anything else going on."

"What about work? They're cool with it?"

Booker looked away and didn't say anything. I brought my plate and glass over to the sink and cleaned them off.

"Nothing? Okay."

I brushed my teeth and got my things together. I had made a list after all. Keeping one in my head wasn't going to be enough, so I wrote it all down. I checked it over once more before crossing off the last item – toothbrush – and throwing it into the trash. I will never be able to explain why I couldn't just throw it out without wasting the time and ink to cross it off. But that's what I did and that's what I always do.

We walked the short walk to the truck and were happy to see it still there and intact, not stripped or gutted or towed away, leaving an empty parking spot to puzzle us. That's always a relief, having the vehicle you will be driving in the last place you left it, with all of the parts where you left them and all of the air in the tires the way you left them. I pulled the key out from my backpack and opened the driver's side door.

When we had first taken the truck, it had a whole string of keys attached to it that presumably belonged to the driver. At our first stop, I looked over all of them and decided that we could leave them behind. Something about holding on to someone else's keys made the whole thing seem a lot dirtier than we meant for it to be. Leaving them behind at a random fucking Pemex in the middle of nowhere was not very helpful at all, but at least a little part of our consciences had been cleared.

I got in the driver's seat and started it up. The rumbling of the engine shook the entire frame, and our seats vibrated like we were on one of those motel mattresses that you see in movies and that you don't think actually exist. The familiar feeling of the vibrating truck, as unimpressive as it may seem, immediately flooded my brain with a sense of nostalgia. I don't know if nostalgia can occur after only a couple of weeks have passed. If it can't, then it was whatever you would call that feeling you get when a time and a place become present again in your memory. I looked over at Booker, and I could tell that he was feeling the same thing. We smiled at each other like a pair of creepy idiots.

I pulled out of the parking lot and toward the nearest gas station. Not a Pemex. After we had filled up, we found a self-service car wash and treated the truck to the cleaning we had promised it.

"This thing is a lot bigger than I realized, now that I'm washing it," Booker observed.

"Yeah, no kidding. It didn't even feel this big while we were painting it. Right?"

"Agreed."

I was already half-soaked from all of the water and soap suds that had been sloshing around. Booker continued to talk while I sprayed the back door.

"But maybe that's because we were so freaked out and rushed then. Whereas now, we're just about to start a nice little journey. No stress. No rush. So it feels a lot bigger since we're taking our sweet time."

"Yeah, maybe. I'm a little stressed though."

He shook his head.

"Why? Bad memories of getting your ass handed to you?"

"Not that. More like…this thing is still stolen, yet we're taking it out on a long ass trip. We could get seriously fucked if we get caught. Like even if we get pulled over."

"I'm sure it'll be fine."

"Fine? No. I looked it up."

He stopped whatever he was doing, which might have actually been nothing. It was taking so long that it felt like I was the only one washing.

"And?"

"And...we'd be seriously fucked, okay?"

"Quantify *fucked*."

"It all depends where you get caught. But generally, if you can prove that you *didn't* steal it and you *didn't* know that it was stolen, which we can't do, you're still looking at one to two years in prison."

"For driving something you didn't know was stolen? No way. I don't buy it."

"No?" I said. "You don't buy it?"

"Nope."

"Well, okay then. We are all set! You fucking idiot."

He laughed.

"What's your point? Do you not want to take this beautiful thing on the road? You want to take my shitty car instead?"

"I'm just saying..."

I didn't know what my point was. Booker nodded and waited for me to continue.

"Look," I said. "I'm just saying that if something goes wrong, I am blaming you. Okay?"

"Oh, sure. No problem, Blake. That sounds great to me."

I finished hosing off the remainder of the soap that was still clinging to the truck. And then, as though we had arrived at some logical conclusion as a result of our discussion, we hopped in the cab and made our way toward the freeway.

10 East. We had a hell of a way to go.

Nine

I've always had a thing for rum. But I'm not a goddamned hipster about it, and I try to not discriminate. I like rum from all countries and regions, or at least the ones that are supposed to make rum. I don't think anyone really makes rum anywhere outside of the Caribbean or Central America, but if they do, that might be something I'd stay away from. But once you get inside that region, I'm ready for whatever. I'll try it all.

Cuba is probably my favorite. I'm a Cuban rum fiend. I love it, and I don't even know why. It might be because I know I'm not supposed to have it, like old guys who love their Cuban cigars. Or maybe it actually is *that* good. I really don't know, and it doesn't actually matter. You like what you like. You want what you want. Don't ask yourself why. It's a waste of time.

Me and Cuban rum though. Whew. We're quite the pair. I spent some time in London one summer for reasons that aren't worth explaining since it has nothing to do with rum and it will just lead me down a side path that I don't need to go down right now. I used to go to the store and pick up a bottle and bring it back to my hotel room, just for me. I'd call down to the front desk and ask for a bucket of ice. Sometimes they'd charge me for the ice. That's pretty fucked up. But whatever. I'm not drinking warm rum unless I have to.

They'd bring up the ice, and I'd start to have my own little party. I'd drop the cubes into the glass and open the rum like it was a part of some ceremony. Sometimes I would send a quick fuck-you over the Atlantic and back to my country, sneering at their inability to stop me from drinking this lovely, gold liquid from our Communist neighbor. This embargo has nothing to do with me. The only Cold War that I care about is the one that I'm about to wage on my liver.

For an everyday rum, Havana Club is my favorite. It's almost better than Private Reserve. If I could have done it all again, and there was somehow a way to steal a truck of Havana Club instead, I'd have a hard time choosing what to do. In the end, I'd still stick with the Private Reserve. Mostly because stealing a truck on an island is generally a bad idea.

Doot, doot, doot, lookin' out my back door.

I don't know why we didn't think to bring a CD player or an MP3 player or something like that. It was a long drive, and the truck only had a radio. There weren't any good stations for the kind of music we liked, so we just stuck to the classic rock station. A little Creedence never hurt anybody, as far as I know, but in general the genre did tend to get a little tired. That's not a good ingredient for an eight-hour drive.

"How long have you been nailing that butterface?" Booker asked me.

Tact.

"I dunno. A while. A few months now, actually."

"Getting serious?"

I looked at him as if to say, *fuck no*. Then I said it.

"Fuck no, man."

He laughed.

"I know. I'm just messing with you. Messing with your *mind*."

"About a girl messing with my shit?"

"Yep."

"Whatever, man. When was the last time you hooked up with anybody?"

"Not that long ago, actually."

"Oh yeah?"

I didn't believe him.

"Yeah. There's a chick at work. High school girl – *but legal* – I think, at least. I finger-banged her in her car last week on my lunch break."

"What the fuck?"

He nodded supremely.

"Did you wash your hands before you did it? Oh…and after you did it?"

"Neither," he said and laughed.

"Fucking…nasty. Way to go, man. You keep raising the bar."

"Anytime, Blake. That's what I'm here for."

Doot, doot, doot.

The city was long behind us and it was now replaced by a very dry, boring desert. Cacti, sand, pavement, and sky – that's all we could see in any direction that we looked. It was both boring and stimulating in a way. But mostly boring.

"So, I've got a riddle for you," I said out of nowhere.

Since we *were* nowhere, it didn't seem too out of place.

"Alright, let's hear it."

Booker was usually game for things like this.

"Three men go to a hotel. Or a motel. Yeah, a motel."

"What's the difference?"

"Motel is shittier. Three men walk in, and it's late. They're looking to get a room each. The front desk clerk says he has a deal. He can give them three rooms for $30."

"Ouch. That is shitty."

"Yeah, that's why I said motel."

"$30 each?"

"No, $30 total. Three rooms, $30 total. The men agree and each pay $10, so the hotel receives $30. Following so far?"

"Yep. $30, three rooms, three men, one shitty motel."

"So the men go up to their rooms, and they all settle in. Meanwhile, the front desk clerk realizes that he made a mistake. The special was not three rooms for $30. It was three rooms for $25."

"What kind of fucking motel is this? It sounds terrible!"

"It is terrible. And that's not the point."

Booker scoffed.

"Anyway, the clerk feels bad, so he asks the bellboy to bring up the $5 to the men. He gives him five singles. Five one-dollar bills. The bellboy realizes that he's not going to be able to split this evenly between the three men. He's also kind of pissed because they all stiffed him on the tip, so he decides that he will keep two of the dollars and then give one dollar back to each man. So far, so good?"

"Yeah, got it."

"So the bellboy keeps the two dollars, gives a dollar back to each man, and goes back downstairs. So now…how much did each man pay for his stay at the hotel?"

"Hotel?"

"Motel. That's not the point."

"Okay. Each man? Nine dollars."

"And how much did the bell boy walk away with?"

"Two dollars."

"Alright, so nine dollars times three men equals what?"

"Twenty seven."

"Plus two…equals?"

"Twenty nine. Ah fuck."

"Where's the other dollar?"

"What the fuck?"

I smiled and looked out the window somewhat happily. I love it when things work the way I want them to. Booker did what everyone always does. He tried to walk through it again, certain that he just made a quick mistake.

"Nine times three, that's twenty seven, right? And two…nine…" his voice drifted off.

"Here, I'll say it again. The men originally paid $30. The clerk gave the bellboy five dollars to give back to the men. He kept two, each man got one back. $10 minus $1 equals $9. $9 times three men equals $27. The bellboy only has $2. $27 plus $2 equals $29. Where is the other dollar?

"Tax."

"What?"

"Was it like, extra tax or something?"

"No, man. Haha. It wasn't extra tax or something. I just told you all of the variables. This riddle isn't about them paying for something I didn't tell you and you having to guess what that is. Like, oh, the man went out and bought a candy bar, and I didn't tell you, and that's where it went, you dummy. How did you not know that he got a candy bar I didn't tell you about? Haha. It's all right there. Nine times three is twenty seven. Add two, you get twenty nine. They originally paid thirty. What happened to that missing dollar?"

"Fuck this shit, man. I don't care. It already hurts my brain."

"You do care. If I don't tell you, you're going to be thinking about this later on, still wondering where the hell it went."

"No, I won't."

"Yeah, you will. I mean, shit, I don't even remember the answer half of the time. It's a fucked up little riddle. I hate it. I mean, I love it, but I also hate it."

"Fuck you, man. Why'd you have to start this shit? Why couldn't we just talk about whatever else we normally talk about?"

"Alright. Take it easy. It's just a riddle."

"Fuck that. I don't know where the dollar went. Up someone's asshole."

"Nope."

"I don't care."

"Yeah, you do."

"No, I don't. They're all cheap assholes. So they lost a dollar. Big fucking deal. They're staying a night in a hotel for nine bucks."

"It's a motel."

"Fuck that motel, and fuck you too."

Doot doot doot.

There's something about driving that makes me want to get to where I'm going as quickly and as efficiently as possible. I hate taking bathroom breaks or food breaks. I hate what my dad calls "dilly-dallying" – probably because he hates it too and I'm slowly turning into him. If I'm sitting around the house, I really don't mind if I do nothing for hours at a time. But if I am going to do something, I become an efficiency expert. I suddenly care so deeply about not wasting time even though it is the premise that most of my life has been built on. It's weird.

Booker is not exactly the same as me here, but luckily, he didn't complain about it too often. He pretty much just went with the flow. And since on this trip, I was the one who was driving, we were able to make good time. I think that's what it all comes down to for me. Making good time. And if you think about it, that's a really dumb phrase. Like you made the time. No one makes time. It's not even real, which I guess means that we all "make" time. It's quite the riddle.

Doot, doot, doot.

We were starting to see signs of civilization at around six o'clock. It seemed like we were getting closer to Phoenix, thank God. It was a long stretch of nothing for a while. Booker may have fallen asleep for a bit, and I just drove in silence. The radio station had turned to static a while back, and I had just shut it off.

So it was encouraging to see buildings, gas stations, and other things that you normally expect to see when human life is present. To add to that excitement, it seemed like this was going to be one of the first times that we got to a show on time. Not that it really mattered, since Brand New probably wouldn't get on stage until at least nine o'clock. Still, it was good to know that we weren't total fuck-ups driving across state lines to miss the whole reason we made the drive in the first place.

We pulled up to a parking lot near the venue. There was a guy collecting money, and we had to negotiate with him for a little while. He didn't want to take us in. The truck was too big, he said. Fuck that. There's no such thing as a vehicle too big for a parking lot. We ended up agreeing to pay double. That seemed fair to me, but he acted like he was getting a raw deal. I told him to get over it. Like it was his fucking parking lot and I was stealing money out of his pocket.

As I stepped out of the truck, I squinted my eyes and tried to see if I could notice the Private Reserve logo showing through anywhere on the side wall.

Nothing.

Painting that truck was a hell of a chore. By the time we got the paint from the hardware store and had found a place to park, I think it was already ninety degrees out. The sun was just *beating* on us, and we were in the middle of some dusty, vacant lot. I still don't even know where we were. Some place outside of Tijuana. It was not a friendly looking junction. I assumed that at any point, a car full of Mexican gangsters would pull up and kidnap both of us. They'd set the truck on fire and pour the paint down our throats, or something fucked up like that.

Every time the wind blew, swirls of dust would scoop up off the ground and slam into the side wall. Sometimes it would bounce back and hit me in the eyes. So I was squinting not only from the sun, but also to avoid these rogue blasts of sand that were pounding me in the face. These were not exactly prime painting conditions. I was in such a rush to finish I really didn't care how it looked. I just swiped paint across that logo as fast as I could. But as I stood there in that parking lot in Tempe, I realized that it actually didn't turn out that bad. It definitely looked like it was cheaply painted, but it did the job. It covered the logo. That's all we really needed it to do.

Doot, doot, doot.

"This place is alright," Booker shouted to me.

The first band was on stage. Even though we were outside of the main area of the venue getting drinks, it was still pretty loud. They didn't sound too bad, but they also didn't sound too good. That's why it was drinks time.

"Yeah. A lot of Zoneys though."

"Well, yeah. What do you expect? We're in their territory."

"Yeah. Actually, think about it. Except for people traveling with the band, we're probably the only two people who aren't from here that came here to see them."

"Good point. Why would anybody drive to *Tempe* – and where would you even drive from – just to see a show?"

"Like us."

He smiled.

"Yeah, like us. Why would anybody be as stupid as us?"

"Don't worry, man. These people chose to live *here*. We're not the stupid ones for driving out for one show. This is temporary for us. This is permanent for them."

"Except maybe them," Booker said as he nodded to a group of fifteen or sixteen-year-old kids. "They probably didn't choose to be here either. Their dumbass parents did."

"Well, it's *their* dumbass parents, not mine. They've still got some of those dumbass Zoney genes in them. I don't. I drove here. In my dumbass stolen truck from dumbass Puerto Vallarta, dumbass Mexico."

"Dumbass," Booker replied.

As expected, Brand New didn't come on until sometime after nine o'clock. We were already buzzing pretty hard, or at least I know I was. Booker switched to beer at some point, like an idiot. Beer at a concert means you'll be in the bathroom half of the time, pissing it all out. Liquor is the way to go. Always liquor. Always rum.

Jesse came out on stage and welcomed the crowd before they started to play. Sometimes a band will just walk out and play a crazy fast song to get the crowd hyped up. And then when it's done, they calmly introduce themselves. Jesse took the other route and asked everybody how they're doing and if they were ready to hear some jams. Then they started to play some jams. The word "jams" was not a part of what he really said. I don't know what he said, actually. I was drunk. That's my jam.

Booker and I shoved our way to the front of the crowd. We were older and larger than most of them, especially the skinny, little emo kids that you would expect to see at a show like this. *Especially* in Arizona. It didn't take much effort before we got within a few people of the fence. I was already soaked in sweat. Some of it was mine, and some of it had probably just rubbed onto me. There was that familiar concert smell of people who smell like cheese hanging around in the air. I never really understood that. Why is there a cheese smell when sweaty, young people start singing along to a band? I know I don't smell like that when I sing and sweat.

Brand New went through their library, hitting songs from their first album, songs from their latest album, and songs from in between. It was the usual way you would perform a concert if you had more than one album. I always think it's funny when I see a headlining band that has released only one album. They end up playing the whole thing because that's all that they can do. Maybe they can slip in a cover or a B-side that you've never heard, but usually that's not an option. If the B-side was any good, it'd be on the album. If it's not any good, they don't want to play it. There is rarely a middle ground here.

So as a fan in this situation, you know when the show is nearing the end. The album has ten tracks. You've heard nine. Spare me the drama of an encore, band with just one album. I know what's coming. Unless that motel clerk from the riddle is in charge of the math at the show. If he's there…then who knows? All bets are off when that guy is involved.

I had to step away at some point to go to the bathroom. My bladder was just too full. When I came back, Jesse was talking to the crowd. The band was just kind of wandering around on the stage like they weren't sure if they were supposed to be there anymore.

"Does anybody have any food? I didn't get to eat today. So I'm kind of tripping up here, all light-headed."

The crowd roared back with varying versions of '*Yeah!*' or '*We love you, Jesse!*' People started to throw things on stage. Mostly candy bars. Someone threw an apple, and he caught it out of what looked like sheer instinct. He didn't even turn his head to look at it as it almost whizzed by his head. He just threw his hand up there and caught it. When it hit his palm, he turned his head slowly in amazement. He was staring at the apple long enough for people to start laughing. Booker laughed. I laughed.

"Did you guys just see that shit?"

The crowd exploded with noise. We all saw it and felt like we had to let him know that we saw it. Booker let him know. I let him know.

"And who the fuck brings an apple to a show? What else you got back there? Celery sticks? A pic-a-nic basket?"

Then he did what any hungry person with an apple would do. He started eating it. Then the band started up, seeming like they were sick of waiting for him. He rolled into the next set of lyrics while he was still eating that apple. There were probably bits of it all over the microphone.

At some point, Jesse took the back of his shirt and pulled it over his head. He wore it like it was a hoodie, but without the hood. He had the words *HI MOZ* taped on his guitar. The first time I saw that, I didn't know who he was saying hi to.

He sang the lyrics differently than they were recorded for the albums. It made it hard to sing along, but it also made the experience feel unique. He mumbled things about being a great band and how their record label was lucky to have them. He did all of these things that I had seen him do the other times I had seen them play. It was all expected, and that was comforting to me. Some things don't need to change for them to be good.

Booker and I screamed along to all of the lyrics throughout the entire set. By the time the lights came on, my voice was hoarse and my jaw was sore. My lower back was tight from getting pounded by the crowd. My knees were creaky and wobbly from standing and bouncing all night. My shirt was a different color than it was when I had entered the venue. My shorts might have been too. I had probably lost two pounds of sweat, but all of that water was still clinging to my body, absorbed into the fibers of my shirt, pants, socks, and underwear.

Good thing I brought that change of clothes I had on my list.

Check.

Ten

I've always had a thing for rum. Rumpelstiltskin. He's a good man. And so are you.

Rum isn't like whiskey. No matter what anybody tells you, rum on the rocks isn't as good as rum with something else. You can try it. It's alright. But it wasn't mean to stand on its own. Rum was meant to be mixed with something else. Like coke. Or punch. Or both.

Rum is meant to be a part of something bigger than itself. Rum is a lover, not a fighter. Rum isn't selfish. It gives itself up for the greater good. Rum is selfless. It's emotionless. Rum is really just there to make sure that everybody else gets their day in the sun.

If you put rum in a glass with just ice, the ice will take center stage. That's just what rum does. Rum is a giver.

Rum doesn't want you looking at it. Rum doesn't want you to notice it for its beauty or its clarity. Rum wants to hide in the bottle. It doesn't want your attention. It doesn't want anybody's attention. Rum doesn't stand on the shelf and say, *"Hey, look at me!"* That's not rum's game. Any rum that seems like it's doing that is probably not that good of a rum.

I didn't make these rules up. These are just observations. Field notes from a longtime admirer. You can listen to them, or you can ignore me. It really doesn't matter. This is just how it is.

After a show, your ears ring. Sometimes you don't notice it for a while. You usually don't really notice it until you get home. Depending on where you live, where the show is, and how you got there, that could be an hour. It could be two. Your ears might still be ringing.

It's a crazy thing to me. I heard in a movie once that the sound of your ears ringing is the last sound those bits of your eardrums make before they die forever. I don't know if that's true, but it scares the shit out of me if it is. And if it isn't, then it's a bastard of a line to put in a movie for no reason. I think it came up because a bomb went off.

Well, yeah. A bomb going off might fuck up your hearing. But a concert? That's normal wear and tear. Don't make me feel bad for listening to music a little louder than normal.

What am I supposed to do, wear earplugs? I've tried that. They're uncomfortable. They always feel like they're going to fall out. And when they don't, they feel like they are never going to come out. There's no happy medium with those things. It's better to just leave them alone and hope that the line in the movie was made up.

Booker was walking in front of me as we left the venue. He was wearing a plain t-shirt and a pair of camouflage shorts. I didn't even notice that he was wearing camo until then, or if he ever wore camo. Maybe that's the point.

He turned around and looked at me.

"Did you see that?"

"No, what?"

I didn't see anything unusual. He must have been talking about a girl or a group of girls or a poster of a girl. Or maybe he just thought of the word *girl*, and it caused him to blurt out that question.

"Those girls. Did you see them?"

"Yeah, man. Shit."

"Right?"

"Oh yeah."

I nodded. A lie of a nod. But what was I supposed to do? Ask him which girls he was referring to? What was the point?

"Fuck."

"Psssh."

Phoenix is always hot. It didn't take the night off when we were in town or next door in Tempe. We left the venue a little after eleven. It still felt like eighty degrees, though I could be wrong. Maybe it was in the seventies. I'm not a meteorologist. It was hot, whatever it was. It really didn't matter. I was soaked in sweat, and there was no chilly reprieve to step into. Just some more warmth that wasn't likely to go away. Knowing that I was sleeping in the back of a cargo truck later that night didn't make it any better.

Booker and I decided to go get something to eat. Even though it was the weekend, we didn't really know where to go in Phoenix, so we figured food was a good starting point. It turned out to be an ending point for the night as well, but that wasn't the plan. We found a Denny's nearby and reluctantly walked in. There's no reason anyone ever needs to describe a Denny's unless you've never been to one before, because they are all the same. And if you haven't been to one, there's no benefit in understanding what a Denny's is like. Just imagine a shitty diner without any semblance of personality. Bam. You're at Denny's.

The menu had some specialty items that must have been new. They were in a little promoted section off on its own panel. Fancy shit.

"Did you see this?" Booker asked.

"Yep," I said, dismayed. "The *rock star* menu."

"At Denny's."

"Yep."

"What are you gonna get?"

"Oh, good question, Mr. Booker."

I did my best impression of an overeager local news reporter talking through the menu.

"I was considering getting the *Hearts on a Plate*, now doesn't that sound tasty? Mmm, yes. Or maybe this little dish inspired by the *Plain White T's*. Those boys are lovely."

"Mmm, yes. That does sound delightful back here in the studio, Blake."

"But, Mr. Booker, I think I am going to settle on the *Taking Back Bacon Burger Fries*. And a bottle of Pepto Bismol."

"I keep an extra roll of toilet paper in my desk drawer if you need it."

"I sure will. Back to you."

"Stu, with the weather?"

Our waitress came over partway through our mockery. I could tell she didn't have any sense of humor. I ordered the *Taking Back Bacon Burger Fries* with a straight face. Booker got the *Moons Over My Hammy*. We each got a glass of OJ. When they came, Booker pulled out a flask and dumped the rest of what I think was vodka into his cup.

"What a bunch of sell outs," I moaned, thinking about the stupid meal that was going to come out in a few minutes.

"You think so? I'd take the money if I was in a band."

"You would?"

"Hell yeah."

He had a pretty serious face on, or rather, it was the same face he always had on, but with a serious look on it.

"From Denny's?"

"Dude, from Payless Shoes. I don't give a shit."

"Alright."

"Look. There are all of these hipster assholes out there trying to stay true to whatever motivation they pretend they have. The music. The art. Whatever. That's total bullshit. Every single person who starts a band does it because they want to get ass, they want to get money, and they want to get to do whatever they fuck they want for as long as they can."

"I'm sure there's an exception," I said, trying to think of one.

"Don't even try. I've already tried. If anybody told you that they started or joined a band for anything other than a personal, selfish reason, they're full of shit. They might believe the lies they're telling. They really might. But it's all bullshit. All art is selfish. And most music isn't art. So just imagine what that makes all musicians."

I looked out the window for a bit, and Booker continued.

"They'd all take the money from Denny's. All of them. It just depends on the price tag."

"I don't think that's true."

"Oh yeah?"

"Yeah. Think about it. Think about…Bob Dylan."

"He's a prick."

"Okay. I don't like him either. But try to imagine him taking some money from Denny's. Any amount of money. I bet he'd turn it down. Every single offer. Turn it down. He's too good for Denny's."

"Man, *we're* too good for Denny's, but look at us. We're here."

"Touché."

"Really, though, you're right. You are. But there's a reason he'd turn down the money. And it's not because he's too good and that's that. He'd turn it down because it would hurt his image, and he uses that image to get bigger bids of money for more expensive buy-outs. I guarantee it."

"Hmm…"

"Think about it. Why the fuck would Bob Dylan turn down free money? Because he wants to make more free money from someone else, and this amount of free money from these assholes would get in the way of a bigger amount of free money from somebody else."

The argument had a few holes, but for the most part it was true. At some point a few years ago, Bob Dylan decided he was a painter. I think you can decide to be a painter. I did it once. Anyone can be a painter. All you need is paint and something thing to put the paint on.

So Bob Dylan decided he was a painter. The man wasn't even a good songwriter, in my opinion. And he sure as shit wasn't a good singer. And now he added painting to the list of things he wasn't that good at but that people were going to fawn over anyway. His paintings sell for thousands of dollars. Five and six digit price tags, all bought by a bunch of other assholes that I can't even begin to imagine without getting angry.

He was only able to do this because he didn't sell out and take money all along the road to where he got to. Maybe he did at first, maybe he didn't. I am not a Bob Dylan historian. All I know is, now? He held out now. For the big money of the art world. A world with deep pockets and way too much pretentiousness to call bullshit on itself. Denny's couldn't put down enough money to compromise his authenticity. But some asshole with a blank wall sure could.

"Fucking prick."

"Exactly."

Booker looked like he had just accomplished something.

"So, hell yeah, I would take money from this shithole and tell them my secret recipes and all of that shit. I'd do that every day of the week."

"Damn."

Our waitress came over shortly after.

"Hey dude, your *Taking Back Bacon Burger Fries* are here!"

The waitress looked at him and then at me. She didn't say anything. I guess Booker had said it for her. She placed the plates down on the table and walked away without a word.

"They actually look pretty good," I said. Booker agreed.

They tasted like somebody had dumped a cheeseburger onto a cutting board, chopped it up, and threw it on top of a pile of French fries. The guys in Taking Back Sunday might have had a good recipe after all. And a little bit of money in their pockets too.

Both of us had to stop in the bathroom before we left. Thanks, Denny's. I sure felt like a *rock star* after that meal. Maybe a has-been rock star. Bloated, depressed, and full of regret.

We walked outside where it was still fairly warm even though it was well past midnight. We didn't really have a place to go or anything to do. Last call was at two o'clock, and that was already getting somewhat close. We were tired from the show and more so from the long day of driving. In one of the most anti-climactic things that I could have imagined doing, we decided to just tuck ourselves into the back of the truck and go to sleep. We didn't discuss what we were going to do the next day. We had options, so we could decide later. For now, we both just wanted to sleep.

The truck was still parked in the same lot because that's what parked vehicles typically do. They stay where you leave them. There was a note on the windshield under the wiper. We were going to have to park somewhere else before we shacked up for the night. They were going to start towing early in the morning, though it didn't say how early. Probably too early for us to want to deal with it. So Booker hopped in the driver's seat and drove us out into the Phoenix night, which is not at all glamorous, if it sounded like it was.

We found a wide alley that had a few cars parked in it. They were decent-looking cars, not cars that you might expect to see rats crawling in and out of. Cars with windows. We decided that this was an alley that we could trust for the night. Booker pulled up the passenger side of the truck so close to the wall that I had to get out using the driver's door. I shimmied my way over and out to the street. My legs felt like bricks. As I attempted to land on them, my knees almost buckled beneath me. We walked around back and unlocked the door, sliding it up quietly to avoid drawing any attention to ourselves. Our sleeping bags were laid out almost exactly as they were when we threw them in there before leaving L.A. Eight hours on the road, and they didn't move at all. That didn't make sense, but we just ignored it.

We shuffled around for a while and got as comfortable as we could. We were lying on the metal floor of a truck. No sleeping bag could disguise that. When the rustling stopped, the silence slowly washed over us, but not in a romantic way. It just did. Or rather, it tried to, but the ringing in our ears kept it away.

"It just keeps ringing, doesn't it?"

"Yep."

"Like a fat girl's phone on opposite day."

"Nice."

"Like Helen Keller's phone on a regular day."

"Haha, you gonna keep going?

Booker paused for a bit. Even though it was dark and I couldn't see him, I could imagine his face as he strained to come up with another quip.

"Like Pavlov's living room."

"Shut the fuck up, man."

"What?"

"Just shut up. You…shut up."

"Not bad, huh?"

"Shut up. Pavlov. Fuck you, haha."

"I bet his wife hated him."

"I bet those dogs hated him. Who cares about the wife?"

"A whole bunch of bitches, hating Pavlov."

"C'est la vie."

"What are we doing tomorrow?"

"I dunno. Let's just see how we feel."

"Alright," Booker said, sounding strangely anxious.

The ringing pulsed back into my ears. I heard a car slowly drive by the entrance to the alley, but it didn't do much to cut through the tinny hum echoing through my head.

"Because, I mean…I could stay out here a while longer, you know."

"In Phoenix?"

"Nah. I mean, sure, whatever. I just meant I could stay out on the road."

"So you're Jack Kerouac now?"

"I don't know who that is. Who is that?"

"You know who Pavlov is but you've never heard of Jack Kerouac?"

"Why, did they work together?"

"What? No. Never mind. We're not *on the road*. We're not actually doing anything here. We're just…I mean, shit, we're laying in the back of the truck."

"Our truck."

"Yeah, right. Our stolen truck. Our stolen, Mexican truck."

"Our stolen, Mexican truck."

"Uh huh."

"Well, I'm just saying. I could stand to be away from home for a while, if you're looking to not go back right away. Like, I could stay out as well."

"Don't you have to go to work? You didn't answer me before when I asked you."

"When did you ask me? At the show?"

"No, at my house."

"Oh, yeah, I know. I didn't answer you on purpose."

"Did you quit?"

"I don't want to talk about it."

"What? Really? You quit? When? Today? Yesterday?"

"No, man. No, I..."

He paused for a little bit.

"I just don't want to talk about it."

"You don't want to talk about the fact that you quit, or you don't want to talk about why you don't want to go back to work?"

"I don't want to *talk* about it. Okay?"

"Alright."

The ringing came back. We eventually fell asleep, or at least I know I did.

Eleven

I've always had a thing for rum. It is an appetite that doesn't have an end. It is consistent and it is unhealthy and it is mine. And at the time, as someone in my early twenties, that almost seemed like a problem. But it wasn't. Not to me, at least.

It wasn't about getting drunk, but I did that all of the time too. And it wasn't about needing it, which I also probably did, though I didn't want to admit it. It was about something else. It was about love, maybe. Pure, syrupy, fermented cane juice. Bottled up, labeled, distributed, and sold as the loveliest word I can think of. Rum. The thing I had for rum was love.

One time I had a dream that I was going to give my girlfriend a bottle of very expensive, highly sought-after rum. Actually, it was for her father. Also, she didn't exist other than in this dream, nor did he. Didn't matter. He was going to get a bottle of something amazing. It was a rum that I had never tasted. The Louis XII of rum if there ever was such a thing. In my dream, there was. And it was wrapped up, ready to be given away. I had so much anticipation, so much hope and longing for the moment it was going to be opened. I was praying that I'd be there when he popped the cork out. Realistically, had it not been a dream, I'd have damned well expected it. It was a gift that you obviously share with the person who gave it to you, and if you don't, then you're just an asshole. And my dream girlfriend's dad is not an asshole.

In my dream, though, we never tasted it. I don't know why. We just never got around to actually opening it. I imagined the taste and smell of it. I had to. I could see blurred visions of buttery notes just tracing along the air in front of me, like taste expressed as an image. It was a trippy, fourth dimensional dream. I sat there itching for him to just open that bottle. The girl – whoever she was – she didn't matter at all. Just him…his hand…that bottle.

I don't remember how I woke up, but I'm sure it was with disappointment. Maybe even regret. I had the bottle in my possession at some point, and I had chosen to turn it into a gift. I had opted to give it away. Why would I do that? Who could ever want that bottle as much as me? I had created this situation and this bottle of rum. It was just a dream. In my own head, in my own subconscious. I had made something perfect, and then I gave it away.

That dream has to mean something in some very deep and touching way. It has to mean that I am a devastatingly tragic human being or that I have no clue how to appreciate good things when I have them. Or that I secretly like to give gifts even though I generally think of myself as a selfish person. Or that I don't actually like rum despite telling myself that I do.

Blasphemy.

The sun must have risen in Phoenix at some point, and we didn't notice. At least not based on the amount of light that we saw. There was a sliver that was peeking in through the very bottom of the truck bed where the door met the floor, but it was so thin and unnoticeable that you could have otherwise assumed it wasn't even there. The only reason we really knew that the day had begun was the noticeable change in the temperature. In the back of an all metal truck, parked beneath no cover or tree branch or any other shade-producing object, you're bound to notice a change in weather. It was warm when we went to sleep, and that was in the dark of the night. With the sun above, probably aimed directly at our poor metal roof, we really started to feel it. Or at least I did. I can't speak for what Booker did or did not feel. All I know is that I woke up with a line of sweat rolling down my temple.

Booker shifted around in his bag when I slowly rolled up the back door of the truck to get a sense of what was going on in the world around us. I only opened it about a foot, afraid that someone would be right there on the other side waiting for us. Like a cop, with his little cop stick, tap-tap-tapping in his palm. *Hey boys, whatcha doin' in there?* Or a little family of zombies looking for some brains, like the apocalypse had hit us overnight and it was now time to pay for our mortal sins. Or just some homeless guys. Or a meter maid. Anything could have been on the other side of that truck door, so I opened it with caution.

On the other side was just a bunch of fucking sun. Booker was rubbing his eyes and moaning, adjusting poorly to the changing conditions of our shitty little sleeping quarters. He asked me what time it was. I just ignored the question altogether, but not intentionally. He asked me again, and I felt kind of bad.

"Oh, it's 10:30. We slept a while."

"Yeah. It doesn't feel like it though."

"That's because we slept on the metal floor of a truck bed. We probably have bruises and internal bleeding all inside our torsos and underneath our shoulder blades."

"Jesus, man."

"Sorry. I didn't sleep well either."

Booker got out of his bag and slowly crawled over to where I was perched by the door.

"I bet if you went outside, took a few breaths, and came back in, you'd realize how much this truck smells like a big fucking pile of Denny's."

"Oh shit. That's so gross. I bet you're right."

We put our clothes on and went outside into the already hot Phoenix morning. It didn't feel that hot though, since the back of the truck was at least ten degrees warmer inside. Outside there was a breeze. There was light. There was no unknown Denny's odor. It was almost refreshing, albeit Phoenix.

We walked a few blocks and found a coffee shop, and we bought their version of breakfast. Booker kept talking about cuts of meat on the walk there, but I can't remember why or to what extent it mattered to either of us. While eating breakfast, we started to come up with our plan of action. Our next steps. I was thinking we'd drive around Arizona for a bit and then head back once we got bored, which was probably going to be after fifteen minutes or so. It looked so terrible on the drive in. I couldn't imagine spending much more time there. Not on purpose.

I had a piece of fruit on a fork, but I wasn't eating it. I was just staring at it. Booker put down his coffee on the table and also stared at it while starting to talk.

"How far do you think it is to Denver?"

"No idea. My gut says it's far even though it feels like it shouldn't be too far. Maybe like…twelve hours?"

"Shit, you think so?"

"No idea. Look it up."

"My phone doesn't have the Internet."

"Yeah, I know. Alright. I don't have much battery though, so I don't want to look it up. It's probably like twelve hours."

"Did you bring your charger?"

"Yeah, the car charger. But I haven't used it since we got here last night. It's not that bad. I just get anxious when my battery level starts to drop kind of low. Even a little bit. It gives me a lot of anxiety."

"See? This is why I don't want one of those things."

"But you have a phone," I said.

"Yeah, but it doesn't have any features like yours. It doesn't do anything other than text or call or take shitty pictures that I can't send anywhere. So the battery lasts forever. It doesn't even tell me how long the battery is actually going to last for, like yours. It just has a few blocks that show how much battery I have."

"Simpler times."

"Whatever. I don't have anxiety over my fucking battery bars."

"They're not bars. It's a percentage."

"Even worse. You have battery percentage anxiety. It's so bad that you can't use the thing to look up something on the Internet, which is the whole reason you have the thing in the first place."

"You don't get it."

"I don't need to. It's stupid. Here's how I see it. You have a phone so you can use the Internet. But, the Internet takes up your battery power. You get anxious over your battery power going away, so you don't use the Internet. Instead, you just carry around a phone that loses battery power and gives you stress. Meanwhile, while you aren't using your phone, I'm not using my phone either. So neither of us are using our phones. And the difference between the two of us is about $50 more a month that *you* pay and some completely unnecessary stress that *you* carry around, all because *your* battery percentage might be fading away if you use the thing for what you got it for."

"Google says fourteen hours."

"Wait, what?"

"That means I was probably right. It's probably like twelve. They always estimate as though you're an eighty-year-old woman driving your Buick, stopping at every rest station to take a four minute piss."

"How did you find that already?"

"In the time it took your post-modern ass to make fun of me and my anxiety, I already looked it up. See?"

I held the phone out across the table and showed him my screen.

"Oh."

He picked up his coffee and took a long sip, slurping loudly. His gesture seemed to show that he didn't give a shit about something, even if his not-giving-a-shit about my phone didn't turn out to be the informed side of the argument that ended with him feeling kind of stupid about it.

"Why did you want to know? Do you want to go to Denver from here? Is that what you were getting at?"

He smiled.

"I quit my job, man."

I shook my head.

"You're incredible."

"It feels pretty good."

"Well, yeah, of course it does. You're away from reality right now. It probably feels fucking amazing."

"Please. Don't start to tell me about being away from reality. You're the one living in some master plan where you don't go to college but have your parents pay for it."

"Fuck you."

"How does your plan end well at all in any way? I don't think it can. At least mine is just a job. I'll find another one when I get back. If I go back."

"If you go back?"

"Let's go to Denver. You've got nothing to go back for right away, and neither do I. Let's drive to Denver."

He was being very forward. More forward than he usually was. He was being a goddamned, unemployed asshole. He wasn't usually this direct, but now he had this nothing-to-lose mentality. I could feel it come out in every word that he said.

"Denver?" I asked.

"Denver. Come on. Let's drive to Denver."

"Hmm."

I finally ate the piece of fruit that had been sitting on my fork for the past five minutes. It was honeydew melon. It could have been worse. Cantaloupe is always worse, for example.

"You know I hate unplanned things."

"Yeah," he nodded. "Just like you hate your battery anxiety, right?"

He had a point. I was always so worried about having a plan, about making a list, about checking things off. I sometimes avoided doing things that I'd probably very much like but that I just didn't see coming. I liked knowing what my future was going to be, and I had a hard time being spontaneous. Ironic, of course, compared to the big things in my life where I had no sense of what my future might actually turn out to be like. But it didn't matter. The little details right in front of me were what I felt the need to control. The big things could be nebulous and scattered. I knew I had to break that habit. It wasn't healthy to try to control everything. It just gave you stress. And battery anxiety.

The drive to Denver was not planned. The drive to Denver did not make any sense. It had no purpose, no prospect. I don't even know why he wanted to go. But maybe that was okay, even though I knew in my gut that it wasn't. Not the way that I lived. Not in my paradigm. This was a challenge.

I decided that I could use a challenge.

"Alright," I said. Booker smiled wide. "But I'm driving."

"Obviously."

In the bottom of my fruit cup was a piece of cantaloupe. I pierced it with my fork and took a bite. It wasn't good.

"This cantaloupe tastes like shit," I said, almost accusatorily.

"Dude. No kidding. We're in fucking Phoenix."

"Oh."

"Yeah."

"Fucking cantaloupe."

He laughed.

We stopped by an ATM before getting back in the truck and starting the drive out to Denver. I had never been to the city before. I knew nothing about it other than the fact that people can never talk about it without mentioning its altitude, like it's an interesting fact that's worth talking about. The mile high city. Big fucking deal. Did you know that Mexico City is almost 8,000 feet above sea level? They don't run around yelling about the mile-plus-another-half-a-mile-high-city that they live in. At least not in English. At least not that I'm aware of.

Leadville, Colorado is over 10,000 feet up there. Why we don't hear about that? La Paz, Bolivia is more than 12,000 feet in the sky. A tank of a hundred and fifty centipedes has even more feet. Denver. Get over yourself.

We headed north on 17. It was a dusty, terrible-looking highway that immediately became depressing after about fifteen minutes of leaving the city. It was going to be a long day. Somehow the sun was mercilessly beating directly into the windshield even though we were driving north, and that didn't make any sense to me. Somehow even the sun evaded logic in Arizona. I was taking some solace in the fact that once we got on 89, we'd be passing the Grand Canyon on our way to Colorado, but that didn't turn out to be very promising at all. It was too far to our west for us to see much of anything.

Instead, we passed through a place called Tuba City about an hour later. Booker made a joke about the women there being horny, and it took me way too long to get it.

Tuba City had its own airport. There were no signs for it, but if you paid attention, you could tell that it was an airport because it was the place with the most tires buried halfway into the ground. I think that was to help stop the planes from driving off of the runway and into the highway. Lots of other places in Tuba City had tires in the ground too, but the airport had the most. I tried to imagine what kind of plane flew into an airport like that and who the people flying there were. It was too hard to imagine, so I stopped trying.

I had always assumed that all of Arizona was filled with cacti. That's what I had always seen in pictures and postcards, so I figured it was true of the whole state. Deserts and hills of cacti and more deserts and more cacti. It even had multiple shapes of cacti. Big ones, little ones, ones with arms, ones without arms that just looked like big, spikey penises, little round ones that looked like spikey testicles, giant ones with arms that didn't look like genitalia at all and therefore weren't funny or worth mentioning. Tuba City didn't have any cacti, and neither did almost all of northern Arizona. It was very disappointing. I wanted to see some legitimate cacti, and I barely saw any at all.

Tuba City belonged on the brochure to Hell. It looked like the place that people from Nogales hear about and thank God that they don't live in. If you've ever passed through Tuba City, you know what I'm talking about. The roads into town had significantly less wear on their surfaces than the roads leading out of town. Even though this seems statistically impossible, it is all right there for you to see if you ever sin so badly that someone sends you there. The highway passes right through the center of town, so you get to see everything that they have to offer without taking a detour.

"This is my favorite hue," Booker moaned.

He was referring to the piles of sand that lined the sides of the road. They were a reddish-brown color that we later agreed looked like big lumps of cinnamon. This was the kind of stuff that we had to talk about. It was a thrilling little city, Tuba City.

In town there was a small shopping center with a movie theater and a tuxedo rental shop. There was some sort of a grocery market and a Szechuan restaurant that looked like it hadn't been open for months. A ragged, stray dog was wandering around in front of the door, probably hoping that someone would hit him with a car. We drove around the parking lot trying to find a place to get some food. While we were waiting at the stop light, an ATV sped over the dirt hill behind us and crossed over the road. This seemed like a regular thing. Maybe he was going to rent a tux and he was late. Or maybe he was the projectionist at the movie theater. Or maybe he was about to commit suicide. It could have been all three, really. Tuba City.

We stopped at a fast food place and tried to order something to eat, but there was some sort of confusion and no one came out to help us. An old woman there tried to teach us how to say a few words in Navajo, but it didn't work out so well. She just kept telling us the difference between the word that means *yes* and the word that means *crazy*. It sounded like the same thing. She just kept smiling while trying to explain the difference. It helped me to understand a bit about what was going on there. We went to a gas station instead and bought some beef jerky and chips. I was going to fill up with gas, but the station was all out of it. I didn't realize that this was even possible. There were a few cars there, their drivers just scraping off bugs from their windshields. I got back in the truck, and then we got the fuck out of there.

"Tuba City," I declared. "Never again."

"Never say never," Booker replied as he smiled.

"No. Never."

The road turned into a long stretch of even more boring road along highway 160. We passed a few hitchhikers that probably died somewhere along the way and a dead dog or two. Monument Valley was off to the left, but we ignored it and kept on going. 160 turned into 191. 191 meant that we were in Utah. Woo-fucking-hoo. Five hours down, and all we had to show for it was a single state boundary and the names of a few places that we hated. Utah didn't look any different for a while. Just a bunch of desert again. You could have told me that we were still in Arizona, and I'd have believed it. We drove for over twenty miles in Utah, and I counted only five cars that we passed. This was empty country.

The truck kept humming along, unafraid of the elevation gains, dry heat, sand, whatever. It didn't care. It was a truck from Mexico. This was all no big deal as far as it was concerned. This was nothing at all. This could have been Mexico. Anything other than Mexico was a good day for a truck.

The sun started to set right around when we hit Moab, which was at least a place that I had heard of before. Arches. There were a bunch of arches that we couldn't see at all, of course. We stopped off at a gas station and had our first proper meal since I couldn't even remember when. The word *proper* is a stretch, but consider it in context.

Moab at least had tourists, so their gas stations had *some* amenities. A microwave classifies as an amenity in my book. We made some frozen burritos and sat down at a table outside of the little store. We were staring down at the ground as we ate with almost pure disappointment and regret filling our entire bodies.

"Pretty sweet idea for a trip, Book."

"Ha ha ha. Shut up, man. We're almost there."

"Not really. We still have another four or five hours to go. If we leave right now, we won't get there until after midnight."

"That doesn't make this a bad trip. You're talking about it like we had some better plans that we skipped so we could do this instead, and then it turned out all shitty. This hasn't been that bad. Right? What has been so bad about it?"

Booker was always like this, fairly optimistic. Cheery. Not seeing the negatives like I see it. He saw Tuba City with the same human hardware that I saw it with. But he didn't see it as the shitty, washed away city that I saw. He saw it as a funny story. A place that he was glad he didn't live, maybe, but nothing negative. Certainly nothing personal.

We were very different people in that way. He didn't get down about things like that. I always did. I let it hit me in a way that I probably shouldn't. I let things like this bother me even though they were nothing. This trip, it was nothing. It was fine. And a good thing, really, though I didn't know it at the time. But it irritated me then.

It didn't bother Booker at all. He was just happy to ride along. Sometimes I wished I could be like that. Instead it just bothered me so much. I wished I was doing something better with myself. I always wanted to be doing more than I was doing. I didn't understand why I was never satisfied. I still don't understand that.

I must have been quiet for a while. Booker was looking around as though he had said something awkward and didn't know how to get us back on track.

"Sorry, man. I don't know what just happened. I just kinda blanked out for a bit," I said.

"You blacked out?"

"No, no. Blanked out. Like just tuned out for a while."

"Oh, alright. Glad I am being such good company."

"It's not you. I'm just a little worn out, is all."

"Need me to drive?"

Normally I'd refuse the help, but it didn't sound like a bad idea at the time.

"Yeah, maybe. Or maybe we can just call it a day and chill here for a while? Like for the night?"

That was uncharacteristic of me. I was usually the guy who made us keep on pressing and pushing. Like I said, I never took breaks. I didn't even realize that I had it in me to make that suggestion. Even Booker looked surprised.

"Sure, yeah. We could do that. Moab! Beautiful place to spend a night."

"Moab. Because less ab just won't cut it," I said.

"Really?"

"Sorry."

"Yeah, we need to take a break. Let's go find somewhere to drink."

We went back inside the gas station and asked the attendant where we could find a bar, but he wasn't very helpful at all. He directed us to a liquor store, which was better than nothing but not exactly what we were looking for. We decided to go there anyway. We'd buy a bottle each and find somewhere to park the truck for the night. I got a bottle of some Nicaraguan rum. Booker got something else, something that wasn't memorable enough for me to recall. Not rum, obviously.

We found a campground really close to the liquor store. They let us drive in and park for just $12 for the night. It seemed like a good deal, but I later realized that $12 might have been a lot of money in Utah. It might be more than some people in Utah make in a week. I have no idea. Utah seems pretty backwards, so I can't imagine that they make much money. Twelve dollars to spend the night was okay for a rich, unemployed Californian like me, so I happily shelled it out.

We drove the truck back to an empty spot that seemed to be where the guy at the front booth told us to go, and we parked. Booker and I climbed into the back and pulled out our sleeping bags. We laid them out on the sand. We wadded up our pillows and rested our heads against them, propped at an angle to let us to drink without spilling all over ourselves.

The stars were ridiculously clear. The sky was purple and black and basically how the sky is supposed to look without light pollution. We talked for a while about bullfighting, about vegans, and about overpopulation. And we drank. We talked about overcrowding in prisons and the practical limits of modern skyscrapers. And we drank. We talked about what it was going to be like when one of our parents died. We just talked like we do. It was effortless, meaningless, and somehow purposeful.

I now look back on that night and realize that everything I was doing was fine. It was alright. I didn't need to feel rushed or unaccomplished or empty. I was living, I was breathing, and I was becoming myself in a way that only I could. It didn't matter that I was doing it by driving through the middle of nowhere to get to a city that I had no business getting to…in a truck that I had no business driving…to start something that I had no business starting. I was doing what I was doing, and it was alright. I didn't realize it then, but it really was alright.

I fell asleep first. Booker put the cap on my bottle before he fell asleep too.

Twelve

I've always had a thing for rum. I've also always had a thing for blowjobs, in case you're wondering what to get me for Christmas and you don't want to be cliché.

I woke up at some point in the middle of the night, my body shivering and shaking. My head was propped up at the same angle as it was when I first stretched out. My neck was all kinds of fucked up. I rolled it around a few times to try to pop some of the kinks out, but it didn't work.

My sleeping bag wasn't doing a great job of keeping the chilly night air away from my body, but I was too lazy to get up and do something about it. I don't know where all of the heat from the day went. I know that this is what is supposed to happen in the desert, but I still wasn't expecting it at the time. Though I wasn't expecting to fall asleep out there either. I looked around and couldn't see Booker. He must have gone back to the truck.

I curled up into a ball to try to warm up, and eventually I fell asleep again. I woke up when the sun came up later that morning. There is no avoiding an early wake-up call when you're sleeping outside. I walked over to the truck and flung the door as far open as I could with one pull.

"You just left me out here?"

Booker was lying on top of his sleeping bag. He was rubbing his eyes and making some yawning, moan-type noises.

"Yeah. What'd you want me to do? Spoon you to keep you warm?"

"You could have woken me up when you came in here."

"You could have woken yourself up, man."

"I did at some point."

"Okay. So what?"

"What time did you come back here?"

"What's with all of the fucking questions?"

"It's not that many. I was just wondering."

"Well, I don't know. Time o'clock."

"Thank you."

I went off to the side of the truck that wasn't facing another group of campers. I leaned against the wall and unzipped my fly. The ground was so caked and dry that it had a hard time absorbing much of anything. I had to spread my legs wider than my normal stance to make sure my stream didn't run into one of my shoes.

"Do you want to get something to eat?" Booker asked, walking around to where I was standing.

"Not really."

"There's a diner in that main part of the city that used to be the Moab courthouse. Want to eat there?"

"How do you know that?"

He smiled.

"I used your phone to see what was around here."

"Ah, fuck. Did you charge it?"

"The truck was off."

"Dude!" I yelled.

"Calm down. Let's go get breakfast."

"Fuck you. Let's just get out of here."

"Breakfast first."

"I'm not hungry."

"Then get a coffee."

"I hate you."

"I don't care. I'm hungry."

The courthouse diner turned out to have a pretty decent-looking breakfast menu, so I ordered something after all. Booker kept giving me a smug, I-told-you-so look. I tried my best to ignore it.

It looked like it was going to be a nice day out. The sun was bright, shiny, and happy. There were a few little, seemingly insignificant clouds on the horizon, but don't try telling that to them. I'm sure they thought they were significant. The air was crisp. Crisp air is always good. Stale air is never good. You'd be pretty disappointed if you walked outside on a nice autumn day, took a deep breath in, and realized that the air was as stale as a YMCA locker room. Crisp is definitely the way to go.

For us, 70 East was also the way to go. It was about a half of an hour north of the city. I figured that once we got on an interstate, we'd see some actual amenities. It had been a while since we had been on a real freeway. We had been driving on all of these state highways, and they all had nothing but animal crossing signs. No convenience stores or gas stations or anything useful. Just animal crossing signs.

A sign would warn of deer crossing for the next eight miles. We'd drive those eight miles. Then another sign would warn of deer crossing for the next six miles. So we'd drive those six miles. Then another sign would show up, but this time it would be a bigger-looking deer. Booker figured it was an elk. Twelve more miles. Okay. Then another sign would tell us that we were entering a deer migration area. That's much more intense than a deer crossing area. The entire deer population was going to walk across the damned road.

70 East was a proper freeway, in that it had a divider and multiple lanes, but that was about it. There was nothing to see. We passed through Grand Junction at the same time that we realized we had crossed into Colorado. It was not that grand of a junction. It was your basic, every day junction, as far as I could tell. We pulled off to get some more gas and a few things to snack on.

The landscape before Grand Junction and the landscape after Grand Junction were two very different things. Before, it was basically an extension of the Utah desert. At one point we passed a sign that read: NO SERVICES FOR 65 MILES. It was that kind of a stretch of road. After Grand Junction, it started to look like what I expected Colorado to look like: more trees, more mountains, more crispness, and whatnot. It was funny to me that a city could be the physical divider between two very different worlds. If I had to be stuck on the 70, I would prefer to be east of Grand Junction, nine times out of ten. That one extra time would be there just to remind me how much better Colorado was than Utah.

"This looks legit," Booker said as we came up to the Eisenhower tunnel.

It was a little after ten o'clock. I had heard that the tunnel had alarms to stop any trucks that exceeded its height limit. A part of me was afraid that we were going to set those off even though there was no way that our truck was that big. Still, what a way that would be to end our run. Blocking traffic on either side of a two mile tunnel, all because we were too stupid to realize how tall the fucking truck was.

We started to approach Denver at just about noon. It was a welcome sight to see those buildings and that skyline. There was more to it than I had expected. I had come to assume that most skylines would be relatively underwhelming. Even L.A. has a modest strip of buildings that makes up its downtown. It's not that impressive. Granted, the corridor that runs along Wilshire Boulevard from Westwood to Century City is probably more packed with high rises than the entire Denver downtown area, but in context, the shapes of the buildings against the expanse beyond it was impressive.

We had just come down off of a long descent from the height of the Rockies and down to the plain that the main parts of the city sat upon. The mountains were impressive. Big, sheer cliffs and mounds of snow. Winding roadways. Tunnels. Curves. Typical mountain shit. But it just seemed nicer since it was in a place that I had never been before. There were very informative, but also very informal, highway signs that cautioned drivers on their descent down the hill. I think one of them said something like, *Don't be fooled, You ain't down there yet.* I'm barely exaggerating.

I had never been to the city before, so I didn't have any idea what to expect. All of that driving – eight hours from L.A. to Phoenix, seven hours from Phoenix to Moab, five hours from Moab to Denver – all within about thirty hours. It was exhausting when I thought about what we had done. Then again, our drive out of Mexico was just as bad and, in many ways, a lot scarier. At least this was somewhat leisurely. That said, we were driving across multiple state lines without any sort of registration or documentation. It was a stolen truck. We hadn't put much thought into that aspect of the trip. We just kind of ignored that part.

Seeing the Denver skyline was affirmation that we had at least arrived at our next destination, even if we didn't have a reason why it was our destination, nor did we have any idea what we'd be doing while we were there. We were without a plan in a brand new place. Thank God my phone had been charging the whole drive, or I'd have had a nervous breakdown.

When I was younger, I remember watching this show called *Denver the Last Dinosaur.* I don't remember anything about it other than the name and that it was animated, I think. That name always came back to me anytime anyone said the city's name. I would just think of that show. I wouldn't think of anything in particular since I couldn't remember anything about it. Just the name. *Denver the Last Dinosaur*. Apropos of nothing, I thought that this would be a good time to mention this.

Booker and I decided that we should get a real, sit-down meal, since we didn't really know what was going to be ahead of us and we might very well leave Denver a few hours after we got there. Any opportunity to eat some real food was an opportunity that we knew we should take. We were going to spring for something a little more substantial. Something a little less embarrassing than that Denny's back in Phoenix, hopefully. Something that wouldn't send us straight to the toilet. At least that was our goal, but you never know what you're getting into until it gets into you.

We found a place that looked like a mix between a bar and a restaurant. Some people call those gastropubs now. I don't think they were called that then. I also don't think I'd ever be caught calling some place a gastropub. I really prefer to not be a douche bag if at all possible, and the word *gastropub* is the gateway drug down that path. It doesn't even sound appealing. Whoever came up with the term should be neutered. We don't want him to procreate and produce more people who produce words like *gastropub*.

Booker ordered a beer, and I did the same. It can't be all rum all the time, believe it or not. After perusing the menu for far too long, we put in an order for a basket of fries, a plate of nachos, and two burgers. Our Olympic training diet had begun.

"I could feel my asshole pucker as soon as you placed the order," Booker complained.

He didn't like the restaurant that we chose. He said that it looked like we were both going to walk away with dysentery.

"Shut up, man. This place is fine."

I gestured around us and waved my arms wide at the room we sat in, mostly by ourselves.

"What's wrong with this? Huh? It's fine."

"It's puckering, Blake. I can't help it."

"I don't even know what the fuck that is supposed to mean. Just…shut up. It's fine."

"We'll see."

I changed topics.

"So, anyway. We're in Denver now."

"Yup."

"Denver. Good old Denver."

I paused for some inevitable comedic timing, and then I said what he already expected me to say.

"What exactly are we doing here?"

We had driven the whole way from Phoenix, a destination that we really had no reason to arrive at anyway. Now there we were, somewhere in the middle of the Rockies with a truck, two sleeping bags, and no plan that I was aware of. Maybe Booker had something in mind, I thought. Maybe he was just waiting until we got there to tell me about it. I thought that maybe it was one of these things that I would have opposed had he told me about it earlier, but now that I was there, I'd be more inclined to go along with it. I hated those kinds of things, but only because they made me realize that my protestations were often unnecessary. They made me feel embarrassed, but I generally liked the outcome of whatever he ended up convincing me to do.

"Beats me," he said.

Well, never mind.

"What do you want to do?" he asked.

"How the fuck am I supposed to know?"

The waitress came by with our beers and set them on the table. Then she set down two coasters. She put my beer on the coaster in front of Booker. And then she put his beer on the coaster in front of me. Then she slowly slid his beer across the table to him and then slid my beer across the table back to me. It was painful to experience.

I took a sip of my beer and smiled. It had been a while since I had a beer. Booker did the same, and he let out that typical *ahhh* that you hear in Coke commercials. Or beer commercials.

"I've never been here before," I started again after another sip. "So I, of course, have no idea what we could actually do. I know very little about Denver. I know their sports teams. I know that they have a lot of beer here. I know that without a railroad, this city would have never existed. That's about all I know."

"I've heard good things about Boulder."

"Yeah, me too. But how about we stay in this fucking city, huh? We just drove forever to get here. I don't want to drive somewhere else just because we couldn't think of something to do here."

"Good point."

"I mean…why the fuck did you suggest we come here? Of all places? You just wanted to get up and go to Denver for no reason?"

"Yeah. Pretty much."

"Pretty much."

"It seemed like a good place to visit."

"Yeah. Why not. Let's drive to Denver."

"Yeah. Why not?"

"Fuck, man."

"What?"

"Just…whatever. Let's figure out something to do."

Our fries came to the table. Not on their own. The waitress brought them for us. Fries in Denver don't have autonomous mobility yet. They're still static.

"Hi, sorry," I said to the waitress before she left the table.

She had a look on her face like she had somewhere better to be, but there were hardly any people in the place, so I figured that was just her general look, which was unfortunate.

"We just got into town earlier today. We're looking for something to do. We didn't plan anything…"

"No?"

"Not at all…"

I shot a sideways look over to Booker to try to indicate that he was the one who didn't plan anything, but she didn't pick up on it. She probably thought I had a shifty stare or I was nervous or I was trying to pick her up like she was a prostitute.

"You didn't plan anything at all?"

"Nope," Booker responded proudly. "We wanted to be uninhibited."

I didn't know that he knew the word *uninhibited*. I was almost positive that she didn't.

"Right," I said. "So we're looking for something to do. To inhibit us, now that we're here."

"Inhibition is the goal," Booker added.

The girl looked at us and frowned. I couldn't blame her.

"I think the Rockies are playing this afternoon. That's not far from here. You could try to get some tickets maybe. They never sell out."

"They never sell out," I repeated.

I looked over at Booker.

"Sounds like a killer time. Anything else?"

She gestured as though she was going to be thinking about it, but she spoke way too soon for that to be the case.

"No, not really. Try the Rockies. They've got cheap beer there during the afternoon games."

She walked away and went back to the kitchen.

"Well, that was very informative," I said to Booker.

"It was almost too much information, if you ask me."

"Not sure where to begin, really."

"Yeah, exactly. Whew."

Our nachos came. Almost immediately after, the burgers did too. We hadn't made any progress on the fries yet, so just like that, we now had a table full of food in front of us. I suddenly got the uneasy feeling that my stomach had shrunk over the past few days due to the lack of food and that I'd get full before I even made it to the burger. I had food-buyer's remorse.

"Cheers," Booker exclaimed, as he raised his nearly empty pint and clinked it against mine.

"To Denver," I said.

We each took a large sip.

"I hope something awesome happens here."

"Fair enough," I replied. "So do I."

I got about halfway through my burger, which was better than I was expecting, and then I had to make a trip to the bathroom. The bathroom was actually very clean and well decorated. It almost stood out. Booker was waiting outside the door when I opened it. On my walk back to the table, I worried that the waitress was going to clear the plates away since both of us weren't there. But when I returned, everything was still in its place. Crisis averted.

I finished everything that I had ordered, including my half of the nachos. Eventually, when he got back, Booker did the same. Our stomachs hadn't shrunken. I felt like we had accomplished something. We ate a full meal. It was a victory.

We walked outside and into the bright, midday sun. Denver claims to have over three hundred days of sunshine a year. They also get multiple feet of snow per year. Somehow I don't believe that those two statistics can live alongside each other, but the Denver tourism board disagrees. That day, it was definitely sunny. I don't know if it was one-out-of-three-hundred-sunny, but it was sunny. Up there on the list for sure. My eyes felt like they would melt if I looked any higher than a few feet above the pavement.

We drove the truck over toward a bunch of numbered streets and found some decent parking that seemed too easy to obtain. Booker mentioned that our parking luck was not the "something awesome" he had toasted to earlier. We decided to not go to the Rockies game right away. We figured we would get stuck with very few drinking options and they'd probably all be overpriced, generic beer. Even for a day game, ballpark beer prices are unfair.

We found a couple of local-looking mini-breweries nearby and ducked inside to see if we could get some tastings. I had been wine tasting in Santa Barbara before, where tasting is all you do, but I had never been beer tasting. For some reason I assumed that this was something one would do with beer even though I had no idea if that was accurate.

It was. The first place we visited had a fairly badass, biker-looking girl behind the counter, willing to pour us samples in oversized shot glasses. She called it a beer flight. Alright. She explained that they were ordered – from left to right – from the lowest ABV (alcohol-by-volume) to the highest. When she said this, both of us began to stare at the right side of the line-up.

"How much is in that tar-looking one all the way at the end?" Booker asked.

"Same amount as the rest. I didn't short you on any of it."

"No. I mean, I can see that. I meant how much alcohol is in it?"

"Oh, the *ABV*?"

"Sure. The A-B-V", Booker mocked. "How much A-B-V is in that one down there?"

"More than you can handle, boy."

"Are you guys in a fight?" I asked.

I always liked to ask this in awkward situations to make it even more awkward.

"It's 14.4%," she said flatly and walked to the other end of the bar, even though nobody was over there.

"Fuck, man," I said. "That's a very strong beer."

"Uh, yeah it is. Boy."

"Boy," I muttered.

"What's this one called again?" Booker shouted down to the other end of the bar.

She didn't look up, move, or flinch. She just stared down at whatever she was looking at, for at least a good ten seconds. That's a long time in an empty bar during the middle of the day. Then she came over to us, smiled, and pointed to a placard on the wall behind her. She leaned forward and onto the bar, her already swooped shirt collar tugging down a bit further as she leaned, her breasts pushing further into both of our sightlines. As she leaned a little further, the collar pulled even more. She smiled at us and didn't say anything. I think she might have been bi-polar. Or a lady serial killer.

The beer was called *Swamp Water*. It didn't taste too bad, considering the name. By the time we had finished the flight, I was already starting to feel a slight buzz. This was great news as far as I was concerned. We paid our tab and walked back out into the sun. My eyes began to burn again, even worse than before. I had just gotten acclimated to the moody darkness of the last place.

I kind of wished we had stayed. I wanted to see more of that crazy girl and her body. I kept imagining her going into the back room and punching an empty cardboard box, crying, and then getting wet from it. And then doing it again. I sometimes have an active imagination when it comes to the ladies.

The next brew pub wasn't as eventful, nor did it have anything interesting to look at. Their beer was decent but nothing special. Then again, I don't know my beer all that well. It just seemed pretty bland and unspectacular to me. Booker was just trying to get drunk. I think I was too. It was the middle of the day during the week, so I guess that's both unusual and unsurprising. If you're drinking at that time, it's probably not just for a quick one. It's for a purpose.

We moved on down the street. The game was probably in the fifth or sixth inning, if I had to guess, but nobody made me guess so I can't say for certain. People were milling around outside of the park, but there wasn't much going on. We decided to give up on the idea of going to the game altogether, as it was getting to be too late for it to be worthwhile. Neither of us really cared that much about baseball anyway, let alone the Colorado Rockies. If I can remember when a team was created, I am not interested in paying money to see them play. They could pay me to watch them play. That arrangement would be fine for me. The inverse is not.

We wandered around the downtown area for a while that day. We stopped in and out of random little bars and places to eat. I don't really remember much about most of the places, but then again, there wasn't really all that much to remember about them anyway. That is, until we wandered into the Marquis Theatre. I remember that place very well.

Booker and I were pretty drunk by the time we sat down on the stools at the bar. There was no one else in the venue other than us and the bartender, from what I could tell. It was maybe five or six o'clock. The place looked kind of like a dump. Most concert venues outside of L.A. look like shit to me. I don't know why that is. You'd think they would try to make them look a little nicer, maybe do some remodeling here and there. Something.

Maybe this is because they are primarily there for the music and the people who want to listen to the music. Those people don't usually care about how a place looks. Most of the time, they are either drunk by the time they get there or looking to get drunk shortly thereafter. Painting the walls and putting some nice things on them would be lost on about ninety-five-percent of the crowd. I just happen to fall into that picky five-percent that would like a little bit of visual enjoyment to accompany my audio for the night.

The Marquis didn't give a shit about any of that. From what I could tell, the place must have been built for an entirely different purpose before somebody decided it would be a good place for a music venue. The bar was tucked against one wall. The stage was essentially on the other side behind a big, looming wall that blocked most of what you might want to see or hear. Not that I would be expecting to sit at the bar and watch the band, but the wall was so offensively *there* that I couldn't help but be annoyed by it. And there wasn't even a band playing when we got there. It was early in the day. Pay attention to me.

If it wasn't for the selection at the bar, I might have convinced Booker to walk out after our first drink. It was kind of weird just hanging out there. There was no reason for us to be there. Booker and I have argued about this a number of times since, but I'm almost convinced that they didn't even have any music playing when we got there. It was that kind of desolation. Forget about the fact that there was no band playing. They didn't even have music coming in over the speakers.

The bartender looked at us and probably thought we were as weird as we thought her venue was. She didn't say much to us at first. I ordered some Ron Zacapa, which was an amazing find at a shitbox like this. Booker pulled for another beer. The fact that I was finally switching over to rum made me both happy and a little concerned. I didn't think it was a great idea, but I was pissing every eight minutes, and I needed to stop pouring the beer straight through my body and into the toilet. I needed something that was going to stick around a bit.

A bedraggled-looking girl stumbled in from outside and took a seat at the stool next to the stool next to Booker. She ordered something and immediately took her phone out and started texting. Meanwhile, Booker and I were talking about my dad.

"He just loves that video poker, huh?"

"It's not that he loves it on its own," I said, trying to make sense of the fact that it actually did seem from our conversation that my dad loved video poker. "I think he just really likes playing it when he's there."

"How's that any different than what I just said?"

"You made it sound like my dad was going to leave my mom for a video poker machine. He doesn't *love* it. He just likes to play when he's in Vegas. In fact, I don't even think he likes to play in Vegas as much he just really likes to play at that one bar in the Orleans where he can watch the band and order drinks at the same time."

"Unlike this place," Booker said, tying the conversation back to its origin.

"Right. Very much unlike this place. This is the opposite of a place that my dad would leave my mom for. This is the kind of place that my dad would see and then immediately decide to renew his vows with my mom."

The girl two seats down from Booker put her phone back in her purse and turned to look at us.

"Your parents are getting divorced?" she asked Booker.

Clearly, she had been paying very close attention. He looked at me and then turned his body to face her. She was wearing mostly black, to the point where I couldn't really tell you what she was wearing except that I remember it was black. Her hair was black too. Her eyes were very big and round and actually pretty, though the rest of her wasn't all that great.

"They're trying to work some things out right now. That's all."

"What's the matter?"

"Yeah, Booker, what's the matter?" I repeated.

"Oh, it's just his work. His work is getting in the way."

He took a long sip of his beer and just sat there for a little bit. The girl didn't say anything in response. She didn't gesture, move, or indicate that she was alive in any way at all.

"What does he do again?" I asked, fully aware of exactly what his dad's job was, but pushing him further into the awkward conversation that had just begun.

"He's a lathe operator," he said plainly.

The girl raised her eyebrows.

"What's a lathe?"

"It's something that a woman like my mom just can't compete with anymore, okay?"

I laughed out loud, so loudly that the bartender looked up from whatever she was doing at the other end of the bar. I couldn't help it. Sometimes I didn't know how the fuck he came up with the things he said. On the spot like that, and deadpan too. It takes a certain mind and skill.

"Cheers to that," the girl said listlessly. She raised her drink to her mouth.

Booker held out his glass toward her, but she didn't notice, so he brought it back to his lips before it got even more awkward.

He turned back to me, and we tried to start talking about something else. It didn't get too far before the girl interjected and asked a stupid question completely unrelated to what we were talking about. It happened over and over.

"Which one of you is from Minnesota?"

"Why don't you like dogs?"

"Have you ever eaten creamed corn from a can?"

That one threw me. I had forgotten that creamed corn even existed until she brought it up.

"What is the point of creamed corn?" I asked her back.

"It's good."

"I think it is an abomination of a vegetable."

"Nah," she said.

"What is the point of it?"

"It's corn," she said. "Corn has no point."

"No. Like, what is the point of making it that way? You like corn, but you don't like to chew? You want to eat something that tastes like corn, but, you know, you also want to be able to hide bodily fluids in it without somebody noticing?"

"Why would you want to do that?"

She looked like she was offended.

"Why would you like creamed corn?" I asked.

"That's a fair question," Booker added.

"Who even came up with it?"

"God," she said decisively.

"God invented creamed corn?"

"Yes."

"I don't think that's true. I think it was just some guy."

"God wasn't just some guy."

"Right," I said. "The creamed corn inventor was just some guy. God was a different guy."

"No. He was God."

A guy walked in and sat down on the other side of the girl. Maybe he was God. It was interesting timing if he wasn't. I had ordered another drink and was mostly done with that one too. The conversation kept on rolling. Booker and I just kept responding to her, trying not to seem angry, bored, or frustrated. We had no reason to be any of those things. At worst, we were just a bit sarcastic, though it was all going way over her head anyway. The bartender kept to the other side of the bar. She apparently didn't want anything to do with this situation.

"I had my license suspended," the girl slurred.

I already knew why, but I met the obligation and asked her why.

"DUI," she said.

"That's not good," Booker lamented.

"Did you do any damage to your car? Or did you just get pulled over?"

"Just got pulled over. And now I can't drive anywhere."

"How did you get here?"

"I walked."

"Ah, we drove. We have a big truck outside. We drove it here all the way from Phoenix. We left yesterday and got here this morning."

"What's in Phoenix?" she asked.

Booker looked at me and smiled.

"We were at a show."

"A show?"

"Yeah, like a concert. A gig. You know. A show. Like you'll see tonight."

Suddenly, the girl perked up and actually looked like she had a spine, not just some rope that connected her head to her ass.

"You guys are in one of the bands?"

"Yep," Booker responded, smiling. "We are definitely in one of the bands."

"No kidding?"

"Why else would we be here this early?"

He used the classic diversion tactic. Instead of answering with a lie, you answer with a slightly related question that implies the lie without having to say it. And it makes the questioner feel stupid for asking. I do this all the time when I'm trying to get away with something but I know that what I say might get revisited later on.

"What band are you in?"

"Not the opening band, but the one after."

She leaned over and starting looking at a piece of paper on the bar with the line-up for the night.

"As Green Pastures Burn?"

Booker looked at me, and I could tell he was wondering what he should say. What a shitty band name. I could feel him about to say yes, so I interrupted.

"No, we're before them. They added us somewhat last minute, as an extra act."

She looked at me, her eyes somewhat lifeless. They were still very pretty even though they could have belonged to a corpse.

"Really?"

"Yeah. We're good friends with the promoter. Bob."

"Bob?"

"Yeah. Bob Arum. The promoter."

Bob Arum is in fact a promoter. A boxing promoter. He is the only promoter whose name I knew and whose name I was positive she did not know.

"Yeah, our friend Bob," Booker added.

She settled back into her seat a bit and seemed to buy it.

"So what's your band name then?"

Booker looked at me and raised his eyebrows. There was an extra awkward pause as we sat there and all waited for him to say something. It took a while. I was cringing, but I couldn't look away.

"Tuba City," he finally declared.

Fuck.

"Are you kidding me?" she asked.

Down past the girl, the guy who wasn't God started to laugh. He had a weird look to him, some kind of mixed ethnicity. I couldn't tell what he was, but at the time I thought that maybe he was Asian. We found out later that he was half-Irish and half-Mexican. I was way off.

"No, ma'am. Not kidding at all," he said. "We're Tuba City."

He said it so slowly that he almost stumbled over his words. Anyone who was paying attention could have realized that it was probably the first time that he had ever said it.

"I play drums."

"I don't believe you!" the girl shouted.

She stood up from her chair and marched over to the bartender. I sat up a little straighter, unsure what was about to happen. The guy at the bar looked at us and waved the hang-loose sign back and forth our way. This further solidified my incorrect guess that he was from somewhere beyond the Pacific. I changed my guess to Hawaii. He didn't really look like it, but it was more convincing to me at the time.

"Did you hear what these guys are saying?"

She was right in front of the bartender, almost shouting in her face.

"No, what?"

The girl turned, looked at us, and threw her hand out angrily down the length of the bar as she pointed.

"These guys are in Tuba City."

The bartender looked at the paper on the bar for a few seconds and looked back at the girl. She nodded, and the girl continued.

"They got added on last minute by the promoter. They're playing tonight. Here. Right?"

She looked over at us and raised her voice.

"Right?"

"Yep."

"Yeah."

"Uh huh."

"Bob set you guys up?" the bartender asked.

Booker looked at me to answer. I didn't know what else to say.

"Yeah. Bob said we were going to go on right before As Green Pastures Burn."

"Why did you get here so early? Doors don't even open for another hour. And you've already been here a while."

"He told us not to be late," the new guy said. "He said that this place was a good venue and that we shouldn't fuck it up by being late."

The girl was just standing there staring at us. The bartender looked down at the line-up and back again at us. It felt like it took five minutes for her to open her mouth and speak.

"Well, why didn't you say something earlier?"

"I dunno," I said.

She looked back down at the flier.

"Drinks are on the house, boys."

She walked back over to where we were sitting and started to pour up new versions of whatever we each had. Booker looked at me as though he had just walked in on his parents fucking. The girl walked back over and sat down in her seat again. She motioned to the new guy to sit in the seat between her and Booker. He got up and did as she commanded.

"You guys," she said, "are one of my favorite bands. Ever. Like ever."

"Is that right?" I asked.

"Oh yeah. Totally. I love bands. I mean, I love your band. I hadn't ever seen any pictures of you guys, so I didn't know what you looked like. But I love your music, like so much."

"What's your favorite song of ours?" Booker asked.

I jabbed him in the ribs. Fucking idiot.

"Dude, don't put her on the spot like that," I said, trying to laugh it off. "I'm sure she likes all of them the same amount."

"I honestly don't remember the names to songs. I just remember the feelings I have when I hear them," she replied.

Not a bad answer for a bullshitter trying to bullshit a bullshitter. I almost bought it.

"So, what are your names?" she asked.

"I'm Blake."

I waved.

"I'm Booker."

He nodded. We both turned a bit and looked at the new guy in between us and the girl.

"I'm Pedro Bay."

He turned, looked at us, and sent a *hey* head-nod our way. His name confused me even more about his ethnicity. I had no idea how Bay was spelled at the time. I was imagining it was spelled *Bé*. Like that makes sense.

"I'm Maria."

None of us really cared about talking to her anymore. We cared about the fact that we had free drinks, at least for a round.

"I'm gonna go to the bathroom."

She got up and walked away. The bartender finished setting up our drinks. She smiled the kind of smile that includes a direct flash of eye contact for each of us, which is hard to do without seeming awkward. Then she slowly walked back to the other end of the bar where she was perched before. This gave us some time to talk to our new band mate.

"Nice job, dude," I said. "Is that your real name?"

"Yep. You guys?"

"Yep, both of us."

"Nice."

"You're a pro!" Booker yelled.

"What do you mean?"

"You just went along with us without even flinching. That's pro status."

"Are you kidding? She was too easy."

He looked back at the bartender and lowered his voice a little, but more in the cartoony way where it sounded a bit more nasal and really didn't get that much quieter.

"I just don't know how this one back here got suckered into it as well."

"No shit, right?"

"Yeah, I was pretty sure we were fucked when she walked down there. I still don't understand how that worked out."

Booker nodded and took a swig of his beer.

"Where did you come up with that band name?" Pedro asked.

"It's Booker's favorite place in all of America," I explained.

"It's a real place?"

"Yes, unfortunately."

"Sounds great. Sorry to steal some of your action here, by the way. That was kind of shitty of me, but I couldn't help but play along with you guys."

"Not at all. Don't worry about it. We're just fucking around anyway. You're more than welcome to join our *band*. As long as no one here is from Tuba City, I think we're clear," I said.

Pedro raised his glass up in the air, and we did the same.

"To Tuba City!" Booker announced.

The bartender looked up at us and smiled.

Things got messy soon after. The drinks kept coming, and they were strong. Strong like ox. Even Booker switched over to harder stuff – I think it was whiskey – once we found out they were all going to be free. Somehow the bartender never showed us any signs of disbelief. She just kept pouring them for us, and we kept throwing them back. Maria wandered around the bar area, sitting infrequently and mostly just shuffling her feet and asking the same types of scattered questions she began asking when we first got there.

Throughout the next hour or so, we established a few key items. Pedro Bay was the drummer. Booker played bass. And I sang. None of this was related to any actual skills that the three of us had. This was just what we always thought we'd do if we were in a band. Even though this was all fake, it seemed to make sense to base the details on something that we could all remember. I was surprised that everybody didn't want to be the singer. I thought that's what everybody always wanted. I guess it was just me. Shallow me. Shallow like ox. Booker surprised me a bit on his choice too. Bass. I guess he kind of was a bass guy at the time. I didn't realize it then.

People started to slowly fill in the venue. We realized that at some point, something might happen that might make us have to pay for our growing bar tab. As soon as the first band showed up, or the promoter, or who knows – *anybody associated with the venue's management* – we were probably fucked. Fucked like ox. But we were so drunk and so greedy to stay drunk that we strung it out as long as we could.

The first band started to set up their gear on stage. I realized that if we were actually in a band, we probably wouldn't still be at the bar continuing to get hammered. We'd be out back doing something band-like. Tuning our instruments, maybe. I don't know. I'd be tuning my voice. *Mi-mi-mi-mi-mi-mi-miiiiiii.* Like that. We stood up and said goodbye to Maria who was still claiming ownership of the bar stool that she first chose, even though she was barely sitting on it. Anytime somebody came over, she zoomed right back and announced that it was hers. You can't really argue with that, and no one did.

"So, we'll see you in a little bit. But from up there."

"Yeah, we've got to go out back and get set up," Pedro added.

"Okay!" she shouted, even though it still wasn't that loud in the venue.

A few people around us raised their eyebrows. Or at least I imagined that they did. We started to walk out toward the front door. The bartender stopped us. The moment of truth had arrived.

"You can go out back. See that door over there?"

She pointed off to the side of the bar.

"It leads to the equipment area. You can load in there. Where's your van?"

"Across the street," I said.

There were no windows at the front of the building, so there was little risk in the lie.

"Alright. You can pull it out back in the alley. If you head out the side door, one of you can prop it open while you drive up so you don't have to knock and wait for someone to open it for you."

"Cool. Okay. So right through that door?" I asked, double-checking for some stupid reason in case she wanted to change her mind and decide to make us pay for our two hours of drinking.

"Yep. Good luck."

She flashed that smile again.

"Thanks."

I motioned to the guys, and we all shuffled back through the door and into a dark hallway. The hallway led to another door. That door led outside. We passed a very small loading area. I realized at that moment that it was the first time I had ever been backstage at any venue. It was a lot less impressive than I thought it would be. Then again, this venue was pretty shitty, so maybe it wasn't a great example of what it generally was like.

As we walked outside, I felt a huge wave of relief sweep over me. We had escaped. Escaped like ox. It could have turned into a pretty ugly situation, but instead we just got to make off without a trace. I started to imagine their disbelief when As Green Pastures Burn came on. They would announce their name and it wouldn't be Tuba City. The bartender would start scratching her head. And then cursing. Maybe silently. Or maybe out loud. Maybe both.

"How'd you get here?" Booker asked Pedro.

"I took the light rail."

"You live in Denver?"

"Nah. Just got here. Never been before."

"What are you up to now?"

"Nothing, really."

"Weren't you going to see those bands play?"

"Nah. I just walked in because I didn't have anything to do for a while."

Booker looked over at me, and I had an idea what he was going to say next. I gave him a nod of approval. I don't even think it was as much of a nod as it was a look. I just looked at him.

"We've got a truck parked a few blocks away that we stole in Mexico about a month ago. We've got nothing else planned for the rest of the night."

"Or the week," I added.

"Or maybe ever."

We turned the corner of the venue and started walking down the sidewalk.

"You want to come along with us?"

"In a stolen truck?"

"Ha, yeah. It's kind of a long story."

"I'm listening."

"Some delivery driver moved in on a group of girls that we were probably going to hook up with," Booker said, as though that was an acceptable reason to steal.

"So you stole his truck?"

Booker nodded.

"Yep. It was self-defense."

"What was in it?"

"About five hundred bottles of rum."

"Shit. Got any of it left?"

"We had to ditch it before we crossed the border."

"We threw a huge party and made some money though."

"Is this a real story? Or is this like your band story you told that girl?"

"No, this is real."

"Because I don't have any free booze to give you."

"It's real."

We approached the truck a moment later. Booker waved his hand in a grand gesture, as though it was the Taj Mahal or Pedro's first time at a strip club.

"This is our baby."

And there she sat. Faded and dusty white. Plain-looking. Boxy. Filled with two sleeping bags, two pillows, and nothing else. Pedro eyed it curiously for a moment. And then he smiled.

"You like it?" I asked.

He nodded.

"This is our home on wheels for the next however long. We have no plans, at all."

I shot a look over to Booker again, and he laughed.

"Nope, we don't."

"You're more than welcome to join us."

"We have no idea what we're going to be doing, but it will probably be a lot like what we just did. Hopefully a lot of drinking and music."

"And maybe pretending that we play music. So we can do more of the drinking."

We all laughed, and I shook my head. What we just did was way too easy. Everything about this trip was just way too easy.

"You guys really don't mind if I hang around with you?" Pedro asked.

"Nah. Not at all."

"You're a part of the band, man!"

"I am the drummer, aren't I? Every band needs a drummer."

"That is true. You are indeed the drummer in our band."

"What would Tuba City be without the drummer?"

"Tuba City Unplugged."

"Yeah. That's no good," I said.

Pedro looked at the truck a bit more and then clapped his hands together.

"Do I need to get a sleeping bag or something, or do you guys have a big, gay mattress laid out in the back?"

Thirteen

I've always had a thing for rum. I took my thing to a rum festival once. That was a hell of a hangover. I've spent plenty of Saturdays drinking from the time I woke up, but it usually involves some sort of midday meal break. Without food, there's no good way to keep going and fight off the spins. That festival didn't give me the chance.

I take that back. There was food. Mostly Cuban food. I just didn't get around to eating it. There was too much rum to choose from. Too many people to talk to. It was rum overload. I couldn't think about the food.

It wasn't that great of an experience. No one else seemed to give a shit about the food either. Everyone was either there to get completely shitfaced or to be a snob, sipping and spitting and using words that no one uses when they're enjoying themselves. Overall, there were very few sippers. It was mostly one big mess of drunk assholes. I've been around that crowd enough, and it usually doesn't bother me too much when it just happens to turn out that way. But these assholes paid an entry fee to be allowed to be assholes. It was an organized event of assholes, like an asshole parade. I was just one of many assholes.

And I'm not an asshole either. I'm not an angry or belligerent drunk. Most people can't tell if I'm really lit, if I just started drinking, or if I'm not drinking at all. I have a high tolerance. And even when I'm drunk, I'm pretty good at keeping it under wraps.

The asshole parade doesn't do that. The asshole parade is all about the lack of control. They feed off of each other. They get boisterous. They are there to annoy everyone, or they aren't having a good time.

Good drunks can sit there and let the world spin around them. They can smile and relax. They know what they're doing is a good time, and they don't want to make a big deal about it. They just want to enjoy it. The asshole parade has horns and trumpets and fucking whistles and streamers. They're screaming. They're stomping. *Look at us, we're drinking!* Some of their enjoyment actually comes from knowing that other people know that they're drinking. They're exhibitionists. Like I said, they're assholes.

After that festival, I vowed to never go to another organized drinking event again. Bars are okay, of course. Except on New Year's Eve, St. Patrick's Day, and sometimes Halloween. But all other days are okay. Beer festivals, rum festivals, wine festivals…they can all go march along without me. I'd rather drink a little more quietly and disconnectedly. I'd rather form my own opinions of how I feel and what that means. I don't like the crowd. They probably don't like me either. And that's fine.

Pedro had his own sleeping bag. I can't remember where he got it from or why he had it so readily accessible. All I really remember is that we woke up that first morning, and it didn't feel too weird. There was a moment when I realized that it wasn't just Booker and I in the back of that truck, and it felt a little bit odd. Like, who is here? And why is he here? And why is it not a girl? It didn't matter for long though. It wore off pretty quickly when I realized that I was again sleeping in the back of a truck. Whether or not there was a stranger in there with us was somewhat immaterial. Sleeping in a back of a box truck will change your perspective on a lot of things that you used to think were weird.

I woke up earlier than the other two, and I let myself outside. I found a quiet alley to take a piss. The morning was crisp but not cold. Or maybe it was warm. I don't know. There is no way that I would remember the details of that morning over any other morning unless it had something to do with what happened to me next, which it didn't. But for the sake of having some details to go along with this story, I'd like to remember it as a crisp morning.

Ah, yes. So crisp. I remember it well.

In the daylight and with sober eyes and senses, I realized that the Marquis Theatre was not as remote as I thought it was when we first wandered in. It was just a few blocks away from Coors Field. It was on the same road, more or less. It stood there in broad daylight, almost naked-looking. Just staring back at me. Like, *Hey, Blake. I'm the Marquis Theatre. Can you hand me a towel?*

How the hell did we get away with that? All those free drinks, all that talk of being the opening band. We somehow either guessed the promoter's name or called bullshit on the bartender who had no idea what his name was. It all worked out too perfectly, like it was supposed to happen. But nothing is supposed to happen. It just happens. So that just happened.

I took a turn down a side street and began to pass numbers. 19th. 18th. 17th. Those kind of numbers. I passed brick buildings and more brick buildings. Small ones. Slightly less small ones. Ones that looked like they had restaurants in them. Ones that looked like they could have had anything in them. Ones with apartments on top of them. I turned down one of the numbers and kept walking. More bricks. More sizes.

I found out later that this area was called Lodo. *Lo* as in Lower and *Do* as in Downtown. I suppose that's an alright way to name a part of a city, or at least no worse than any other way of naming it.

If I was the guy in charge of naming parts of towns, I'd call this part Brick. It could be a wide ranging area, and that would be fine. Basically any part of the downtown area where the buildings were predominantly brick would be a part of Brick. It wouldn't even need to be contiguous. It could be a few blocks here, separated for a while by some other part of the city. Then it could turn back into Brick again. Brick didn't need to be connected. Brick wasn't particular like that.

I turned back up another street and started to pass numbers again. Most places were closed and showed no signs of when they would open again. I tried for a few moments to remember what day it was, but I gave up when I realized that it didn't matter. It was probably just a day when places didn't open up that early. That could be every day. It didn't matter.

I got back to the truck and stood at the entrance to the alley where we parked. We had now parked this truck in two different alleys in two different cities without encountering a problem either time. No disturbance, no garbage trucks honking horns, nothing. I know that this isn't exactly scientific proof that we were not going to have any problems in the future, but it struck me as I stood there on that definitely crisp morning that there is something very official and okay about an unmarked, white box truck being parked in an alley. Ask anyone around. It's probably supposed to be there, but they won't know for sure. It's a truck. They park in alleys. That's kind of what they do.

We were inconspicuous without even trying. Hiding in plain sight, as the phrase goes, though the word *hiding* implies that you're trying to be concealed. We were just trying to find a place to park and pass out. We didn't think much beyond that. Karma must have been busy taking care of someone else at the time.

I stood there for a while and just stared at the truck. My mind started to wander back to Mexico. I started to get deep. Real deep. I was fixating on a set of melancholy, introspective thoughts of the rum we stole and the party we threw and the girls we almost got to fuck but didn't get to fuck that first night. It was deep and heartfelt. I imagined the breasts and asses that we didn't get to squeeze. The asses that got away. I stared up at the sky. Why, Lord?

My thoughts went to eating all of that shitty food from those shitty convenience stores and how long the drive through the desert felt to us. I thought about that delivery driver and how shitty it all turned out for him. He got it the worst.

I must have been standing there for at least five minutes. That's a long time for someone to stand in one place doing nothing for no reason. That certainly crisp Denver air blew through my hair as I got all deep and introspective and thoughtful. I was like a fucking statue of emotion. I was a monument to our theft. I was an iconoclast. I don't even know what that is, but I think I was it.

I walked around to the front of the truck and hopped in, closing the door quietly so as to not awake the guys as they slept in the back. I lay down across the bench seat, my head pressed against the passenger door, my knees slightly bent and leaning against the seat back, my feet connected to my ankles like a normal human being. I closed my eyes and started to fall asleep. My walk was a false alarm. I wasn't ready to wake up for the day just yet.

I had a dream about a guy that I used to talk to at the gym. This was back when I gave a shit about how I looked, or at least enough to exercise a few times a week. I was actually in pretty good shape at one point, at least by my standards. There was a faint line that indicated where my abs were. It was not a six-pack though. It wasn't even the carton that held the six-pack. Think of it as the receipt that you threw away from your trip to the grocery store when you considered buying a six-pack but instead bought some chips and salsa. That's the faintness of the line I was developing back when I cared enough to try.

This guy was pretty old. He had to be in his seventies. There I was, barely getting my ass to the gym, and this retired guy was dragging himself in every day. I never saw him doing anything there though. He would just hang out in the locker room. My guess is that he swam for maybe fifteen or twenty minutes and then just showered and changed for two hours on either side of that. I have no proof. Maybe he just changed the whole time. When I would go, I used to show up at around the same time, give or take an hour or two. And without fail, I'd always see him just walking around the locker room. He was always some degree of naked, as old guys in the locker room tend to be.

I dreamt that we were outside of a concert venue, though I couldn't remember which one. It obviously didn't really matter. I was outside with some friends, but I couldn't find them. The old, naked guy was outside too. He was leaning up against a wall, his knee bent and his right foot flat against it in some kind of James Dean pose that he somehow pulled off (despite the fact that he was probably as old as James Dean would have been if he hadn't gone through that intersection that day and if nothing else had killed him for the next sixty years). Mathematically I realize that this doesn't add up, but just go with it. It was a dream.

We were talking about restaurants that we've eaten at. That wasn't a topic that we had ever talked about at the gym, as far as I could remember. I was telling him about the nicest places I had been. I was explaining them to him with a pandering detail that I was almost embarrassed about. At one point I started to pat him on the head when I explained in detail the importance of this particular restaurant that I was describing. I kept patting him on the head. Very understandingly. He didn't say much. That's all I can really remember about it.

I woke up for a little while before falling back asleep. I wondered why I was thinking about him. I didn't even know his name. I used to think that his name was Joe, but that was entirely made up. Joe was a decent old guy name, so I had some chance of being correct. Good old Joe. James Dean Joe.

Once, he had told me a story that I always thought was pretty interesting. As I lay there half-groggy and in between bouts of sleep, I thought of it and I started to smile. He was old enough that when he went to school – and he went to a private, Catholic school – it was still alright for teachers to get physical with the students to keep them in line. Physical, like beating them with a ruler, a stick, or with their bare hands. Not physical in any perverted way. You pervert.

Back then, it was considered a sin to say your prayers and do the little holy cross motion over your head and chest while using your left hand. Maybe that's still the case. I don't know. Back then, the nuns always made you do it with your right hand. The problem was that Joe was a lefty. He was born that way. Ten-percent of the world is born lefty, you know. Not sure why God messed that one up. Because that means that there is a one in ten chance that in order to respect the Lord, you're going to have to do something that feels unnatural to you. That makes sense.

Anyway, Joe was a lefty by nature, so it took a lot of beatings for him to get used to this new way of doing things. But just like the church trying to get people to pray the gay away, sometimes you just can't shake your nature no matter how hard someone tries to make you. Joe just couldn't stop using his left hand for certain things. So, he made a compromise.

From eight o'clock until three o'clock, he used his right hand as his primary hand. He wrote with his right, and it looked terrible. He prayed with his right. He turned pages in a book with his right hand. He probably ate sandwiches with his right hand. You get the idea. Anything that he did while he was in school, he did with his right hand. And then when he got out of school, he'd use his left hand.

Back home at the dinner table, he picked up his fork with his left hand. He played guitar with his left hand. He shot his dad's gun with his left hand. He jerked off lefty. He unhooked bras lefty. He was a lefty for the things that he did when there was no one to tell him not to. He was a righty when he was being watched.

When he became an adult, these mannerisms carried over into his everyday life. He used a different hand for each thing that he had to do. But as he explained it to me, this wasn't a blessing. He wasn't ambidextrous. He just had a designated hand for each task that he had to carry out. Sometimes his brain would mix things up, and he'd have to consciously remember which hand was the good hand for the thing that he needed to do. So sometimes, he told me, he'd be sitting there for a few seconds immobilized, unsure of how he was supposed to proceed.

All of this derived from this stupid idea that it was wrong to praise God using your left hand, as though you were made with two hands but only one of them was divine. How fucking stupid.

I fell back asleep thinking about that, trying to remember which hand I used to pat him on the head, wondering if he'd have patted me back with the same hand or if God would frown upon us both. Or if God really cared at all about which hand you used for whatever you did.

I woke up a few hours later when Pedro opened the door to the cab and started to shake my foot. I remember thinking that there was something weird about him. He didn't know me. We had just met the night before, while drunk. He had probably sobered up, but it didn't make a difference. He still felt comfortable enough to come find me and make sure I woke up by grabbing my foot. I didn't mind it. I just didn't think I'd have done the same if I were him. I'd have hung out for a while outside of the truck, debating if I should just ditch the two weirdos that I was hanging out with. It'd be a short debate. I'd have left before they had a chance to wake up and awkwardly convince me to hang out. I'd have never seen them again.

In fact, I would have left way before I fell asleep in the back of a stolen truck with two guys. I would have never put myself in that situation.

Not Pedro. From the look of him, his face smiling dopily down by my feet, he didn't seem like he was in a hurry to get away from us. Or to get anywhere, really. He looked like he wanted to hang out until there was something better to do…and then probably turn it down to hang out with us some more. I hadn't met anybody like him before. I still haven't.

"You ready to wake up?"

I was staring down at him by my feet, not saying anything for maybe fifteen seconds before he asked me that.

"Guess so. What time is it?"

"I dunno. Noon. Booze o'clock. Let's get hammered."

"Just one speed, huh?"

"Yeah, boss. I just want to get going."

"Alright. Is Booker up?"

"Yeah, pretty much."

"Alright."

I swung my feet under the steering wheel and down by the pedals, sitting upright as best as I could. Little stars started to shoot across my eyes, white flecks of dizziness. They enveloped most of my vision for a few seconds. I just sat there staring forward. They went away a little while later. I hopped out of the cab and onto the pavement. The absolutely crisp air from earlier had been replaced by a slightly balmy breeze. I had slept for so long that the wind had abandoned one adjective and replaced it with a new one. The wind was cold like that sometimes.

Booker was standing at the back of the truck, leaning against its corner. It didn't look comfortable.

"What's the plan, man?" I asked him, clearly ignoring what Pedro had suggested earlier.

"Pedro wants to get drunk," he responded, clearly not ignoring what Pedro had suggested earlier. "So how about we do that? I could do that."

"Uhh…yeah. Yeah, I could do that, I guess."

"Don't guess. Just drink," Pedro chimed in.

I looked at him and frowned.

"You're on a mission."

"Yes, I am."

"Don't let me get in the way then. We'll get drunk."

"Yeah!"

He shouted with happiness like he was a little kid. It was almost contagious.

"Book, do you think we can keep the truck here all day or what?"

"Probably not all day. We should move it in a few hours. Let's try to find an alley on our walk to the bar or wherever we're going. Then when we come back…I mean, then *let's* come back and move it to its new spot for the night."

"So we're staying here another night?"

"Yeah, man. Denver. Why the fuck not?"

Pedro was pacing back and forth by the wall, smiling.

"We should try to do what we did last night," he added. "But again."

"Again. Sleep in the back of the truck? Yeah, that was pretty sweet."

"No. Get free booze by pretending to be a band."

Booker looked at me and winked.

"Don't wink at me," I warned him.

"Pedro and I were talking about this earlier this morning. I bet we could pull this off again if we wanted to."

"Are you serious?"

"The band," Pedro reminded me.

"We just have to convince some dumbass women that we're in a band that's about to play, and I bet we'll get some VIP treatment again."

"Nope. That was pure luck. That is *not* going to happen again."

"Dude, you're wrong. Think about it. These people have no idea what most of these little bands sound like, let alone what they look like. They could look like anyone. Like us. They could look like us, and no one would ever know the difference."

Pedro was just standing there nodding. It was a solid contribution.

"Yeah, I believe that part, but I don't think we're going to get free drinks out of it again. I think that was a one-time deal. That was luck. That's it."

"*Luck* you, man," said our new friend.

Booker looked at him and shook his head.

"Don't say that again," he laughed. "But really, Blake, you might be right. But I don't think you're giving this genius idea we accidentally ran into the credit it deserves. I think we have a pretty good chance of a repeat."

"I already learned my lesson about being greedy, remember? I got my fucking ass kicked when I wasn't satisfied with having a good time and knowing when to walk away. No thanks."

Booker turned to Pedro to explain.

"We tried stealing some money from a bar in Mexico, and these dudes beat the shit out of old Blake's face. He used to be a good looking guy. Now he's…this," he said, pointing to my face and shrugging.

"It happened right here," I added, showing him the wall of the truck where they had pinned me.

"So we just don't do it here then," Pedro replied. "We just have to find the right place."

"Yeah, Pedro, there you go! We just need to find the right place."

"What kind of place is that?" I asked. "A music venue with some strung out chick who couldn't stand being called out on not knowing what she was talking about, to the point where she will pretend she is a fan of our very obviously nonexistent band, and a bartender who didn't give a shit about anything, at an empty but somehow welcoming venue that partners with a promoter whose name we randomly guessed?"

"Yep," Booker almost shouted, though it was quiet enough that it warrants a comma and not an exclamation point. "That's not luck, man. That's every goddamned music venue in this city and in this country. Probably everywhere. Music people are self-righteous pricks."

"Mmm-hmm," Pedro confirmed.

"They would much rather pretend they *knew* that we were in a band than admit that they had never heard of us or didn't know who we were. That's not just that place last night. That's *every* place."

"Yeah it is!" Pedro insisted.

I thought about it for a bit. They had a good point. People who are into music – or even people who claim to be into music – are about as stubborn as people can get when it comes to being out of the loop. They will pretend to know something they don't know, just for the sake of not being bested by someone else. I've seen it dozens of times. It's a well-known phenomenon. It doesn't have a well-known name, or at least not yet, but I think it's still a phenomenon.

"Alright. Okay. Let's just see what happens then?"

Booker started to smile. He looked straight at Pedro as his smile grew.

"I don't care," I added. "This is a win-win for me. I am either right, or I get free booze. So, I'm in."

Pedro came away from the wall and walked toward Booker with his hand in the air. Booker slapped him five and looked at me with his eyes crossed and his tongue half-hanging out of his mouth. Pedro didn't see it, though I don't think he would have even understood that Booker was mocking him even if he did. This guy was weird. But at the same time, there was something genuine about him. Something endearing and honest and likeable. You couldn't get mad at him, I could tell. Not for long, at least. He was like a dog.

Good Pedro. Good boy. Sit. Drink. Give me paw.

I went into the back of the truck and changed into the clothes that I had worn two days earlier. I only had two changes with me, so this was about as fancy as I was going to get. These were the clothes that I had soaked through with my sweat at the show in Phoenix. They smelled like it. My hair was a matted mess and my skin was so oily that when I rubbed my fingers across my face, there was a noticeable glisten on my fingertips. I was going to need a shower at some point, or at least I was hoping for one. This wasn't Mexico. Someone was going to kick us out of their bar if we kept our hygiene streak going in this direction. Pedro somehow looked pretty clean, but we had just met him the day before. For all I knew, he could have walked straight out of the shower and into that venue. Booker never looked clean, so I didn't even bother looking at him.

We wandered back into the Lodo area. There were bricks and shapes and numbers. It was like I already knew the place as I told the guys to take a left, keep going straight, stop at stop lights, all that kind of stuff. I was an expert on this part of town based on my single, hazy-eyed walk a few hours earlier that nobody actually knew about. We found a bar that served food. For a while I was pretty sure it was the same place that Booker and I had been to the day earlier, when we first got into town. Booker assured me that it wasn't. I still think it might have been. We are not receipt keepers, so I doubt we'll ever know.

"So what's your deal, man?" I asked Pedro right before I took a big bite of my burger.

Ketchup squirted out of the side and onto the plate. I had no regard for manners at this point in the day. I smelled like I was just coming from the gym, but I looked like I had never stepped foot inside of one. That's one of the worst combinations of sight and smell that a man can embody.

"I used to mow lawns for my friend's dad in the summers," he said, and then he took a bite of his burger.

He grabbed a fry and stuck it in there while he was chewing.

"Uhhh. Okay. That's your *deal*?"

"I don't know what you mean by that."

"I mean, like, what are you doing in Denver if you're not from Denver and you have no reason being in Denver and you don't know anybody in Denver?"

"Oh."

He kept chewing and started to nod a bit.

"I thought you were asking why I knew so much about two-stroke engines."

I must have not been paying attention to what he and Booker were talking about, because Booker was nodding and looking at me like I was an asshole.

"Nah, that makes sense. Sorry, did I just totally cut you guys off?"

"Yup," Booker confirmed.

"My bad. I wasn't paying attention."

"Nice."

"Yeah, sorry."

Shit. My mind wandered sometimes.

"Anyway, I meant like, what's your deal? What brought you here and why are you here?"

"I just wanted to get out and explore a bit. I didn't have much going on, so I thought I would hit the road for a while."

"Is everybody trying to be Jack Kerouac lately? What the fuck is that about?"

"Who's that?" Pedro asked.

"Right?" Booker retorted. "Blake is obsessed with the Jack Kerosiac guy. He's been yapping about him nonstop since we got on the road."

"Whoa, first of all, dude, how did you fuck up the pronunciation of his name about two seconds after I said it?"

"Kerosian?"

"Shut up. Second, I haven't been talking about him the whole time we've been out here. I mentioned it one other time."

"You sure?"

"Yes. Positive. *And* I only mentioned it because *you guys* have been talking about getting out on the road, hitting the road. Road, road, road. It just seems very..."

"Kerosian?"

"Yeah, you dumbass. Very *Kerosian.* Like he's fucking Armenian."

"Ah, dude," Pedro chimed in. "I hooked up with an Armenian girl back in high school. She was short. Maybe not even five feet tall. Huge boobs though. Amazing rack."

"Amazing for a short girl or just amazing amazing?"

"Amazing amazing."

We all sighed. It was obvious that we were all in our own ways feeling the pains of our respective dry spells.

"Where's she at now?" Booker asked.

He obviously had the longest dry spell amongst us.

"New Jersey."

"Ah, fuck. Hey Blake, wanna go to Jersey next?

I just looked at him while I took another bite of my burger. I think it was buffalo meat.

"So is that where you're from then? New Jersey?"

"Naw, man. I'm from Omaha."

"For real?"

"Yep."

"That sucks." I paused. "Doesn't that suck?"

"It used to."

He smiled and waved his arms around, gesturing as though he had finally made it somewhere better. There were bits of food stuck in between a few of his teeth, and it made me realize that there might be the same thing going on in my mouth. Then I remembered that I didn't care.

"So, this is you. You're Pedro Bay. You know about two-stroke engines because you used to mow lawns, and you're from Omaha, Nebraska. And you used to fuck a big-titted Armenian girl from New Jersey. That's who you are. Oh, and you know nothing about the beat generation."

"Nope, boss. Una problema."

"Oh, you have heard of the beat writers?"

"No. No idea what the hell you're talking about there. The correction is on my whereabouts. I mean, my original whereabouts."

"You mean that you're from Omaha?"

"Right."

"So you're not from Omaha even though you just told us you're from there?"

"No, I am."

"This is a great conversation, guys."

"No kidding."

"Omaha, Texas," Pedro explained.

"There's an Omaha in Texas?"

"Oh yeah, there is," he said.

"No shit? Alright. Well, whatever. It sounds worse than Omaha, Nebraska, so now I feel worse for you than I did before."

"No sweat, man. I grew up there but then moved to the east coast for a bit when I got older. Then I decided to leave. And now I'm here."

Booker eyed me and smiled.

"That's very Kerosian, don't you think?"

"Fuck you."

I rolled my eyes and stuffed the last bite of my burger into my mouth. Booker and Pedro took care of the check for some reason. I played on my phone for a bit, trying to figure out where we should go next. The sun was still shining overhead, presumably. There was a roof in the way so I couldn't be sure until I stepped back outside. But if the scene outside of the windows was to be trusted, it was going to be sunny out there.

"How about we go to Boulder?" I offered.

"What's in Boulder?"

"I dunno. A college."

I scrolled around on my phone while they stared at me.

"Rock formations."

"Sounds pretty fucking legit."

"We've got time, don't we?" I asked.

They both agreed.

So we drove to Boulder. The truck was getting a nice tour of North America. I bet its old owner wouldn't have taken it to all of the places that we were taking it. Its old owner was selfish and lame. He'd just take her back and forth between the same places. The warehouse. The shops. The hotels and resorts. The fucking Pemex station.

Not us. We took this baby to all new worlds. Like the sarcastically-fabulous city of Phoenix and the actually-so-far-so-good city of Denver. And the still-not-sure-but-optimistic-about-it Boulder.

It was a short drive compared to what we had been doing. I think it took maybe thirty minutes. The truck rattled and hummed along, seemingly unfazed by all of the miles it had rolled over in the past few weeks. I suppose that's what vehicles do. They drive. It just seemed to me that if you had asked me to travel from Puerto Vallarta to Los Angeles to Denver, and I was a car, I'd be pretty annoyed. But maybe that's why I was born as a human and not as a car. I'd be a bitch of a car.

We spent the day in Boulder wandering around the main downtown area. It was pretty small and had a Third Street Promenade kind of feel to it, but in a good way. We weren't interested in shopping, so we zigzagged around until we found a place where we could start drinking. It was, after all, already a few hours past Pedro's definitively announced "booze o'clock." We were behind schedule. The sun started to go down behind the Flatirons before we realized that they were the rock formations that we were supposed to care about. It was getting dark, and we had no way to account for what we had done with ourselves all day. It still was a couple of hours before it was nighttime, but it was the right time to make a move if we were going to make one.

We started to ask around for a music venue. Everyone kept referring to the Fox, as though we were fucking idiots for not having heard of it before. There was a level of indignation over the fact that we didn't know where live music was played in this little college town. That attitude just didn't sit right with me. I liked Boulder up until that point. After that started to happen, I got over it. It was cool, but not that cool. Sorry, Boulder. Your people ruined it for me. You're still in fucking Colorado. Don't act like you're better than what you are.

Nevertheless, we made our way over to the Fox, which, as it turned out, was pretty much right across the street from the campus of the University itself. Technically it was across the street from a deli and market. But the back of that deli was facing the back of something else, and that thing was across the street from the campus. So it was third cousins with the campus.

The Fox had a retro feel to the outside of it. In fact, a lot of Boulder had a cool vibe to it, despite the aforementioned people. It almost felt like it was separated from the rest of the world, the world that I had lived in. The altitude and those looming mountains blocking it from the west coast gave the whole city an aura of isolation and purity. It wasn't just the clean air. It was something else. I guess that's why they call places Big Sky and shit like that. It really does feel wide open. I felt it more in Boulder than I did in Denver.

From the looks of it, Pedro didn't feel anything. He had somewhat of a lazy eye even when he was sober, or at least when I assumed he was sober earlier in the day. A few hours of drinking later, his eyes were playing chase around his head. It made him look a lot drunker than he was. Then again, I was drunk too, so my barometer was not properly calibrated. He could have been damned near poisoned, for all I knew. It didn't matter. He was upright, and no one gave him a hard time about it. That's all that matters.

The Fox let us in early even though we didn't have tickets to the show and there was nothing else to do in there other than watch a show. We told the guys at the door that we were on a road trip from Los Angeles and that we were checking out historic music venues all across the country. The Fox was at the top of our list, we told them. It had some truth to it. They let us in to look around. It was a medium-sized venue. Maybe six hundred people could fit, if I had to guess. That's decent. It was somewhat U-shaped, which seemed to make a much better fit for people than the place we had been to the day before, with its awful layout. This one actually made sense. I bet that no one at the Marquis would have believed our road trip story if we tried to sell it to them there. No one would travel across the country for that shithole.

After our little walkabout, we went over to the bar in hopes of getting a drink, but nobody was there. Some girl came over and asked us if we were doing alright, which I took as our cue to leave. I headed for the door and assumed Booker would be following behind me. I turned around about five or ten seconds later. I looked back, but neither of them were anywhere in sight. That was mostly because I was standing behind a support beam. I looked around the beam and saw Pedro talking to the same girl that I was pretty sure had just passive-aggressively kicked us out. I walked back and could overhear a bit of what he said as I got closer. It sounded like he was trying to negotiate a way for us to stay. My stomach sank a little. I didn't know him that well, but I had a good idea of what he was trying to do.

"Here he is now. Where'd you go, Blake?"

"I was off behind that support beam over there," I said.

Everybody looked over my shoulder at the beam and nodded.

"Why'd you do that?"

"Thought we were leaving."

I put my hands on my hips.

"You're doing it, dude," Booker said.

I took my hands and put them in my pockets. He always made fun of me when I put them on my hips. He insisted that only women and out-of-breath soccer players waiting for a free kick or a substitute were allowed to do that. He was probably right, but I apparently thought it was comfortable enough to do it fairly often.

"We're not leaving, buddy," Pedro announced. "Ky-Kylie right here said we can stick around a bit."

"Uhh," said the girl.

"I think it's Karen," Booker added.

"It's Kylie," said the girl.

"Damned right. Like I said, Kylie, we can stick around a bit, right?"

"I don't know…what do you guys want to do exactly?" she asked.

"Drink," I tried to say quietly, but it was loud enough that everyone heard me.

The fact that it was quiet made it sound really pathetic and desperate. I wanted to say it again and with more enthusiasm, but the moment had already passed.

"Well, uhh, the bar doesn't open for another thirty minutes or so. You guys could walk around outside for a bit and come back when we do open, if you want. Do you already have tickets?"

"Outside schm-outside, why can't we stay in here?"

Pedro was starting to sound as drunk as he looked. I took my hands out of my pockets and put them on my hips again. Booker eyed me hard. I kept them there.

"Nah, it's alright," I said. "We can walk around outside for a bit, right Booker?"

"Yeah, man. No problem. We'll come back in a bit."

"But wait," Pedro moaned.

He wouldn't give it up.

"Can't we just hang out a bit longer? As I was saying while Blake was over hiding behind that pole over there, we're one of the bands playing here. We just got here a little early."

The girl eyed him very cautiously before she spoke.

"Tonight's show is a solo. There's no opener."

"Ah," Booker mumbled.

"So unless all three of you are a one-man acoustic band, I think you might not be telling me the truth right now."

"Whoa whoa whoa, Kylie," Pedro stammered.

I was about ready to walk away and just go outside and leave the two of them there to haggle over what was going to amount to nothing with the poor girl, but he began to speak again before I had the chance.

"I didn't say we were playing tonight. I said we're one of the bands playing here. Soon."

"Is that right?" she asked, obviously humoring him.

"Yep. Well, okay…I mean…I hope we are."

"Oh yeah?"

"Yep. Our promoter is really trying to book us here as an opener if you have a drop-out or some additional time before your already-booked openers in the next week or so, while we're in town. We're running a guerilla west-coast-slash-mountain-time-zone tour right now."

He paused to catch his breath, and he could see that she didn't believe a thing that he was saying. In these types of situations, there are two ways that you can approach your next move. You can give up and swallow your pride, realizing that you didn't convince her that your story was true. You can walk away. Laugh it off. Move on. Or, you can forge forward, knowing very well that she probably isn't going to bite, but refusing to give up on the fabrication that you committed to.

Pedro forged forward.

"We played at the Marquis last night," he said.

This got her attention for some reason. Her eyes opened up a bit.

"Is that right?"

This time she didn't sound like she was mocking him as much.

"Yeah. We went on right before As Green Pastures Burn."

"No kidding?"

"Yep," Booker added. "They were dickheads, by the way."

"Who? The Marquis?"

"No. As Green Pastures Burn. They were lame. The guys at the Marquis were solid."

The girl put her hands on her hips as she asked her next question. Instinctively, I took my hands off of mine. Booker laughed.

"So wait a minute…are you guys actually for real?"

"Uh huh," Pedro said, defiantly.

"What's your name?"

"Pedro."

"No, your band name."

"Oh. Tuba City."

"How come I've never heard of you?"

"Because our promoter is a lazy cokehead," Pedro countered immediately.

The girl laughed.

"They all are."

"Tell me about it," I added, trying to get into the mix.

She looked over at me, and it looked like she winced. I decided to not say anything for a while after that.

"So, alright. Well, I don't work in the office, so I don't know anything about booking and all of that…but you guys can hang out a little longer if you want to."

"Nice!" Booker cheered.

"Just don't do anything fucked up, alright?"

"Yeah, no problem, Kylie. We just want to hang out a bit until the bartender gets on."

"Right. Alright."

She started to walk away and toward wherever she originally came from.

"Just don't do anything that will get me in trouble. Okay?"

"Of course."

"Thanks, Karen," Booker said and smiled.

She smiled back and walked away.

"How the fuck did you guys just do that?" I asked.

"Do what?" Pedro asked me back.

"Uh...convince her that we were in a band and to let us stay here even though we don't have tickets and the venue isn't open yet even if we did."

"Dude, what? Who cares about tickets? We *are* in a band. Our truck is parked out front. Our promoter is a cokehead."

"His name is Bob," Booker reminded me.

"Right."

"Want to make ourselves some drinks?"

Pedro was already walking over to the bar as he asked.

"Dude, didn't you just hear her?"

"Yeah, I heard her," he said, as he made his way around to the back of the bar and faced me directly. "But I'm not Pedro, some guy you just met who listens to what people tell him to do."

"Oh, you're not?"

"Nope," he said, grabbing a plastic cup from under the bar and placing it in front of him. "I'm Pedro. The drummer in Tuba City. You've known me for a long time. You know that I don't listen to what people tell me to do."

He splashed a bunch of some clear liquor into the cup and looked up at me intently.

"No ice?"

He shook his head.

"There is no ice. Bartender didn't come in yet. Just booze and mixers."

He splashed some coke on top of it and stuck his finger in to stir it around.

"Tuba City," I said.

It had a decent ring to it after you said it a few times, though I had only said it once then.

"Yep."

He walked back around to the front of the bar and put his hand on my shoulder like someone who cared about me more than someone who had just met me twenty-four hours earlier would care about me. It felt no different than if I had known him for years.

"And dudes in bands don't listen to chicks named Kylie who tell them not to get them in trouble. Dudes in bands do whatever the fuck they want."

"That's why they're in the band," Booker added.

"Why do you keep adding little one-liners in there, man?"

Booker laughed.

"Because tonight is the Pedro Bay show. He is on fire right now."

Booker slapped Pedro on the back.

"Look at this motherfucker! He got himself a drink. He doesn't give a shit. He's in the band."

"It's warm," Pedro said, displeased and grimacing as he sipped.

"Yeah, but it's free."

"True that."

I walked slowly toward the back of the bar, looking around as I did.

"Stop scoping things out, man. You're in the band too. You're a badass. You're Blake from Tuba City. The fucking band."

Pedro was very reassuring.

"So act like it."

I tried to imagine that what he was saying was true. It did feel pretty empowering. Like I wasn't myself and like anything I did wasn't really attributed to me, but rather to this persona of a person who I wasn't. It made it feel like there wasn't that much of a risk with anything if I was pretending to be someone else. I stood at the corner of the bar and looked out at the stage. It was mostly dark, with just one dimly lit overhead light spreading a faint fan of brightness onto some drop cloths and equipment. In a few hours there would be a crowd in here, cheering for some guy on that stage. All of that gear would be gone. It'd be just him and some lights.

If that guy was where I was right then, he'd probably go behind the bar and get himself a drink. He'd know that he was the reason this place could keep their lights on another day. He'd know that they adored people like him, even if they didn't know who the fuck he was. They needed him. He gave their entire business a justification. This was the music venue, and he was the musician. Pedro was telling me that I was the musician too.

Maybe I was.

"Make me a rum and coke while you're back there," Booker ordered.

I looked at him, and back at the stage, and then at the bar in front of me.

"You're just the fucking bassist, man," I laughed as I picked up a plastic cup. "Make it yourself."

Fourteen

I've always had a thing for rum. I read somewhere that rum founded our country. I say *our* as though you are a citizen of the United States just like me. Maybe you're not. Sorry. I will write something relevant for you and your citizenship later. By founded, I don't mean that the founding fathers were not actually historical figures, but rather that they were powder-wig-wearing bottles of rum. No. That would be cool but not very likely, as rum cannot talk or make laws or sign declarations. I mean that the money that rum brought in is what bankrolled the origins of America.

But, I didn't claim it. I just read it. I may have read it on the Internet too, so it may be entirely untrue. I am far too lazy to look it up on any official source – which would still be on the Internet – so I am just going to let that statement hang out there and perhaps solidify into what you remember one day as a fact. And then maybe you will communicate this on to someone else. And then they will do the same. The circle of lie.

So I've always had a thing for rum, and so has America. And so it's very fitting that in what felt like the heart of this country, rum was beginning to have a thing for us. And that thing was an extremely pleasant bout of luck, amongst other things. But mostly luck.

That night at the Fox turned out to be a very good turn in the right direction for us. I decided to take Pedro's advice and embody the swagger that comes with being in a band. At least for a little while. I didn't see any reason not to give it a try. We were in a new city where we knew nobody. There was no reason that we couldn't be what we were pretending to be. But it wasn't going to be believable if we didn't act the part. So we did that, or at least we did to the best of our abilities. It's not like we had been in a band before and actually knew how we were supposed to behave. As far as I'm concerned, there's nothing wrong with making it up as you go. So that's what we did.

The solo guitarist put on a really good show. It was as solo as it gets. Just him, a chair, and his guitar. One guitar. Not a change of a bunch of different guitars, with different guys coming on the stage to help him prep.

Nope. It was just him. It was as though he had traveled there entirely on his own, producing his own show all the way through. It felt very authentic, which of course belies a great deal of irony to the situation, as we couldn't have been any further from authentic. But, whatever. He didn't know that. And I had never even heard of the guy, so I didn't owe him anything.

The crowd was really into him. They were overall a fairly mellow group, so we were able to push and shove our way to just about the front and center of the crowd. Again, the Fox was laid out in a way that provided a great view of the stage as long as you were inside and not behind that one beam that I had found. It didn't matter though. We wanted to be up close. The free drinking beforehand and the days and days of drinking before that…it had calloused our temperaments. We didn't care if we upset a few girls on the way to the front and they huffed and puffed and jabbed us in the back with their elbows.

Yeah, I'm taller than you. I don't know what else to tell you. This isn't a class picture. The short people don't automatically get to go in the front so their faces can be seen. In the real world, tall people have advantages. You need to deal with that. Or wear some heels. You do have options that you can take advantage of too. Don't get mad at me for taking advantage of mine.

About halfway through the show, the singer took a break from his set and just started chatting with the crowd. *How are you guys doing tonight,* that sort of stuff. It was nothing out of the ordinary. At one point, realizing that he couldn't ask how we liked the opening band, since there wasn't one, he asked the crowd what other bands they had seen there lately. Everybody started murmuring, and some people would intermittently begin shouting random words that didn't sound like band names at all. It was just a bunch of unnecessary noise, really. It's not like he could understand anything other than what the people right in from of him were saying.

"Tuba City!" Booker yelled, probably a bit louder than most people.

The singer looked over to where we were standing.

"What?" he asked into the mic.

"Tuba City!" Booker repeated, with Pedro yelling along with him, which probably didn't help.

The singer leaned into the mic before asking again.

"Hooba City? Is that like the sequel to Hoobastank? Why don't they call themselves Hoobastank, Jr.?"

He looked out at the crowd to get their reaction, which turned out to be a pretty big roar of laughter. It wasn't that funny, but whatever.

"No! TUBA. CITY. That's our band!"

"Tuba City?" the singer repeated.

"Yes! That's us!"

Booker waved his arms around the area where we were standing.

"Hey, everybody," the singer said, smiling. "We've got Tuba City here. Give it up for Tuba City!"

I couldn't tell if he was mocking us or if he was just trying to get the crowd going, but it didn't matter. The crowd began cheering and screaming as though they had not only heard of us before, but, like, they loved us. The singer looked a little surprised, but then he went along with it.

"Right on, guys. Welcome to the show. Tuba City!"

The crowd cheered again, and the singer started to strum his guitar and lead into his next song. Booker looked back at me and raised his eyebrows so high that I think they brushed against the ceiling. Pedro was staring straight forward at the stage, jumping up and down, even though no one else was. I was laughing. I looked over to my side. A group of girls were looking at us and smiling.

Tuba City had been released into the wild.

The show went on for quite a while, maybe ninety minutes overall, which is pretty long for a solo guitar show. The guy must have been tired at the end. If he had been on the road doing this in different cities every night, he must have really developed some stage endurance. After his last song, the lights came up and everybody started to file out into the street. There was no encore.

As usual, some people stuck around after the show hoping to find valuables on the ground – guitar picks that he might have thrown out but that I am pretty sure he didn't throw out, and things like that. Some people actually wait around to try to hang out with the band. But the band never wants to hang out. And even when they do, they don't want to do it in front of the stage. They want to be out back. Everyone knows that, but not everyone acts like they know it when the show ends. They act like the band – or the guy or whoever they came to see – is going to just walk out front and start talking to whoever stuck around. That never happens.

But we've all done it. I've done it. Booker has definitely done it. And that night, some people did it. Though some people stuck around waiting to see if they could talk to another act, maybe one that was a little more attainable. Us.

Unbelievably, those girls that were smiling after our little band name announcement were still hanging around, and one of them was eyeing Booker pretty hard. He was fairly oblivious, which never happens when it comes to girls. That's how I knew he was wasted. I don't even know why we hadn't made our way out into the street yet. I think maybe Pedro was in the bathroom. It doesn't matter. That extra minute or two made a big difference in what happened next.

The girl walked over to Booker and started to ask him when and where we were playing next, as though we were a real band. I still had a hard time pretending that I wasn't, you know, pretending. Booker did not have this issue. He immediately came up with a story, and, as a good friend would do, he introduced me to her and to the rest of her friends. Her friends were not at all interested in me. So I ended up looking around at the stage, the bar, and the rafters…and ultimately greeting Pedro a little too excitedly when he came back. Meanwhile, Booker and the girl were getting a little cozier with each sentence that passed. That's some pretty impressive velocity. Within a few minutes, they started to make out, or whatever it is called now. Her friends looked away.

I didn't really know what to do either, so I just stood there and talked to Pedro. His eyes were pretty lazy looking. I couldn't even tell if he was looking at me, but it didn't matter. He could hear me, so the talking did what it was supposed to do. You don't need eyes to talk. Most people know that. Except maybe people without eyes or ears. They probably don't know that.

"So what do you want to do now?" I asked.

"These chicks don't wanna hang out?" he asked me back, referring to the girl's friends.

"Ha. What do you think?"

I nodded in their direction, and they were on their phones, their faces pointed straight down.

"If they won't talk to each other, that means they probably don't want to talk to us either."

"Right."

"So what do you want to do then? Just let them go at it until they get tired of it?"

We looked at Booker and the girl, and they just kept making out. It was getting kind of weird. There weren't a lot of people left in the venue. I was pretty sure that a bouncer was going to come over and tell us to get the fuck out. And then the whole band thing would come up. And then it would get awkward.

"Dude," Pedro said loudly as he poked Booker in the ribs. "Take your girl and let's go outside before they kick us out."

"You read my mind," I said.

"Alright, alright," Booker mumbled.

We walked out past that support beam and to the street. It was chilly out – not crisp – and there were groups of kids smoking and leaning against walls and doing what people do after a concert. Booker's girl was off saying something to her friends, and he had an anxious stare beaming from his face. I knew what he was thinking. It was Puerto Vallarta all over again. He wasn't going to get any ass. It was just going to be another night where a group of girls ruin it.

But that didn't happen. Instead, the girl said goodbye to her friends and came back over to us. For the record, that never happens.

"So what's up?" she said, as she grabbed Booker's arm and pulled herself close to him.

"Fuck," he said.

We ended up heading out to some dive bar where they just sat and talked and made out while Pedro and I stood up and leaned against the bar, talking nonsense about who knows what. It didn't matter. I was sipping on some more rum, this time just on the rocks. Pedro had a beer. He was new. I didn't hold it against him.

Last call rolled around much quicker than we expected, and the inevitable moment of truth came. But it didn't matter. The girl was his. She wasn't planning on going back to wherever she should have been going back to. She was going back with him.

The unfortunate thing, of course, was that we didn't have a place to go back to. We just had the truck. And even if he was able to convince her to sleep in it, and even if she believed that for some reason none of our instruments and gear were in there even though we were supposed to be some legitimate band, there was still the matter of what do with the other two guys who were supposed to be sleeping in there as well.

But it turns out it wasn't a problem. Sort of.

I woke up the next morning the same way I had woken up the day before, lying down across the cab of the truck, my knees bent and propped against the steering wheel. I stretched my legs out as best as I could, and I felt some creaking in my joints. It can't be good to sleep with your knees bent two nights in a row. Then again, I do lots of things that can't be good for me. I looked outside and realized that we hadn't tucked the truck away into a discreet alley. It was just parked on the street. No one seemed to notice or care.

I stepped out of the cab and onto the pavement. I tried to remember what the hell had happened the night before. I got really curious. What happened to the girl? Was she back there? Where was Pedro? Did he leave us? Did we even have his phone number? Was he gone?

I walked around back and slowly slid the door open. Then I started to laugh. All three of them were in there, all passed out on top of the sleeping bags, all wearing way less clothing than I would have guessed they'd be wearing. Pedro looked like he was fully naked, but I couldn't really tell. There was a pillow blocking what would have given me a better view. Better, meaning clearer. Not necessarily *better* better. The girl was topless and with a pair of panties on, her clothes rolled up in a ball behind her head. Booker was in his boxers and socks, which seemed uncomfortable to me. I hate socks. And I hate sleeping in them even more.

I stood there for a while and just looked at all of them, careful to not draw too much attention in the street behind me. It was probably not okay for a group of naked people to be chilling out in the back of a stolen truck in the middle of a random block in downtown Boulder. I mean, maybe it was okay. I don't know. I didn't want to find out.

The girl had a decent rack. For a little while I was dumbstruck and just staring at her breasts while everybody continued to sleep. What the fuck had happened? I decided to wake Booker up and get some answers. I tapped him on the foot until his eyes started to flutter. He looked at me down by the door. He squinted and shifted around. Then he looked over to his right at the girl next to him. He let out a mixed moan of satisfaction and laughter.

"She totally did both of us," he whispered.

"At the same time?"

"Nah. Me first. Then Pedro."

"Are you kidding?"

"Nah, man," he smiled.

"What'd you do, just watch?"

He sat up a bit and inched toward the door.

"I just passed out after I was done."

"So what did Pedro do while you were fucking her? He watched you?"

"Oh, no. I didn't fuck her. She just went down on me."

"What about him?"

I nodded toward Pedro.

"I dunno. Probably the same thing. I'm sure I would've woken up if they were fucking."

"Yeah, I probably would have too."

I scratched my head and looked behind me to make sure that nobody was looking in at us. Or at them, really.

"So the two of you got blowjobs from this random girl in the back of the truck?"

"Heh," was all he said.

"This girl who is still passed out here, without her shirt on."

"Yeah. Yeah."

"The fucking truck, man."

"Almost," Pedro added.

Neither of us realized that he was awake. I think there was a chance that he didn't either, until he spoke.

"More like…the sucking truck."

"Nice."

Booker began to climb off of his sleeping bag and out to the street where I stood. He pulled his pants over to him and put them on, one leg at a time. Two at the same time would have been weird, like he was a girl. Pedro shuffled around, probably trying to find some pieces of clothing that he could put on. Eventually both of them came out and stood in the potentially crisp morning air, neither one wearing a shirt. The girl kept sleeping through it all, and I kept staring at her chest.

"What the hell are we going to do with her?" I asked.

"Maybe she can give you a blowjob too," Pedro suggested.

"Fuck, man. She was good?"

They both nodded.

"Damn."

"Maybe we can just leave her in the back and go get some breakfast?" Pedro asked.

"Yeah, I'm actually pretty hungry already."

Booker stretched his back and rubbed his stomach.

"What? We can't just leave her in the truck!"

"Why not?"

"Dude," I said with my eyes probably bugging out of my head. "This truck is *stolen*."

I whispered the word *stolen* in case anyone was listening, as though two shirtless guys in the street behind a partially opened truck with a nearly naked girl inside wasn't cause for enough concern.

"We can't leave her in it and just go out and eat somewhere."

"Well…"

"Well what?"

"Well…I'm not waking her up!" Booker snapped.

He ran away like he was a little kid. He hid somewhere around the front of the truck.

"Ah. Fuck," Pedro deadpanned.

He crawled back into the truck and started to shake the girl's foot. Booker didn't come back. He just stood on the other side of the entire thing, looking around in the street as though he didn't know us. Shirtless.

"Wake up, girl," Pedro crooned.

"You don't know her name, do you?"

"Heh," was all he said.

"Wake up, little girl," he sang to her.

I looked around behind me again.

"Maybe you shouldn't call her a little girl. In case someone hears you."

Pedro laughed. I looked up front and saw Booker smoking a cigarette. I don't know where he found it. He didn't normally smoke, and he definitely didn't have his own pack of butts.

"Hey!" Pedro yelled.

It was so loud that it echoed off of the metal walls and out the door. The girl moaned and started to move around. Her breasts jiggled a bit. She opened her eyes and caught a glimpse of Pedro. Then she mumbled something. It didn't sound positive, whatever it was.

"What time is it?" she asked.

Fair enough. You can't really tell in the back of a box truck.

"Time to get out of here."

She looked down at her bare chest and shook her head.

"Dammit."

"Yeah."

He moved away from her and toward the left wall of the truck, the driver's side, that is. He picked up what appeared to be his shirt. He pulled it over his head and then walked back to the door, ducked under it, and came back outside. In the bright sun I could see that it was actually Booker's shirt. No matter. As long as it wasn't the girl's shirt, it was probably alright.

"But really, what time is it?" she asked again.

"But really. It's time to go."

Ruthless. I looked around the side of the truck. Booker was sitting on the curb, his belly rolled up and hanging over his belt a little.

"You're an asshole," she said, as she began putting her clothes back on.

She pulled her shirt on first, as girls do. Then her pants. I've seen guys get dressed that way, and it always makes me confused. That's the girl way to get dressed.

Before her shirt went on, she had to find her bra. It was somewhat near where her feet were when she was sleeping. She was leaning forward on her hands and knees, reaching for it just a few feet away from where Pedro was standing. I was a little bit off to the side of the truck door, but I had a decent view of her breasts as they swung freely toward the ground, her back slightly dipping in a reverse arch. I started to think about if there was a chance that she would blow me too. Her breasts, hanging down, brushing against my legs and hips and maybe even my balls. Her hair covering her face but not getting in the way of her mouth. Her eyes closed. Or open. It actually doesn't matter. I wouldn't see them anyway. Her left hand stroking from the base of my dick and up to her mouth, her mouth bobbing up and down, her tongue doing whatever it does when a girl is doing that. I can't really tell, usually. All of this was running through my head. I started to get hard, just watching her there in front of us.

Then she put her bra back on, and I felt an unnecessary flicker of regret, as though there was anything that I could have done in that situation to stop her from getting dressed and putting her body back into hiding.

"You guys are both assholes," she said to both of us.

"Why? What did I do?" I asked.

"Whatever," she said.

She pulled her pants on, and somehow her shoes were on almost immediately after. It usually takes me about two minutes to get my shoes on. I am terribly slow in that department. She slid out of the truck, and with a tight grip on her purse – which also seemed to come out of nowhere – she walked past me and toward the sidewalk. Booker stood up as she walked his way. She waved her hand as though to say, *Don't bother*, and he sat down as though to say, *Okay, I won't*. She walked down the sidewalk, and all three of us watched her ass as she did. It was alright. The rack was definitely the selling point.

"Breakfast time?" Pedro asked.

"Heh," was all I said.

Fifteen

I've always had a thing for rum. One time, I had so much that I thought it sent me to the hospital. That's not to say that I can't remember if I went to the hospital or not. I definitely went. I just thought at the time that I had seriously damaged one of my organs by drinking too much. It turns out it was just my appendix, and it had nothing to do with rum or drinking. Thank God. Just an appendix. You don't even need that thing.

It was a Monday afternoon, and I had gone out hard the night before. I don't even think I was twenty-one yet, but that didn't really matter in my world. I still went out. Hard. I was sitting around my house the next day eating a salad, and my stomach started to hurt. I thought that maybe I had contracted some type of immediate food poisoning, or maybe my body was rejecting the fact that I was eating something healthy.

I lay down on the floor for a while, but it didn't get much better. I vowed to never eat a salad again. The pain kept lingering no matter what I did. It felt different than food poisoning. I started to doubt my body's ability to keep up with my life. Maybe I did just overdo it and I had some failing organ somewhere in there, half-full with rum and unable to function properly.

I used heating pads. I used pain killers. I was puking. I was shivering. It was pretty awful. I lasted through the night, and in the morning I went to the emergency room. It was at a University-run hospital, so they had all kinds of people helping and asking questions. The type of people that maybe otherwise wouldn't be there in a normal hospital. I am pretty sure I was asked how much I weighed at least seventeen times. There was very little coordination. It was concerning, but I didn't really care all that much since I figured they still had to take care of me one way or another.

They ran me through a series of tests and MRIs and all kinds of things. I had to drink some chemicals that made my insides glow so that they could figure out what was going on in there. That was a trip. It tasted pretty chalky going down. They told me that I might feel some warmth inside when they put me under the MRI machine or whatever it's called. I sure as hell did. It felt like someone poured an unstoppable stream of hot tea down my throat. And it didn't stop at my stomach. It kept going. I felt it in my intestines and eventually down to the very end of my asshole. It felt like I was going to just let it all out on that bed. It was really weird. My mouth tasted like I was sucking on a pile of metal.

I sat around in my little ER room for a long time. I don't think I was admitted into surgery until about seven o'clock that night, but I had gotten there sometime around nine in the morning. That's a long time to wait in an ER. There must have been a better place for me. My situation wasn't that much of an emergency if I was able to sit there for ten hours. I bet someone died in the hallway while I just hung out and waited. Stupid hospital. Then again, I'd have been pretty pissed if they kicked me out for someone else with something more serious. I believe in the "first come, first served" rule when it comes to anything where I was there first.

At some point in the afternoon, a homeless guy came in to the ER after getting in a fight. I was in Santa Monica, so I guessed that he was probably down by the beach when it happened. I never got to see him the whole time I was there, but I overheard about ninety-percent of what he was talking about. It was pretty entertaining. I actually took notes so that I'd remember what he said. I thought it was *that* interesting. I thought maybe I could use them in a story when I got out. I never did though.

Meanwhile, in Colorado, there weren't that many homeless people. Not nearly as many as there were in Los Angeles. My guess was that in the winter, most of them died. It's probably a lot like trying to keep a citrus tree in a place where it always frosts. It's not going to make it one of those years. The conditions are just too harsh. You may as well move it somewhere warmer where it belongs. Like Los Angeles.

We left Boulder later than morning after getting that breakfast the guys kept asking about. In the end, it was nothing special. It never is. Breakfast is a means to an end. Any place where they make a big deal about breakfast is not the kind of place for me. I eat in the morning for one of two reasons: I need to sober up, or other people are doing it and I don't want to just sit there and watch them eat. Otherwise, I'm fine to wait until it's sandwich or salad time.

We drove back to Denver with Pedro riding bitch and Booker hugging his body against the wall. His head was leaning out of the window like it had been for so many other times up until that point. Not even that rogue bug that flew into his mouth could have stopped him. He was like a dog. And Pedro was like a dog. In some ways, I was like a dog too. On a mission to drive this thing somewhere. I don't know how that makes me like a dog, really, but I don't want to be the odd man out in this story.

"So, Pedro," I started, right around the time that we could see the skyline, which is pretty much as soon as you get on the freeway on your way out of Boulder. "You wanna hear a riddle?"

"Ah, fuck!" Booker yelled. "No. No, you do not."

"Hey man, let him answer for himself."

"What kind of riddle?" Pedro asked.

"Who cares. It's not a good one. It's a fucking trick."

"Dude. It's a riddle. It's supposed to be a trick. That's what a riddle is."

"Fuck your riddles, man."

Booker pushed his head fully out of the window, using the wind to block out the sound of my voice.

"What's that about?" Pedro asked.

"He's just a dumbass and can't stand it when he doesn't understand something...which is *all of the time.*"

Booker leaned his head back inside long enough to reply.

"Fuck you and fuck your riddles."

Back out his head went.

"I think I'm gonna pass. This time, at least," Pedro said.

I shrugged.

"Your loss."

A few minutes passed, and nobody had said a word.

"Is this part of the riddle?" Pedro asked.

"What?"

"This whole...act. Is this a part of it?"

"No," I laughed. "Don't you know what a riddle is?"

"I don't know if I want to know, man."

"You don't," Booker offered, raising his eyebrows as a convertible passed in front of us.

The car's top was down, and there were a couple of girls inside. It didn't feel warm enough to be driving around with the top down, at least not by California standards.

"You should follow them," Pedro advised.

"Good idea."

I kept my arms perfectly still on the wheel as the car switched lanes ahead of us and sped off down the road. I lifted my foot slightly off of the accelerator. Pedro shook his head.

"They're getting away."

"What are they, bad guys? What do you mean, *getting away*?"

"They're getting away," he muttered. He looked over to Booker.

Booker continued to stare out the window.

"That's too bad," I said.

We exited the freeway and headed toward downtown Denver again. There was no good reason behind that decision. I assumed that if we skipped by the city, it would have to mean that we had a destination further east to visit. Which would have been a bad idea. What's east of Denver before you get to the ocean? A bunch of fields, and then what? Chicago? That seemed a little too far.

I parked the truck in a regular metered parking spot, though it hung over both sides by at least a foot. We found a bar that was open and serving beer at happy hour prices even though it was a little earlier than happy hour proper. I ordered two beers for the guys and a rum on the rocks for myself. The bartender questioned my order.

"Are you for real?"

"Yes. I am for real."

"Really?"

"Yeah, what?"

"Never heard anyone get rum on the rocks before."

"Well, congratulations. You just met me. I like rum."

"Guess so," he said.

"I've always had a thing for rum," I said.

"Guess so," he said again.

I shook my head and looked away. The table we had chosen looked like a little island in a sea of empty tables. There was a guy by himself at a table alongside the wall. There was us. And that's it. Bars in Denver always seemed to be empty during the day. That's probably a good thing.

"Tell him how we got the truck across the border," Booker said, nudging my shoulder as I sat down.

"Ha," I said, thinking back on it.

"It's legitimately stolen, right?" Pedro asked, implying that there was another way to steal something.

"Yeah, it's stolen," I said, nodding.

I took a sip of my rum. It was pretty bad.

"So how did you get through the Border Patrol?"

"Oh, we drove it," I said.

"Right. But you aren't its owner. Do you have the registration?"

"Yeah, actually. It was in the glove box. Apparently that's not just an American thing. Mexicans keep their documents in their glove box too."

"It's too warm down there for gloves," Booker reminded me.

"So you drove up to the border. They ask for your registration. And you give it to them."

"Yeah, pretty much."

"Wasn't it in Spanish?"

"Yeah. Oh yeah, definitely. It's a Mexican registration. It's out in the truck now if you want to see it."

"No, I believe that part. I just…I don't get it. Didn't they realize that you aren't whoever it says the vehicle belongs to?"

"I don't think they thought about it. They were more concerned that we were driving a box truck across the border and that we were white. They thought we were coyotes or something."

"Coyotes?"

"You ever watch *The Shield*?" Booker asked.

"Nah."

"Booker learned the term *coyote* from *The Shield*," I explained. "It's a guy who transfers illegals across the border and back."

"Awesome fucking show," Booker added.

"Yeah, it is," I agreed. "Anyway, they thought we were driving this truck with people in it, or something, so they made us open up the back. They had an officer get in, walk around, tap on walls, all that shit. They were assuming we had people stashed away somewhere in there. Like we had hidden them under the metal floor or in the walls. Like they were drugs and we melted them down to fit into a vehicle."

"But all we had was an empty box truck that used to be full of rum," Booker said with a smile.

"That's it?" Pedro asked.

"Yeah, man. They didn't even really look at the registration or the license plate or any of that. I don't think they even asked for my I.D."

"Yeah. They didn't," Booker confirmed.

"So you just drove up, let them poke around the back of the empty truck, and then they let you in the country?"

"To protect and serve. And not think or question. It was ridiculous. We were shitting ourselves on the way there. We figured we were going to get hassled and arrested and raped and thrown in prison and then raped some more...and it turned out to be the biggest anticlimax I think I've ever experienced."

Pedro was smiling, but he looked concerned.

"What were you going to say if they did ask you whose truck it was?"

"I came up with a plan," Booker blurted out, clearly eager to be the one to tell the story. "If they started to give us a hard time, we were going to start looking really panicked and tell them that we got robbed and taken hostage while on spring break, and these Mexicans drove us around for a while, tied up in the back of the truck. And then when we got near the border, they told us that if we didn't drive the truck over the border, they'd kill us, but that they didn't tell us why or what we were supposed to do after we got over the border, other than to park the truck somewhere. And if we ever wanted to live, to never tell anyone about it."

"We even went so far as to get some cheap rope and rub it across our wrists and arms to make it seem like we were really tied up."

"Shut up!" Pedro exclaimed.

"Yeah. That shit hurt too. Remember that?"

"Yeah. It's hard to give yourself a rope burn when you don't want one. Not that anyone ever wants one, I guess."

"Anyway, the way we figured, we had no clothes, no suitcases, no nothing. All of our stuff was presumably still at the resort that we had never checked out of. The details of our story would have added up. They could have called the hotel, and they would have confirmed that we disappeared when we said we disappeared."

"We were also pretty drunk when we made the whole story up. But it seemed good enough to stick with it. And we didn't really have another choice anyway. We couldn't just walk across the border."

"Why not? You can do that still, can't you?"

"Not without a passport, you can't. We had left them with our bags and all of our stuff in our room back in Puerto Vallarta. You can't just *walk* into the U.S. without a passport."

"But," Pedro smirked, "you can just drive a *stolen truck* without a passport right on in."

"Apparently?" I asked aloud, and Booker nodded.

"Crazy, huh?"

We all took a drink.

"Yeah," Pedro said. "That is about as crazy as it gets, I think."

"But it worked. Looking back on it, I mean, it wasn't that bad of a plan, considering the situation we had gotten into. We were hundreds of miles away from the only identification that could let us back in the country.

We were driving a truck we had stolen. We were carrying cash from a party we had thrown where we essentially sold all of the stolen rum."

"And we stole that cash too," Booker added.

"Yeah," I laughed. "So we're like three-time felons in another country, with no proof of citizenship, hanging around a border town with a freshly painted, stolen truck and a wad of money. So why not just drive that thing straight toward a row of armed police officers and let them interrogate us?"

"Turns out, they were just confirming we didn't have any people stowed away. They didn't even ask us what we were doing with an empty truck in the first place."

"Unreal."

"Yep."

"And now you're in Denver."

"Yep."

"In a band," Pedro reminded us.

"In Tuba City," I said, proudly.

I took a sip of my rum, and it tasted better. The ice was melting a bit, weakening that initial kick.

"Speaking of…what venue are we performing at tonight?" Booker asked.

I raised my eyebrows.

"You really want to push this thing as far as it can go, don't you?"

"I do," he admitted. "I think we're just seeing the beginning of where this can go."

"And where's that?"

"Fuck if I know, man. I'm just saying, we're seeing the very beginning of it right now."

"Or maybe we just saw the end of it."

"Don't be such a downer. Look at what good things we've seen so far. Two nights of free drinking. Two different cities. Two blowjobs."

"One girl," Pedro added.

"Hey, if we can make tonight a third night of free drinking, I'll be more than happy with that."

It was true. I thought that the free drinks part was actually somewhat realistic. The girl thing seemed like a fluke to me.

"Because you don't want a blowjob," Booker declared.

"No, because I don't think that's going to happen. I don't even know how whatever happened last night happened. That girl must have been out of her mind to get in the back of a truck with two guys who said they were in a band. She may as well have been wearing a shirt that said *You Can't Rape The Willing*."

Pedro snorted and almost spit out a mouthful of beer onto the table in front of us. He coughed out a half of a sentence.

"Our first band shirt!" he said in a high, strained voice.

"Anyway, I don't know any other venues around here. I guess we can try to find another one and see how it goes."

I remember saying this thinking that it would be enough to get the conversation to move on to something else. My hope was that they'd get too drunk and forget all about it later on.

"Or we could try the Marquis again," Booker continued.

"Yeah...or we could do that. That seems like a terrible idea though. They already know we're not in a band."

Again, me trying to get out of the conversation.

"As terrible of an idea as driving through the border without a passport in a stolen truck?" Pedro asked.

"Not that terrible, man."

I paused for a moment and thought about it.

"I guess you're right. It really isn't that bad of a plan, if you think about it."

Booker had been staring down into the bottom of his glass, but that line caused him to look up.

"Are you serious? I was just joking."

It may as well have been me asking myself that. I had no idea why I was going along with this conversation, let alone actually entertaining the idea of doing it.

"Yeah. I mean, we told them we were in a band. We told them we were being promoted by a guy named Bob. They seemed to buy the whole story. Who's to say that they won't buy it again?"

"How do we explain our mysterious disappearance the other night then? And why the promoter they work with – who I am guessing they've since talked to – has no idea who we are?"

"I dunno, man," I said. "How were we going to explain ourselves when we crossed the border? We had a story ready, but we didn't even need to use it."

Booker looked at me skeptically, even though this was originally his idea in the first place.

"So you're saying that we should just go back to the Marquis and tell them the same story and expect to get free drinks and blowjobs out of it?"

"God, man. With the blowjobs. I am not suggesting we are going to get blowjobs tonight. Get over it."

"Hey," Pedro chimed in. "Leave me out of your negativity. I am going to remain optimistic that I will maybe get a blowjob tonight."

"Whatever. That's fine."

"Every night is an opportunity," he said.

"Okay. Who cares? That's not my point."

"What is your point then?" Booker asked.

"Look, goddammit! It was your stupid idea to go back to the Marquis! I don't think it's a good idea, but I also don't really give a shit what happens if we do go back. What are they going to do? Kick us out?"

"Yeah."

"Who fucking cares? So what? So we go to another bar. Big fucking deal."

"Calm down, dude."

"I'm just saying, it worked once. They were fucking idiots. So maybe, who knows? Maybe it'll work again."

"That's it?"

"Yeah. That's it. That's my plan. I don't think we need a Swiss fucking watch, Walter."

"Nice," Pedro nodded. "I love that movie."

"Me too. So let's do that. Okay?"

Booker was staring at me and nodding, almost creepily.

"Alright, man. I think that's a good idea."

"Why are you staring at me like that?" I asked.

"Stuck in a daze right now," he said, his voice trailing off.

I smacked him on the arm. He didn't snap out of it, so I ignored him.

"Look," I said, turning to Pedro. "I don't know how this is going to go, but I think you have a good point. We had no idea how our border crossing was going to go, and it turned out just fine. We prepared for the worst – we even gave ourselves rope burn for no reason – and we didn't need to do anything. We could have just driven up there and winged it."

"Well," Pedro reversed course a bit. "Not exactly."

"What do you mean?"

"Maybe you guys needed to take the time to get the rope, to rub it on your arms and your wrists and whatever. Maybe you had to do that to delay your arrival to the border, so you would get the perfect set of circumstances that would allow you to cross through without a problem. Maybe if you hadn't done that, you would have been stopped by a different officer, and he would have asked for your passport, and you would have had to come up with a story, and shit…we wouldn't even be sitting here right now, you know?"

"A butterfly effect," Booker whispered, still staring at me like a complete freak.

I shook his shoulders until he finally snapped out of it.

"Jesus, man. I hate it when you do that."

"Yeah, me too," he said.

His eyes focused again. Even though he was still looking at me, it was different now. He was present.

"So we're just going back to the Marquis to try this all again?" he asked.

I turned away from him and looked over at the bartender. He was wiping down the counter even though he hadn't poured a drink since he gave me ours, twenty minutes earlier.

"Guess so," I said.

Sixteen

I've always had a thing for rum. Even before I knew what good rum was, even before I had any sense or taste at all, I still gravitated toward it. The first time I got sick from drinking too much was from rum. Well, sort of. It was from Captain Morgan Parrot Bay. That's an embarrassment to the world of rum. A travesty to the word itself. Even parrots are offended that they're associated with that shit. Something that smells like sunblock and tastes four times worse should never be sold as a consumable beverage.

Nevertheless, I didn't know this when I was younger. I went to a party when I was a freshman in high school. I don't even know how I got invited, now that I think of it. Everyone else there was a senior or in college. And I was this fourteen-year-old kid. I had just turned fourteen about a month earlier. And I was trying to be Johnny Coolballs or whoever I thought I was at the time.

Someone asked me if I wanted a drink, and I was like *yeah, yeah, of course,* like I knew any better. Parrot Bay and warm diet coke. How about that? *Yeah, yeah, of course*. How about a few of those? *Yeah, yeah, of course*. How about having to lie down at around midnight in some random guy's house so you could make the room stop spinning, except it'll just make it worse? Yeah. Yeah. Of course.

I woke up at around 5:30 the next morning and realized that I had a soccer game I had to get ready for. I didn't play for my school's team. I don't know if I was good enough – I probably wasn't – but I had never tried out. I just played for a local in-town league, as they called it. Not sure why they called it that. It wasn't like it was in any particular town or not in any other town. But whatever. That's what it was called. My game was at seven o'clock. I was hungover and exhausted. I somehow got home in time to shower, get dressed, and make it there on time. I played miserably. We lost 1-0. It was our only loss of the season, as it turned out.

I blame the Parrot Bay. That shit should have never been concocted. Captain Morgan would be ashamed that his terrible product cost my team that game. I didn't hold it against rum though, as I knew from my younger days and from my dad that rum was not the enemy. Coconut was the enemy. Fucking Parrot Bay.

When we got to the Marquis later that night, we walked in and headed straight toward the bar like the unsurprising booze fiends that we are. I saw a bottle of Parrot Bay up on the shelf. I wanted to reach behind the bar and just slide it off of the shelf and onto the ground. What the fuck was it doing there? It was making me mad. I looked away and noticed that Booker was looking pretty nervous.

"Chill out," I said, channeling my inner Johnny Coolballs again.

"We're gonna get kicked out, man. They're gonna hand us the bill and kick us the eff out of here."

"So?"

"Yeah, so?" Pedro repeated.

"I don't want to pay the bill for the other night of drinking before we even start our tonight of drinking."

"If they hand us a bill *and* kick us out, we're not paying the damned bill. And if they hand us a bill and they *don't* kick us out, we can kick ourselves out. It's that simple."

"I guess so. It just doesn't seem like a good idea to be here."

Booker looked around as though some guy was going to come up and grab him by the collar and stick his foot up his ass.

"Whatever."

I didn't want to deal with this. Normally he's about as laid back as a person can get. Near horizontal. But every now and then he gets swept up by some kind of anxiety or fear or concern or something, and it damned near paralyzes him. I never really understood it, but I can tell when it is happening. And like the good person I am, it just pisses me off. I never feel sympathetic or consoling. I just get annoyed and usually tell him to *shut up* or to *man up* or some other verb combined with ascension.

I walked up closer to the bar and realized that there was no music playing, just like the first time we showed up. There were more people there than the first time, but still not enough for us to blend in. I was wearing the exact same clothes as I wore the last time, which didn't help. The same bartender who was there the last time was there again too. Shit.

That was actually my hope, that it was just going to be some other girl or guy back there and the whole problem would just evaporate. No such luck. She looked up from whatever she was doing behind the bar, which was probably just wasting time by unnecessarily rearranging bottles, and she looked right at me. Then she smiled.

"Hey, rock star," she said.

I overheard Booker let out an audible gasp, but I didn't turn around to look at him.

"Hey yourself. What's up?"

Johnny Coolballs, back on the scene.

"Sorry I didn't get to see you guys perform the other night."

She smiled again. I figured she was being sarcastic, so I just went along with it. I didn't know what else to do.

"Yeah. You missed out. Can I get a rum and coke?"

Why not, I thought.

"How about for the other guys?" she asked, nodding to Pedro and Booker, both of whom were standing at least a few feet behind me when I turned around to look at them.

"Couple of beers," I said, as though you don't normally say what kind of beer you want when you ask for one at a bar.

It was like I was saying, *Who gives a shit what they want, I want a rum and coke, woman.* Booker and Pedro came up alongside me like two scared, little puppies. Because they were dogs earlier, if you recall. Now they were puppies. Baby dogs. The bartender came back with my drink, and then she sloshed two beers on the counter. I pulled out my wallet and started to thumb through my very obvious lack of bills. It was going to be a credit card kind of night.

Or at least that's what I thought. She waved it off.

"On the house, boys."

I nodded, JCB style. I had no idea what was going on at the moment, but I was acting like it all made a lot of sense to me. Booker was looking bewildered as he grabbed his beer. I almost wanted to slap him in the balls to get him to snap out of it.

"So what happened the other night?" I asked.

"Are you serious?" she asked me back.

I don't know what I was thinking, and I immediately regretted opening my mouth. I had taken it too far. I was already wanting to retreat back out the door and run away down the street, leaving any trace of JCB behind. My confidence wore off very quickly. She started shaking her head and smiling.

"You know that girl that was sitting here talking to you guys at the beginning of the night? Maria?"

I nodded.

"She had a seizure or something like that. I've seen it happen before. Maybe it's not a seizure, but it's some kind of spasm-type thing. You guys didn't see the ambulance lights out front?"

We all looked over to the right at the thick, black wall. There were no windows. She was a bartender, not an architect.

"Nah, we must have missed that. Damn. A seizure?"

"Yeah, something like that. She's alright. She's always alright after they happen, but I always freak out when it's happening anyway."

"You're saying *always* like it happens a lot."

"I've seen at least three."

"Jesus," Booker whispered.

"So anyway, I was out front with her while they were loading her in the ambulance. Must have taken longer than I thought. I came back in, and you guys were already off the stage and that Green Pasture bullshit was on. So I didn't get to hear you play."

She smiled a genuine, sweet smile. I smiled back. Unbelievable.

"Well, it's your lucky day," Pedro announced.

I cringed. I had a terrible feeling that I knew what he was about to say.

"We're playing again tonight!"

I looked over at him with my best mad dog stare that I could make. Because I was a dog too. And he was a baby dog. I couldn't fucking believe him.

"Really? How'd you pull that off?" she asked.

"Yeah, how *did* we pull that off?" I repeated while still staring at him.

I looked back at her and then back at him again.

"Easy," he said as he took a sip of his generic beer whose name was never disclosed. "Bob hooked us up."

"Bob," I said. I turned back to the bartender and managed a weak smile. "Good old Bob."

"Well, I hate to jinx it, guys…but I think that Maria might be coming back in tonight," she said.

"Who's Maria?" Booker asked.

I rolled my eyes.

"The girl you guys were talking to the other night."

She was way more patient than I would have been. Or than I was.

"So she just goes out a couple of days after having a seizure? Isn't that a bad idea?"

"I dunno," the bartender replied. "Life goes on, right?"

"Hell yeah, it does!" Pedro blurted out.

He was already most of the way through his beer. I could tell by the way he moved his wrist that he was debating whether or not he should just chug the rest with his next sip. He tipped his head back, and I looked away. We had only known each other for about forty-eight hours, but I already knew with certainty that he was going to be getting shitfaced again.

"She's gonna be pretty excited that you guys are here again. She kept saying how big of a fan she was of your band!"

"Yeah. We love it when we get to meet real fans like that."

"Totally makes our day," Booker added.

I looked at Pedro, and his eyes were already starting to get lazy. The left one was drifting. He tapped his glass on the bar.

"Can we get another round?"

The bartender nodded and pulled out some new glasses. Booker hadn't really made much progress on his beer, probably because he was just barely getting over his brief stint as a nervous, little pansy. He started to sip faster to try to catch up to us.

"How often do you see Bob?" I asked, trying to get a better idea of how big of a pile of shit we might be stepping into.

"Barely ever anymore. He hardly comes in. Why? He around?"

"Oh, no. I mean, I don't know. I was just wondering if we'd see him."

She pushed my drink over to me.

"It's been a while, that's all."

"I could ask Marty to give him a call if you want?"

"No, no. No, that's alright. Marty. Yeah, don't worry about it. I was just wondering if you saw him much."

"Nah, not really," she said. "Hey, look. I gotta go, you know, do my job over there."

She motioned toward the other side of the bar where some meathead looking guys were moping around empty-handed.

"No problem."

"I'll be back in a bit. Don't pay for any drinks," she added as she walked away. "If anyone else comes by and tries to serve you, just tell them you're already being helped. Okay?"

"Yup. Okay."

I couldn't tell if she was in on our scam or not. Did she know that we weren't an actual band or was she just doing what she thought was her job? On one hand, maybe she knew but just didn't give a shit. She'd keep serving us drinks anyway, because it wasn't her bar, and she had a perfectly good excuse if it ever blew back her way. Maybe she liked that we were pulling a hoax and she was there to help us out. On the other hand, she might have actually believed us.

I never found out the truth. It didn't matter anyway. Free drinks are free drinks. However they come your way, you take them. That's about all you really need to know in this type of situation.

We kept pounding them back until the first band started to load on stage. It was about that time on the first night that we decided to cut out and avoid getting caught. By that point, I think Booker and Pedro had split at least a dozen beers, and I was probably on my fourth or fifth rum and coke. It wasn't exactly blackout territory, but we had been drinking before we got there, so the effects were piling up. Pedro looked like he could either pass out in the middle of the floor or ride a dirt bike in circles along the walls. He was simultaneously lethargic and energized. His eyes were beaming in two different directions, and neither one knew that the other wasn't following along. He looked pretty bad. Booker looked how Booker usually looks.

Then Maria walked in the door. None of us noticed at first. We were watching the band set up and run through their meager, little sound check routine. She came up to me and grabbed my arm.

"What the fuck are you doing here?" she asked.

I turned and looked at her. When I saw her face, I had to smile.

"As I live and breathe," I said.

"What?"

She looked more focused than the first time we saw her. Or maybe I was more drunk than I was then.

"Nothing," I replied.

"Doing nothing? Aren't you guys playing somewhere tonight? I think I saw it on the Internet."

"On the Internet?"

"Yeah."

"We don't have a webpage."

"Then it was on Facebook."

"We don't use Facebook."

"Twitter."

"Nope. What's that?"

"It's a new thing. You'll see. MySpace."

"I heard that's going to die soon."

"I saw it somewhere."

"No, you didn't," I said.

"Yes, I did. Are you playing here? Is that why you're here?"

"No. We came here to try to find some creamed corn. But they didn't have any. And then we got stuck getting drunk at the bar instead."

That was me trying to be charming, but I was too drunk and I didn't think about the fact that my little tidbit of a memory from that night wouldn't mean much to a girl who left in an ambulance.

"You're playing here," she yelled. "I knew it! I knew it!"

"Hey, keep it down," I whisper-talked.

It was too loud with the sound check and the conversations around us to whisper-whisper, and yelling back would defeat the purpose of what I was saying. Whisper-talking was my best option.

"Jackie!" she yelled toward the bar, teaching me the bartender's name in the process. "They're playing again tonight?!"

Jackie nodded. Then Jackie smiled.

"You fuckers," she said and punched me on the arm.

"Us fuckers," I said.

"Well, lookee who we have here," Booker said as he strutted over to us.

"Biff Tannen," I said. "As I live and breathe."

"What?"

"Nothing."

"How's it going, Maria?"

Thankfully, he remembered her name this time. Though it wouldn't have really mattered if he didn't, I'm guessing.

"Much better today. You guys going up next?"

"Yep," he confirmed. "Right after these guys."

"Hell yeah!" Pedro yelled from about ten feet away.

He wasn't talking to anyone else, and he wasn't glued to the floor, but for some reason he didn't come any closer. He was a weird dude.

"Can't wait to see you up on stage," Maria exclaimed as she lit up a big, wide smile.

"Oh yeah," Booker replied. "Me too."

The opening band started to play, and I felt like shitting my pants right where I stood. Even though logically, I could have remembered that I had no reason to ever come back to this venue or this part of Denver or even the state of Colorado again in my life, I was drunk. Logic was evasive. I was worried about how the hell we were going to get out there without getting our asses handed to us by security. I wasn't in the mood to get beat up. And then try to drive away drunk in our stolen truck. The situation had about eighteen bad angles, and they were all pointed right at my face. The guys didn't seem to be fazed.

When Maria went to the bathroom, Booker leaned over and detailed what he was thinking.

"Let's do it," he said.

This did not instill in me the kind of confidence that I was hoping for.

"Do what?"

"Let's go on stage and perform as Tuba City."

I frowned.

In less than an hour, I had gone from Johnny Coolballs to Johnny Scaredy-Cat. Meanwhile, Booker, a few beers deeper, went from oh-shit-we-are-going-to-get-asked-to-leave to the embodiment of the Nike swoosh, more or less.

"How are we going to do that?"

"I dunno," he said.

"Great."

"How about we start loading some gear onto the stage when this band is done?"

"What gear?"

"Let's go take a look," Pedro suggested.

"Take a look where?" I asked.

I was getting annoyed, and their suggestions were not making me feel any better.

"Back stage. In the alley. Who knows? Let's go look."

"Jesus fucking," I said.

I didn't bother to finish the sentence. Booker walked away and went toward the bar. He started to talk to Jackie. She was nodding. Then she yelled out a name, and a security guard came out of nowhere. *Shit.*

But it was alright. He led us over to a door along the wall that he opened without using any keys. In other words, we didn't really need him for anything. It was the same door that we went through the other night. It led to the alley. When we got partway down the hallway, the cool air hit my face. I relaxed a little.

"Can we just leave?" I asked Booker.

He shook his head.

There were random people milling around out back. One of them could have been Bob, for all we knew, since all we knew was nothing. We walked all the way back where Booker peeked out the door.

"There's a van right there with the door slightly open."

"Thanks, scout. Good work. So what?"

"Let's use their gear."

"Fuck you," I said.

"Fuck you!" Pedro bellowed.

His voice echoed in the alley outside.

"Goddammit, Pedro. Keep it down."

"Keep it down!" he yelled.

I sighed as loud as a stage actor would sigh. It was too loud for normal life, but I was trying to prove a point. It didn't work.

"Don't be a pussy, Blake," Booker demanded.

I remember it clearly. I remember how he looked at me when he said it. He almost stared right through me, like I was getting in the way of him and his childhood dream. It was more intense than I had ever seen Booker look before. I was probably just hammered, but it resonated with me.

"Alright," I said. "But whose van is it?"

"Beats me."

He leaned out the door and shouted out loud to the empty alley.

"Hey, whose van is this?"

The alley didn't respond, because it was made of brick and pavement, not vocal chords and brains.

"Looks like it's ours," he said.

Pedro took the initiative by stepping out into the alley and walking toward the van. He swung the door open. I half-expected there to be people sitting inside of it, giving him dirty looks. Maybe one them would come out and take a swing at him. Instead, there was no movement, no sound.

"Anyone in there?" I asked.

"Nope," Pedro replied, his head already well inside the van. "Just our instruments!"

Booker stepped out, and I did too. The cold night air slammed into me with a velocity that I didn't quite expect. I got a little bit dizzy. I continued walking toward the van anyway. Pedro was all the way in, near the back, wiggling around a case that was blocking what looked like a drum set.

"Dude, the drums are staying on stage. We don't need to bring that out there," Booker wisely advised.

I don't know how he thought of that right then. I have to give him credit there. I would have unloaded whatever instrument I thought I could play. I would have rolled out a baby grand piano if that was my thing. I'm not great in impromptu situations. Pedro readjusted himself and grabbed a guitar. Booker had a bass in his hands. I had nothing. I was still standing near the door.

"Hey, pussy," Booker snarled at me. "Your microphone is already on stage, but I think you ought to walk in with this as well!"

He tossed something at me, and I instinctively moved out of the way. It clanged against the pavement and rolled around a bit before I could tell what it was. It was a tambourine.

"Thanks, man," I laughed. "This is exactly my speed right now."

"I can tell."

Pedro and Booker emerged with their guitars gripped in their hands, the straps hanging down and flapping against their bodies as they walked back inside. I followed behind them, my tinny tambourine making slight chink-chink noises with each step that I took. When we got inside, the house music was on, and a few of the guys from the first band were filing back down the hallway. Booker nodded at each of them as they passed by. They nodded back. Camaraderie.

Booker got to the door and paused to look back at me as I walked closer. He smiled.

"Let's do it," he said, almost maniacally.

"Fuck," I muttered.

Booker walked out into the venue like it was the living room at his parent's place. Like he didn't give a shit at all. Pedro and I followed behind him. I don't think I had that same aura. We walked up on stage and started to get into position, like this was a tryout or an audition or something where you didn't tune your instruments at all before you started to play. The other band had just cleared the stage. Usually there was at least a ten or fifteen minute break between acts. Everybody gets a chance to go to the bathroom, get another drink, have a cigarette, whatever. Yet there we were. Almost ready to go. But to go and do what? I didn't have a clue.

I had always had problems being in front of a bunch of people, but a funny thing happened as I got up there. My fear just kind of melted away. I felt numb, but in a good way.

I know that people sometimes say that in moments of extreme pressure, their true instincts come out. Like the mother who lifts a burning car off of her baby, or whatever that bullshit story is. I'm sure that has never happened, by the way, but for some reason people love to talk that one up. Did that ever actually happen? I doubt it. I guess it doesn't matter. The symbolism is what's important.

Heroics can come out when all of your options are exhausted. You can do the things that you always wondered if you'd be able to do if you had to do them. That's why people care. That's why they let you talk about some unbelievable thing that no woman or man could ever do. That car is a symbol. A symbol of an obstacle. An obstacle that can be overcome.

This moment was my burning car. This tambourine, as gay as it was, this was my superhuman strength. Or my adrenaline. Or whatever supposedly gave that woman the ability to free that baby from that car. My tambourine freed me from my fear.

That, or the rum.

"Check, check," I said loudly into the microphone. "Chickity check yourself before you wreck yourself," I added.

A slight murmur of laughter hummed across the crowd. I looked back at Booker who was trying to figure out how to plug his guitar into the amp. Pedro had somehow already plugged his in. He started to strum it but without a pick, since we hadn't thought to grab those from the van. The guitar shrieked and thundered without any discernible rhythm. I looked out in the crowd and spotted Maria, staring up at us while almost everyone else wasn't paying a damned bit of attention.

"Check, check," I said again. "I ain't paying that check."

I extended my left arm out toward the bar and pointed at Jackie. She pointed back. The crowd hummed a little louder. It felt pretty good. Booker finally plugged the bass in. I knew this because I heard the feedback as he got the plug halfway in. It was unmistakable. He pushed it in all the way, and the feedback stopped. He slung the guitar over his shoulder and fiddled with the strings a bit. It sounded much better than Pedro's attempt.

"Check, one. Check, one. Check, one."

I was just saying whatever I had heard people say at all of the other shows I had been to. I didn't even know where the sound guy was or how that whole arrangement worked. We were probably supposed to be communicating with him in some way. Instead I was just saying things in the mic, and it wasn't getting any louder or quieter. He was probably wondering what the fuck I was doing.

Pedro started to slam away at the drums. It didn't sound any better than his attempt on the guitar. It might have even been a little worse.

"Check, check, Czech Republic!" I belted out. "Check, check, checker game," I said more quietly.

I was trying to simulate the sound check guy changing my audio levels. Booker started to thump away on the bass. I looked back at him with the mic gripped tightly in my left hand. The tambourine was in my right.

"Hold up, brother," I shouted.

Booker let up for a bit. I looked back at Pedro seated at the drums, and he gave me a thumbs up. The guitar he had brought out was lying on the floor, still plugged in. I walked over, picked it up, and slung it over my shoulder. It felt good.

"Check, check, checker cab!" I shouted. "Are you guys ready?!"

The crowd had started to pay attention to our fake sound check, and I actually got a decent response back. I looked back at Booker and Pedro. They both looked about as ready as I could have expected them to look in that situation.

"Alright then. Maria, are you ready?"

I looked straight at her, and she lit up.

"Hell fucking yeah I am!"

Everyone around her turned and looked at her. Then they turned back to look at me. I dropped the tambourine on the floor. It went chink-chink-chhh.

"Tell them who we are, Maria!"

I had a moment of doubt. I had almost forgotten our damned name. And now I was banking on her not forgetting it too. We were her favorite band though. Her favorite made-up band.

"Tuba City!" she shouted.

Thank God.

"That's fucking right!" I spit into the microphone. "We're Tuba City! We're from Los Angeles!"

That line got a few cheers, but I barely noticed, as I was getting wrapped up in the moment.

"We were just out in Boulder yesterday for a show at the Fox. And now we're here. And we're so happy to be here! Right?"

I turned around to the guys.

"Yeah!" they both yelled, as though there was anything else that they could say at that point.

"So Denver," I yelled, doing my best lead-singer-of-a-band impression that I could possibly do. "Are you ready to rock your fucking faces off?!"

The crowd yelled back a loud jumble of noise that sounded mostly positive, so I kept going.

"Alright! Enough of that self-promotion bullshit. This song is called…Yeah!"

Pedro, that drunken genius, led off with four claps of the drum sticks, just like a real band would. It felt like for a second, for just a tiny split second, that everyone in that crowd was leaning slightly forward and on their toes, excited and ready to hear us play. On the fourth clap of the drum sticks, Booker started in on bass, plucking and pulling with a snapping force. And then I began to violently grab strings on my guitar as fast as I could. And then Pedro began slamming the drums like they had bullied him in elementary school. We were vicious to those instruments.

And it sounded like a homeless guy fell down a flight of stairs with a shopping cart full of cans, bottles, and large metal objects. It was terrible. I had just assumed that we would make something that sounded *something* like music. It absolutely did not. The crowd immediately turned on us and began to shout and cover their ears. It was incredible to see.

I started shouting random words that didn't rhyme or that maybe weren't even words. I pulled my face right up next to the microphone and screamed. I looked over at Booker, and he was jumping all around his side of the stage. I couldn't even tell if he was touching the strings anymore. My voice and my guitar were horrendously loud. Pedro's drums were the exact opposite of rhythmic. It was atrocious. I couldn't even continue to sing or scream or whatever I was doing. I just started to laugh.

After what might have been the most abominable stage debut of a fake band in the history of all fake bands, which may not be that deep or storied of a history at this point, I kicked the microphone over and tossed my guitar off of my shoulder and over my head. It slammed on the stage floor and probably made a better noise in doing so than I had made in the thirty seconds I attempted to play it.

"Fuck you, Denver!" I yelled, and I walked off the stage and toward the hallway.

I heard Booker drop his bass, and I assumed that he followed behind me. I was hoping Pedro did too, but I wasn't going to turn around and try to find out. I just kept walking.

I got outside, and there was a group of emo-looking dudes all gathered around the open doors to the same van that we had just raided. They looked up at me with immediate scorn. I looked behind me and saw Pedro and Booker about halfway down the hallway, heading toward me laughing.

"Did somebody jack your gear?" I asked as I kept walking outside.

"What the fuck do you know about that?" one of the more emo-looking guys snapped at me.

He had that kind of hair style where you plaster half of it across your face in a weird arrangement of sharp angles. He looked like a fucking idiot. It made me smile.

"I know that some dudes are up on stage using shit they obviously don't know how to play."

Booker and Pedro came out right behind me.

"I'm guessing maybe that's yours?"

"Fuck!" one of the guys yelled.

Another one started to walk inside, and he motioned for the others to follow him.

"Thanks, man," another one offered to me as I walked away.

"No problem, buddy. You should keep that door locked."

"No shit," he said.

As soon as they were all inside, we started to run down the street. There was no way I was going to stick around for the aftermath of that mess. I ran with drunken speed. The street lights, car lights, and shop lights were blurred by my eyes. I ran and ran and ran, and Booker and Pedro followed right behind me. After a little while, I actually recognized where we were. Number streets and bricks. Somehow I had navigated us back toward familiarity without even trying to.

I ran around the corner of the next block, and I could see the truck ahead of me. It was still parked in the same undersized parking spot that I had chosen earlier in the day. No tickets. No tow truck. No boot. Just our sweet, sweet truck. I stopped running, and the guys caught up a few seconds later. We all huffed and wheezed and panted as we walked down the sidewalk. Booker and I both started laughing. We walked behind the truck. Pedro sat on the rear bumper step. He looked up at the sky and smiled.

"Tuba City," he said, slowly.

"As I live and breathe," I replied.

Seventeen

"I've always had a thing for rum."

Pedro was leaning against the front of the truck. I was standing across from him.

"What do you mean *a thing*?" he asked.

"You know, like I've always had a thing for it."

"Yeah, you just said that."

"Right."

"What does that mean?"

"A thing. Like…I've always had a thing for it."

"Jesus," he said. He turned toward the back of the truck as best he could without moving from his position against the grill. "Your boy is making no sense!" he shouted back to Booker.

"How am I not making sense?" I asked.

"He never does!" Booker yelled back from somewhere behind the truck, wherever the gas tank was.

"What thing are you talking about?" Pedro asked again.

"A thing. Like a love for it."

"A love for rum?"

"Yeah. I can't love rum? Why not?"

"Whoa," he started. "You can love whatever you want, man. I don't care. I just don't know why you wouldn't just say that you always had love for rum, rather than just saying you always had a thing."

"What's the difference?" I asked.

"Between a love and a thing?"

"A love?" I asked.

"Your boy is making no sense!" he shouted again.

"Never!" Booker shouted back.

"Fine," I said, and I walked away.

We were at a gas station somewhere in Utah. It was a little bit after Interstate 70 dumped into the 15. Right before a place called Beaver. That fact entertained us for about an hour of the drive there. I walked into the food mart and went over toward the coolers to get a water. Occasionally I drank the stuff, but only when I had to.

We had been driving for almost the entire day. This was our second stop to fill up for gas and food, except nobody really wanted food this time around. The last gas station had made us second guess ourselves there. Pedro had essentially given up his claim to Denver and hit the road with us for the indefinite future. Outside of Boulder, there really wasn't another place around that we wanted to spend any time driving toward, so we decided to try to make it to Vegas in a day. We left early in the morning on a Friday. It was Friday the 13th, actually.

"Are you ready to go there, Socrates?" Booker jabbed.

"Huh?" I asked.

"You were standing there for like three minutes, just staring out in the sky like a fucking mongoloid or something."

"Do you think Socrates was a mongoloid?"

"You either looked deep in thought or mentally retarded."

"Oh. That's not good. I was just replaying the other night in my head."

"What night?"

"Night before last. You don't want any food?"

"Nah."

"Me either," Pedro added.

"Alright. A bottle of water it is."

So we drove off. I tried to bring up the riddle somewhere along the way, and they both shut me down. It was becoming a sensitive subject, so I backed off and let it go. At least for the time being.

"Why were you thinking about the other night?" Booker asked.

"What, I can't think about things?"

"Okay," he laughed. "Yes. You can think about things. Sorry I asked, commander."

I was being a little touchy, but I couldn't tell why.

"I was just thinking about that shitty pizza place."

"Mario's?"

"Yeah. What a bunch of fucking assholes. That's probably why I'm annoyed right now."

"It wasn't that bad..." Booker started to say, but I cut him off.

"Yes. Yes it *was*."

After our first and last "show" at the Marquis, we went out to get something more to drink and eventually, something to eat as well. The drinks came from several different bars nearby, though I can't remember any of them by name or where the hell they were. One definitely had some sort of organized line dancing going on, I remember that. We stood on the sides and watched in amazement, or at least Booker and I did. I didn't realize that people actually did that in public. Maybe Pedro was used to it. He didn't seem as surprised.

Afterwards we went to eat at a place called Mario's Two Fisted Pizza, or something that sounds about that ridiculous. We got there at maybe one in the morning, and it was packed.

"So what was so bad about it? I thought the pizza was pretty good."

"That heavy metal thrash music was just awful. I feel like it just put everyone in an aggro mood. It's probably why you stormed off."

"I didn't *storm* off."

"Yeah you did," Pedro added. "You got pretty sassy and you stormed away."

"See?" I said. "I blame the music."

"Was it really that bad?" Booker laughed. "I did wander away like a little bitch. That's not usually like me."

Everyone in the restaurant had a snarl on their face, which is a hard thing to do when you're also eating pizza. The whole thing had a gimmicky feel to it. The guys behind the counter were absolute dickheads. When we tried to order, they were about as pretentious and unfriendly as they could be. It was like a shittier version of Dick's Last Resort but without any warning or disclaimer.

"I didn't realize that people even liked metal anymore," I said.

"Maybe it's a Denver thing."

"Well, whatever. I've decided that if you like metal, you are not allowed to prepare food for me anymore."

"Seems fair."

"So, did we even tell you how we found you?"

"Not really. Pedro told me about the clues you started to find."

"Oh, the pile of pizza crust on the set of stairs down the street?"

"Yeah," Booker laughed.

"Some clues," I said, looking at Pedro. "That could have been anyone's. We were right next to a fucking pizza place."

"Denver seems like the kind of city where people don't just leave their crust on someone else's stoop. That seems more like an L.A. thing."

"Pedro, it is not an L.A. thing," Booker said. "But it is a *me* thing. When I'm feeling sassy."

"Still a clue."

"Dude, whatever. *You* had no clue. You went to sleep behind a bunch of fucking bushes on that outdoor mall road."

"Not true," Pedro retorted. "I tried to sleep. But then you crawled back there and kept me awake."

"Sounds romantic."

"Oh yeah," I said. "Very romantic. We were having a great time until this group of dudes walked up and started macking on these girls."

"Macking?"

"Yeah, I don't know where that came from. You know what I mean though. They were throwing down game."

"Who are you right now?" Booker asked.

He had a point. I didn't usually talk like that. I still don't.

"I blame Mario. Anyway, these dudes kept going on and on to these girls about how they were jewelers and how they wanted to take them back to their shop to try on some necklaces and whatever."

"Pearl necklaces," Pedro snorted.

"I didn't even think of that. Maybe that's what they meant. I thought they meant real necklaces."

"Okay. And?"

Booker was keeping the conversation moving, which wasn't entirely necessarily since we still had a few more hours on the road. We had just passed a sign that told us we were two hundred miles away from Las Vegas. You know you've been doing a lot of driving when seeing a highway sign that tells you that you're within two hundred miles of your destination makes it seem like you're almost there.

"So Pedro gets this great idea to take off one of his shoes and throw it at the guys."

"It seemed like a good idea at the time," he said, trying to defend himself but laughing as soon as he said it.

"Yeah, great idea. The guys were like, *what the fuck was that? Who's there?* Then they threw the shoe back with perfect aim. Hit Pedro right in the side."

"At least I got my shoe back."

"Sounds like I missed some really good times," Booker said.

"That's not all. We ended up taking another nap, or at least trying to, in a big park somewhere. We couldn't find you, and we didn't want to leave you out there on your own."

"So you slept in a park?"

"We tried to."

"Why didn't you guys just call me?"

"Battery was dead," I said.

"Oh, you must have been freaking out!"

"Too drunk. But I would have been, yeah."

"So you slept in a park?"

"Only for a little bit. Then the sprinklers went off and it woke us up."

"That's not what happened," Pedro countered. "A cop hit me in the ribs with his nightstick and told us to move along."

"What? That didn't happen. We woke up from the sprinklers."

"Night stick," he insisted.

"Sprinklers."

"What were you doing this whole time anyway?" I asked Booker.

"I don't remember anything, man. I just remember you guys waking me up and my neck being hella sore."

"Ha. Well, you were sleeping in the middle of that alley with your head propped up in the air. I'm not surprised at all."

"It was really weird," Pedro added. "You were on your side, and your neck was perfectly in line with your spine. Like you were sleeping on some invisible pillow."

"Sure as shit didn't feel like a pillow. It's *still* sore."

"Well, no shit. Anyway, that was it, really. Just some shoe throwing and park sleeping. You didn't miss much."

We never did figure out what it was that we had been fighting about that made him stomp away. After we found Booker, we all walked back to the truck and passed the fuck out almost instantly. It was something like five in the morning. We slept through a good amount of the next day and took it relatively easy after we did wake up. It had been a rough few days, and we all needed a little bit of a break. But that only lasted a little while. We started to feel antsy, or at least I did. That was when we made the plans to head out to Vegas the following morning. And that was what brought us to that gas station near Beaver.

Pedro fell asleep when we were only about thirty minutes outside of Vegas. He was snoring pretty hard, so I felt free to talk about him openly.

"What do you think his deal is?" I asked.

"Beats the shit out of me, man. I like him though."

"Yeah. I do too."

"Did you see the tattoo on his arm?"

"Yeah. Is that a Sobe lizard?"

"I think so. On a skateboard."

"I mean…you know. Whatever."

"Yeah. Did you see the other one?"

"No," I said, and Booker laughed. "Where is it?"

"His other arm," he said.

"What is it?"

"I don't want to ruin the surprise."

"Come on."

I looked over and tried to see if I could lift the sleeve of his shirt to see it.

"Dude!" Booker almost yelled. "Watch the road. Don't wake him up!"

"What is it?"

Booker laughed again.

"I think it's another Sobe lizard. But this one is on a snowboard."

"Shut up."

"Really."

"What is this guy's deal?" I asked again, rhetorically.

Then I slapped him on the leg a few times. He wiggled a bit and his snoring stopped for a few seconds, but he didn't wake up.

"Pedro Bay," Booker stated.

"Founding member of Tuba City," I added.

Booker nodded.

Vegas is a shit show no matter when you go or what you plan on doing. Even if you go for a work conference – though I have never done such a thing – you will end up getting wrecked and making an ass of yourself. It's a terrible vortex of humility and manners. It's a travesty of a city. It is America at its best and worst. The only thing worse and more American is how Americans act at all-inclusive resorts in other countries. Beyond that, it's Vegas. Then it's Boston on St. Patrick's Day. Then Halloween pretty much anywhere in the country. Then your city if your team wins the Super Bowl, unless you're Indianapolis, because you're boring as hell. Then it's a four-way tie between single women at weddings, the stand-by line for the *Price is Right*, Costco on Black Friday, and Never Ending Pasta Month at the Olive Garden. The rest of America is alright to me. God bless it.

When we got there, we parked the truck somewhere far enough away from The Strip that it wouldn't get us into any trouble, or at least that was the plan. To write about Vegas without giving the context of time would be inappropriate. More than any other city in this country that I've been to, Las Vegas has had a different feel, look, and general vibe that is all defined by the year you went there. There are definitive lines in the sand – unintentional pun – that run along certain years or events. Before or after the recession of 2008. Before or after the City Center was opened. Before or after they tore down that place with the wooden roller coaster and clowns, where they ended up building the City Center. And other defining lines that would have been defined before I was old enough to give a shit about Las Vegas.

This was 2007. This was after the roller coaster place was torn down but before the recession hit. That meant that the City Center was still just a bunch of metal rods sticking out of the ground. There were lots of wooden boards separating the pedestrians on the sidewalks trying to go from the Monte Carlo, where nobody really goes, to the Bellagio, where nobody goes to do anything other than look at those glass flowers in the lobby and the real flowers behind them. I always thought that the guy who has the job of arranging all of those real flowers in the back was a pretty lucky guy. It's a pretty cool job if you like flowers. Which I do.

Vegas in 2007 was pretty legit. It wasn't a semi-ghost town like it was in 2009, and it wasn't the bloated mess that it has been ever since people started to waste their money again. The monorail probably existed back then. But like today, nobody used it, so I couldn't really tell you for certain if it was around when we were there. Even if you confirmed that it was, I still don't know if I would believe it. The thing hides behind giant buildings. It's practically not there even when you know that it's there.

Anyway, we parked the truck somewhere undesirable and took a taxi in the year 2007 to get to a place on The Strip that probably still exists today. It is roughly in front of the Imperial Palace, which, now that I think of it, should be torn down any day now. If it hasn't been yet, I don't know what they are waiting for.

We weren't going to the IP though. We went to some shitty, little bar right in front of it that has beer pong tables and slushy machines that fill up giant plastic beer bongs for like $40. This was Pedro's first idea as soon as he woke up. It wasn't his worst. We each got a slushy drink. Mine was in a plastic cup that was shaped like a guitar. It even had a strap that I wore over my shoulder. Pedro had the classic beer bong, and Booker, unsurprisingly, chose the biggest one they had. The douche bag one with the strap that goes around your neck, because it is just too heavy to carry without it. America.

It didn't take long for us to start telling any girls we spoke to that we were in a band. Nobody seemed to care or believe us. In retrospect, I am realizing that it didn't help that I was wearing a guitar that I was drinking out of. They must have thought we were joking, and somehow that offended me, even though the real band that I was insisting I was in was actually a fake band that we had fully made up. But who cares. I had been on a stage. On a tour, sort of. In another state. And no one believed me. So fuck them.

We bought a pitcher of beer and played a game of beer pong, with me on one side and Booker and Pedro on the other. I don't remember who won or if anyone won. We were getting hammered, and no one around us seemed to give a shit that we existed. Everyone was just there to listen to the shitty 80's music that was playing and to watch frat boys play beer pong and high-five each other when they made their shots. That's what you do when you play, so I don't know why I am getting snotty about it now. It just seemed kind of annoying. It made me miss Denver. And even more, it made me miss L.A.

I think it was having the same effect on the guys as well. We were just having a shitty time, so we left and went to another bar. It didn't take long for us to realize that no matter where we went, we were going to be dealing with the same general population. A bunch of douche bags. I killed what was left in the guitar that I was drinking out of. I threw it on the ground like I had just finished a set. Things were very spinny at that point. I remember thinking that I wanted to call Harper to see what she was up to, like that would have amounted to anything other than a feeling of regret the next day. I was the only one who hadn't gotten off during the trip, so I was probably just backed up.

We spent a while wandering around on The Strip, telling anyone who would listen that we were in a band. No one cared. It really started to piss me off. So I combatted that the best way I knew how, and that was with more alcohol. I got so drunk that I even started to tell people about our stolen truck, like that was a good idea. Still, no one listened. At some point I gave up and just decided that I wanted to go back to the truck. It was maybe one in the morning, which in Vegas terms is early bird dinner time. What a failure.

"You don't want to try to get into a club?" Pedro asked one last time.

"Dude. I have been wearing these same shorts for almost a week now. What club is going to let me in?"

"I'm sure we can pay a bouncer or someone to let you in," he suggested.

"And me too," Booker added.

He looked worse than I did, somehow. He was generally a messy eater, so there were all kinds of rubbed-out food stains on his shirt that were starting to take on a permanent look. There might have even been a bit of those Taking Back Burger Fries somewhere on there.

"Ehh," was all Pedro said in response.

"Right."

So we went back to the truck. In a city with so many hotel rooms, it almost seemed ridiculous that we were going to spend the night laid out on a metal floor. But that was our plan. Besides, one hotel bill is more expensive than no hotel bill. Pedro was the only one who seemed willing to pay to stay somewhere else, but he wasn't going to do it on his own.

Oh, the truck. She was beautiful in her ugliness, like some women can be at times. When we finally got back, we must have been walking for over an hour. We were desperate to see her. She sat so humbly in the parking lot of a very stereotypically seedy-looking drive-up motel. I honestly don't know how we found the place and then how we decided that this was where we wanted to spend the night. I think it was because we wanted to stay out of sight and under the radar.

Fair enough. Except we did a terrible job of doing that. Pedro was antsy, and it was clear that he did not want to fall asleep. We were all lying on our backs staring up at the pitch black ceiling. We had the door closed entirely. At some point in the trip, we realized that we were not going to die from a lack of oxygen if we closed the door all the way and that it was probably safer if we did.

"How about we go back out?" Pedro said slowly.

"You can go if you want."

"Yeah, man. Don't let us stop you."

"I don't want to go out on my own."

"Why not? You were on your own when we met you. What's the difference?" Booker asked.

"That's not the point," he said.

He seemed a lot whinier than he had been yet, and I was almost getting annoyed that we had invited him along with us. I was too dizzy to care.

"What's the point then?"

He hemmed and hawed, or whatever that phrase is, for a little while.

"I don't like where we're parked," he finally admitted.

"What?"

"It's shady. You don't think it's shady?"

"It's Vegas," I said flatly. "Everything here is shady."

"I don't like it. Can we move the truck somewhere else?"

"Are you kidding?"

"You don't even have to get out of the back," he offered. "You can just lay here, and I'll drive us somewhere else."

"Dude. Why?"

Booker sounded as annoyed as I felt.

"I just don't like it here. I can't explain it."

He paused for a bit, and no one said anything.

"I'm going to move the truck," he said decisively, and he started to get up and head toward the door.

"To where?" I moaned.

"Just somewhere else. Don't worry. It'll be quick."

The keys were jingling in his hand. I realized that I had no recourse at that point unless I wanted to get up and take them away from him.

"Whatever, man. Fine."

"Thanks!" he yelled over the noise of the door sliding up.

He hopped out and slammed it shut, probably waking some dirtbag in the motel or interrupting whatever despicable act he was committing. In actuality, it probably wasn't that bad of a motel, but I like to pretend that he was right and that it was a place we should have tried to escape. I heard the front door shut and the engine roared to life. I hadn't been in the back of the truck while it was running until that point. It was very loud, certainly louder than it was outside.

"How drunk do you think he is?" Booker shouted to me.

The truck lurched into gear and answered for me.

"Ah, shit!" I yelled.

Pedro hadn't driven the truck yet, and for all I knew, he had never driven a car in his life. The truck jumped forward, and Booker and I slid uncontrollably toward the back door. The sleeping bags provided no grip on the smooth metal floor.

"Why is he going for– " Booker started to ask, right as the front end of the truck climbed over one of those speed-bump-parking-stopper things at the end of a parking spot. The whole truck jumped up in the air, and we got tossed right along with it. There was another small bump and then a jolting crash as the truck slammed into the wall of the motel. I heard glass shattering, and I assumed it was the windshield.

We had stopped moving, it seemed. Booker and I took that as an opportunity to climb out of the back and see what the hell Pedro had just done. He was standing outside of the cab, the driver's door open, his hands almost comically on top of his head like he had just witnessed a terrible bout of luck.

"What the fuck was that?!" I shouted at him.

"Shit!" he yelled. "Shit!"

"What the fuck, man?" I asked as I ran up alongside him to inspect the damage.

"I thought I was going in reverse! Shit! Shit!"

The hood of the truck had driven into part of the wall. It didn't knock it down entirely, which is somehow what I was expecting even though that wouldn't have made much sense. There was glass strewn across the hood, not from the windshield but from the motel room window itself. There were bars on the window that were bent in and jutting out in a few different directions. The truck itself looked largely unharmed, but I couldn't really tell since the part that would have been most damaged was half-buried into the motel wall.

"Jesus, man!" Booker yelled, looking frantically around the parking lot.

Nobody was outside other than us, which seemed hard to believe.

"We've got to get the fuck out of here!"

"Run?" Pedro asked.

"No, man. Drive! We can't leave the truck behind! It has our prints on it!"

It seemed like a legitimate concern at the time. In hindsight, it is pretty unlikely that this crime would warrant a fingerprint dusting. We had seen too many movies.

"Give me the keys!" I yelled, before realizing that it wasn't possible. "Never mind. It's running. Right. Get in!"

Booker went to run around the front, like an idiot, realizing immediately that he couldn't without climbing over the hood. He ran around the back, closed the door, and jumped in the passenger side. Pedro was just standing there with his hands on his head.

"Get the fuck in, man!"

"Shit!" he yelled, before turning around and looking back at the parking lot.

"Get in," I said more calmly.

He snapped out of whatever shock he was in and jumped in the cab, assuming his seat in the middle. I looked around the parking lot once more, saw no one, and got in right behind him.

I put the shifter in reverse – which was very easy to do and very difficult to mistake for being two gears lower – and eased back slowly, thinking that the whole building might fall down if I went too fast. Pieces of glass and wall began to crumble and fall on the asphalt. The front tires bumped up against the speed bump that I had already forgotten about. I stepped heavily onto the gas, and the truck bounded over it, the three of us almost coming up out of our seats in doing so. I backed up without any regard for what was behind us. I threw it into drive and peeled out and into the street. The truck heaved and swayed. I imagined sparks flying out from the back even though there would have been no reason for that to have happened.

I was extremely drunk, and the immediate trauma of what Pedro had just done only served to wake me up, but not sober me as well. I raced for the freeway, somewhat aware of where it might be while mostly following my intuition. I don't know what anyone was saying that whole time until we got to the on ramp. I was fiercely focused on getting the hell out of there. The reality of what we were doing at that very moment didn't really hit me until a couple of days later. I was fleeing the scene of an accident while drunk, in a stolen, foreign, commercial vehicle that I illegally sold alcohol out of.

By some godly miracle I found an on ramp and entered the freeway, heading south on 15. We all sighed some form of relief when we realized that we might have actually made it away, at least for the time being.

Whatever excitement Booker and I had felt when we first stole the truck was now feeling like nothing in comparison, though this wasn't anywhere near as positive.

"Pedro, you fucking idiot," I started in on him. "What the fuck is wrong with you?"

"I'm sorry," he said with a real sadness in his voice. "I don't know what happened."

"All because you didn't like the fucking parking lot?" Booker demanded.

"I'm really sorry."

"Jesus," I said. "We need to pull over at some point and see how much damage you did to the grill."

"Why?" Pedro asked. "The truck is running. It doesn't sound like it is having any problems."

We all paused to listen, and it was true. The engine sounded just fine. There were no squeaks or shakes or anything that wasn't already there.

"Because I need to know how bad this thing looks in case we get pulled over. I need to be able to make up some story about what I did."

"Dude," Booker reminded me, "if we get pulled over, we are fucked anyway."

"Right. Dammit."

I thought for a moment. I didn't like to be wrong.

"Well, I still want to know how bad it is."

"Me too," Booker replied. "There's got to be a gas station up ahead somewhere that we can pull off at."

We looked for one, and the next exit looked like it had a place that we could stop. I was concerned about getting out of the city and, more importantly, out of the state entirely. I didn't think they would be able to chase us across state lines for something like this. But I didn't know who *they* were or what *they* were allowed to do, so it was really just an impulse to run that was driving me forward.

We stopped at the gas station and parked along the side. We were near a street light but not facing anything other than a wall, which seemed ominous, considering what we had just been through. I stepped out of the cab and came around to the front of the truck. The grill was bent in right at the center, but not too badly. The bumper was pinched in a bit more. Neither looked in danger of falling off or deteriorating any further. The hood was a little scratched but not structurally altered in any way. The windshield had no cracks. We all looked at each other, and then I laughed.

"Pedro, you fucker, you are NEVER allowed to drive this thing again."

"Agreed," Booker stated.

"Agreed," Pedro concurred.

Booker started to look around the gas station.

"What?" I asked.

"There are no other trucks here," he said quickly. "Let's go to another station."

"Why?"

"Come on, let's go," he said.

"Go where? Why?" I asked again.

I hate cryptic bullshit, and he knew it. There's no need for mystery among friends.

"We need a new license plate," he declared. "So can we go?"

We got in the truck, and I started to drive back toward the freeway.

"That's not a bad idea, actually."

"Have you done this before?" Pedro asked, jokingly.

It felt too soon for him to be joking and possibly enjoying himself, but I was too drunk and tired to try to make him feel bad about it.

"Yeah, of course," Booker replied, completely serious.

"What? When?"

"Dude," he said, addressing me. "We're already on our fourth license plate for this baby."

"Since when?" I asked.

I couldn't believe it.

"The last one I got was in Denver."

"No, you didn't.

"Yes, I did."

"You did?"

"Yes. We have a Colorado license plate right now. You didn't notice?"

"What? No! I had no idea. I just assumed…" I trailed off, realizing that I had never stopped to think about what license plate we had at all.

"What, that it was the Mexican one still?"

"Yeah."

"Ha! Come on, man. Are you kidding?"

"No."

"How do you think we crossed the border? With a Mexican license plate?"

"Where did you get a U.S. license plate from?"

"Some other truck. The day we painted this, I bought a couple of screwdrivers from the hardware store, and when I found a commercial truck with a California plate, I snagged it."

"No shit?"

I was simultaneously impressed and embarrassed. I hadn't thought about any of this. I was a terrible criminal.

"Yeah, man. Then when we got back to L.A., I swapped it with another one so we didn't get tied to that first one somehow."

"That makes sense," Pedro added. "But if the owner called and reported his license plate stolen, wouldn't that mean that the one you had would be flagged for the police to keep an eye out for?"

"Well, yeah. But that's why I swap them, not just steal them outright. I figure it's less likely for someone to notice that they have a different license plate number than to notice they have no license plate at all."

"Right," I said. "I've been climbing in and out of the back of this thing for almost a week now, and I never paid any attention to it. At all."

"Exactly," Booker said. "So when we got to Phoenix, I swapped it again, just to try to be safe. And then again in Denver."

"Damn. I am impressed. And scared."

That was just for comedic effect. I wasn't scared.

"Thanks," he said. "And thanks."

We pulled over at another gas station where we saw a truck parked alongside the building, minding its own business like a truck at a gas station would. Pedro and I went into the little convenience store to make sure the attendant didn't get suspicious, and Booker did whatever it is that Booker did. When we came out, he was leaning against the hood, hiding most of the damage. He nodded as we got closer and then turned away to get back in the truck. It would have been a pretty cool moment, but the back of his shirt got caught on a twisted piece of the grill. It pulled him back a bit before it let go, and he stumbled forward. At least he tried to look cool. That's what counts.

We got back on the freeway and started heading south again. The enormity of the desert night made me realize how long of a drive it was going to be and how drunk I actually was. It started to seep into my eyes, my head, and my hands. Driving all the way to L.A., which somehow was our de facto yet unspoken plan, was too dangerous. Even for me.

So instead, we made it up the long hill that leads you out of Nevada. We crossed the state line back into California. We drove for another ten or fifteen minutes before we found an unassuming exit where we could park. The road was poorly maintained, which was promising for us. As we headed farther down, I saw an unpaved path that led behind a decent-sized hill. This was going to have to do for the night. I backed the truck in, just in case we needed to make a getaway. That made sense at the time. As though we were going to flee from the police if they came and found us.

We all got out of the cab and climbed into the back. Pedro didn't say a word. I think we were all somewhat happy to be back there again. It was almost four in the morning now, a proper night in Vegas after all, even though we ended up on the side of the road in California as a result.

Eighteen

I've always had a thing for rum. It has gone way beyond the point where I know one rum from another. I try my best to not be a snob about it. I don't go around tasting rum and offering my tasting notes to whoever will listen. I don't talk about the buttery palate or the faint notes of a charred oak barrel. I don't compare viscosities or mouth feels. I don't say *full-bodied* unless I am talking about a big girl, and I don't think it is any of your business if I want to talk about a big girl, for that matter. I don't insist that my rum should be *experienced* in glassware of certain shapes or sizes. I don't do any of these things.

It is sometimes almost embarrassing how much I've learned about it. Because it's okay to be an expert on wine. You get your own word. You get to be an oenophile. That's pretty cool. It's the same thing for people who love beer. Sometimes they make their own beer. They go to beer events. They're considered hobbyists. Hobbies are acceptable things to have. Even people who love scotch or whiskey will earn a certain amount of respect when they tell you how much they know. There is something noble in having that knowledge, with having any of this knowledge. These are all acceptable forms of alcohol to know a lot about.

But if you know a lot about rum, you just sound like a guy with a problem.

Maybe I am. But I do know a lot about it, and I don't see any reason in pretending that I don't. I just try to not be offensive about it. I don't need you to know that I know a lot about rum. I need me to know it.

I almost always order rum when I go out. That's a given. Sometimes I let them pour me the house rum, and sometimes I call the rum that I want to drink. It really depends on what they have. Just asking what kind of rum a place has will usually tell me all that I need to know. If the bartender looks at me a little weird, I know that they probably don't have anything worth asking for.

I know enough about bar culture to know a place that I should be calling my rum from a place that is going to serve me whatever is cheapest, just secretly re-poured into the more expensive bottle that I see on the shelf. That said, I have on occasion tried to call my rum in a place that is just going to take my extra money and laugh at me.

The problem for them is that I know when they are doing this as soon as the drink hits my mouth. No matter how drunk I am, I can taste the difference between whatever shit they are serving as their house rum and the Zaya Gran Reserva that I ordered. Zaya doesn't leave a burning taste in my mouth. Zaya doesn't make me wince. So when I order the Zaya and it tastes like I am drinking a vodka and Coke, I know that I made the mistake of calling my drink in the wrong place.

And then I don't go to that place anymore. Or if I do, I order a little more carefully, and I certainly don't tip. Sometimes I will even underpay or walk out on the bill. You don't get to fuck with me when it comes to rum. It's not about the money either, though I understand that is what would irritate most people. It's about the goddamned drink. I ordered the more expensive rum because I *like* it. Not because I want to impress somebody or because I want to try something new.

So when the drink is given to me and it doesn't have what I wanted in it, you have to understand that I am going to retaliate. I may go to your bathroom and piss in the flower pot next to the toilet. I may open a tab on an expired credit card and leave it behind at the end of the night. At the very least, I will be leaving you a negative review on Yelp. This is a fair warning to the cheapskate bar owners of the world. You can fuck with me on any number of things. Rum, you cannot. Rum is my backyard.

I was in the middle of explaining this to Pedro at one of my favorite restaurants in L.A. when I realized that he probably didn't care at all about rum. He seemed more like a guy who just liked alcohol in whatever form it came to him. This was a number of years ago, so my knowledge was much less than it is now. I had never had Zaya before, for example. Maybe I was talking about the difference between Captain Morgan and Bacardi Gold. I don't know. It doesn't matter. The principle is the same. I started to taper off my obsessive explanation for fear of losing him entirely. He was already looking straight at me but with that look that makes you think he wants to be looking around the room at anything else.

"Anyway, man," I said, realizing that I sounded like quite the fanatic. "I just don't like it when people fuck with me."

"Who does?"

"Not me. So anyway, what do you want to do today?"

"I was thinking we could take Tuba City out on the road again."

"But we just got back here. Like, not even twenty-four hours ago. I don't want to drive that thing just yet."

"It doesn't have to be far. I meant in L.A."

"But taking the truck?"

"Yeah. Well, I mean, that part doesn't really matter, but I think it makes it more fun. I just want to go out and try to get more girls and more free drinks."

He was a man of simple needs. I could be too. But not usually.

"Heard that. But I don't know."

"Why not?"

I thought about it a little bit. Something didn't feel right, doing that in L.A.

"You know that phrase about not shitting where you eat?"

"Ah."

"Yeah, I think it's that. Like, I go to the clubs here pretty regularly to see real shows. I don't want to jeopardize that by getting kicked out of one of them and never being able to go back to see some band I really like when they do come through here."

"Do you really think that would happen?"

"I'd kick someone out if they pretended to be a band and swindled me for money. Or if they went on stage and made asses of themselves."

"Yeah, no, I get that. But like, do you think they are going to know who you are if you go back for a show?"

"I have to show them my I.D. when I want to get a wristband, so yeah. They'll know who I am."

"Right. Okay. But like, why would they know your name in the first place?"

"Well, if we got kicked out, what if they make me show them my I.D.? Like if we get arrested or something."

"Yeah, I guess. But how about we just don't get arrested doing this? That doesn't seem too hard to avoid. I don't want to go somewhere if we think we're going to get thrown in jail for it."

"True."

It still didn't feel like a good idea. Then again, none of this was. None of what I was doing with my life was.

"Besides," he added, "it might be better to develop some sort of a following in at least one city so we could do this more often and not have to run away after each show."

The way he called it a show, it was like he thought we were actually becoming a touring band.

"I guess. This is easy for you to say though. These aren't your hometown venues that you're risking."

"I don't have hometown venues, man."

"Good point."

I realized that he wasn't going to be able to understand what I was worried about.

"You know," he said, leaning back in his chair a bit. "For someone who is so concerned about his mortality, you certainly do a whole lot of nothing with your life."

"Whoa whoa whoa, man. What the fuck is this? Are you my psychologist now?"

"Listen, I'm just saying. I've only known you, what, a week?"

"We met on Monday."

"Okay, so less than a week. Even better. So in that time, I have heard you talk about how we could die at any moment and how it's so crazy that you could be alive one minute and dead the next and you'd never know the difference. And you'd never know it's coming."

"I said that?"

"A couple of times."

"I must have been drunk."

"Right."

"It's so true though."

"Right. So true. Right. So, for a guy who I have only known for a few days and who has been saying all of these romanticized things about life and death and fate and whatever bullshit you and Booker talk about when you think I'm asleep…"

He paused for a moment and smiled.

"I didn't realize you were awake. Sorry about that."

He shook his head.

"If you really are that worried that you might die at any moment, why do you care about anything at all?"

"Because I can't be a nihilist."

"I don't know what that is, but that sounds like an excuse to me."

"Alright. Look, I don't know, okay? I'm scared of dying."

"Who isn't?"

"Lots of people. But the thing is, I'm not that afraid of it. I am just worried about the fact that it can happen at any time and that I might not be doing what I want to be doing when it does," I said.

"That's my point," he whispered as he leaned forward again, putting his arms on the table.

He got right up close to me.

"Back up, man," I said, and I leaned back in my own chair.

"Let go, Blake."

"Let go of what?"

He smiled and kept leaning forward.

"Of whatever you've got that is making you worried about not being able to get into a music venue because you pretended you were in a band. Who gives a fucking shit? If you died tomorrow, you'd be mad that you paid for your drinks."

"No, I wouldn't be. I'd be dead."

"Well, I'd be mad then."

"I don't care if you're mad if I'm dead."

He leaned back in his chair again, seeming annoyed.

"Like I said. You're the one obsessed with your mortality, not me. You're the one who keeps talking about doing what you want to do and not doing what you think you *should* be doing."

"I believe in that," I said, defending myself.

"You don't act like you do. I mean, you do sometimes. Sometimes you just don't give a shit, and you...you steal a truck full of rum in Mexico and you drive it out of the country. That's living. That's where you're in sync with your beliefs. But then other times, you don't do jack shit, and it's because you're worried about what is going to happen next."

"You're saying all of this like you know me so well. How do you know that this past week hasn't just been an anomaly?"

"Look," he said. "The only way you can make sure you don't die full of regret is to just do whatever the fuck you really, really want to do. Right then, at that moment. You have a choice, and you choose for today. You don't choose for tomorrow, and you don't choose for next week, or next year. Or next whenever. You choose for today because maybe today is the last day you'll get to choose for. That's how you live and die with no regret."

"It's so paralyzing," I said.

I closed my eyes to take in what he had just said. It was maybe one of the best pep talks I had ever heard in person, and it was all to support the dumbest, most worthless decision that I didn't want to make.

"Everything can paralyze you if you let it," Pedro said.

And then it hit me.

"You're absolutely right."

He leaned forward again.

"I drove the truck into the motel on purpose," he whispered and then laughed loudly.

It was an awkward laugh that just burst out. It was packed with nervous energy, but it rang full of truth.

"You are a crazy motherfucker."

"You know what it was? I just wanted to do something that I would probably never want to do again. It just hit me. I got the keys to the truck, and I saw that shitty motel, and I hated it for whatever reason. And I thought, *I want to drive the truck right into it.* So I put the thing in drive, and I did it."

"How did it feel?"

"It didn't feel like anything at all."

"So you regret that now instead? You followed your instinct so that you wouldn't regret not doing something, and you end up getting nothing out of it but regret?"

He shook his head.

"No. I didn't say that. I don't regret anything I did."

"But it didn't make you feel like you wanted it to make you feel."

"No, man. You're missing the point."

"What's that, then? What is the point of driving someone else's truck through a motel wall if it isn't going to achieve something for you?"

"See, that's what you don't get. I wasn't looking for a feeling that I wanted to get out of it. I was just looking to *do* something that I wanted to do. It suddenly came over me, and I wanted to do it. So I did it."

"It's that kind of thinking that gets people thrown in jail," I said.

"It's your kind of thinking that makes your life like a jail," he replied.

"Damn."

"No offense," he added.

"No, I get it. Just...damn."

"Look at me," he demanded. "I'm sitting in some restaurant in L.A. with a guy I met in Denver who I barely know at all."

I started to say something about him thinking he knew me well enough to judge the way that I lived my life, but he stopped me before I began.

"I have nothing with me. I have no clothes, no car, no nothing. I left behind just about everything I have to come on the road with you guys because it just seemed like the right thing to do."

"But what if it isn't?" I asked.

"How can it not be?"

"What if things go terribly here? What if you die because of something we decide to do?"

He sat back in his chair again.

"I don't see that as any worse than whatever other life I might be living, where I also might die at any moment because of something else I decided to do."

"Damn," I said again, but this time I smiled.

Pedro didn't move or say anything in response, and we just sat there for a little while, looking at each other. It was a very important moment in my life. It was the kind of moment that I could tell actually mattered, even while it was happening. He had not only proven his point, which is sometimes very hard to do when arguing with me, but he also had changed the way that I was thinking about the decisions I had been making. And the ones that I would be making in the future.

"Well?" he asked, after what was probably a longer silence than either of us had realized.

I nodded slowly a few times before replying.

"There's a place on the east side of the city that I like but that I don't go to that often anymore. It's always pretty dark there. I think we can try there tonight."

"What's your favorite venue in L.A.?"

"One step at a time, man," I said.

"Alright," he laughed. "Sorry."

"Don't apologize. You're fucking amazing."

"Eh," he said.

We ordered another round of drinks. Each sip tasted like it was being swallowed by an entirely new mouth.

My phone rang, and it was a number that I didn't have in my contacts. I recognized the area code, but I couldn't remember where it was from. The last four digits were 2-7-4-9, which felt familiar to me. Turns out, it wasn't at all. All of that existential talk had me feeling very aware and present.

"Hello."

"Blake?"

"Uh huh. Who's this?"

"It's Maria," the voice claimed.

"Who?"

"Maria. From the Marquis."

I had to think a bit before I remembered what the Marquis was. I was still hung up on the meaningless 2-7-4-9.

"Oh, what the hell? Hi. How did you get my number? Did I give you my number?"

"No, you didn't. I got it from Jessie."

"Who's that?"

I didn't know anyone named Jessie that I could think of. Male or female. Jessie or Jesse. Other than Uncle Jesse. But I didn't know him personally.

"The bartender at the Marquis. You don't pay attention to anything, do you?"

"How did she have my number?"

Pedro was eyeing me curiously. The only parts of the conversation that he could hear involved me questioning why someone was calling me. For all he knew, it could have been anybody. The police. My mom. His mom. Uncle Jesse.

"She got it from Booker."

"Interesting," I said. "Isn't her name Jackie?"

"Oh yeah."

"Well, anyway. Hi. What's up?"

"Just wanted to see how it was going. Seeing if you guys were planning any new shows or anything."

"New shows," I repeated, deliberately for Pedro's sake. "Yeah I think we're going to perform tonight."

"Oh yeah? Where?"

"Not in Denver. We're back in L.A. now."

"Oh. Where are you performing? I've been to L.A. before."

"We're playing at one of the places at The Echoplex."

"Oh yeah. I've been there."

"You have?"

"Yeah. It's in Echo Park, right?"

"Yeah. I mean…you could have guessed that though."

"Whatever. I've been there. There's The Echo and then there's The Echoplex. Which one?"

"Uh. The Echo."

"So, is it cool if I tweet that you guys are going to be there?"

"If you what?"

"Tweet."

"What the fuck does that mean? Text?"

"No, tweet. Like on Twitter."

"What is a Twitter? Didn't you mention that the last time I saw you?"

"Yes," she moaned, but she didn't actually sound annoyed.

She sounded like she was secretly happy that she was on the cutting edge side of something that we weren't. If only she knew Booker a little more, she'd realize that her grandmother was probably more cutting edge than he was. I think he still had a rotary phone in his bedroom.

"What is it?"

"It's blah, blah, blah," she said, but actually explaining what Twitter was.

"So you created an account for our band?"

"Yeah," she chirped happily. "It was a big thing at South by Southwest this year. All of the bands that were there started creating their own Twitter accounts. So I figured I'd create one for you guys since you didn't have one yet and since we knew each other."

"You went to SXSW?"

Sometimes I speak in abbreviations and acronyms.

"Yeah, I've gone a few times."

"That's pretty legit," I said.

"Yep. So I can tweet about your show tonight?"

"Yeah, sure. Whatever. I mean, we don't have anyone who would actually know about us on Twitter though, so what difference does it make?"

She laughed.

"You don't get it. But that's okay. I'll just tweet it anyway."

"Alright."

"I have a lot of followers, you know."

"Okay. Cool."

"Anyway, good luck! Is it alright if I text you later?"

"Yeah, sure," I said, mostly confused about what was happening.

"Okay, bye!"

She hung up.

"What was that?" Pedro asked.

I did the best job I could trying to explain what we had just spoken about. Pedro seemed to get it more than I did.

"That's pretty sick, man. We have our own publicist. And it sounds like she's connected."

"I guess."

"That's a good thing. Maybe we'll start to get a following!"

"I doubt it," I said, and I took a big gulp of my drink.

"I hope our fan base is mostly chicks," he added.

"Right."

We finished our drinks and went back to my place. Booker texted me to let me know that he'd be coming by to meet up in about thirty minutes, so we just hung out in my room and drank some more rum. Booker showed up later than he had predicted, which I had predicted myself. He was barely through the door when I hit him with my first question.

"Why did you give that bartender in Denver my phone number?"

"Nice to see you too. Hey, Pedro!" he yelled over my shoulder.

He walked by me and went straight for the kitchen. He pulled a glass out of the cabinet and some ice out of the freezer as he began to answer me.

"What happened? Did she call you?"

"No, that girl Maria did."

"Oh, right. That was the point."

"What was the point? You knew she was going to give it to her?"

"Yeah, I knew. She asked for your number so she could give it to Maria. So I gave it to her."

"What? Why?"

"Uh, you're welcome," he said, and he walked into the living room.

Pedro was in there just sitting on the couch, the bottle of rum on the coffee table in the middle of the room. Booker took a hold of it and poured some into his glass.

"I'm not thanking you for that," I said.

"Whatever, man."

"Guess where we're going tonight?" Pedro asked Booker, changing topics.

"Where?"

"What's the name of the place?" Pedro asked me.

He had a great memory.

"The Echo."

"Oh yeah? We're going as Tuba City?" Booker asked.

He slapped his hands on the coffee table, pretending it was a drum set.

"Yeah, he's going along with it!" Pedro shouted.

In the most monotone voice I could possibly use, I confirmed the plan.

"Yes. I had an epiphany today. Things are going to be diff-er-ent now."

"Don't say it like you're some kind of retard, man," Pedro scolded.

He turned to Booker.

"We had a moment earlier today."

"How sweet," Booker laughed.

"What'd you do all day anyway?" I asked him.

"Oh, I hung out with that girl from work that I told you about."

"The teenage one?"

"Whoa, man. She's of age."

He turned and looked at Pedro.

"I think!"

Pedro lifted his hand up for a high five, and Booker slapped it enthusiastically.

Dumbasses.

"Nice to hear that you're getting some more ass while trying to set me up with a crazy one that lives halfway across the damned country."

"Whatever, man. You've got your own game. I didn't stop you from reaching out to the butterface today. Or anytime this week, for that matter."

"Well, I couldn't exactly invite her over while I was with Pedro all day."

"Are you guys in a fight?" Pedro joked.

"Shut up."

"Man. The honeymoon from the epiphany wore off pretty quickly on this one," Pedro complained.

"Sorry. I just…I don't know. I don't know how I feel about this whole Twitter thing."

"What?" Booker asked, his mouth half-full with an ice cube.

"Oh, don't even get me started. You're going to hate it."

"Then don't start," he said.

I didn't say anything for a little while, and the two of them continued talking. I went to the bathroom. I had this habit of lifting up my shirt when I was alone in the bathroom. It was my way of taking inventory of the different muscles, or lack of muscles, that I had. It wasn't looking too great, and I realized that we had been treating our bodies pretty poorly for the past few weeks. Worse than we usually did. I sat down and tried to take a shit, hoping to lose some weight and look better afterwards. Nothing came out. I ended up peeing sitting down. I checked the mirror again, and it still looked the same. It would have been better for my ego if I hadn't looked at all.

I looked at my eyes for a little while. They still looked alright. They were a little bloodshot, which I expected, but they weren't too rough. I stared at myself for a while, and I got into a real fixed type of stare that I was having a hard time breaking. I wondered if I was going to die right then and there.

I didn't. When my stare finally broke, I thought about the conversation with Pedro from earlier in the day, and I decided to just relax and bit and let the night take us wherever it was going to take us. I flushed the toilet and walked out. I didn't wash my hands because I was at home, and I had nobody that I was trying to impress.

Nineteen

"I've always had a thing for rum."

"What is that supposed to mean?"

Jesus. These people. I don't get why they don't understand what I am trying to say when I say that. It's a romantic declaration. It's a fucking statement. It's something you're supposed to hear and then just sit there and listen to. Maybe listen to some more about it after you nod. Something like that. Instead, most people just ask me what I am talking about like it wasn't clear in the first place.

Maybe it's not. I don't know. It seems pretty clear to me. I'm enamored with rum. And I want to tell the world. Shout it from the mountaintops and all of that kind of stuff. It's a big part of my life. What's so hard to get about that?

We were at The Echo, which is attached to The Echoplex, at least as far as I can tell. I don't know if I have ever been to it, but I always just assumed that the whole thing was The Echoplex and The Echo was just a part of it. Maybe it was the other way around, and The Echo was the parent while The Echoplex was the child. Writing the word *echo* too many times makes it not look like a word. Echo. Echo. Echo. Echo. Ironic.

I was talking to some guy at the bar because apparently I had nothing better to do.

"Nothing. I just like rum a lot. I thought you were asking me what I was ordering because you heard that I called that specific rum for my drink."

"No. I was just asking."

"Got it."

This was going really well. I waited silently for the bartender to serve me my drink, and then I walked away as fast as I could. Booker and Pedro were talking to two girls who looked like they couldn't be old enough to get into a place serving alcohol. Or any place that wasn't a high school.

"Hey, man! Guess what?"

Pedro could be very giddy sometimes. It almost made him seem a little feminine.

"What's up?"

"These girls heard of us," he said. He nodded toward them as though I couldn't tell which girls he meant.

"Heard of who?" I asked.

"Tuba City," the girl closer to Booker said.

"They told you to say that, huh? That's good."

"No," the girl said. "I saw it on Twitter. My friend re-tweeted that you guys were going to be here."

"What the fuck does that mean?" I asked, not realizing that I didn't care until after it came out of my mouth. "Actually, never mind. I don't even want to know. So your friend knows about us?"

"Yeah," the other girl said.

She leaned over toward Pedro and smiled.

"We know what you're doing, and we think it's fucking awesome."

"You told them?"

"No," the girl replied for him. "Everybody knows."

I started to feel those pangs of panic that you feel when you think you're going to get in trouble for something you shouldn't have done.

"Everybody?"

"Yeah, what?" Booker asked.

"Well, not everybody. But everybody that read the tweets."

"The whats?"

Booker looked really confused, like an elderly woman using a laptop.

"Dude," I started. "Don't worry about it. It's like a promotional website or something. People are using it to talk about bands and movies and things. Right?"

"Uh, yeah. Sort of," the other girl said.

I don't remember which one said it, to be honest. One of them was the girl and the other one was the other girl, but neither of them really mattered all that much. They were entirely interchangeable as far as I was concerned.

"So everybody on this website knows what we're doing?"

"Yeah."

"What are we doing?" I asked.

Pedro looked at me and nodded like I was a mastermind criminal prosecutor or a detective. The girl rolled her eyes.

"Ah, that's helpful," I added.

"Whatever. We know that you're not a real band, but that you're pretending to be one so you can get free drinks and have some fun."

"Damn," Booker muttered. "This is on that webpage?"

"It's not just a *webpage*," one of the girls lashed back.

"Okay, chill. Whatever. It's on this Twitter thing?"

"Yep," they both said.

"Hmm."

I started to think about this, and I realized that we probably had nothing to worry about. Whether everybody was using this thing or if no one was, and whether our secret was out or if no one had a clue what we were doing, it didn't really matter. We weren't going to get in trouble for something that was publicly known, and we weren't going to get caught if no one knew. There might be some danger in that middle ground, but from what I could tell, this was all largely irrelevant.

"So, can I get you ladies some drinks then?"

They looked at each other and smiled.

"Finally!" one girl said to the other.

"Hey, I was going offer! We just didn't get to that part yet."

Pedro looked confused but realized that he was getting edged out of his relevance with these girls.

"We can *all* get them drinks," I said. "I just meant, can I, as the singer of Tuba City, head over to the bar and get them something to drink? On behalf of all of us. The band. Tuba City."

I paused for a moment and thought about it before continuing.

"You know, it may help me if you come with me and make it seem like I really am in a band. For the bartender, you know?"

"You really are in a band," one girl said.

"Yeah, you are," the other agreed.

"Right. Alright. Then let's go to the bar."

We walked over, and the girls were somewhat hanging all over me, which is not what I was expecting. They seemed too young for me to be too comfortable with it, so I just pretended in my own fake rock star way that they were fans that I couldn't be too bothered by. That seemed to work. Within moments of being up there, I was recognized as the singer of a band that was performing later. Recognized, of course, by one of the girls that I was with. Shortly after, people around us started listening and paying attention. These girls and their shrill voices made sure of it.

It wasn't more than a minute before the bartender felt obliged to give me something and to give it to me free of charge. There were people watching and listening to the interaction. People who suddenly got excited that I was there. Me. Blake Caldaro. The guy who had been there just a few minutes earlier and who got snubbed when trying to make some small talk about rum. *You've always had a thing for what?* Rum, motherfucker! Now get out of my way. I've got some free drinks to take away from here.

People are funny. They are so fickle and so concerned about things that they didn't care about moments before they decided that they cared about them. At their essence, most people just can't stop themselves from joining the bandwagon. On some psychological level, I think they need to be a part of the group. Even the people who say they don't. They do. They just refuse to admit it.

It's true that people generally *want* to be unique, to be considered original, to be independent. It's a part of their ethos. This is what it means to be a person in this modern world. You're a free thinker. An individual.

But they're not. Not usually. A friend of mine used to tell me that most people are sheep. Anatomically, this is not correct. I've checked. But metaphorically, I kind of get it. Yet, we all fight against the concept that we are so similar to someone else, or a group of someone elses. But in the end, what does it matter? We're designed to be very similar. Why is it a failure to live up to our design?

All of those people at the bar – all of the ones who were listening, paying attention, and feeding into the idea that this bartender needed to do something to recognize the otherwise unknown guy who suddenly became important – they are exactly what I am talking about. It's a sort of mass market approach to decision making. We don't form too many of our own opinions, but we don't need to. We just react to what someone else thinks. We don't realize that we do this because we like to think that we have our own original ideas. But this is how ninety-five-percent of our decisions are made. Like dominoes.

So whether I decided to walk back to Pedro and Booker or if I was subconsciously drawn back to them because of a popular opinion that I should, I can't say. But I did walk back, and I did have some free drinks in tow.

"No shit?" Booker asked when I got back.

"No shit, my good man," I replied.

I looked back at the bar, which wasn't more than twenty or thirty feet away, and I saw a few people talking and nodding over toward us. I realized that it if this thing started to gain momentum, we were going to have a hard time determining the difference between the people who legitimately knew that we were illegitimate and the people who illegitimately assumed we were legitimate. Not that that latter group was doing anything wrong. They just didn't know any better. They assumed that we were the real deal. And then there were other people who knew that we weren't, but they pretended that we were. It was going to be difficult to keep it all straight.

"What are you ladies doing after the show?" Booker asked.

"Probably homework," I answered.

They both scoffed.

"Homework is for people who care," one of the girls replied, clearly not understanding what I meant or why I said it.

"Jesus," Pedro mumbled.

He took a big sip of his drink. I followed him and did the same. A group of guys walked by and raised their cups to us, like a salute. Again, I couldn't tell if they thought that we were a real band or if they had been reading these apparently effective tweets that Maria had written and they were helping the cause. I suppose that in the end, it didn't matter. We were just there for the free shit. Staying in character was to our benefit.

The night took an interesting turn after the first band left the stage. I couldn't tell if it was just my paranoia or maybe the alcohol or maybe both, but it felt like there were a lot of people watching us. Wondering why we were still in the crowd. Maybe wondering when we were going on stage. It started to feel like the right time to get out of there. That isn't what happened, of course, because Pedro and Booker were intent on milking every last drop out of this rather than just walking away when it was still going well. They were not the types to retire like one of those athletes who hangs it all up at his peak. Barry Sanders, they were not. They were more like Brett Favre, wringing the thing dry and then wringing it some more until they damn near ripped it apart. And then texting some dick pics to seal the deal.

"When do you want to go up on stage?" Pedro asked Booker, and I overheard.

"No, no, no," I started.

Booker put his finger up to my lips like I was a child. I kissed it. He still held it there, unfazed.

"Hang on now, man. This is what the people here are expecting."

"No, it's not. They are expecting a real band."

"Are you sure about that?" he asked. "They are all looking at us. The people at the bar are all getting us free drinks. The girls in the crowd are all eye-fucking us. We are supposed to go up there and entertain them."

"Or we could just walk out the door and go to another bar and enjoy the fact that we got what we came here for?"

"What was that?" Pedro asked. "Just to get drunk?"

"Yeah. I mean, no. It wasn't just to get drunk. We had a good time, right?"

"It's not over yet," Booker stated. "We have to go up there."

Pedro turned to me and wagged his finger.

"Remember what we talked about earlier."

The bastard. He knew that I was feeling very sensitive that day. I was afraid of my mortality, and he just called me out on it.

"Ahh," was all I could say.

"I'll go ask someone where the loading area is," Booker shouted and walked away.

He came back way sooner than I had expected.

"You change your mind?" I asked with hope.

"It's over there."

He pointed toward a door off to the side of the stage. Obviously.

"Fuck."

Pedro smiled and slapped me on the back as we started to weave between the people in the crowd and over toward the wall.

"I hope you've been practicing lyrics," he said.

"Oh yeah. All day."

"Good!"

We walked out back, and sure enough, there was a bunch of gear just sitting there. Like someone had planted it there for us to take.

"Man!" Booker yelled. "It's like that girl Maria just tweeted all of this here, or however that works!"

"I don't think it works that way," I said, but I had no idea how it did actually work.

"I think there are already drums up on the stage," Pedro said.

"Yep, there are. But what happens when this band comes over and they want their instruments and they realize we're taking them on stage?"

"Well, hold on," Booker paused, looking at the stickers on the gear. "I don't think these are for the next band anyway. Yeah. They are for the one after."

"Okay. So then the next band…they are probably getting ready to go on?"

"No, that's us. That's what we're doing."

"Thanks, Pedro. I get that. I meant the actual other band."

"That's us," he repeated.

"Okay. Fine. That's us. But remind me, guys. Why are we doing this? We could have continued to get some more free drinks. All those people were totally buying into it, whether they knew or they didn't know. But now we're going to go on stage and ruin all of that and get ourselves kicked out?"

"That's the idea, yeah."

"Why?"

It didn't make sense to me. The good thing was going to end, but we were going to be the ones ending it. It seemed stupid and counter-productive.

"Because that's what this is," Booker yelled emphatically, slamming the guitar that he was holding down on the floor. "This is about us being something. Whether or not that is real, we still have to go through with it. We can't just walk away from it."

"Why?"

"Because that's not what this is. This is something else."

Plainly stated.

"I'm too drunk for this," Pedro blurted as he walked out on the stage with a guitar, just like at the Marquis.

We didn't have a choice but to follow him, but first I wanted to get one thing clear with Booker.

"This isn't a thing."

He looked at me without a smile or a flinch. He stared at me for a few seconds before opening his mouth.

"You're wrong," was all he said.

He walked out on the stage with a guitar. I looked around for a tambourine, but I couldn't find one, so I went out there with nothing.

The crowd was a mix of mostly young people and a few older-looking hippies on the fringe and the edges of the room. People started to take notice that we were up there. The lights hadn't dimmed because of course we weren't at all coordinated with the light guys or whoever usually does that stuff. People in the crowd, though, they started to cheer and wallop and make weird, encouraging noises. A lot of them were looking directly at us. It was almost intimidating, knowing that in a few moments we were going to significantly disappoint them with our lack of musical talent. I took some confidence in knowing that people were out there expecting an utter failure. In fact, they were looking forward to it. But they were by far the minority. The rest of the crowd was just going to hate the hell out of us.

"Check, check," I said flatly into the microphone.

I wanted to get a sense for the volume. The last band seemed very over-modulated. My voice sounded okay to me though, so I continued a little louder.

"Check, check, check mate."

I looked back to the sound board, and the mixing guy looked at me like he was watching a ghost. I turned away. The realization that he was there made me nervous.

"Check one, check two, check three, check four. Check your woman on the floor!"

I looked back at the guys, and they were both ready. But I had no plan. I didn't know how to start this whole thing off. The last time we played, if you could call it that, I was so surprised by how terrible we sounded. I was really expecting that we'd be better, that we'd at least sound something like music. It was going to be hard to get into this, knowing how bad it was going to be.

"Check book!" I yelled. "Travelers cheque!" I shouted.

I made sure to pronounce it with a Q-U-E at the end of it. The crowd appreciated that.

"Check-in McNugget! Checks in the mail! Anton Chekhov!"

I had been thinking of these earlier in the day, but they were hard to come up with on the spot. I was pausing for a few seconds in between each shout, but the crowd was engaged somehow. I decided it was time.

"What's up, everybody?!"

The crowd gave a mild type of roar. I always hated it when bands or performers tried to get the crowd to make more noise. It seems too desperate. I refused to do it.

"We're a band from right here in Los Angeles. Have any of you heard of us before?"

The crowd didn't really make much noise. I realized where I had gone wrong.

"Our name would help, wouldn't it? We're Tuba City! From right here in sunny fucking L.A.! Anyone out there heard of us before?"

There was a huge cheer from the crowd, or at least it sounded way bigger than I was expecting. I was floored. Those riding on the bandwagon and those pretending all got on the same page, and they cheered for us.

Us. A trio of nobodies.

Someone in the crowd yelled loud enough for me to hear.

"Where are your tubas?"

He had a good point.

"We left them at home! We'll bring them next time!"

The crowd cheered again.

"Well, fuck yeah then! You guys ready?"

I turned back to Booker, who looked as serious as he did when he went out to the stage. Pedro was holding his drum sticks high above his head like he was under arrest.

"Then here we go! L.A., you are in for a motherfucking explosion of noise like you've never heard before. Let's go!"

I looked back at Pedro, and he did the drum stick count off.

One, two, three, four. And noise. And then more noise. And then shouting. And then booing. It was hysterical. I wasn't nearly as drunk as I was when we were in Denver earlier in the week, but I was lit enough to not care again as soon as we began. It lasted all of twenty or thirty seconds before Pedro gave up and ran off the stage and toward the side door.

Thirty seconds is a long time for a cacophony.

I kept yelling whatever the hell nonsense I was yelling. Booker threw his guitar down and followed Pedro. I stayed on stage, maybe too long, and then ran off after I no longer saw either of them. There was no way I was getting stuck up there by myself with that mic and nothing else. Fuck no.

As I was stumbling toward the door, I saw security finally start to make some moves toward us, so I hurried away and scooted out the back. To this day I still don't understand why there wasn't somebody closer to the stage who could have stopped us. Or at the Marquis, for that matter. It all seemed way too easy. Like when you accidentally sneak some liquids onto a plane and you find out after. It makes you question the idea of security in general. What are they actually doing? Did our performance seem normal enough for them to not budge? That would be a sad testament to the music scene that we have created, but maybe that's all there is to it.

I don't remember how we got out into the street or back to the truck, but thank fucking God we did. I started the engine before I think my ass was even fully on the seat. We sped off and up the road, much more intuitively than our sprint out of the Marquis and into the Denver streets. I had a general idea of where we were and which direction we wanted to head. It really didn't matter anyway. We just needed to get away as fast as we could. We laughed and shouted and whooped like we had done so many times already in the truck. Our beautiful, beautiful truck.

We drove for a couple of miles and stopped off at a bar that Booker and I used to drink at during the summer after we got out of high school. We each had a fake I.D., and this place barely gave a shit enough to check them.

They had a decent selection of rum behind the bar. I was very excited, so I chose something that I hadn't seen before. I ordered three of them even though it was pretty expensive for someone like me, a guy with no job and no real source of income. But, I figured that a night of free drinks was worth celebrating. With some drinks.

"Where are we playing tomorrow?" Pedro asked as we waited for the bartender to finish pouring.

"How about the El Rey?" Booker suggested.

Our drinks arrived, and we all cheers'd.

"That place doesn't really have a great bar. Also, they are kind of legit."

"The Echo is legit. I like The Echo."

"Yeah, that's not what I mean. I just can't imagine the El Rey letting us get away with this."

"Good point."

He rubbed his chin like a stereotypical man in thought.

"How about the Fonda? Same thing?"

"Yeah. Kind of intimidating. I love that place too."

"Yeah," he said.

We both stared forward. I was thinking about a solo acoustic show that I saw there once. The show ended with the singer getting the crowd to split into two groups, with the left side of the room singing one part of the chorus and the right side singing another. It resulted in this really trippy, syncopated melody, and it turned out sounding really good. Now, every time that I hear that song, I think of that performance and how we all helped finish it off. That's what I was thinking about. I don't know what Booker was thinking about. I only have access to my own brain.

"This is nice, guys. Real nice. What other places do you want to reminisce about?"

Pedro was smiling when he said this. He was almost always smiling. He almost always looked drunk too. They went hand in hand.

"Sorry, man. It's hard to think about places in L.A. in this context."

"Whatever. Just pick another place," he said.

"I think we are aiming too high. To be honest."

"Yes. Be honest," Pedro repeated.

"I think we are. I think The Echo was too big. There's no way we should have been able to do that. That is a legit place. What the fuck were we thinking?"

"It worked, didn't it?" Pedro asked.

Booker nodded.

"It was a fluke."

"No, it wasn't. How can you say that?"

Pedro didn't really know what he was talking about, and I knew that I was right. Booker kept nodding.

"Blake's right. That was not supposed to happen. Their security fucked up, or something. They have way too many shows for this to not have happened before."

What he said made me wonder if this was something that had, in fact, happened before. It never crossed my mind. By that time, I had been to maybe a hundred shows in my life. I think that's a good sample. And I'd never seen a rogue, fake band just take the stage and pretend to perform. Not even at a smaller venue. It just didn't happen.

"Do you think that we were able to get up on stage because the security was just that bad? Or was it because no one had ever had the balls to try it before?"

"Maybe both," Booker replied. "Either way, I think you're right. We can't continue to do this. Not even at a smaller place like the Hotel Café or something."

"I like that place too," I added.

"Yeah. Me too."

"Very nice, guys. *Where* are we going?" Pedro demanded, in his jokey, happy sort of way.

"I think we could do any of these places, but we can't get back on stage. We've got to avoid that from happening again."

"I like that part," Pedro mumbled.

"It isn't the point though, is it?"

"What do you mean?"

"Well," I said. "Tuba City should be the best band in the world that you never, ever hear. Because obviously, we have no talent. We have no musical instruments. And we have no songs. We have no business being up on stage."

It was a sobering thought for our drunk minds.

"But that doesn't really matter. Because Tuba City is all about the experience *before* the performance. We should never be around to actually perform. What we did tonight was reckless."

"Wise words, oh drunken master," Booker mocked. "But you are right."

"We got carried away. All of the hyping it up and the drinks and the girls, that's what this is about. It's the access that we want, right? Not the actual performance. Because we can't actually perform. We suck. Like we are legitimately terrible."

They were both nodding now.

"In fact," I continued, "by us going on stage, we might be calling too much attention to ourselves…and all for something that we don't even really care about. We care about the booze and the girls. Right?"

"Right."

"I like the stage part," Pedro insisted.

"What do you like more? The stage part or the free booze and blowjob part?"

"Alright," he said.

"So let's focus on that. And let's do our best to avoid ever getting put in the position we got stuck with in Denver."

"Tonight shouldn't have happened," Booker confirmed. "We got really lucky."

"We did. So let's agree to not get up on stage again unless we *absolutely* have to. Okay?"

We all agreed. Then we all began to drink our drinks and talk a little more loosely about the night. Even though we said we weren't going to do it again, it was still exciting to talk about it. We did, after all, just get up on a stage in front of a decent-sized crowd and embarrass the hell out of ourselves. It was a good story. We just couldn't tell anyone about it.

"What if we get forced to go back up on stage?" Pedro postulated. "There's got to be a better way to get out of it, right?"

"Can't we just run away?" Booker asked.

"I'm sure we could. But isn't there a better way, maybe?"

They both thought about it for a little while and came up with nothing. I had something in mind, but it seemed like too much of a stretch. I was getting pretty drunk, so I threw it out there anyway.

"What if one of us pretends to have a seizure while we were up there?"

Pedro started laughing. A lot.

"Like that girl, like your new girlfriend?"

"Yes, you dick. Like a person who has real seizures."

"Whoa, Blake. Don't get so defensive over your new girlfriend."

"Fuck you, Booker, and fuck you both. She's not my new girlfriend."

"Uh huh. Sounds like you just got upset that we made fun of her seizures. Your new girlfriend's seizures."

"No," I said. "It's just not cool to make fun of people who have seizures. That's fucked up."

"It was your idea to pretend to have one on a stage in front of people. Isn't that fucked up?"

"Yes. But that's not malicious."

"Oh. Well, pardon me. Your fake seizure is all good. But my comparison to a real seizure, which was only mentioned because you came up with the idea of faking one in the first place, mine is not okay. Is that right?"

"That's right."

"How does that make sense?" Booker asked.

"Because you're a dick. And I am not."

"Fuck you, Blake."

"Fuck you too, Booker."

"Fuck you guys," Pedro added.

We all cheers'd.

"And fuck your new girlfriend too," Booker threw in.

I punched him on his non-drinking arm while he cackled an annoying laugh just to get under my skin.

"Hey, her tweets are what got us all of our free drinks tonight, don't forget that. So give it a rest. We have her to thank for all of this."

"I don't want to hear about her tweets, dude. That's your girlfriend. Keep them to yourself."

"Fuck you again, Booker."

"Fuck you too, Blake."

"Fucking fuck, dudes. Can we talk about something else? Like where the *fuck* we are going tomorrow?"

"Oh, right."

We all thought for a bit, though I don't know what Pedro was thinking about because again, I can't read minds. But since he didn't know any places in the area, I could only assume that he wasn't thinking about much.

"How about that guitar shop in Venice? That's a cool little spot. Super low key."

"McCabe's?" I asked.

"Yeah."

"That's in Santa Monica."

"Jesus, guys. Come on."

"Just saying. It's not in Venice. It is pretty cool though."

"Really small."

"Yeah. Do they have a bar?"

"I don't remember."

"Fucking Christ! What is wrong with you guys?"

"I think they only have shows on the weekends," I added, ignoring Pedro's outburst.

"What? This is how we make decisions," Booker explained.

"Yeah. Chill out, dude."

"Jesus."

"You say that a lot."

"You make me say it a lot."

"Touché. Anyway, Booker, you brought up the Hotel Café before. That sounds like a good place for us. I think they have shows almost every night of the week. I think."

"Indie Hollywood bitches will be all over us."

"There we go," Pedro said, a little more cheery than his last few additions to the conversation. "Now we are talking."

"We've been talking this whole time," I noted.

"Fuck you, Blake."

"Fuck you too, Pedro."

The bartender was wisely at the other end of the bar, ignoring our terrible conversation and probably thinking about something more interesting. Or maybe not. I have no idea. Like I said, I can't read minds or anything like that.

Twenty

I've always had a thing for rum. Just like I told that girl with the whatever eyes in Mexico, and just like I tell everybody else who will listen, which is usually nobody. It's been me and rum, and rum and me, for as long as I can remember. I like it that way. Maybe one day, people of the world will appreciate rum as much as I do. Maybe they'll get over the Johnny Blues and the Macallan 25s and the whatever elses out there that other people salivate over.

Or maybe not.

I don't care. This isn't supposed to be the start of some social movement. I don't say that I've always had a thing for rum because I want people to agree with me. Nothing about what I like is any better than what somebody else likes. I mean, I *personally* think it is, of course. But that's not the point. The point is that I have been infatuated with rum since I first knew what it was. This book is but a chapter in the story of our love. I've always had a thing for rum, and I always will. If the state of California would let me marry it…I wouldn't. Because I have a thing for girls too. A man can love more than one thing, you know.

I like to carry around a flask. I feel that it makes me look distinguished, like I'm a gentleman. Some of that class goes away when I reveal that on my flask is a hand-painted silhouette of a devil dancing in front of flames, holding a pitchfork and smiling. That does make me lose some of the class. But most of it remains, because like I said, a flask is a distinguished accessory.

I also like to keep another flask in the center console of my car. That's probably not good for the quality of the rum that I keep in there, but it is good for the ease of access that I have whenever I am away from home and I forget my carrying flask. I usually keep Cuban rum in the one in the car. Because I don't think it's enough to illegally store alcohol in my car, I also need it to be from an embargoed state. I'm pretty sure that when you double down on the risk, it effectively neutralizes it. Two negatives make a positive. I learned that years ago.

The next night at the Hotel Café was much more subdued than our time at The Echo. The venue itself is low key and a lot smaller too. It is basically one medium-sized room with a bar in one corner, a door that may or may not be permanently closed, some bathrooms, and a stage, all in the other corners. The lighting is very dim and the bartenders are a little too cool for their own good. But not in that moustache-wearing way that bartenders are too cool today. In a 2007 kind of way. Whatever that was. I can't remember.

Maria had called me earlier that day and asked me how the show had gone the night before. She kept talking about the Twitter account and how many people were tweeting and re-tweeting and whatever else people do on there. She made it seem like it was going well. She sounded happy about it, so I let her be happy about it.

"Where are you guys playing tonight?" she asked, so committed to the idea that I really couldn't tell if she knew we weren't a real band.

"We decided last night that the Hotel Café would be a good place for us tonight," I said.

"I've never been there."

"It's decent," I explained. "But it's not like the other places we've been going. It's more of a folksy, indie kind of place."

"Ohh," was all she said.

"It looks like the kind of place that someone big is going to get discovered at."

"Really?" she asked.

"No, not really. It is way too small. No one big would ever come from there."

"You guys are going to be big one day."

"I hope not," I said.

"Me too," she said.

Maria agreed to tweet more about our performance that night if I agreed that I wouldn't forget her if we did become a big act one day. I felt comfortable agreeing to that, considering that the whole point of the band was to not ever be big, or to ever even be real. The very idea of calling it a band was starting to grow on me, even though all we had amounted to so far was a pair of embarrassingly brief moments on stage where we proved that we had no musical talent in any part of our bodies. Those moments – and the flock of people that had started to pay attention to us – those were our accomplishments. It was probably more than I could say for the rest of my life up until that point.

When we got to the Hotel Café, Pedro was in a fairly somber mood. I couldn't figure out why, and I don't think I ever figured it out. I asked Booker if he noticed. He didn't. Booker never noticed anything like that. He was about as much of a dude as you could be when it came to feelings. They were just not a part of his general take on life. Only in rare instances did some empathy poke its head out. Maybe just to get some air.

We decided to leave the truck behind for the night. Something about it felt wrong, but my argument had been that there was no real reason for us to roll up to such a small venue with such a big vehicle. I had been getting nervous about taking it everywhere we went. It was, after all, still a stolen truck from another country. There were moments during that time where I had some common sense. But much like Booker's empathy, they were brief moments. This night was the only night from when we first took it out to Phoenix until the final night that we had to give it up that we didn't use it in one way or another.

If it wasn't raining that night, it was raining another time I went to the Hotel Café. Either way, I can describe what it is like when it rains and you are going to that venue. It is wet. There is an overhang alongside the building where people smoke cigarettes and do whatever else people do outside of music venues. The entrance actually faces an alley and not a main street, adding to some of the allure of the place. It feels really intimate, like you weren't even supposed to know that it was there. I would imagine that a lot of people don't know about it, nor do they know who they're going to see when they do show up. It has a spontaneity that you can feel when you walk up.

It didn't seem like it that night when we walked in. At the bar were a couple of faces that looked familiar but that I didn't actually recognize. Like I had seen them before, but I didn't know who they were. It turned out that was exactly what was happening. The crowd was a decent size for a Monday, maybe forty or fifty people. Of that, I think that maybe ten or fifteen were from The Echo the night before. At first it seemed like a coincidence. Music heads tend to travel in packs. I rarely ran to consecutive shows, but I assumed that there was a revolving crowd that you'd begin to recognize the more often you went out.

As we went up to the bar to get a drink, I made eye contact with a guy who gave me a very knowing head nod. I nodded back. Then I looked at Booker, who shrugged.

The guy leaned over and said something to the bartender. The bartender looked our way and then looked back at the guy. Then he walked away and poured someone else a drink. I later found out that the guy had tried to tell the bartender that we were in a band, but the bartender didn't seem to give a shit. That reaction made sense, in actuality, but at the time I felt like our mojo was gone, and it was because we didn't have the truck. I was filling with regret. When the bartender came by, I ordered a drink. He poured it for me and then asked me if I wanted to open a tab or pay cash. Like I was a mere mortal.

I said *cash.* I was reaching in my wallet to pay when another guy, a different one, pushed the hand that was holding my wallet down and told me not to worry, that it was on him. He then nodded to the bartender and said the same thing. *On me*, he said, more or less. The bartender looked at me and then back at the guy, and then he walked away again to help someone else.

"He's always a dick," the guy said to me.

"That's good to know."

"You're not paying for a drink tonight, don't worry, man," he reassured me.

I didn't feel so assured. But then again, who the fuck was this guy?

"So what's going on?" I asked him, awkwardly.

"Beats me," the guy said.

He was probably my age, but he was dressed much better than I was, like he was going to be somebody one day. It reminded me that I was probably going to continue to be a nobody.

"Cool."

"I dig what you guys are doing," he said, not quietly.

"Right on. Thanks."

I looked around for Booker and Pedro, but they were too far away for me to bring them over and create a diversion. I wanted to walk away.

"I've got some buddies down in San Diego who were up here last night at The Echo. We all saw you guys."

"Oh yeah."

I didn't know what else to say.

"One of them had heard about you guys on the Internet."

"On Twitter?" I asked.

"I don't know. Whatever. He said that you guys were going to do something like what you did."

"Yeah. We're not very good," I said.

"You should have seen security afterwards."

"Oh?"

"They were fucking flipping out. Some of those guys looked like they were just stunned. Some of the other ones looked like they saw the whole thing happening but just couldn't do anything about it. It was funny as hell."

"We got the fuck out of there as soon as we could," I admitted.

"Makes sense. You should have seen it though. The crowd was cheering for you guys. I mean, not all of it. Shit. Actually, most of it wasn't. But there was a group of maybe, I don't know, maybe like this size here," he said, waving around at the crowd at the Hotel Café. "And they were all chanting *Tu-ba! Tu-ba! Tu-ba! Tu-ba!*"

"No shit?"

"Yeah. My buddies were joining in. It was funny as hell."

"That's what we're here for, I guess."

I was feeling very humble. It seemed unreal to me – a crowd of people chanting for a bunch of no ones. For us. We didn't even have our own instruments, let alone our own tubas. We wouldn't even know how to play them if we had them.

"My friend who had first heard about you text me today and told me you were gonna be here, said he saw it online. So I figured, what the fuck, why not come out and see it again?"

"Oh," I said. "We're not going to go on stage tonight."

I expected him to look disappointed, but he just nodded.

"Yeah. It's too small here. You'd get killed."

"I don't even think that door back there opens either."

"I think it does."

"I don't think so."

"I think it does," he repeated.

"Thanks for the drink, man. I'm gonna go find my friends."

"No problem."

I went over to Booker and Pedro and asked them why they didn't come over and bail me out.

"We thought you knew that guy," Pedro explained.

"What? Booker, you know I don't know that guy. Come on."

"Whatever, man. I didn't want to get in the middle of that gayfest that you had going on."

"He wasn't gay. He knows about our band. He was at The Echo last night. He bought me this drink to say thank you for the good time last night."

"Sounds gay to me," Booker muttered.

"No shit?" Pedro asked.

"That's exactly what I said. Also, fuck you, Booker."

Someone went up to the mic on the stage and started to introduce the next act. We stopped talking and started listening, but that didn't last long. Another guy came over and started talking to Booker. I tried to catch his eye a few times, glad that I wasn't the only one who could get stuck in a potentially homosexual conversation, but he refused to look at me. He probably knew that I'd be staring his way.

Free drinks kept on coming. Every time I went up to the bar, somebody came over and bought me one before I could order, or at the very least, before I could pay. I was starting to think that we were going to have to go up on that stage just to give them what they were hoping to see, but every time I explained that we weren't going to, all I got was an agreeing face nodding along to my explanation. I remember wondering what Maria had posted online. Everybody seemed to be on the same page, like buying us drinks was a part of some bigger thing, but we didn't know what that thing was. It was an uneasy feeling, but one that faded away the longer it carried on.

The first guy who bought me a drink was talking to Booker when they pulled me in to join the conversation.

"He thinks we should go down to San Diego later this week," Booker blurted out.

He was looking pretty sloppy.

"Why don't we?"

"What's in San Diego?" I asked.

"I've got these buddies down there," he replied.

"Yeah, you said that before. That's cool. I think we're probably okay in L.A. for now though. We've been traveling a lot lately."

Booker waved me off like I had no idea what I was talking about. The guy then went on to tell us why he was pushing so hard for San Diego. He seemed to think that we had a big following down there already. The conversation started to feel a little too surreal, so I walked away and sat down at a table with my drink. We weren't a real band. There was no way that we could have a real following in a real city. This guy was an idiot.

I had both of my hands wrapped around my glass when a couple of girls came over and started to chat with me. They said they knew that I was the singer in a band and that they really liked singers. I kept my hands pressed on my glass, like they were going to steal it away from me if I loosened up.

"Everybody likes singers," I said. "So what?"

"So," one of the girls said. "That means that we really like you."

"Uh huh."

One of the girls kissed me on the cheek. I didn't move. I wasn't accepting that this was happening. The other girl started to rub my leg under the table. Then the one who had kissed my cheek leaned back over and started to kiss my ear. I suddenly perked up.

I had a girlfriend in high school that used to start to kiss my ear right before she was going to go down on me. I don't know why or how that started, but she would do it every time. It got to the point where even after we broke up, I would get really turned on by the feeling or sound of a girl kissing my ear. I couldn't help it. It triggered thoughts in my head that I was going to get something that the girl most likely was not planning on giving. It was a terrible response to have, but I had no way of avoiding it.

"You like singers?" I asked.

"Yeah, we both do," the girl kissing my ear said.

The other girl was still rubbing my leg. I was getting annoyed that it was just my leg, but I knew that I had no right to expect anything else. A minute earlier, I had never met them before. Neither of them knew about the stimulus effect that the one girl was having on my ears. For all they knew, they were just being cute or whores or whatever they were trying to do.

"Where are you from?" I asked.

"South Bay," the ear girl whispered.

"Do you want to go to San Diego later this week to watch us perform?" I asked.

I figured what the hell, why not.

"What day?" the girl asked into my ear as she bit down slightly. The biting didn't do it for me, but she didn't know that. The other girl ran her hand all the way up my leg and brushed against my dick. She didn't care for the small talk. I didn't care that she didn't care.

"I don't know yet. It'll be on Twitter."

"On what?" the girl rubbing my leg and now the head of my penis asked me.

"Twitter. Look it up."

I turned my head so that the other girl's mouth was away from my ear, and I looked into her eyes. She was very pretty. But blonde. Not my type.

I got up from the table and took my glass along with me as I walked toward the stage. I felt like I was bulging out of my pants. With all of that ear play, I had to focus on something else or I was going to lose control. It had been a while. For some strange reason, I wasn't interested in whatever those girls seemed like they wanted to do. I didn't trust them. But I did want to use them to build an audience.

I was obviously pretty drunk. Under normal circumstances, I wouldn't turn down a girl for just about anything. Let alone two girls, if that's what they were suggesting. I couldn't tell. It was a weird night, and I was still trying to accept the idea that this was all happening. I went outside and hung out with the cigarette smokers under the awning for a while. A few of them gave me knowing nods, and I nodded back. I was polite, but I didn't engage in any conversation. I was having a hard time understanding what I was supposed to be doing.

Booker and Pedro didn't seem to be very concerned. No surprise there. They were walking around, talking to whoever would listen. By the end of the night, they were convinced that we were going to have a crowd of people driving down from L.A. to go to a show at an unplanned venue in San Diego some time later in the week. A venue that, according to some well-dressed guy that we had just met, would also have a bunch of our San Diego fans. Our San Diego fans. What fucking San Diego fans?

Just a week earlier, we drove the truck to Denver to see what the city was all about. To humor a drunk girl who wouldn't leave us alone at a bar, we pretended we were in a band. A random guy at the bar pretended he was in the band too. We then decided to continuously pretend that we were in a band. The random guy came along with us and left Denver almost as soon as he had gotten there. And now, just a week had passed and we were talking about a trip down to San Diego to go meet our growing fan base, a fan base that supposedly spread using something on the Internet that none of us had ever heard of. That thing, by the way, was being handled by the same drunk girl that we were lying to back in the Denver bar in the first place.

The details continued to run through my head for the rest of the night. Seven days seemed too short of a time for something like this to have happened. Granted, we were talking about a handful of people in a small L.A. venue that seemed to recognize us. It's not like we were selling out arenas or signing with a major label. But we were getting some of the perks that I assumed came with being a legitimate act. The free drinks kept coming. There were girls – more of them than I had ever seen Booker have luck with, for sure – and there were dudes who liked us too. And these dudes were not cockblocking or being douche bags about it at all.

People were recognizing us. I had lived in the same city for over twenty years, and no one had ever recognized me anywhere that I went. And now, suddenly, because of one little thing that we did while we were driving around a stolen truck through the middle of the country, I was a guy getting his dick rubbed by a strange girl in a venue that I'd been to maybe a dozen times. No one had ever rubbed my dick there before. What had changed?

Seven days. I just kept thinking about those seven days. Were we geniuses? Or was it just dumb luck? And more importantly, wasn't this whole thing just going to completely blow up in our faces?

"Seven days," I mumbled as we walked back to the truck after the show had ended.

"You're a mopey bitch tonight, huh, man?" Booker asked, meaning to sound concerned, in his own way.

"I just don't get how this is happening," I said.

"Who cares?"

"I care, man," I replied. "It doesn't make sense to me."

"Who cares?" Pedro repeated.

"I said I care?"

It came out as a question, but I didn't mean for it to.

"Right."

I really couldn't figure him out. He was a weird guy.

"Anyway," Booker continued. "We need to talk to your girlfriend and get her to tell the Internet that we're going to San Diego later this week."

"Uh huh."

"We should do it later in the week though. Let's maybe try somewhere on the Westside before we go all the way down there."

"Let's bring the truck," I said.

"Is that why you're being so mopey?"

"Maybe."

"Who cares?" Pedro asked.

"You're so fucking weird," I said.

I looked him right in the eyes after I said it. He smiled.

"Who cares," he said.

The next day, Maria called me again and helped me pick out a place for us to go that night. We chose Temple Bar, which is now something entirely different. I think was just a closed-down business for a while. It used to be one of my favorite places to go. It was about as eclectic as a place in L.A. can get without boasting about how eclectic it is. They had a pretty good selection of rum too, which was really all they needed for me to care about them. I was also impressed that Maria had even heard of the place. For someone who had been to L.A. what seemed like one time, ever, she sure as hell knew a lot of venues in the area.

Maybe she did her research on the Internet and she knew nothing about them from her own personal experience. It seems like something you could do and get away with it. I don't know though. She seemed authentic to me. I really couldn't tell, but I also didn't care. The fact that she chose Temple Bar was good enough. If it was the Internet or her brain that told her to suggest that place, it really didn't matter to me. It was a good suggestion either way.

Booker and Pedro spent the day together while I hung out at home and took care of a few things in my life. My actual life, that is, where I had a bedroom at my parents' house and a car in the driveway and all of those regular things that people generally have. Most notably, I had to do some laundry. Wearing the same clothes for almost a week was a nice, little experience that I could check off on some list later in life, but it was beginning to bother me. I'm sure it was bothering the people around me too. I also had to get some of my demons out, as I had been running on full for over a week and those girls from the night before kept running through my head.

In the sober light of the next day, I started to question why I didn't let those girls continue on and see where it led. There was a part of me that knew why I didn't, but I couldn't understand or acknowledge that just yet. It didn't matter anyway. I had to get all of those hormones and whatever else was floating around in there out of my system. Maybe twice, even. And there was no way I was doing that while hanging out with Booker. Somehow he always knew when I wanted to jerk off. And then it made me feel weird knowing that he knew. I wanted to preempt that and just deal with it while I had some time to myself, even though he probably knew that's part of why I wanted to have some time to myself that day anyway.

Just in case there was a chance for me to not waste all of that good energy on a couple of unappreciative Kleenex, I texted Harper to see what she was up to. I waited patiently for another five minutes. After not hearing from her, I got on with it and took care of myself. It was a utility jerk, nothing more. There was no romance, enjoyment, or fun to any of it. I just had to clear it out. I felt much better afterwards, with only a slight hint of regret that lingered for a minute or two.

That night at the Temple Bar was very much like the night before at the Hotel Café. A few people that we had now seen for the third consecutive night were there. It made me start to wonder if they had any other life other than going out and seeing shows. Then again, I had no right to question the value of other people's lives, so I let it go. I didn't see those two whores from the night before. I felt okay about that, as that would have made me somewhat nervous. The guy with the San Diego friends was there, and he bought me a drink again. This time, he assured me that he was not gay and that this was all part of what Tuba City was starting to mean. I didn't know what he meant by that, but I decided to relax a bit. If a guy wanted to buy me a drink, I wasn't going to stop him. Free is free.

We got pretty good at playing the part of a band that wasn't actually performing at the venue that night. For the second night in a row, I watched as Pedro and Booker wandered around the crowd, talking happily with what seemed like lots of interested people and potential fans of ours that we didn't even know we had. There was a buzz going around the crowd, and it all seemed to focus on us. When someone would ask if we were playing that night and we told them that we weren't, some people would nod and smile, and some people would look disappointed. When we told them about our show in San Diego, they all perked up. It was starting to feel less weird and a little more regular.

We were a band, maybe. Sort of. Maybe. Or at least there were people who thought that we were. And there were other people who knew that we weren't but pretended that we were. That all had to count for something, even if it was just free booze and attention. There could be worse things in life than getting that on a regular basis.

I decided that maybe San Diego was a good idea after all. I was in the bathroom and standing at the urinal when I decided to text Maria to see what she thought about it. It was the perfect place to initiate a conversation away from the guys. She said that she thought it was a great idea. She had some venue ideas again, but I hadn't heard of any of them before.

I wasn't too familiar with the city even though I grew up just a couple of hours away. I didn't really like it, to be honest. It was too perfect-feeling. I liked L.A., full of its flaws and mistakes, its scratches and cuts. For a city that has the stereotype of being so plastic and superficial, if you've ever spent any time in L.A., you realize right away that it has an underbelly. San Diego, on the other hand, is like a big, perfect breast implant. You can't really dislike it, objectively speaking, but at the same time, it's hard to tell what there is to like about it. If perfection is your thing, then San Diego is probably pretty nice, I guess.

I went back out to the bar to get another drink. I stood alongside the far end, somewhat near the back of the venue. I looked around for Pedro and Booker, but I couldn't see them anywhere. My phone vibrated. It was Maria again. She was going to start tweeting about our show in San Diego. She said that we had over a hundred followers now. That sounded like a lot to me. I had never had a hundred of anything.

I put my phone back in my pocket and looked up. The bartender saw me from across the room. He gave me a pretty big thumbs up. It looked a little odd. Then he held up his finger to ask me to wait a moment. I was already waiting, so that didn't seem to me like it was going to be a problem. When he was finished with whatever he was doing, he came over and apologized for the wait.

"No problem," I said.

"We just always try to serve the artists before the rest of the crowd," he said somewhat quietly, but loud enough so that I could hear him.

"I see."

"So what can I get you?" he asked as he smiled, opening both of his hands in front of his chest as if to reveal a hidden treasure. "We've got it all."

"I've always had a thing for rum," I told him.

"Oh yeah?" he said.

Twenty-One

I knew we were getting somewhat close to San Diego when I saw those two white, half-dome looking things along the coastline, sometime after Orange County ended. I remember people saying that they looked like breasts. I didn't think they did, or at least not very much like the breasts that I've seen. If I ever see a pair that look like those two buildings, I might have to seriously question my taste in women.

Rather than spend the night in the truck, I had made plans to stay with some friends of mine who lived in north San Diego County. I get that the county is pretty big, like Los Angeles, but I never understood why the people there make it a point to call out the fact that there is San Diego proper and then the North County. I guess it's not much unlike L.A. and the valley. Something about it insinuates that it is lesser than the rest of the area. That's kind of unfortunate. I'm sure it's just fine, but I don't live in San Diego, so I don't know if that's true. For the record, the San Fernando Valley is just fine too. I lived there at one point in my life. It's not for everyone. It's not for me. But it's just fine.

My friends in North County actually lived pretty far east and away from the ocean. San Diego without the ocean is not what you think of when you think of San Diego. It's more like the rest of California. It's not that sexy or exciting. They lived on an avocado farm. Really. I didn't realize until they moved there that people like me or my friends could actually live on a functioning avocado farm, but apparently they can.

My friend's dad bought the property as an investment, and he let his son live there. In return, my friend has to manage the farm. That's a pretty good arrangement for both of them. By comparison, my dad paid for my college education, and I used the money to instead fund my drinking habit. One dad in this scenario is responsible for producing a shit load of avocados, and the other is responsible for producing a shit head of a person. Both of them had good intentions. One of them just had a better son.

That said, I felt like I was doing alright for myself, at least that week. I could kind of say that I was in a band, and even though we didn't make any music, we got to drive around and effectively tour like a band. That's not a metric ton of guacamole, but it is somewhat of a decent story. Dad was going to have to settle for that.

It had been a couple of days since the night at Temple Bar. According to Maria, there was a lot of activity on our Twitter account. We kept getting more and more followers as word started to spread about what we were doing. I asked her at one point if she thought the venues would catch on to this, but she seemed to think that there was no risk. Being that I didn't really understand how whatever she was doing was working, I trusted her and left it alone. Unless we got kicked out of a club before we did anything wrong, I wasn't going to worry about it.

"Do you think one of us will get laid tonight?" Pedro asked, facing me.

The sun had nearly set, and we were getting closer to the main part of the city.

"No."

"Yes. Yes!" Booker countered.

"I agree with Booker," Pedro decided.

"That's good. Don't ask me then."

"I won't."

He waited only a few seconds before asking about it again. He was about as predictable as the swallows of San Juan Capistrano. That's a local reference.

"Really?" he asked.

"Yeah, why don't you think we could get laid tonight?"

"Because it's San Diego, man. The girls here are all perfect. The guys probably are too. We are outclassed here."

"That's true," Booker admitted. "But that doesn't really mean anything when we're in a band."

"Right. Yes. *The band*. But I still don't think any of us are going to get laid tonight. We're staying on an avocado farm. Who the hell is going to come all the way out there to fuck us?"

"I was thinking about that, actually. Why are we staying there again?"

"I haven't seen them in a while. I kind of want to stop by. I still haven't been to the farm yet, and they've lived there for almost two years, I think."

"So why don't you tell them to come to the show…" Booker started, and I interrupted.

"The *show*?"

"Whatever. The *show*. And then they can go back to the farm. We stay in the truck."

"And get some ass," Pedro chimed in.

"Right," Booker continued. "And then we go up to the farm tomorrow. How about that?"

"I feel bad. I already asked them if we could stay there. They probably got an air mattress set up and all of that shit. You know how couples who live together are. They do that kind of stuff in advance. They're thoughtful. It'd be pretty shitty for us to change plans this late."

"I've never even met them," Booker reminded me.

"So?"

"You know how I get with new people."

"You'd rather sleep in the back of the truck than meet some new people? Come on."

"Kind of."

I could tell that his anxiety thing was kicking in again, so I let it go.

"Let's just go to the venue and see how it goes. Okay? If we are in no shape to drive anywhere, let's commit to getting totally fucked up and crashing in the back of the truck. And if one of us is sober enough to drive a bit, let's go up there."

"That could work."

"Or not. I really don't care," I decided. "I'll just feel like an asshole if I tell them that I'm not stopping by."

"Maybe that's better than showing up drunk with two guys they've never met before," Pedro suggested.

"Yeah, maybe you're right. It was probably a bad idea to ask them if we could stay there."

"It's not a *bad* idea," Booker backtracked.

"Maybe it is. It doesn't matter. Let's just do this *show*, or appearance, or whatever the hell this is going to be. Why do we call it a show? We don't perform. That feels weird."

"We're a band," Pedro reminded me.

"Yeah."

"We are."

"Okay," I said. "We're a band. Doing a show. In San Diego."

"Yep."

"No air mattresses," I added. "Though it would be nice to have one for the back of the truck, now that I think of it."

We all nodded. Maybe for the next trip, I thought.

There were probably thirty or forty people who knew who we were that night, right when we got there. It was fucking impressive. And by the time the night was over, there was another hundred or two who knew who we were as well. The well-dressed guy wasn't there, but his friends all let us know who they were. They kept buying us drinks. I got drunk pretty fast, and I had to ask them to slow down. When they wouldn't, I started farming off my drinks to other people who were also there to see what we were going to do that night. The bartenders seemed to want to get in on the action. They started offering up free drinks to anyone who was with us. It felt like a strange conspiracy. It didn't really make sense, but I was too drunk to think about it.

Though we had agreed just a few days earlier that we would try to avoid getting up on stage, somehow it happened again. It was after the second band had finished their set. I don't know what led us up there, but before I realized it, we were on the stage and in front of the whole crowd. People were chanting our name. The band name, that is. Not our people names. I don't think anybody cared enough to know those.

"Tu-ba! Tu-ba! Tu-ba!"

Nobody cared about the *City* part, either. It was too hard to chant. Too many extra syllables.

The room was spinning, a lot. I reached over to pull the microphone out of the stand, and I stumbled a little bit. Pedro shouted something incoherent. The crowd cheered. There was a legitimate response happening. For us. It had nothing to do with the stupid little rhymes or jokes that I tried to make during my fake sound check. There were people in the crowd who came there that night just to see what we would do. Like we were a real band, but without the songs. Or the talent. Or anything that a band possesses. But still somehow like a real band.

We had an *actual* following. The Internet had turned our fake nothing into a real something.

"Tu-ba! Tu-ba! Tu-ba!"

In the midst of all of the chanting, I had a moment of clarity. I went over to Booker and then to Pedro, and I explained to them what we were going to do. Even if the bartenders and the crowd and whoever else out there thought that this was fun to watch, there was going to be someone out there who felt ripped off. The venue owner, the manager, the promoter, or the next band…someone was getting a raw deal out of our good fortune. There is no free lunch, as old people say.

"Are you guys ready to fucking rock?!" I yelled.

It sounded like the entire crowd roared back at me. *Yes, we are*, they roared. *We would like you to fucking rock, please*, they suggested.

"Well, alright then! We're Tuba City. We're from Los Angeles. And we're…"

I fell down onto my side and started to shake. Not for real, not like something had actually happened to me. I fell with intention. I heard a few people gasp and scream in the crowd. There was a pretty loud murmur that was bouncing off of the walls. I kept shaking on the ground, kicking a bit and thrashing around. Pedro stood up and nearly knocked over the drum set that he was behind.

"Is anybody out there a doctor?!" he shouted.

Of course, nobody replied. Doctors don't go to venues like the one we were at. Not on a weeknight. Not to see a fake band…or a real band. At least not good doctors. The kind of doctor that would volunteer his or her services in a situation like this was probably doing something much more respectable at the time.

"He is having a seizure!" Booker yelled.

He jumped toward me and landed on his knees beside my convulsing body.

"Fuck!"

This was in reaction to the pain that he felt from landing awkwardly on the stage floor. This had nothing to do with me.

I tried to stay in character as much as possible, but I wanted to laugh so badly. What a moron. Pedro rushed over, and the two of them started to try to pick me up. That is something you would never do to someone who was having a real seizure, but it was nothing that anyone there was going to question. They started to drag me off the stage while I continued to shake and convulse as best as I could. Pedro fell down at one point, and I fell on top of him.

I kept shaking and kicking. The crowd was abuzz with confusion. Some people thought it was a legitimate seizure, and they didn't know what to do. Some people knew that I should be left alone to ride it out, but they didn't want to say anything. Some people had to have known that it was a hoax. And then some people probably didn't realize that it wasn't part of an act, but they knew that we weren't a real band, so it all felt a little strange. Nobody *really* knew what had happened until they started talking about it on Twitter later on.

We escaped out the side of the building. Some woman who looked like she worked there offered to call an ambulance. She went back inside, presumably to do that, and we were able to somehow run off and get the hell out of there before anybody else came out. The truck was really close to the venue, but we were too drunk to just get in and drive away. Instead, we got in the back and pulled the door shut so that nobody would see us.

"Oscar-worthy!" Booker announced.

"Thank you, thank you."

"How the hell did you come up with that?" Pedro asked.

"What? I suggested it the other night."

"You did?"

"Jesus, yeah. You don't remember me talking about it?"

"Negative."

"Fucking genius," Booker cheered. "Really, man. Awesome fucking idea."

"Thanks. Sorry if I kicked either of you."

I was too drunk to know if I had or not.

"Whatever," Pedro said. "If you did, it was worth it."

"Yup," Booker agreed.

I texted Maria later to tell her what had happened. I tried to make it sound like an homage to her, realizing after I sent it that it might actually sound really insensitive. She didn't seem to care. She said she already knew anyway.

"How?" I asked. "Twitter?"

"Yeah. This stuff moves pretty quickly online."

"I guess so. Did people buy it?"

"Some did. Some pretended like they didn't, but I think they did. And some knew the whole time. They loved it the most."

"Yeah?"

"Yeah. I think if you have to go on stage again, that's probably better than actually performing."

All of a sudden, I realized that in my drunkenness, I had let my guard down. Or that she had.

"Wait a second," I said.

"What?"

"You know that we're not a real band."

"What?" she asked.

"Come on."

"What?" she asked again.

"You just said that if we had to go on stage again, blah blah blah. Why would you say it that way if you thought we were a real band?"

"Oh," she said.

"Oh?" I asked.

She started to laugh.

"Whatever, Blake. So what?"

"So nothing. I just didn't realize that you knew."

"Really?"

"Yeah. You knew?"

"What kind of fucking idiot do you think I am?"

"I mean, there are a lot of people out there who don't know."

"Right. Sure. But they haven't been talking to you and setting up your Twitter account and reading what people tweet about you and…and are you serious? You thought I thought you were a real band?"

"I just didn't think about it," I admitted.

I was pretty drunk, and the conversation was starting to confuse me. It made sense that she would have known. I just hadn't considered it.

"Well, I knew. Obviously I knew."

"Did you know the whole time?" I asked.

She laughed again.

"No, Blake."

I wasn't too drunk to not pick up on her sarcasm.

"Even when we first met?"

"Even when we first met," she confirmed.

"So we weren't your favorite band."

"You weren't a fucking band!" she yelled.

"Oh yeah," I said. "I'm pretty drunk."

"No shit."

She laughed again.

"Well," I said, realizing what this all actually meant. "Thank you then."

"You're welcome. You idiot."

I told her that I was going to get off the phone so I could figure out what we were doing next. We didn't have to hang out in the back of the truck for the rest of the night. It was still early, and we ought to make the best of the free liquor that was sloshing around in our stomachs.

"Remind me to tell you something tomorrow when you're a little more aware of yourself," she said.

"Okay."

"Have fun."

"Okay."

She hung up the phone. I stared at it a while. I was a goddamned idiot for not realizing that she would have known. And I was also somewhat in awe that she was still doing all of this for the purpose of whatever it was that we were doing. She believed in it as much as we did. That felt good.

We went out to some bars in the area, and nobody bought us drinks. That was okay. We barely needed any. We found a dartboard and played darts for a while, hitting the wall almost as often as we hit the board. Darts should never be allowed where alcohol is consumed. Then again, nobody wants to play darts just for the hell of it while they're sober. The safety hazard may be a necessary evil if darts should continue to exist in this world. But still, it seems like a bad combination. Someone should look into this.

When the bar closed down, we went back to the truck and passed out in our sleeping bags. There were no girls that came back with us. Pedro had a chance with one that he was chatting up at the bar, but she just ended up leaving without giving a reason. That's the worst kind of rejection. The unexplained and never-to-be-explained abandonment. She seemed too pretty to want to spend a night in the back of a box truck with three dudes anyway. In fact, even the ugliest of girls might not want to do that, so it probably didn't have anything to do with her looks. She just happened to have a brain in her head.

I never called my friends in North County to tell them that we weren't going to be staying with them. Their air mattress probably sat alone on the guest room floor, or wherever those things go when you plan on having guests over at your avocado farm ranch house. We did stop by the next morning, and they didn't seem to mind. Inside, maybe they were angry. I couldn't tell. On the outside, they seemed to just shrug it off. If it were me, I probably would too.

I can't be bothered to hold a grudge. It's too much effort. And when you have thirty acres of avocados to maintain, maybe you can't be bothered to get mad about a drunk friend not bringing his two other drunk friends over so they can all sleep on your floor and piss in your toilet.

When you have thirty acres of avocados to maintain, your life is probably very different than if you don't have thirty acres of avocados to maintain. Most of us will never know though.

We were at the farm that next morning. Pedro was off talking to my friend about the backhoe that he had just rented to rip out some trees on the north side of the property. Booker was inside, lying on the couch. I was sitting on a rock, trying to take it all in but generally just feeling like a hungover mess. It was sunny and bright. There was virtually no shade where the house sat on the property. It was a terrible place to have a hangover. I walked around to the back of the house where the sun wasn't directly beaming. One of their dogs followed me over there. I ignored him. I didn't ask him to follow me, so I didn't feel bad about not giving him any attention. He probably never had a hangover, so he wouldn't understand. But I didn't care.

I gave Maria a call.

"What was that thing you said you wanted to tell me?" I asked.

She was impressed that I remembered.

"So, I don't know what to make of it. I think it's bad news though."

"What is it?"

"There's a guy who has started to tweet you guys. He says he knows about the truck."

"What? What does that mean?"

I was worried, but also confused. And hungover. And still not really sure what tweet meant.

"Not about where it came from. He's saying he knows about what happened in Vegas."

I had told Maria about what Pedro did. I also told her why he did it after I found out, but I didn't tell Booker. That didn't seem like something I should tell him. He liked Pedro, and I didn't want him to start to think badly of him for doing something that he just wouldn't understand.

"What exactly is he saying?"

"Let's see. He said, *I know what happened in Vegas, with the truck.*"

I started laughing.

"So basically, exactly what you just said."

"Yeah."

"Nice. *I know what you did last Vegas.*"

"Huh?"

"Nothing. Anything else?"

"No."

"Hmm."

I thought about it for a while. The dog finally started to walk away.

"He probably has to know something, right?" she asked.

"Are you sure it's a he?"

"Yeah. I mean, the picture is of a guy. So unless it's a girl pretending to be a guy…but I don't think that's a thing that girls do."

"It's usually the other way around."

"Right."

"What does he look like?"

She made some noises, the kind you would make if you were squinting to look at something.

"He has sunglasses on, so it's hard to tell. He's a white guy. He has a moustache."

"Sounds like my dad so far."

"He looks kind of like a cop," she said.

"Ughh," I blurted. "Really?"

"It says he's from Las Vegas too."

"A cop? Does he have a uniform or something?"

"I can't tell. It's just his face. And his name."

"What's his name?"

"Well, his Twitter name, I mean."

"Right, okay. What's his Twitter name?"

"At Debt Peters."

"What?"

She repeated it for me.

"At Debt Peters? Why does that make him sound like a cop?"

"Det, like *Detective*?" she tried.

"Okay. Why the *at* part?"

"Oh. Right. That's how Twitter works. Everyone has an *at* symbol before their name."

"Why?"

"That's how it works," she said.

"Alright. Det Peters," I said.

"Like one word. DetPeters."

"Alright. Detpeters."

"No, not like a single word. Like DetPeters," she said.

"Whatever. I am way too hungover for this. So we have a cop in Vegas that is posting on the Internet that he knows what we did with the truck?"

"Yeah, I think so."

"Shit. How would he know how to find the Twitter page?"

"I was thinking about it this morning. I don't know though. If someone saw the license plate, that wouldn't get them here."

By here, I assumed that she meant the website and that she was in front of a computer.

"Right. And we got rid of that license plate anyway."

"Is there anything on the truck that says the band's name?"

"Nope. It's just white. Did you ever see it?"

"I didn't."

"Oh. It's a beast."

I paused and thought about the truck for a bit. I got up from where I was sitting to go look at it around the corner of the house. That beautiful fucking truck.

"But I love it," I added.

"That's nice."

"Can you message him back on there?"

"Yeah, of course. But should we do that? What if he is a cop?"

"If he's a real cop, why is he posting on the Internet that he knows what we did? That seems fake."

"This thing is so new though. It may end up being how cops catch criminals in the future."

"We're not criminals!" I shrieked, way louder than I meant to.

"That's not what I meant. I just mean that you don't know if a real police officer would use this or not. They have – especially in Vegas, I bet – they have cybercrimes units. I bet they already know about Twitter, and they're using it to track down all kinds of people."

"Well, great. Maybe you should stop using it then. I don't want some Vegas cop coming to arrest me for a hit-and-run in a stolen truck!"

"I guess I can stop," she said.

She sounded sad about it. I could tell that she was really liking her part in all of this. Even through my hangover-induced headache, I was feeling a little guilty for suggesting it.

"Well, wait. He's in Vegas?"

"Yeah, that's what it says."

"Let's think about this then. Can he cross state lines to come arrest us? If I'm in California, can he really do anything about it?"

"He can call another police department there, can't he?"

"And tell them what though? There's a Twitter account where some girl in Denver…"

"Some girl?" she interrupted.

"Sorry. Sorry. Some wonderful lady. Where some wonderful lady in Denver is posting updates about a group of guys who are pretending to be a band, and they crashed a truck into a Las Vegas motel, and he needs their help arresting us?"

"It does sound pretty unrealistic."

"And what? They follow the posts you make and show up to a venue, and they arrest us? No way. The more I think about it, the less I am worried about it. Even if the guy is legitimate. He can't touch us from Las Vegas. No way. No way."

"So I can keep tweeting for you guys then?"

"Wow. That's all you care about, huh? Yeah. Yeah, keep tweeting. Fuck that guy. DetPeters can tweet all he wants. I don't even know what I am saying, but whatever. I think that's right. He can tweet all he wants. It won't make a difference. Especially if you're writing all of these things for us."

"What do you mean?"

"Well, it'd be like trying to arrest a rapper for rapping about selling drugs and shooting people and whatever else they rap about in rap songs."

"Damned kids these days," she added.

I laughed.

"You know what I mean though. You didn't actually do any of this, and I didn't write any of this. So unless this guy can come across state lines, show up to a show, and prove that the truck he's looking for is the truck we have, when we have different plates on it and when we're not the people making these posts to the website? I mean…no way. No way."

"No way," she repeated.

After I got off the phone, I went inside to talk to Booker. I explained to him what was happening, and he seemed to care less than I did. I think his actual response after I finished telling him what I thought was a simple, *Okay*.

Okay. I didn't bother telling Pedro. We had consensus between Booker and me. Even though Pedro was the dumbass who actually drove the truck into the wall, it didn't seem like it was his problem.

My hangover was starting to wear off. I felt bad about how I had treated the dog, so I went back outside and tried to find him. He was lying in the shade behind the house, right where I was standing earlier. He looked up at me with a hopeful twitch of his head.

"Yeah, buddy. I'm here to play with you."

He thumped his tail against the dusty ground like he understood what I had just said.

Twenty-Two

I've always had a thing for rum. I went to Barbados once, on that trip I took to St. Lucia. The islands are so close together in the Caribbean that you kind of owe it to yourself to visit at least two while you're down there. Unless you don't like moving around a lot, or if you hate using your passport. Then maybe just stick to a Sandals resort. Or just buy a poster of a white sand beach and stare at it while you drink chi-chis that you made in your blender at home.

From what I can tell, Barbados is only known for a few things: sugar, rum, beaches, and Rihanna. It is a great place for any of those reasons, but there's really just one draw for me. No offense, RiRi.

Barbados is a good place to visit. They don't love Americans there, but it's not as bad as Antigua. At least what I know of Antigua, which all comes from the one time I read that book by Jamaica Kincaid. Maybe I got the wrong message though. I was admittedly confused from the start. I was reading a book about an island, written by a person named after another island. Come on.

I've never been to Antigua, but that's mostly because the book says that the locals crush glass and put it in the food that they serve to tourists. That's one way to get me to not visit. I am personally not a fan of crushed glass. I find its taste to be bland and overrated. Also painful. Barbados, on the other hand, either doesn't have a book that discourages people like me, or it is just generally a better place to visit. I would imagine it is a bit of both.

Their rum is fantastic. It's some of the best that I've ever had. One of the few very things that I can remember in detail about the time that I spent in Barbados was a fish festival that I went to. It didn't sound that appealing to me, but everyone said that it was a good time, so we tried it. It was on a Wednesday night. I don't usually go this route, but that night, I smoked a big joint that I bought from a guy on the beach before I went. That might have been part of what I liked about it there. I was pretty damned high.

For me, the best part of the fish festival was the rum that I was able to buy and the stoop that I sat on, drinking alone and watching the locals dancing in the street to some music that seemed to be coming out of nowhere. They had a bunch of stalls and carts, all selling different kinds of fish that they caught in the bay earlier in the day. I didn't bother with any of it. I was just sitting there taking it all in. High. Watching people dancing. It made me want to dance, but I knew that I was too white to try it there. It wouldn't go over too well even though I'm not that bad of a dancer. Besides, they had a good thing going on. I didn't want to be the reason that they wrote a book about how much they hated people like me.

So I just sat there sipping my rum straight out of the bottle. The fish festival took place on a dirt road. When it started to rain, I figured that everyone was going to duck under some of the awnings of the nearby buildings. No one did. They just kept dancing. So I just kept sitting there. It seemed like the right thing to do. The only precaution I took was to cork the bottle when I wasn't drinking from it. I didn't want watered down rum.

The road was in poor condition. Just walking down it, I almost twisted my ankle a half a dozen times. I didn't understand how people were dancing on it. But they also lived in these shanty hut things that had holes in the walls, corrugated metal roofs, and doors that didn't fit the full frame of the doorways. I guess you just dance on whatever the fuck you have to dance on when that's all you have.

Barbados was a good place to visit. I'd go back, as long as they don't write a book about the place before I get there. I won't do any harm, or at least I'll try not to. I'll be a good white boy. I promise.

When we left San Diego later that day, I asked Booker if he would drive. In retrospect, it was pretty fucked up for me to do that after I just found out that we might be getting chased by some cyber cop, but it didn't cross my mind at the time. I just wanted to relax and lean my head against the wall, and that's all that I was thinking about. We were somewhere near Newport Beach when my phone started to vibrate. It wasn't a number that I recognized, but it had a 310 area code, so I knew it was in L.A.

"Yo?"

"Yo back," a guy said.

"What's up?" I asked.

"I got your number from Maria," the guy said.

"Who is this?"

"My name is Trey Levio."

Pedro looked over at me and stared at the side of my head while I was talking.

"Alright. Do I know you?"

"No," he said plainly. "Not yet. But I want to meet you. And Booker and Pedro too."

"Oh. You got my number from Maria?"

I was annoyed at her. I didn't want her just giving out my number to random people from the Internet who wanted to meet us. Especially after this cop thing she had just told me about.

"Yep," he said. "She resisted for a while, but then I explained to her why I wanted to talk to you guys, and she realized it'd be a good idea for us to get in touch with each other."

"Okay. So do you mind explaining that to me too? Because this is a really fucking pointless conversation so far."

"Oh, you didn't talk to her about it?"

"About what? I am about to hang up here."

"Okay, sorry. Sorry!"

There was a pause. I think I had scared him off. I wasn't usually that curt with people, but I was just not in the mood to put up with some random babbling from a guy I'd never heard of. He may as well have been a telemarketer.

"It's fine. Just tell me something already," I said.

"So, I'm Trey Levio. I'm a band promoter from L.A. I've been hearing about you guys for the past couple of days, and I like what you're doing. I mean, I think it's pretty bad for my business, but overall I think it's funny and awesome, and honestly, I am getting a little sick of what I do anyway."

"You're a band promoter for real bands?"

"Yeah. Not big bands. Smaller acts. But I have connections. I book shows. I do all of that stuff."

"So why are you calling me? You want to book us for a show?"

I started laughing. It sounded so stupid.

"Yep, exactly."

"You know we're not a real band, right?"

"Oh, yeah. Yeah. No, I totally get it. Totally get it. That's what's so good about it, right?"

"About what?"

"About me booking shows for you guys. People won't expect it to be fake. They'll actually think it's real. We'll get some advance money. We'll get to hit the road, if I line up a couple of gigs. I mean, if you're into it, of course. I think it could be pretty sweet."

"Wouldn't this just ruin any credibility you had?"

"Oh, totally."

He said it so nonchalantly that I could tell he really didn't give a shit about what he was doing. It almost seemed like he was looking for an excuse or a way to get out of it. Why else would you sacrifice your career? Just for a laugh? No way.

"You're for real?" I asked.

"Yep. I mean. Yeah. I talked to Maria, and she said that maybe it'd be a good thing if we all met. She said you guys were heading back from San Diego right now."

"Jesus, Maria."

"You're not interested?"

"No, I mean…let me talk to the guys. We can probably meet up. Where in L.A. are you?"

"Oh, I can meet you wherever. I'm in Los Feliz, but really, you name it. I have wheels."

"Alright. I'll call you back."

I got off the phone and explained the parts that the guys didn't already figure out from my end of the conversation. They were both very much in favor of a meeting, so I threw my caution out the damned window and called the guy back to tell him that we could meet up. I also called Maria and told her to check with me before giving my phone number out to anybody else in the future. I didn't want random people being able to call me. That was how things would get out of control. That is, more out of control than they already were getting.

We met with Trey at some random office that he said we could meet at, in Century City. It was his friend's place, the business office of some importing and exporting company. It was a Saturday afternoon, and no one was going to be there. It was a small office with a decent board room table, so we sat there and began to talk. None of us had ever been in a real office like this before. It felt a little intimidating, and it certainly put us out of our element. For the first few minutes I worried that this was all part of a set up. Like that Vegas cop had put this guy up to this and we were all going to get arrested.

"What's up, dudes?" he asked as he greeted us when we first arrived.

"You have anything to drink?" Booker replied.

Trey smiled.

"Of course."

Trey was a pretty normal-looking guy. He was tall, thin, and had normal guy hair. There really wasn't much that I could describe about him. He was a generally average white guy. That day we met, he was wearing a Brand New sweatshirt. It was black, and it just had the band's name, some squiggly lines, and other random things to fill in the space. I remembered seeing that exact sweatshirt on a merch table once, but I didn't buy it because it looked too small. It seemed to fit him alright though, probably because like everything else about him, Trey was a normal size too.

He had brought a bottle of rum along with him. It was a bottle of Pyrat XO. There was a kitchen on the other side of the main door to the office, and he came back from there with four tall glasses and a bag of ice. He filled the glasses about half way with ice before splashing the rum over the rocks. There was no mixer. You don't need it with Pyrat XO, so that was alright. I don't know if or how he knew about me and my infatuation with rum or if it was just a coincidence, but it started everything off in the right direction.

"You really like that phone or what?"

Pedro kept playing around with the conference phone at the center of the table. He was like a little kid, fascinated by everything around him. The phone, the chairs, the video conference camera.

"It's pretty legit. Do you use this for work?"

"Fuck no, man. I don't work here. This is my buddy's office."

"He lets you come up here?"

"More or less. I just thought it'd feel more official if we were at a table that wasn't in my apartment, you know?"

"Fair enough," I admitted.

Booker kept asking about the other bands that Trey had promoted and the groupie situation. Everything for him was about the groupie situation, whatever that was. I sipped the rum and tried to talk business terms, but I didn't have any terms that I wanted to discuss. He seemed like an alright guy. Very friendly and good-natured. He seemed like he just wanted to help us do what we were already doing, but better.

We spent about two hours in that office, just drinking and hanging out. In his mind, he had already been working on a tour of sorts.

"Like an actual tour?" I asked.

"Yeah, more or less."

"Which one is it?" Booker pushed.

Trey laughed.

"More. Sorry. I say that a lot. What I mean is…yeah. An actual tour. Just don't expect it to be awesome or anything. I can get you bookings. But we have to work together to get the people to show up."

"That's what the Twitter is for," Pedro reminded him.

"Oh yeah. The good old *the Twitter*."

Trey knew more about the smaller venues up and down the west coast than I thought anybody could possibly know. Not just the names of venues but names of managers, good nights to perform, bad nights to get stuck in a city without a hotel, places to eat when you had some money, all of that kind of stuff. He was legit, and the more time we spent with him, the more I liked him. He had an infectiousness to his personality that didn't get old even after hitting the road with him, which is what we ended up deciding to do on that afternoon.

"Can you guys give me a few days to get everything sorted out?"

"What's a few?"

"Like three days. Maybe two. I just want to make sure I can book the right places, you know? I've already been looking into it, so I'm pretty sure we're on track, but now that you're in...I just want to make sure I can do everything I was thinking I could do. You know?"

"Sure."

None of us had any plans further than that afternoon, so it wasn't going to be an issue if we had to wait a few days. Waiting was all that we had on the horizon. Waiting for an impulse. So why not wait for someone else to make that move for us?

"To Tuba City!" Trey announced, raising his glass in the air.

We all raised our glasses as well and met them in the middle, over the conference phone that Pedro couldn't stop playing with. The bottle of Pyrat was already empty, and I was starting to feel anxious about the bag of ice that had been sitting on the floor the whole time, slowly melting away. We decided to head out and sync up again a bit later. Pedro hugged Trey when we got to the elevators. Pedro seemed to like hugging people. Trey seemed alright with it too. I am not a hugger, but I will do it if I have to.

The next few days went by pretty quickly. I don't remember much of what we did, but I do know that we didn't go out as the band at all. Booker thought it'd be a good idea to save up our good luck for the tour. The tour, we were calling it. Like it was a real tour.

Trey would call me every few hours and confirm the progress that he was making. He was scheduling what was going to be a week-long trip up and down the west coast, possibly longer if he could get everything lined up in advance. Crucial to this plan was his ability to book these venues all ahead of time. He wanted to make sure word didn't spread and cause damage to his reputation and affect our chances of booking a gig.

When we met in the import or export or whatever kind of office it was, I had laid out all of the details of where we had come from. That included the origins of the truck and how it all had started. Knowing that we were dealing with stolen property, I figured that this guy deserved to know everything up front. If he was still interested in doing this – which he was – then I wasn't going to feel guilty with whatever ended up happening. We agreed to keep the tour out of Nevada, just in case Det. Peters was an actual person who posed an actual threat. We considered hitting the road in a vehicle other than the truck, but we all decided that it was really like the unspoken fourth member of the band. It had to come along with us, or we weren't *us*.

"A Tuba City tour without the Tuba City Express?" Pedro asked.

"Pedro. What?"

"That's what I call it."

"The Tuba City Express?"

"Yeah. Booker, I told you about that. Tell him."

Booker looked at me and shook his head.

"Yeah. Pedro likes calling the truck the Tuba City Express."

"Since when?"

"Since who cares."

He turned and looked at Pedro.

"I told you he was going to think it's a stupid name."

"It's not stupid!"

"Anything with the word *Express* on it sounds like a bus or a train," I said.

"So?"

"So this is a truck."

"Is this what you guys do all day?" Trey asked.

"Basically."

"Yeah."

To imagine what was going on in our minds at the time is a little hard to do now. It all seems very unrealistic and unlikely. I don't know if it was the pace that this all happened that made each new facet seem less unbelievable, or if it was just our young excitement. I had my moments of doubt. I questioned what this all was and why we were doing it, but most of the time, it just seemed to make sense. When things are going your way, most people don't stop to ask why. They just let them keep going their way. Only in hindsight do you start to appreciate what you had, how it got there, and how lucky you actually were. But back then, we were just enjoying it as much as we could.

Trey first secured shows in San Francisco, Sacramento, and Portland, in that order. He added another show in San Francisco right after Sacramento and then a pair of gigs on the same night in Seattle. Trey insisted that there were hot women in Boise. That idea stuck with Booker. It stuck with him so much that later he somehow convinced all of us that spending a night in Idaho would be no worse than a night anywhere else. It seemed like a hell of a drive for just one show, but Seattle was close to eighteen hours away from L.A., so all of it was fairly flung out there. And after the past few weeks of our lives, it really didn't seem all that aggressive or distant.

Committing to Boise meant that a later offer to open at a show in Vancouver had to get turned down, but we all agreed that it made more sense anyway, since the truck was such a liability. Crossing the border was probably a horrendous idea.

We were all sitting around at my place one afternoon. Trey was discussing logistics.

"I like what you guys did in San Diego. We need to do that when you guys get up on stage."

"Do what?" I asked. "The seizure thing?"

"Hell yeah. It throws off suspicion for long enough that we can get out of there."

"But what if someone in the crowd is actually a doctor or knows first aid or anything like that?"

"So?" he asked.

"What if they put their fucking hands on me and try to give me C.P.R. or whatever?"

Booker laughed.

"You don't give C.P.R. for seizures."

"I said, *or whatever*. Whatever you do when you are medically trained and someone is having a seizure."

"I think you're just supposed to sit there and let them ride it out."

I was shaking my head.

"Right. And if they don't? I don't want some motherfucker putting his hands all over me."

"Why?"

"Why don't you pretend to have the seizure?"

"That wouldn't make any sense. You're the singer."

I kept shaking my head until Pedro came up with a good idea.

"Can Maria talk to people on the Twitter thing?"

"Yeah, that's all you do on it is talk. I think."

"Can you ask her to find someone each night who can pretend to be a nurse or E.M.T. or something?"

"Petey, you genius!" Trey yelled as he slapped Pedro on the back.

"It's Pedro."

Trey started laughing. He had been trying to call him Petey here and there, and it apparently was not going over too well.

"Right, right. Okay. Still a great idea!"

Maria said that it would be easier to just write a tweet and ask for someone to help us out at the next show. We'd find the right people there, or at least through a friend of a friend or however it works. It turned out to work way better than we had expected, just like everything else at the time.

On that first night in the Bay, we ended up having nearly a dozen people pretend to be a part of some nursing school outing, just hanging out at the show. I was practically carried fully out the door and shrouded in secrecy by what felt like a legion of supporters. Trey had previously warned the venue that I was having health issues and that there was a very small chance that I'd be stricken while on stage. When it actually happened later, *much to everyone's surprise*, there was a lot less suspicion that we were doing anything deceitful or out of the ordinary. There was even mild sympathy.

Trey brought a sleeping bag and camped out in the back of the truck along with us each night. In Sacramento, he booked a hotel for himself when he had an encounter with a girl that he used to date a while back. She looked like a slut when we first met her. We found out later that she paid for the hotel room, so I had second thoughts on who the slut in that situation actually was. I wasn't going to judge them either way.

On our second night in San Francisco, he was back in the truck with us. We lay four wide, almost shoulder to shoulder. It was tight quarters, but none of us really gave a shit. We were all pretty drunk and out of our minds by the time we lay down to pass out anyway. Trey was actually following us in his car while we were on the road. He didn't ride with us, and he couldn't, even if he wanted to. The cab of the truck didn't have room for much more. So really, he could have slept in his car instead, but I think he just liked hanging out with us and wanted to be a part of the fun.

Maria kept the Twitter updates coming along. By the time we made our way to Portland, we had over four hundred followers. Det. Peters continued to post cryptic but seemingly accurate messages, but none of us worried too much about it. We crossed into Washington and exceeded five hundred followers. We were officially blowing up.

At the first gig in Seattle, there were so many people who knew who we were that it felt like they might have outnumbered those who didn't.

The whole thing was moving along so fast. We felt like we were unconquerable. The free drinks and the attention kept on coming. There was even some cash involved, though Trey insisted that most of it was spent on filling up our gas tanks along the way, which he handled himself.

He was really into the whole thing. You could tell that he was pretty good at his job, or whatever his job used to be. There was no way you could screw over that many venues and still have a chance of working in the industry again. He never really spoke about what he actually wanted to do with himself or what plans he might have after this all blew up in his face. We only assumed that he knew what he wanted and that he was a grown man who could make his own grown man decisions. As long as it didn't negatively impact us, I didn't see anything wrong with him sabotaging his career. He was a young guy, maybe just a few years older than us at the time, so it wasn't like he was going to go hungry if he had to start over and do something else.

We skipped out on the second gig in Seattle altogether. Pedro went too hard at the first one and puked his face off in the alley where we parked the truck. Skipping was our only good option. A two- man, fake band seemed a lot less intriguing. On top of that, none of us wanted to leave him alone in the truck in that state. Not because we really felt that badly for him, but because we didn't want to have to clean up the mess after. It'd be better to nurse it all out and save ourselves the trouble. At some point Trey offered to be a substitute for Pedro. We all rejected that immediately, and he didn't bring it up again.

Maria called me the next morning as we were getting ready to drive to Boise. Pedro was moaning so loudly that I had to go outside to take the call.

"So, I've got some bad news, maybe," she said.

"Det. Peters scaring you off again?"

"No. He keeps posting. I'm just ignoring most of it. It's not that."

"Oh, okay."

"So I think you guys have a copycat band out there now," she said.

"A copycat?"

I had left the truck door open, and the guys all perked up when I repeated what she had just said. Trey walked over to me and put his hands on his hips. He should have known better. Booker came over and shook his head, probably at Trey more than at what I had just said.

"Yeah. People are posting about Tuba City going on stage at the El Rey in Los Angeles and trashing all of the gear. It sounds pretty vicious."

"Vicious?"

"Yeah. Like, they kicked the drums around, a guitar got thrown into a wall. It sounds like everybody got pretty mad, and they had to run out the back door. I guess they got away, it seems. But yeah."

"I wouldn't call that a copycat, really. I feel like they maybe got the idea from us and they took it too far. That's shitty, but that's not…I don't see how that's bad news for us. Right?"

"They called themselves Tuba City up on the stage though."

"Oh. Fuck."

I repeated the main details of the story to the guys. Trey looked mortified.

"That's not good for us at all."

"I'm sure it's not that bad," I said.

"Ask her what the guys looked like," Pedro shouted at the phone.

"No, I'm not asking her that, you moron. She can't see them. It's just people writing about it."

I pulled the phone back to my mouth.

"Right? There aren't any pictures on there or anything, are there?"

"No."

"Alright. Well. I mean, thanks. For calling. I'm gonna talk to the guys, and we're gonna start driving to Boise in a little bit. I'll check in later on."

I got off the phone, and we all talked about it for a bit.

"It kind of pisses me off," Booker said without any emotion.

"I think it pisses all of us off. But what are we going to do about it? It's not like we can copyright the idea of being a fake band."

"But they're doing it for the wrong reasons, it sounds like. We didn't trash anyone's gear. We're not hurting anyone. It's more like a populous movement."

"I didn't know you knew the word populous."

"I don't, really. But I think I used it right. Right?"

"Yeah, you did."

"We're coming from a good place with all of this," he continued. "They're not. It sounds like they're coming from a bad place. That's not what this is all about. This is about getting free stuff and having fun."

"Somebody has to pay for that though," I reminded him. "Besides, you're assuming you know why they're doing this. We don't know why. Maybe they're just like us."

"This is bad," Trey kept saying, staring at the ground.

"Is it?"

Pedro was looking worried too. Or just hungover.

"Look," I said, trying to calm everyone down. "This is what happens when you have a good thing, right? People want to get in on it. We can't stop that. We put this idea in people's heads by doing this in the first place. It is probably going to spawn off other copycats as soon as people realize that we're not in two places at the same time."

That didn't make anyone much happier.

"This is really bad," Trey said again.

He took his hands off of his hips and put them on top of his head.

"You guys are freaking out over the inevitable. We can't do anything about this."

"That doesn't make it right," Pedro whined.

"It doesn't matter," I said. "If we can't do anything about it, there's nothing to worry about. It is just going to be whatever it is going to be."

"Maybe we can tell them to stop."

"No, dude. What? We can't tell them to stop. We don't know who they are just like they don't know who we are. We just have to, you know, go out there and do what we were going to do. Hopefully this was just a one-time thing."

"It probably isn't," Booker said.

"Jesus, guys. You're being way too dramatic about this. I shouldn't have even told you about it. Let's just go to Boise and see if Trey was lying about all of the hot women we're probably not going to see when we get there, okay?"

The topic of women seemed to get everyone thinking a little bit differently. Trey looked directly at me, his hands still on his head, and he smiled.

"Oh, you'll see."

"Good. Alright. Let's go see Trey's stash of hot women he has hiding in the state of Idaho. It's a long ass drive. We really should get going."

I motioned to the truck. Nobody moved or shifted their weight or anything.

"They're coming from a bad place," Booker mumbled.

"Oh fucking well," I said.

Twenty-Three

I've always had a thing for rum. In lieu of a band photo that we didn't have, I had asked Maria to put a bottle of rum up as the band's profile picture on Twitter. She just found a picture of a bottle online and put it up there. I hadn't actually seen the page or the site or any of that, so I didn't know what kind of rum it was. A part of me wanted to log on just to make sure it wasn't something terrible that I didn't want associated to me, but I knew that it was a stupid and vain concern since the whole thing was something that I shouldn't want associated with me. In fact, the picture should never be associated with me in the first place anyway.

To Trey's credit, there were actually a lot of hot chicks in Boise. And they were ones that were more kind of my type too – a little unorthodox, a little weird, but definitely attractive. As if anyone thinks their own type is anything other than attractive. There were also some harsh-looking girls out there too, like any city has. All in all, it was an alright place to stop by.

Both Booker and Pedro had it ingrained in their heads that they were going to get some ass that night. They turned out to be right. It goes back to the concept of penile optimism, in a way. They wanted it so badly that they made it happen. The catch, since there usually is one when it comes to women, was that the girls that they ended up hooking up with were not exactly lookers. They were a little rough. But when the goal is to get ass, and you get ass, that equals success. Even if the ass you got is not ass you'd prefer, that's still a win. Goal setters can't be choosers.

The next day, we started our drive back to L.A. Trey was trying to set up a show somewhere along the way since we were probably going to have to stop at some point anyway, but he wasn't having much luck. We cut back into southern Oregon and started to make our way down through California. Maria called me at some point while the other guys were asleep and I was driving. I could see Trey in my side mirrors, following behind the truck.

"Det. Peters is getting more aggressive."

"Hi, Maria."

"Sorry. Hi."

"How so?"

"He saw all the tweets about the other Tuba City, and now he's convinced that you're a bunch of destructive assholes. He's saying he's going to come find you guys and arrest you."

"Shit. Really? This is all public?"

"Yeah. It's all on there. Do you never look at it?

"No. I thought that would be narcissistic."

"This whole thing is narcissistic."

"Good point."

"Also, some of the followers aren't happy about the trashing of the gear, so you're getting hated on a bit right now."

"No kidding, huh? Twitter hate. Doesn't take people long."

"I think they're just idiots, and they don't realize that they're not you and that you can't be in Seattle and L.A. at the same time."

"You can say something to all of them about it though, can't you? Like, saying how officially we're in Boise or something like that."

"Yeah, of course. I have been. But people are idiots, and they don't read everything. They just see the most recent thing, and they react."

"I guess I get the name of the website now," I said.

"It looks like they might have done the same thing somewhere else in L.A. last night, by the way. There are a few vague tweets that sound like they did it again."

"Fuck, man. I liked the El Rey too. I hope they didn't do it somewhere else that was good. Or anywhere, really. Fucking assholes."

"Det. Peters just posted again."

"Jesus. Is this thing always updating?"

"Yeah," she said. "Of course."

"What he'd say?"

"You won't get away with this."

"That's pretty generic."

"You should see all of the shit he keeps tweeting though. The guy is obsessed."

"Fuck. Any good news at all? How are you doing?"

"Good news. You're over six hundred followers now. And I'm doing well. It's nice here today."

"Six hundred?" I said, ignoring the personal comment entirely. "Wasn't it just five hundred yesterday or the day before?"

"Yeah. You should see all of the notifications I get. It's growing really quickly. Which is good and bad, you know?"

"Yeah. Bad if people think we're a bunch of assholes. I mean, we are. But if we're that other group of assholes. Why can't they just go by a different name or something? Fucking assholes."

We hung up the phone, and I sped up. I was annoyed and tired. Everybody had gotten laid recently, and I still hadn't. I think the last time for me was before we went out to Phoenix, when Harper came over. All of the driving and the sleeping in the truck and the drinking pretty much the rest of the time – it left me with no chance to jerk off. For whatever reason, everyone else was getting lucky and getting rid of it. And I was just building up tension and not releasing it at all. I contemplated pulling off at a gas station and having at it in the bathroom, but ultimately, logic and laziness got the best of me. So I stayed on the road.

We drove down through California and ended up stopping somewhere that I can't even remember. We didn't bother trying to find a place to be a band. We didn't even find a place that sold rum, and I didn't have any in the truck with me. We just parked somewhere that no one would come looking. We hung out, drank beers, and told stories. It was an alright night. Probably as good as any other night, really.

When Trey and Pedro fell asleep, Booker and I had a somewhat serious talk about how we might have done a bad thing for ourselves by being such good friends with each other for so many years. This was the first time in a long time that I had spent extensive amounts of time with anyone other than Booker. It felt good, and I was enjoying it. He agreed that he was too. It made me worried that I was missing out on other friendships that I never bothered to have because I was so comfortable just being around him.

I loved Booker like a brother, but even brothers have other friends. We agreed that we would try to spend more time apart, but then we realized that we sounded like a really lame couple going through a crisis. We lay there for a while, not saying much of anything to each other because there really wasn't anything to say. It was the kind of problem that only became a problem when you called it a problem. Had we never brought it up, it would have never really existed, and there would have been one less thing to weigh on our consciences. But it was out there, lingering like a quasi-gay conundrum. It was the toothpaste that wouldn't go back into the tube.

We eventually fell asleep in our sleeping bags. When we woke up, we didn't mention it that day, nor did we mention it to each other ever again. I've thought about that conversation a few times since then, and my opinion hasn't changed. Maybe we did do ourselves a disservice. We'd never know. I just wished I had never thought of it in the first place. I blame the beer. Rum never made me think of stupid shit like that.

In the morning, we drove back to L.A. At some point on the drive, Maria called me to tell me that our Twitter count had exploded all the way up to nine hundred people. Back in 2007, when no one was using it and Justin Bieber wasn't anybody and tweeting wasn't even a thing that people talked about, we had a following that was mushrooming out like an unstoppable disease.

And it was becoming a divisive thing. More and more people were following us just to hate on all of the shit that the other version of the band was doing. They were showing up in more venues than we were, and they were turning this thing into something very different than we had intended for it to be.

"This might be becoming a problem," I said to Maria.

"I think the Det. Peters thing might be a problem, but I don't think the number of followers you have is a bad thing. I think more is always better."

"Nah, not always. What's weird to me is that in the real world, if you start to do some unsavory shit, people stop associating with you. But on this thing, the more polarizing you are, the more attention you get."

"Why do you think they're doing this?" she asked me.

"Maybe it's that. Maybe they want the attention."

"But why?"

"I have no idea. They're just trashing the stage and leaving, and all of the blame is getting thrown on someone else. So they're not really getting much attention out of this anyway."

"Maybe it's just for the thrill of doing something fucked up. Isn't that why you stole the truck in the first place?"

I laughed.

"No. We stole the truck because I am somewhat obsessed with rum, and I was feeling vindictive after some delivery guy cockblocked us. It had nothing to do with attention. It was just to replace one thing that gives me boners with another thing that gives me boners."

"That's nice."

"Sorry. You asked."

She had brought up a good point though. We didn't know what their motivation was, but it probably didn't matter that much anyway. They were just some random guys who saw someone else's decent idea and decided to take advantage of it. Whether or not they had a purpose was somewhat immaterial, at least to me. The guy who had his truck stolen didn't know what my purpose was, but it still fucked up what he was trying to do.

"Well, anyway. Det. Peters is getting more and more intense."

"How so?"

"He's saying that you should turn yourselves in. To give yourselves a chance to reduce the charges that will be filed against you when he catches you."

"*When* he catches us?"

It was just like the typical scare tactics that you see in all of those cop shows on TV. He was trying to strong-arm us into submission. Or admission. Some kind of mission.

"What if you did turn yourselves in? Like, what if it comes to that?"

"It's not going to come to that," I reassured her. "He can't touch us from Nevada."

"But maybe someone else can. Maybe he gets a warrant or something, and you get busted for all of this."

"Stop it."

"I'm just saying. If there's an easier way out, maybe you think about what that would mean if you took it."

"Come on."

"I'm just saying. There's got to be some way to make this end."

"We can stop this whole thing. That's the only real option."

"Yeah," she said, sounding as sad as she did a week or so earlier when I had first suggested it.

"Look. You're talking about me turning myself in for a hit-and-run so we can maintain the authenticity of a fake band that people on the Internet are buzzing about. It makes no sense. Like…those priorities are all backwards. We should stop the fake band because it actually isn't anything anyway, and then this guy leaves us alone and we live normal lives again."

"But what if he doesn't leave you alone? I don't think he's going to stop pursuing you if you just get rid of the Twitter page. He still wants you for the damage you caused to the motel wall. Getting rid of the page may make him even more determined."

"Doesn't this guy have anything better to do than to try to catch some guys who damaged a fucking wall? Who gives a shit? It's a goddamned wall."

"I bet it's just the principle. Maybe he just wants to *catch* you."

"Well he wants Pedro, anyway. Not me. I didn't do anything," I reminded her.

"You stole the truck in the first place," she reminded me.

"He doesn't know that," I said, and then I sighed.

"It won't make a difference if he finds you guys."

I sighed again. This shit was really wearing on me. Just a handful of days earlier I had never even heard of this guy. A few weeks before that, and none of this existed at all. I was just a guy on a fake spring break trip with my best friend. Now we were stuck in some weird, complicated Internet cop mess. It was starting to feel like there were going to be some serious consequences that we had to either avoid indefinitely or face directly. Neither option sounded very promising.

"There has to be a better way out of this. For the first time in such a long time, I am actually proud of what I have been doing. Of what *we* have been doing. I know it's stupid and it's not even real, but it *is* something. I've never been a part of something before. I don't want to give that up because of how we got here. What we're doing has nothing to do with the bad things that we've done."

I was preaching, and I knew that I was lying to myself about that last part.

"I know," she said.

Her voice was a sad, little whisper.

"I want to see you," I kind of just shouted out.

It was silent for a few seconds. A few interminable seconds that plagued me with immediate regret.

"I want to see you too," she replied, knocking most of the regret out of my mind.

Neither one of us said anything for a little while. I looked over at the guys. Both of them were straight passed out, which was good, because I would have been embarrassed if either one of them had heard me. Mostly Booker. But Pedro to some degree too. I looked in the side mirror and confirmed that Trey couldn't hear me either.

"I've got to figure a way out of this," I said, refocusing on the problem.

"You will."

When we arrived back in L.A., we parked the truck in the same parking lot where we first had left it when Booker and I came home from Mexico. We swapped out the plates and decided to call it a night. We were all pretty beat. Pedro came home with me and slept on my floor. We decided that we would all go out somewhere the next day and talk with Trey about what to do next. The trip that he had planned and that we had just spent the last week of our lives enjoying had come and gone so quickly. In some ways, it felt like we were just priming the pump for the next adventure. In other ways, it felt like something big was looming around the corner. I was afraid of that feeling. I didn't want to encounter whatever it was. It felt like a pile of dog shit. Nobody wants to run into that. Not even dogs.

Pedro and I woke up to the sound of my phone vibrating. A lot. It was sitting on my dresser at a slightly awkward angle that made it vibrate a lot louder than it normally would if it were flat. Maria was texting me. A lot.

More bad news. The copycats are back again

Fourth night in a row. This time looks a lot worse. They trashed the stage at the glass house

Det. Peters is blowing up now too. He's going crazy

Followers are over 1000 now. 1034 exactly. If you wanted to know

Are you awake yet??

I texted her back and told her that I was asleep. Pedro and I went out to the kitchen. He sat down on a stool, and I went to the fridge to get us some water. My mouth was dry. Since we slept in the same room, I could only assume that his was too.

"Are your parents ever around?" Pedro asked me as I was pouring the second glass.

"Not really. They go on a lot of trips. My dad travels a lot for work too. And they're usually just not home."

"My parents are always home. That's why I left, kind of."

"Grass is always greener," I said and shrugged.

I stood across from him on the other side of the counter. I slid his water with my left hand while trying to bring the glass to my mouth with my right hand. I missed my mouth by about an inch. I'm not a good multi-tasker. I like to think that most people aren't either. I finished pushing his glass, and then I readjusted mine to meet my lips. Pedro didn't see any of this. He was fiddling with a coaster.

"I guess so," he said quietly.

When we left the house, it was very grey outside. It was the beginning of May, so that wasn't much of a surprise. I drove to Booker's place and picked him up, and then we drove out to the restaurant where Trey had suggested we meet. The roads were a little more congested than usual, and we arrived about an hour after we had planned. Most of that had nothing to do with the traffic. It was just that kind of day. If Trey was mad that we were late, he was fantastic at hiding it.

"Sorry, man," I started, and he shushed me almost immediately.

"No problem. Sit down, come on, guys. Sit down."

"How you been?" Pedro asked.

We made some small talk for a bit while the waitress took our drink orders and tried to push some appetizers on us. After she left, Trey started to talk business. He was very much like that. Business had a very distinct tone with him. We didn't know him much outside of the business context though, so maybe that was just what his tone was. Business-like.

"So how many followers do you guys have now? Do you know?"

Trey had been asking about the Twitter stuff pretty regularly. He saw it as a great promotional tool once he started to realize how easily it could be used to attract the right kind of attention. He was very right, of course, but at the time he just seemed like a guy who was experimenting with the latest new thing.

"Probably like seven hundred now, right?" Booker guessed.

"What? No. We're more than that," I said.

Trey nodded.

"I dunno," Booker replied.

"Well, then don't say anything when someone asks a question like that. He's obviously asking me. You're like a child that walks into a room…"

"Whatever."

I took out my phone and checked the texts that I had received from Maria.

"1,034. We broke a thousand last night, I guess."

"That's fucking crazy."

"So…cool," Trey moved on. "So I was thinking about it. Do you know how many of those people are in L.A.? Like, can you tell where they all are located?"

"You can tell, but not easily, I don't think. I mean, I don't know. I haven't used it. I can ask."

"Ask," he said, definitively.

"Okay."

Our waitress came back with our drinks. Mine was a water. I wasn't in the mood to get a real drink, not yet. It was that kind of day, like I said. I asked Maria, and she responded a little while later after our food had come out. While we waited for her to reply, Trey had already explained the details of why he was asking

"I think I thought of a way for you guys to get out of this mess with the cop."

"Dude," Booker almost yelled. "That guy probably isn't real! I keep telling you, we don't need to worry about that shit."

He had been saying that all along, anytime someone brought it up. The rest of us weren't as confident.

"Well," Trey continued. "I did some digging around, and it looks like there is a Detective Peters with the Las Vegas P.D."

"Some digging around?" I asked.

"I know some people out there," he explained coolly.

He was mysterious sometimes. I wished I knew people somewhere so I could say something like that to someone at a time like that. But I barely knew anyone who wasn't at the table with me.

"Peters is a common name," Booker reminded all of us.

"Yeah, so is Tiberius," I said.

That was Booker's actual first name, though no one I knew ever called him it. Every now and then someone would refer to him as T, but that was as close as it got. I don't think Pedro or Trey picked up on my joke. There were lots of things that Booker and I said between each other that they probably just ignored. We had way too much history to assume it was worthwhile to ask for clarification anytime we said something that seemed intentionally vague to one another.

"Fuck off," he said, much less vague than I had been.

"Anyway, guys," Trey carried on. "I am starting to think that this guy is the real deal. I've been asking around, and it seems like the real Detective Peters at the L.V.P.D. is one of these real abuse-of-power kind of guys. Like he does whatever he needs to do to get results. He's a real fucker. My guy I know out there, when I asked him if he thought the Peters he knew would do all of that Twitter shit this guy has been doing, he just said *Yeah. Oh yeah.*"

"Well, that *is* very convincing."

"Trust me. After I explained the situation a little more..."

"Wait!" I yelled. "You have a cop friend in Las Vegas, and you told him about our situation?"

"No, no! No. I didn't say I have a cop friend. I said I've got a guy out there. Don't worry. I didn't tell him anything specific, and he is definitely *not* a cop. I was just asking about the Peters guy to a guy I know who knows a thing or two out there."

"Alright."

"Look. The point is, I think this Twitter guy is the real deal. I think you have a real police officer tracking you guys online. I asked my buddy if there was any way that he could cross state lines to pursue you, and he seems to think that he could."

"Shit. Really? I thought you had to hand it over to a federal agent or something like that?"

"Only if it is a federal crime. This was a state crime."

"Pedro's state crime," I added.

"Your international crime," he reminded me.

Everyone liked to remind me of that part.

"Alright. So…fuck. Fuck. What is your idea on how we get out of this? If this guy is a real hell-bent dick about what he does, it doesn't seem like we could just stop using the Twitter account and he'd let us slip away, right?"

"No, right. That's not what I was thinking. If my guy knows what he's talking about, and I think he does, it sounds like this guy is going to try to find you no matter what. Right now, you're just making it easier for him to follow along. If you killed off the Twitter account, he might just drop a net on you the next day."

"That's a terrible visual. A net? And also, is that a pun? Like the Inter-*net*?"

Trey ignored me and kept talking.

"I was asking how many people you have on there in L.A. because I think I came up with a way to use them all to your advantage."

"That's all we have been using them for anyway. It's just a way to get more free shit."

"No, I mean to get out of this situation."

His voice started to tremble a bit.

"Do you guys even care about trying here or what? What the fuck is your problem today?"

I hadn't seen Trey get worked up about anything until then. He seemed genuinely emotional, or maybe he was just annoyed. It was that kind of day, like I said.

"Sorry, man," Booker offered on my behalf. "What's your idea?"

"Goddammit."

He paused and drank some water while shaking his head. I could tell that he was asking himself why he was trying to help us in the first place. I don't blame him. We can be terrible sometimes.

"I was thinking. You have all of these followers. Some of them love what you're doing. They love Tuba City. They love the very idea of having fun at the expense of the institutions they pay into, night after night, that never pay anything back to them. You're like the Robin Hoods of the underground music scene, and people really dig that."

"That's pretty legit. Did you just think of that?" I asked.

"Nah, I thought of it the other day. Anyway, some of them love you guys. And then some of these people who are following you are only doing it because they don't like you and they want to see what you're doing next so they can, I don't know…actually, I don't know why they follow you. That seems like a waste of time. But, whatever. They clearly don't like Tuba City. They're actually getting mad about all of this because they think it's destructive and immature and it's tainting the industry that they've totally bought in to. But the thing is, most of these people aren't getting mad at *you*. They're getting mad at these copycat douche bags who are taking your good idea and turning it into something negative."

"They're coming from a bad place," Booker said.

"Right. So on the one hand, you have some fans of your *work*, let's call it. And then you have some haters of your work. But the haters don't hate *your* work. They hate someone *else's* work that they're disguising as yours."

"Right," I said, looking directly at Booker to see if he had gotten more out of this than I had.

I was vaguely following, but I didn't think Trey had said what his actual idea was yet. At least I hoped he hadn't. I didn't hear an idea anywhere in there. That is, until he said the next thing he said.

"So why don't we do to the copycats what they are doing to us?"

He rephrased himself almost immediately.

"Not us, sorry. To you guys."

"It's an us thing, Trey."

"To us, then," he said.

"Copy the copycats?" Booker asked.

"Exactly!" Trey shouted.

He slapped both of his hands flat on the table.

"Let's copy the copycats!"

"How?" Pedro asked, looking more confused than any of us.

Trey leaned forward. Drama.

"If they want to pretend to be us, then they can *be* us. And if they're us, then they won't mind when we turn ourselves in for the truck accident."

"Ahh...but it won't be us," I said, catching on slowly.

"No. Of course not. It'll be them. Tuba City. The guys who drove the truck into the motel in Vegas. The guys that Detective Peters wants."

"A sting?" Pedro asked.

"It's kind of more like a switcheroo," Trey explained. "Actually, it's kind of both, really. A sting and a switcheroo. A *stingeroo*."

"Okay," I said. "I get the concept, I like it. But how do we get this cop to come find these copycat guys when we don't even know who or where they are? They're just some random, untraceable guys like we were before we started using Twitter and the Internet made us targets in the first place."

"Oh," Trey said with a wide smile. "That's the best part."

He slapped out a quick, little drum roll on the table before continuing.

"I am pretty tight with the new booking manager at the Troubadour. We used to work together a while ago. I was calling around, and they've got nothing booked almost all weekend. He said that if we can get a hundred people in the door, we could have ourselves a show."

"At the Troubadour?!" I shrieked like a little girl.

I loved that venue. I still do. It was so historic. And there were no bad spots in the room. I had seen so many shows there that I couldn't even count them all.

"I know the guy," Trey said, still smiling.

"When you said have *ourselves* a show," Booker asked. "Do you mean our own show?"

"Headlining," Trey confirmed.

"At the Troubadour," I said again, this time a little less femininely.

"Now wait…don't get too excited about it," Trey warned. "You guys aren't going to go on stage or anything. This is all so we can get you out of this jam you're in with this cyber cop."

"Cyber cop," Pedro repeated and laughed.

"I still don't see how a headlining show is going to get all of this to go away though. Do you think that Det. Peters is just going to show up because we're headlining a show at the Troubadour? Maria has been posting where we're playing every night, and he hasn't shown up yet. What makes this any different?"

"No. I mean, we can't rely on his spontaneous attendance, no. This is where your girlfriend comes in."

"She's not my girlfriend," I said.

"Uh huh," Booker nudged me.

Pedro nodded and smiled.

"She needs to reach out to him and convince him that one of you is willing to turn yourselves in for the crimes you committed. But that you're not going to drive out to Nevada because the rest of the guys are avoiding the state entirely. The only way he can get you is if he comes out to the show to intercept you when the rest of the band doesn't have their guard up."

"Damn, man. That's pretty good."

I thought about it a bit more and started nodding.

"Because if she reaches out to him and he isn't who he says he is, we don't have a real problem, and this all goes away. And if he is who we think he might be…"

"I don't think he is," Booker interrupted, but then he smiled and shook his head as he motioned for me to continue.

"… then he will find a way to make that sting happen."

"Exactly," Trey said.

He put his hands on top of his head and leaned back in his chair.

"But wait," Booker asked.

He leaned forward in his chair and put his forearms on the table. I leaned in along with him. More drama.

"We still only have the cop and the venue. How do we get the copycats there so we can set them up to take the fall for us?"

Trey closed his eyes for a moment but didn't move from his backwards lean in the chair.

"Guys," he said as he opened his eyes slowly, trumping any of the table-leaning drama that had been thrown down so far. "You think that Tuba City's promoter can arrange a headlining show at the Troubadour for his band, but he can't get them to show up on stage? Don't you have any faith in me *at all*?"

"But how?" I asked.

"Dude!"

The feet of his chair slammed on the ground, and he leaned forward again.

"I have my ways. Let's just leave it at that. I will get those motherfuckers there. That's my job. Your job is to get your girlfriend to start talking to that cop. You tell her to tell him that we're playing at the Troubadour this Saturday and that he had better find a way to get his ass there."

"Alright. But she's not my girlfriend," I reminded him.

"Right," he said. "And you just turn down ass in every city we go because you gave up fucking for lent."

Twenty-Four

I will always have a thing for rum. I can see how my future will unfold. I will get married. I will have a family. I will find some meaning within meaning, and I will feel happiness. I will achieve what I am meant to achieve, and then not long after that, I will die. I will be okay with that because of all of the things that I have been able to do and see and feel.

I will have a New Orleans-style jazz funeral, but in California. I always wanted one of those, so I know that my corpse will be happy and smiling as the trumpets squeal and the confetti makes a mess of the street. The people who have loved me in my life and who didn't die before me will all be there. They will be celebrating, cheering, and looking like they are having a good time. But the jazz music will only lift their spirits for so long. After the music wears off, they will be crying and smiling and trying to enjoy themselves because they'll know that I wanted them to. But like all people at all funerals, they will just be sad, inside and out. Dying is a sad business, and there isn't anything that anyone can do about that.

And after they carry me down the street, I will be buried somewhere near a tree, if there's still room in California to bury people. I will be in my own little box with a bottle tucked carefully between my folded arms. My body will decompose, because we all do. My skin, bones, hair, and teeth will all turn into dirt, and then later, they will turn into nothing. All that will be left will be the rum. Just a pile of dirt and some rum. And some echoes of a trumpet...

I think about death a lot. I haven't experienced it much in my life, but it doesn't stop me from thinking about it. I worry about not being what I want to be before my time comes. I'm afraid that something unexpected – it is always unexpected – will just take me away. Before I finish this book. Or the next book. Or the next drink. Or the next kiss. Before the next anything. It astonishes me. We live life with so much daily control, yet the most important thing that we face is almost entirely out of our realm of understanding or manipulation.

I don't want to die. I don't believe in anything else after this life, and I like this life that I am living. But all things will die eventually, and we are left with nothing but a bunch of thoughts or stories about what they used to be.

I love the Hemingway line about there never being any end to Paris. It reaches beyond the real and creates an abstraction that can and does last as long as time itself. Paris the city will have an end one day. It is inevitable. But the idea of Paris will never end. There is never any end to an idea or a feeling, or in my case, *a thing.*

I will always have a thing for rum. It is my Paris. But unlike Hemingway, I can die and be buried with my obsession. Knowing that he couldn't do that probably upset him. Maybe that's why he blew his head off. Who knows. That's a crazy thing to do. It would be very hard to hear the jazz music and the sounds of the parade over the sound of a shotgun shell shattering through my skull, so I will just die when I die and leave it at that. Bury me with my rum, and I will be a happy, dead man with my head fully intact.

I was musing on my death while I sat on the couch at my parents' house. They were away somewhere for the weekend. Santa Barbara, probably. They went there a lot when they had time. Or Vegas. But I think it was Santa Barbara that weekend. It was just Booker and I. Pedro was somewhere with Trey, doing whatever it is that promoters do for bands. Getting the word out. Making phone calls. *Promoting*. Pedro was trying to help him however he could.

I wanted nothing to do with any of that. The whole point of this thing was to get a free ride for as little effort as possible, because otherwise it wasn't much of a free ride. Self-promotion seemed to interfere with my ethos there. Maria could run the Twitter account. Trey could talk to whomever he needed to talk to. Pedro could be Pedro. Booker could be Booker. I was going to be me. And being me meant sitting on the couch and thinking about how I might die at any given moment. Being me wasn't the best or most interesting option of the ones that I just mentioned, but I didn't have much of a choice. I was me, and I was okay with that.

It was Saturday, May 5th. It was one of my favorite days of the year, and it had nothing to do with the fake Mexican holiday that most people were going to be celebrating. I couldn't care less about Cinco de Mayo. It was another one of those holidays where people just go out and drink their fucking faces off. The holiday itself was a sham. It commemorates a battle that was lost by the people that we are supposed to be celebrating. That makes no sense to me. We should be celebrating the winners. That's what the rest of the world does. Fucking Mexico.

I wasn't excited about Cinco de Mayo, not in the least. I was amped because it was the day of the Kentucky Derby.

"Are you just going to sit there and stare at the wall all day, or are you going to turn on the TV at some point?"

Booker was in the kitchen washing his hands. I don't know why they would have been dirty, but I am never one to question unnecessary sanitation.

"Just thinking about dying," I said.

"Awesome."

"I'll turn it on in a few minutes."

He came over, sat down next to me, and stared in the same direction that I was staring.

"This is pretty interesting. I see why you do it now."

"Whatever. It's my house. I can think about whatever I want to."

"Uh huh."

He leaned over and turned the TV on. It was already on NBC. I had already turned it on earlier, just in case the remote and the TV both stopped working and it had to be stuck on one channel. I was really looking forward to the Derby, so I took the extra precaution even though I knew that would never be a scenario that would happen.

"I will stop now," I said.

"I. Will. Stop. Now…" he repeated in a robot voice. "Cheer up, man. It's Derby day."

"I know. I'm not in a bad mood. I was just thinking."

"Well, stop. You're a douche bag when you think for too long."

"Good to know."

The pre-show had already been on the air for about two hours. We were about an hour away from post time. There was no shortage of unnecessary discussion about hats and outfits and all of the other shit that the Derby is known for other than horse racing. The weather looked perfect, and the track was graded fast. It looked like it was going to be as good of a day as any other Derby that I had seen. The commentators kept mentioning that Queen Elizabeth was in the audience. The cameras kept showing her just sitting there like there was nothing better to show.

"Show the fucking horses!" I yelled at the TV.

Booker looked over at me and raised his eyebrows.

"She's the queen, dude. Chill out."

"Not my queen."

"Yes. Not mine either. But still. It's a big deal."

"I think it's a waste of time. They should be showing the horses. Or the other races, at least."

"They never show the other races."

He was right. At Churchill Downs on the day of the Derby, there are about twelve or thirteen races that are run, and the only one that makes it on the national broadcast is the Derby itself. Maybe they do that to maintain the illustriousness of the event, or maybe they think that people won't care. I don't get it. I'd rather see a bunch of no-name horses and jockeys competing in any race than see famous women wearing famous dresses made by famous designers. I am not responsible for the programming at NBC Sports though, so it remains what it is.

"This is why I was just staring at the wall," I said.

"Thinking about dying."

"Hell yeah."

My phone vibrated. It was a text message from Maria updating me on the Twitter account, as usual. We were up to twelve hundred followers. Most were in L.A. or San Francisco, she said. And it seemed like a lot of them were going to be coming to the headlining show. I sure as hell hoped so, as we had a lot hinged on this thing. Trey's plan was making me nervous, which was probably why mortality was on my mind in the first place. I always thought about dying when I got nervous. It usually made me feel better.

This thing could fall apart for any number of reasons. A hundred people needed to show up and actually pay money for a show that they most likely knew wasn't going to have any performances. Though I don't think that anything major would happen if we fell short of that number, it still was intimidating. I didn't know a hundred people. I couldn't even name a hundred people. And that was the easiest obstacle in front of us.

Maria had been talking directly with Det. Peters since Wednesday night, after Trey shared his plan with us and I shared it with her. Peters more or less proved to her that he was a legitimate detective. And by that, I mean that he gave her his badge number, and she was somehow able to verify online that he was in fact a real person. That fact was scarier than anything we had done yet. The guy was for real.

Not only was he real, but he was real *and* he was planning on coming to the venue with a team to apprehend us that night. A team. A team! That is more than just one person on some Twitter account. That is a group of adult men who are traveling hundreds of miles with the intent of arresting us. At the time, it never occurred to me that it was quite excessive for him to orchestrate all of this for a simple hit-and-run on a piece of property, but it didn't matter. That was the man that we were dealing with. Like Trey, he seemed to not have any emotional investment in his actual career. He was just riding this thing out for the thrill of it, and he happened to be pretty good at what he did. That was a bad combination for us if the douche bag copycats didn't show up as we were hoping.

Trey was keeping unpleasantly quiet on that topic, but he kept assuring us that he would get them there. Part of me wondered if he really cared who got arrested or if he just wanted it all to go down as some massive spectacle that he could walk away from and laugh at. I couldn't figure out his angle in all of this, and since we hadn't known him all that long, I didn't trust him much.

I felt like there was something slightly off about him. But on the other hand, he had really gone out of his way to help us out with everything, and with very little regard for his own reputation. Maybe he didn't care about that anymore, but it didn't matter. A promoter lives or dies by his rep. As far as I was concerned, what he was doing was sacrificial. Even if what he was sacrificing wasn't something that he wanted.

Mostly, I just wanted to believe that he wouldn't let us down. That he would somehow find a way to lure those guys to the Troubadour that night and that our involvement in any of this would never truly be known. The truck and all of its evils would be pinned on a group of unoriginal pranksters who had no idea what was about to hit them. To me, that was a fair price to pay for stealing someone else's great idea.

For what it was worth, they seemed like a relatively static group of assholes. Unlike our group, who wandered from city to city looking for the next venue or crowd to take advantage of, they stayed right around L.A. On Wednesday, they stormed the stage at the Wiltern, which seemed like way too much of a coup and could not have lasted more than a few seconds at most. On Thursday, they were at Chain Reaction in Anaheim. On Friday, The Glass House in Pomona. Night after night, they stayed elusive, at least from security. The Twitter crowd had begun to identify the differences between them and us, or at least the smarter ones did. That gave me some hope, but I still had no idea how Trey was going to get in contact with them, and even if he did, how he would convince them to show up to a headlining show for their fake fake band.

It seemed too obvious. But maybe that was its beauty. It was too easy to pass up.

"What time does this start?" Booker asked.

My phone started to ring. It was Trey.

"Usually around 3:30. This is Trey, hang on."

Booker looked at the clock and started to walk away.

"I'm taking a shit then," he announced.

"Great," I said. "Hey, Trey. What's up?"

Trey sounded excited and exhausted.

"Did you know that the Chili Peppers are playing at the Fonda tonight?"

"No. That's pretty cool."

"I love them."

"Nice. Is that why you called? To tell me about a band you like?"

"No. I mean, sort of. The show is a little earlier than the doors for our show, so I'm going to try to recruit some people looking to score tickets and send them our way."

"You think Chili Pepper fans will want to come see us? They're a real band."

"They started off like you guys, you know."

"No, they didn't," I said.

"Well, sort of."

"Whatever, man. The Derby is going to start soon, so I've gotta go. Any word about the copycats?"

"Got it under control," he said.

That's what he had been saying for a while but without any evidence or updates.

"Of course you do. Alright, man. Suck my kiss."

"Right on," he said and hung up.

A moment later a text came through from Maria asking me when I was getting to the venue. I told her it was going to be a while since the Derby was about to start.

You should get there early

I explained to her that there was no real reason to get there early, and in fact, if Det. Peters was there early, it could be a really bad idea.

I just think you should get there early

I stopped paying attention to her and turned my phone on silent as they started to play "My Old Kentucky Home". I got chills that ran up and down my arms. I love the Derby so damned much. It always gives me chills.

"Booker, call it quits! The race is about to start!"

He yelled something back, but it was too muffled for me to hear what he said. The program went to a commercial just as he came out.

"A fucking commercial?"

"Sorry, man. They just played the song."

"I could hear it. What did Trey have to say?"

"Something about the Chili Peppers. They're playing at the Fonda tonight."

"Okay," he said, as the commercial faded to black and the next commercial came up.

"Dammit. Sorry, man."

"It's fine. I was just about done anyway."

The next commercial came on, and he looked at me and shook his head.

"Sorry. This has to be the last one."

It wasn't. There were two more. Fucking NBC.

"Finally!"

Booker was rubbing his hands together as we stared at shots of the horses walking up and down the track. They were getting ready to load into the gates.

"Who you going with?" I asked.

"Scat Daddy."

"Hard Spun," I said, nodding.

"Right. What post?"

"Seven."

"I'm fourteen."

The horses started to load into the gates from both sides. For as long as I could remember, the Derby had so many horses in the field that they had to add that little extra gate cart on the side to accommodate all of them. I always wondered why they didn't just make a bigger gate that was large enough for all of the horses that would run. They had a temporary solution year after year. They still do. I don't get it.

My horse loaded in at around the same time that Booker's did. We looked at each other and nodded. There was, as there always is, one horse that didn't seem to want to go in, and he was fucking up the mojo of all of the other horses. They finally got him in, and the camera switched to the straight-on view.

The guy yelled, *"And they're off!"*

Booker and I both shot up to our feet. We stood there with our hands outstretched and wringing the air. 2007 was the year after Barbaro had his botched start at the Preakness, and I remember watching the opening stretch with a lot more focus and concern than I had before. It looked like a clean break as far as I could tell. Our horses were nowhere to be found as the crowd converged. That was neither a good nor a bad sign. It was just a fact.

I leaned down to the table and picked up my glass. I had a Caipirinha. The Mint Julep is the traditional drink on Derby Day, but I didn't like mint or whiskey, so I went for something else. Caipirinhas weren't that popular back then, or at least not in the U.S. This was before it became the Mojito 2.0 and every trendy bar or restaurant had one on their menu. I didn't even know what it was supposed to taste like. I had seen a bottle of Cachaça at the liquor store a couple of years earlier, and I bought it thinking that I would like a sugarcane rum. I didn't. Or at least not at first. But I kept on trying it until it grew on me, and eventually it became my Derby drink.

"And down the stretch they come!" the guy yelled.

Our eyes were bugging out of our heads. Booker's horse was still nowhere to be found. We had only heard his name once during the race, when they were naming all of the horses at the beginning of the first turn. Mine had been out in front for a while, but he gave up the lead and ended up finishing second. Street Sense was the winner, crossing the finish ahead by almost three lengths. It didn't even look close.

"Shit," Booker said.

He was drinking a Caipirinha as well. No other drinks were allowed in my house during the Derby or during the other two Triple Crown races. It was a new rule that I had put in place after Booker had spilled his beer on the remote the year before and I almost had an aneurysm. It was unrealistic, but I was worried that the beer spillage would change the channel or turn the whole TV off. Only short glasses were allowed from there on out.

We watched the ceremonies, the draping of the flowers, and the lady reporter on the horse talking to the little tiny jockey on the back of the winner, using his little tiny jockey voice. It had to be hard to be a jockey until you won a big race like the Derby. Unless being a jockey ran in the family, your parents had to be a little hard on you if that's the profession you chose. Riding a horse, dressing up like a dainty clown with a helmet. It is pretty embarrassing. That's why those guys always cry when they're getting interviewed after the big race. Years of repressed embarrassment are all validated on national television. But instead of getting the last laugh, they just cry and thank a bunch of people. It's somewhat fitting.

Maria had been texting me throughout the race, but since my phone was on silent and on the table, I didn't see any of it until later. She just kept texting about getting to the venue early. I finally sent her a text back telling her that we would be getting there at around six and that it would still be early enough for any of the things that we needed to do, which was pretty much nothing but sit there and worry until something did or didn't happen. I said all of that, more or less.

Trey called me to tell us that he was outside the Fonda and that there were already people lined up waiting to get inside. There were people scalping tickets and people balking at the prices. He was doing his part to try to divert anybody who wanted to see a show but didn't want to pay hundreds of dollars to instead head over to the Troubadour. He said he was having a little bit of luck but that most people who were there that early weren't interested.

"What about the copycats? Do you know if they are going to show up?"

"Don't worry about it," he said.

"I am worried about it. It's a few hours away, and you keep telling me it's gonna be alright, but I have no proof or reason to believe that it will be."

"Chill, Blake. We've got this covered."

"Who is we?"

"Well, me. I've got it."

"Listen," I said, as stern as I could be, which was not very stern at all. "That cop is going to show up, and he is going to be looking for us. If he gets there and we're the only assholes there, you realize that I am getting fucking arrested and thrown in jail for all of this shit, don't you?"

"That's not going to happen. Calm down, okay? He doesn't even know what you look like."

"We don't know that for sure."

"You told me that Maria was taking down any picture that people posted or linked to you guys, right?"

"No, I told you that I *told* her to do that."

It turned out that you can't do that. I don't think I ever told Trey that part.

"Oh."

He paused. I could hear a siren in the distance through his phone.

"Well, whatever. The guy isn't going to see you. We're covered."

"The copycats are going to show?"

"The copycats are going to show, yes."

"You're sure?"

"Yes."

"No, you're not. You're just saying that."

"Calm down, Blake. Have another drink and watch the race. Then start to get ready to head out."

"The race just ended."

"Oh yeah? Who won?"

"A horse."

I shook my head at Booker. Then I hung up.

"Did you just hang up?" he asked.

I nodded.

"Cold."

"Whatever. He just kept telling me the same shit about those guys. *Don't worry. Chill out. They'll be there.* I have no confidence in this fucking plan whatsoever. I got Maria to direct a goddamned police officer to come arrest us, and I've got a self-destructive promoter telling me to show up to the place where the fucking cop is going to be. With the hopes that some random douche bags who aren't smart enough to come up with their own scam will just appear magically on stage and get handcuffed and taken away with the stolen truck that is parked right in front of my goddamned house right now. What a fucking stupid plan!"

"Dude."

"What?!" I yelled, grabbing my drink and shoving it toward my mouth.

"We're not going to get arrested for any of this. You need to relax."

"How the hell do you know?"

I sounded so accusatory that it almost made me feel bad. But he didn't let it faze him, so my guilt never really arrived.

"We're going to be fine. We'll run out the door if it starts to look suspect."

"From a cop?"

"We crossed the goddamned Mexican border with a truck we stole in their country. We drove the goddamned truck across *our* country, sleeping in the back of it like a bunch of fucking hobos."

His tone was getting elevated, but it was just to match mine and to prove his point. I could tell that he wasn't mad, not at all.

"We crashed it into a motel wall."

"That was Pedro," I reminded him.

"He's one of us now. So *we* crashed it into the wall. *We* drove it back here. *We* drove it all the way up and down the coast. *We* got gas at that station in Oregon and then drove off and didn't pay the guy."

"Self-serve makes so much more sense," I added.

I had somewhat forgotten about that incident. We were just a bunch of assholes. We couldn't even pay for our own gas.

"It does. And it was still very, very wrong. The whole thing is wrong. But you know what?"

"What."

"*We* are not going to get caught for any of it. It's just not going to happen."

"You don't know that."

"You don't know that we will," he replied.

"Nice fucking logic. I feel so much better now."

"Drink your Caipirinha and shut the fuck up, dude. We're not getting arrested tonight by some Las Vegas cop that your girlfriend sent out here to find us. It's just not happening."

"And she's just not my girlfriend either," I repeated, for what felt like the fiftieth time.

"Right. Because most girls would slave over a webpage for a guy they only met twice in their lives."

"Fuck you. She's not my girlfriend."

We met Pedro outside of the venue. It was 5:30. No one was in line, and there wasn't even a bouncer at the door yet.

"Where's Trey?" I asked.

"He's still at the Fonda. We were getting a lot of interest over there, so he stayed a little while longer, but he told me to come here so we could get ready."

"How'd you get here?" Booker asked.

"Bus. That orange one," he said, pointing across the street at an L.A. Metro bus. Nobody rode the bus in L.A. Only people with problems rode the bus.

"I still don't get why he's at the Fonda and not the Echo."

"The Chili Peppers are there tonight," Pedro tried to remind me.

"Yeah, I know. But Minus the Bear is at the Echo."

"Fuck!" Booker shouted. "Really? I still haven't seen them."

"Yeah, I saw it online the other day. Not that it matters, because we probably shouldn't go to the Echo for a while anyway."

I shot an angry look over at Pedro.

"Whatever, man. You lived that night. Remember? I helped you *live*."

"I'd rather not live if it means that I get to see one of my favorite bands."

"Maybe we can make it if we go after?" Booker suggested.

"No way, it'd be too late. Besides, you're assuming that we're not going to be in jail at the end of the night."

"Dude. You are such a bitch today."

"Minus the Bear," I sighed. "Fucking shit. We're just going to be here, hoping some dickheads show up and take the blame for us. Just to get rid of that thing."

I pointed down the block at the truck, thirty or forty feet away but still somewhat in front of the venue.

"Meanwhile, today could have been Derby Day *and* Minus the Bear day."

"Oh, they get their own day now?"

"I'm going inside," I said.

I was holding the keys in my hand when we walked through the front door and into the bar area. I had been there early in the past, and usually they wouldn't let us in at all. It seemed like everybody was keeping their expectations low. It wasn't supposed to be a show night. There was a girl behind the bar, but she didn't look like she knew what she was supposed to be doing there.

"Can I help you guys?" she asked.

There was no disclaimer that we weren't supposed to be there, that there wasn't a real band on that night, none of that. Just an offer of help.

"Yeah," I said. "We're in the band that's playing tonight here."

It was a line that I had used so many times in the past month, but it was something that I had never said with any truth behind it.

"Oh, oh okay. You all loaded in?"

I looked at Booker and realized that there was a right answer to the question. I just didn't know what it was.

"Sorry?" Booker asked, buying some time.

"Oh, right," she said. "Your guy was here yesterday. He dropped some stuff off in the loading area out back."

She motioned around the side of the bar and somewhere toward what looked like the stage.

"We haven't had a show for a couple of days, so no one messed with it," she added.

"Gotcha."

"The manager's office is right over there," she pointed, in the other direction. "If you want to drop off anything, like your keys or anything like that, you can go over and say hey. He's probably just sitting on his ass and watching videos on his computer."

"Okay, thanks."

I started to walk back there while Pedro and Booker took seats at the bar. I looked at them both, already sitting, and I opened my palms upward in question.

"We're gonna get a drink, that cool?" Booker asked. "You need us to go and meet with the manager and drop off the keys or whatever?"

"No. I'll do it."

I walked through the door and out into the empty venue. It was dark and almost a little creepy. There was no one in there. It was something that I had never seen before. We had been to other venues where they let us in before anyone else. We had been to the Fox in Boulder where it was just us and the bar. We had been to a few others so early that they didn't understand why we were there. That part was familiar enough, but I had never been this early to a place where I had seen dozens of shows. It was something else to see it completely empty and desolate. There was some quiet, tinny music playing from a speaker somewhere far away. It almost felt haunted.

I walked back toward where I assumed the manager's office was, but I was wrong. I had to wander around a bit more to find it. The girl behind the bar was right. There was a guy sitting on his ass behind a computer.

"You in the band?" he asked, barely looking up at me before looking right back at the computer.

"Yeah. I'm Blake."

I held out my hand to shake his, and he just shook his head.

"Nah, man," he said. "Where's Trey?"

"He's on his way. We're just hanging out at the bar. That alright?"

"Yeah, that's fine."

He was still fixated on whatever he was watching.

"Cool if I leave the keys to our truck here?"

"Sure. There's some pegs over there."

He didn't motion toward anything in the room. He didn't even move his arm or hands at all. I looked around and saw a small shelf with some hooks on it hanging behind the door. I hung the keys up and said thank you before walking back into the empty and mostly quiet main room. What a weird fucking guy. It worried me that he was Trey's contact and one of the people that we were relying on to pull this stingeroo off. The whole thing felt a little wrong to me.

I got to the middle of the room and stopped for a moment to look around me. The stage had one dim, off-white light hanging over it. Other than the monitors and a microphone stand, there was nothing on the rest of the stage floor. There wasn't even a mic in the stand. It was just a stand. It made me wonder if bands had to bring their own microphone or if the stand was so worthless that no one bothered to move it or lock it up. I didn't know these things because I wasn't in a real band and I probably never would be in one. I was just going to be a guy with a decent story on one side of a set of prison bars. I knew which side I wanted to be on, but I didn't know what fate had in store for me.

I stared up at that stage for a while. I started to picture the crowd filling in around me, like I was the first guy there to watch a band that I had always been dying to see live. They would come on stage, and everyone would cheer. I would just stand there silently because cheering is for girls. The singer would make eye contact with me while he sang my favorite lyrics. I'd feel something surreal for that moment, like the world was actually stopping and doing exactly what I wanted it to do. The feeling would fade when he went into the chorus, and when the song ended, it'd be entirely gone. But I'd have felt it. Everything would make sense for just that tiny, insanely brief moment. It would feel like letting go. It would feel like something bigger than what it was.

It was almost always paired with alcohol, or otherwise it would just be a creepy moment where you stared into the eyes of a singing man and you got a weird man-boner for him. It always had to have alcohol involved for it to be legit. A slow pit-pat of footsteps interrupted my fantasy, and I had to look over and away from the stage to see who was walking toward me. My eyes struggled to focus in the dim light.

"Blake Caldaro. As I live and breathe," a voice said.

"What the fuck?" I asked, unable to say anything more profound or friendly.

It was Maria.

"The guys told me you were back here. I didn't expect that you'd be staring up at this empty stage like you were in an upright coma."

"What are you doing here? Is that…is that why you were asking me when I was getting here?"

"Sherlock," she said flatly and smiled.

She walked closer to me, stretched her arms around my waist, and gave me a big, tight hug. I hugged her back, even though I was awkward when it came to hugging and I usually did the one-armed one whenever the situation came up. I used two arms for this one. Her face was buried against my chest, so when I spoke, I spoke with my chin almost resting on top of her head.

"When did you get here?" I asked.

"A few hours ago. Got a flight earlier today. I wanted to surprise you."

She was still hugging me, her face upturned and looking up into my eyes. I felt uncomfortable, as though someone could walk into the room at any time and question what we were doing. I took a deep breath and tried to relax a bit.

"You should have told me. I could have picked you up. You could have come over to watch the Derby with us."

"That's alright," she said. "I'm glad I'm here now."

"Do you want to get a drink?" I asked. "We're pretty early. There's obviously no one here."

I waved one of my arms around. She was still hugging me.

"Okay."

We went back out to the bar. When we walked through the doorway, Booker smiled.

"You found her," he said knowingly.

I must have had a puzzled look on my face, and Pedro picked up on it.

"We knew she was coming," he told me.

“Ah,” I said.

Maria asked the girl behind the bar for two rum and cokes, and I nodded behind her as she spoke. Trey called me shortly after to let me know that he was on his way. Trey never texted me. He always called. I don’t know why that was. Maybe he was just old school like that.

It was light outside, and the drinking was starting to feel really good. I wandered in and out of the front door – there was still no bouncer – to take in some of the fleeting daylight as it crowned over the buildings around us. Every time I came back in and saw Maria, I was surprised at how much better she looked than I had remembered. I couldn’t tell what it was. She had always had very nice eyes, and they were still just as nice. But there was something else that was throwing me off. I don’t think it was the alcohol, though I’m sure that helped soften the lines a bit.

At some point, she took my hand while we were sitting at the bar and held it in hers. I saw Booker look down at it but then look away and not say anything. He was a good friend. In times like that, he knew how to be exactly what he was supposed to be. I appreciated that more than he realized.

Maria had to go to the bathroom, and she asked me to take her there. There was a bathroom right next to the bar area that we were sitting in, but she insisted on going to the other one inside the main venue. She said that she didn’t want everyone to hear her going. I didn’t even realize that there was another bathroom, but I walked with her anyway.

We walked out into the main room where it was still dead empty. After a few feet, she turned around and faced me directly. Then she stepped up on her tip toes and kissed me. Even if I was surprised, I didn’t act like it. She kept kissing me. So I started to kiss her back. I was kissing her with all of the intent of a guy who actually wanted to kiss a girl, which I didn’t realize I was, until I started doing it. To me, she had been looking much better. With the rum in my veins and the excitement of everything that we were about to be facing, I got wrapped up in the moment and I kissed her back like a guy from a romance novel, or at least how I'd imagine they describe one.

The Troubadour has a balcony that I had only been on once, but seeing as it loomed over the entire venue, I knew where it was and how to get up there without having to think too hard. We ran up the stairs, her first, stopping along the way to kiss a few more times. At one point, I picked up her little body. She wrapped her legs around my hips, and I carried her up the stairs as I climbed. We found an empty, flat area behind a section of seats. I sat down, with her body on top of mine. I lay on my back, and she started to pull my shirt off over my head. Then she started to unbuckle my belt. Then she pulled her shirt off over her head.

Her bra came off shortly after. Her breasts were not large, but they looked amazing. I grabbed them as she pushed her body closer to mine and we fell back to the floor. It had been so long for me that I was already pressing up tight against my pants. As she was pulling her pants down to her feet, I pulled mine down as well. We were as naked as we were going to be. My shoes were still on, and her pants were wrapped around one ankle but not the other. It didn't matter.

I was as hard as a pipe but not nearly as thick or long, though it depends on what kind of pipe you're imagining. I had never been with a girl who required so little foreplay, but I wasn't about to complain. I slid into her almost immediately, and my eyes rolled back in my head. She shrieked with what sounded like a little bit of pain. We didn't have to go for too long before I was ready to lose it. I wasn't embarrassed. I considered it a compliment to the girl if she got me off really fast. Still, I felt like I owed her an apology even if I didn't mean it.

"Sorry about that," I said when we were done. "I can get you too."

"Don't worry," she said, as she smiled. "You're the rock star. I'm just the lucky groupie."

We didn't have any tissues or towels or anything, so I just wiped off what I could on the ground. Maria helped me get dressed, assisting me and my one clean hand. We went back downstairs and used the bathroom like we said we would. When we walked back into the bar, Booker looked at me and smiled.

"You found her," he said again, and I laughed.

"He did," she replied.

Trey got to the Troubadour at around 7:30, just as people had started to arrive. They put a proper bouncer on the door to stop people from just wandering inside like we had. Pedro and Booker were getting emphatically drunk at the bar. I think there was a bit of understanding between them that this was very likely the end of something. Maybe the band in its entirety, maybe just a part of it, or maybe our freedom and clean criminal records. Whatever was about to happen, they had decided that they didn't want to face it sober. I can't blame them. I was following suit, but clearly behind in the race.

Maria was walking around the bar area slowly, touching the walls with her fingertips and smiling as she passed along. It was weird, but I didn't care. I was still basking in that post-orgasm euphoria that makes you feel like everything is going to be alright, even if you have no evidence that it will be and past history has taught you that it probably won't be. I felt free. Released and unrestricted.

I felt like myself.

As people started to be let into the venue, the bar area filled up first. Not only because it was the first area just off to the left that you could pass through, but also because there was nobody in the main performance room to go watch. Getting a good spot near the front didn't seem to be a concern for the early crowd. They all just wanted to drink. I was in agreement with them. They were on the right track.

Trey walked over to me and put both of his hands squarely on my shoulders.

"We're gonna be good tonight," he declared.

"How do you mean?"

"We're gonna be good," he repeated.

Then he tapped his hands on my shoulders a few times and smiled, walking away backwards, repeating himself.

"We're gonna be good!" he yelled.

"Good with what?" Maria asked me.

"Beats me. Everything, I hope."

Maria was waiting to get a call from Det. Peters when he was nearby so that they could meet outside the venue and she could identify who the guys in the band were. She had told him to get there at around ten. She said that she wasn't sure if the guys would be there until just before they actually made it up on the stage. Sometimes they just rolled in from the street. It wasn't exactly true, but we were trying to buy ourselves some time for our copycat guests to show up. So far, he hadn't called.

At around nine o'clock, a guy with an acoustic guitar stepped up on stage. He started to strum and play some decent sounding chords. It was enough for me to notice and walk away from the bar and into the main room, my drink in hand. Trey was standing in the middle of the room watching him. A few people were standing in various, separate groups, all facing the stage. The bar crowd started to pour in as more and more people heard the music. His guitar wasn't plugged in to an amp, so it wasn't too loud. The mumbling and conversation that carried over from the bar began to drown him out. Trey arranged for a sound guy to plug him in, and the problem went away.

He wasn't that bad, but I had no idea who he was. Trey later told me that it was his friend, a guy in a band that he had promoted a while back and that was no longer touring. He was the bassist, but he played acoustic and sang when he had the chance. Maria didn't seem too interested, but I was starting to dig some of what he was doing. The whole concept was making me laugh though. A guy with real talent, opening for a fake headliner. People listening, but only politely. They came to see the other band. The one with no talent. My band.

The guy played for what was probably forty minutes before placing his guitar down on the stage and bowing to the crowd. There was a mild round of applause, and then everybody headed back to the bar or the bathrooms. At that point, more people had come in from the street and had filled up the bar area about as much as it could be filled. I didn't understand where all of the people were coming from. A lot of them looked a bit older. They might have been Chili Pepper recruits that reluctantly made their way down Santa Monica Boulevard and decided to give us a try. In total, there were maybe a hundred and fifty people packed in the little, tiny bar area, with some overflow spilling into the main room.

I ran into Booker while he was coming out of the bathroom, and I told him to hang on and wait for me. I went in and let out a stream that lasted for quite a while. He was leaning against the bar when I came out.

"Did you take a shit?" he asked.

"That was all number one."

"Damn. Glad I waited for you."

"Come on," I said, and I pulled his shoulder to follow me.

"Where?"

"Come on."

I walked outside, and he followed behind me. The sun had been fully down for a little while now. The colder night air was pushing in from the ocean. It felt good to be outside. The venue had gotten a little warm with all of the people even though there was still plenty of space to move around. Somehow the body heat had raised the temperature.

"What are we doing?" he asked.

I walked down the block a bit and then stopped. I looked back at him.

"If it all goes right, this is the last time we're going to see the truck."

"Oh. Damn."

He looked past me at the curb where the genesis of whatever it was that we had been doing for the past six weeks was just sitting there, humble and patient. Some of the white paint was chipping off in areas where you'd expect, but for the most part it was holding up pretty well.

"I thought maybe we should just come out and say goodbye to it."

"Uh huh," he said.

"I'm gonna miss it."

"Yeah. Me too. Also, you're kind of being a girl right now."

"I'm trying to have a moment."

"Yeah, okay. I can do that. We can have a moment."

We both just stood there and stared at it. It wasn't our truck. We had stolen it from someone who also probably didn't own it. It was about to be orphaned or maybe brought back to its rightful owner. I had no idea what the future would hold for it, or if it would have any future after that night. Maybe it'd be turned into scrap metal or salvaged for parts. Maybe it would be dismantled and stored as evidence. Maybe they'd send it back to Mexico. Our beautiful, amazing disaster of an idea sat in front of us, as uncertain as anything else in life.

We had spent so many nights sleeping in the back that for a while after, I had a hard time falling asleep in a regular-sized room. Anything else felt too big, too open and vulnerable. The truck felt right. Everything about it felt right. Even though it was so wrong and there was nothing that could change how wrong it actually was, it felt right. The truck wasn't ours. It never was. But a part of it would always be ours, and that was the feeling that filled me as I stood there staring at its poorly painted walls and dusty tires.

"Well," Booker said, after standing there for a while not saying anything. "That was an emotional moment that we just had there, looking at this truck."

"Sure was," I said.

We walked back down the block and into the venue. It was different than a normal show. There were no sound guys walking around, setting things up, and testing out instruments. There were no managers or friends or random people walking to and from backstage. There was virtually no activity on the stage itself, and as a result, everyone was at the bar. It almost felt like the show wasn't happening.

At some point, the momentum began to pick up and things started to move along. Trey enlisted the help of some people that I had never seen before to start bringing out instruments and gear onto the stage. The crowd was beginning to settle into two distinct camps. One was the group that was firmly planted at the bar. Most of them looked like they wouldn't wander out in front of the stage until some music started playing. Some of them looked like that wouldn't even make them move. The other was the group that was there for the music. You could tell. They were all jockeying for position in the fairly open expanse in front of the stage. At the end of the night, they were going to be much more disappointed than the first group.

Trey was organizing various sound checks and equipment tests. He was up on stage testing the microphone, swapping out gear, testing it again. It was all entirely unnecessary, but you couldn't tell the difference by the way he was acting. I wondered where he had learned how to do any of this as a promoter. Maybe just by watching it night after night. But by that logic, a waiter should be a good cook.

Almost like clockwork, Maria got a call just before ten o'clock. It was him. She pressed her phone against one ear and her free hand against the other. I couldn't hear what she was saying. She motioned to me that she was going to walk outside. I started to follow her, and she put her hand out fully, like a crossing guard in front of a school. *No. Stay.* So I didn't follow her. Instead, I wandered around until I found Booker and Pedro. They looked annihilated.

"I think Det. Peters is here," I slurred, not aware of how much I had been drinking until I tried to act serious.

"Oh," Booker remarked.

"Let's meet him!" Pedro yelled, his eyes scanning the room, presumably for a man in a police officer's uniform.

"No. Shut up. We are never going to meet him."

"You don't know that," Pedro said.

"Well, I am never going to meet him. You can meet him if you want to."

"I'm gonna go find him," he shouted and stormed off toward the bar.

I followed behind him, trying to catch up before he made the whole situation get extremely complicated. He weaved to the side of a few people who were shifting around. I got stuck behind them for a bit. It was long enough for him to make it all the way through the door and to the bar.

"Jesus," I said under my breath as I tried to catch up.

As I stepped through the doorway and turned the corner, I almost ran directly into his back. He had stopped dead in his steps and was facing the bar. Booker crashed into me and sent me pushing into Pedro. The three of us were piled up like a human traffic jam.

"What's going on?" Booker asked.

I looked back at him and shrugged. Then I turned back to Pedro and shook his shoulders.

"What are you doing, dude?"

"It's them," he said.

I looked past the back of his head and saw them. They were standing at the bar. There were four of them. Four fucking douche bags.

"We're in the band that's playing tonight, you dumb bitch," I heard one of the guys snap at the bartender.

"I don't think so," she said.

She turned away from them and started to take someone else's drink order. One guy nudged another, and then almost immediately, he reached behind the bar and grabbed a full bottle of Jack Daniels. He swung it over the counter and pulled it down toward his stomach. The guy was wearing a hoodie. I could see that he was tucking the bottle inside it and against his chest. He zipped up the front, and the bottle disappeared from sight long enough for the bartender to not notice.

"Fuck that!" Booker almost yelled.

"Calm down. They were supposed to show up," I reminded him. "Holy shit, where is Trey?"

"Who cares," Pedro mumbled.

"He got them here. I need to tell him. Holy shit!"

Maria walked back in from outside. She gave me a thumbs up and smiled uneasily. I motioned with my head toward the group of guys.

"Is that them?" she mouthed.

I nodded. The one with the Jack had taken it out from his hoodie. He was drinking directly from the bottle and passing it around to the others. They didn't seem to give a shit about anything.

Maria must have been staring long enough for one of the guys in the group to notice.

"Hey!" he yelled at her. "What the fuck are you looking at?"

She looked a little bewildered.

"I…uh. I don't know."

The rest of them turned toward her.

"Are you in that band that's playing tonight?" she eventually asked.

"Yeah, we are. So what?"

There was a bite of anger behind everything that I had heard them say so far.

"I love bands," she said, starting with the same line that she used to charm us back in Denver. "You know…like…I think you guys are just so cool."

She flashed a flirty smile. The guy with the Jack started to laugh.

"Well, don't get your hopes up. I can guarantee that none of us would ever be interested in hooking up with an ugly, little troll like you."

"I wouldn't even let you suck my dick!" another one shouted.

They all laughed. The look on Maria's face made my hands tighten into fists. The blood was pounding through my veins. I shoved myself past Booker and Pedro, and I brought my face right up to the guy with the Jack.

"What the fuck did you just say to her?" I shouted.

"Whoa, bro. What do you think you're doing?"

"Say it again," I snarled. "Go ahead. Fucking say it again."

"You need to back off, man. There's four of us and one of you. You got it?"

I kept staring straight into his eyes. He looked vapid and cold.

"I know how many of me there are. And I'm not afraid of you, you little fucking piece of shit."

The guy didn't flinch. His confidence was way too high. It just made me even more mad, so I continued.

"Don't you ever talk to that girl like that again. Don't you even fucking look at her again. You got that?"

I was just a few inches away from his face. It was taking all of the restraint that I had to not just slam my forehead right into his nose and split the whole thing right open.

"You need to get out of my face," he said flatly.

Pedro and Booker came up next to me and started to pull me away.

"Come on, man," Pedro said, looking at me and not at the guys in front of us. "Let's go."

He started to pull me back, and I kept staring into the guy's eyes. I was so angry, I was shaking. The guy put his hand up and waved a mocking goodbye. Pedro kept pulling me, and eventually we turned away and started to walk back into the main room. Maria put her arm around my waist and squeezed it reassuringly.

"I'm so fucking mad right now," I started, and she shook her head.

"Don't worry," she replied. "They'll get what's coming."

It took a while for Pedro to get Booker to follow us back into the main room. It was like trying to get a dog to stop staring at a cat in a tree. Trey was adjusting the microphone stand when I yelled his name out. He looked up and raised his eyebrows.

"The fucking band is here!" I shouted.

I didn't think about what effect that statement would have. Everybody around me immediately looked right at me and then behind me, like I was hiding something behind me, and then toward the door leading to the bar. Then the cheering began. And the chanting. And the clapping. Trey hurried off stage and left the microphone dangling from the stand.

People from the bar area undoubtedly heard the noise and started to pile into the main room. More chanting. More clapping.

"Tu-ba! Tu-ba! Tu-ba!"

I looked at Booker, who started to laugh.

"Way to go, dude."

He started chanting along with the crowd. More and more people began to push in from the bar until I was pretty sure there couldn't have been anybody left in there. The copycats pushed their way through the crowd and stumbled out to the middle of the floor, just a few feet in front of us. I started chanting too.

"Tu-ba! Tu-ba! Tu-ba!"

I could see them looking at each other. The guy with the bottle of Jack pulled it back to his mouth and pounded down a shot. He passed it to another guy who started to do the same. Then they just rushed to the front of the crowd, knocking whoever was in their way out of the way, and they threw their bodies up on the stage floor. It was less awkward than I figured it would be. If we did that, one of us would have tripped or fallen, I'm sure. The crowd roared as they all stood up on stage. Pedro was shaking his head. Booker and I were chanting.

"Tu-ba! Tu-ba! Tu-ba!"

The guy with the bottle of Jack stood in front of the microphone and held up the bottle in his right hand.

"Fuck you!" he yelled.

He kicked the microphone stand over, and it bounced off the floor and into the crowd. A few people scattered to avoid getting hit.

These guys were dicks.

"We are Tuba City!" the guy yelled into the room. "And we hate you!"

"We hate you too!" Pedro yelled, but it was mostly drowned out by the loud murmurs and shouting from the crowd still reacting to the mic being kicked at them.

Things started to get thrown all over the stage. A guitar, a cymbal, a pair of drum sticks. The same guitar again. I looked around the room, and everybody was pushing back from the stage, seemingly out of fear. We had to take a few steps back to give everybody some room to move. An entire drum was hurled into the crowd, bouncing off of someone's outstretched arms.

Security started to rush the stage, and the guys ran in the other direction toward the back and away from the bar. And that's when it happened.

The first one to get hit was the guy with the bottle of Jack who was doing the yelling. Out from behind the backstage curtain, a linebacker of a man charged through and swung what looked like a pipe right at his stomach. The guy fell down instantly, the bottle of Jack crashing on the floor and shattering. Another man, even bigger than the first one, rushed through the curtain after the first collision and headed straight toward the next fleeing douche bag. He hit him exactly the same way, and it resulted in almost the exact same physical reaction. Two down.

The other two stopped dead in their steps and fell to the ground out of what looked like a sheer instinct to try to avoid pain. It was the smartest thing that they could have done, really. Troubadour security pounced on them as the two huge guys from backstage suppressed the other two guys that they had hit. The first guy to rush through the backstage curtain pulled out a pair of handcuffs from behind his back and slammed them on the Jack guy's wrists.

"Det. Peters," I whispered, loud enough for Booker and Pedro to hear but not loud enough for anyone else to notice.

It was pretty loud in the room anyway. In addition to the house music, which was still playing, the crowd was shouting and screaming and probably wondering what the hell was going on.

"What a badass!" Booker yelled.

"I can't believe he's real," Pedro added.

When the four assholes were properly cuffed and restrained, Det. Peters stood them all up, one by one, and marched them off the stage and out toward the curb. Troubadour security shepherded them along the way as Det. Peters stayed up on stage for a little while longer. He addressed the crowd and thanked everyone for their cooperation. It was a brief and emotionless speech that he seemed to have forgotten he was giving partway through. He stormed off stage and back toward the manager's office. We were not too far away, and I could overhear the conversation.

"Can you confirm that truck out there belongs to the men I just apprehended on your stage?"

"What truck?" the manager asked.

I couldn't see him, but I imagined him to be staring at his computer, still watching whatever the hell he was watching when I was there earlier.

"There is a white delivery truck parked in front of this establishment. I believe it belongs to the four men that I just handcuffed on your stage. Can you confirm that this truck belongs to them?"

The manager seemed to pause and think for a bit. He was probably finishing up whatever video he was watching before answering.

"Yeah, uh. They dropped off the keys earlier. They're right here."

I heard some jingling, and I recognized it immediately.

"Unbelievable," I muttered.

The odds of this all happening seemed so ridiculously low that I wanted to drive to Vegas right then and put it all on red. Or black. Or whatever people put it all on. I wanted to make a bet. I had no idea that this one thing was going to be the difference between tying the truck to the copycats as the dust settled a few days later and Det. Peters realizing that he had nabbed the wrong guys. It almost made me want to hug the manager. Him and his goddamned computer. If he had paid attention to me, for even just a few seconds, we might have been completely fucked.

Det. Peters stormed out of the office and out toward the front of the venue. We worked our way through the crowd, most of who were also trying to follow him to see what was going on. Eventually we spilled out into the street, just as he was confirming the license plate and front hood damage to the truck. I saw him nodding. His hands were on his hips. I looked over at Booker to see him smiling and shaking his head.

"When was the last time you changed the license plates?" I asked him.

"Just the other day. He's not going to have any clue how to trace this back."

"But he can see the damage to the hood. He's got to assume that this is it. That this is the truck that crashed into the motel."

"Yeah. But it's never going to point back to us."

We both paused for a bit.

"You sure?"

"How could it?"

He was right. It really couldn't. Even if he traced back the license plates all the way to their origin, they were never going to implicate us in any way. I breathed a huge sigh of relief, and I felt my shoulders ease forward. As he looked up from his examination of the truck, Det. Peters noticed the growing crowd around him. He straightened out his back and turned to face the on-lookers.

"Party's over, people," he said, using the classic cop line that I didn't think any cops actually ever used. "This truck is now property of the Las Vegas Police Department."

People in the crowd started to mumble, ask questions, and make snide comments. I think the Las Vegas thing threw everybody off. I didn't understand the technicalities of it, but I didn't want to. It was working in our favor, so I pretended it didn't matter.

"The party is over," he repeated, and then he laughed a stereotypical cop laugh.

It was booming and proud and about to precede a mildly funny statement that amused him more than anybody else who was listening.

"Tuba City has left the building."

Booker shook his head.

"Lame."

Twenty-Five

"I've always had a thing for rum."

"I know," Booker responded.

"I don't know why I keep saying that."

"I know. You do say it a lot."

"Do people think it's stupid? When I say that?"

He was holding a plastic cup in his hand. Before he answered, he pressed it against his forehead.

"No."

"Alright," I said.

I wasn't convinced that he was telling me the truth. He knew it too.

"Who cares?"

"Yeah."

"No, really. Like who cares? Say whatever you want to say."

"I usually do."

"So what's the problem?" he asked.

I thought about it for a bit. He kept the cup against his forehead the entire time, looking exasperated. We had been spending a lot of time together. Maybe I was wearing on him.

"I just don't want to be known as the guy who always says the same thing. And then people make fun of me about it behind my back."

"I think there are more important things in life to worry about than this."

"Deep. But are there?"

"Yeah, man. Who cares?"

"I just feel like people don't appreciate rum as much as they should."

"Okay. This conversation is over."

"What? Why? You disagree?"

"No, but I was just wrong. This *is* stupid."

He pulled his cup away from his head and set it down on the bar. Then he picked it up again and took a big gulp.

"I've always had a thing for rum," I repeated.

"Congratulations. I have never had a thing for rum. Who cares?"

"Me," I said.

"Well, okay. Glad we established that."

The girl behind the bar was wiping down the counters. She looked at me, and without saying anything, she made an expression that asked if I wanted another drink. I nodded. She pulled out a bottle and a glass, and she started to pour. Maria was slouched against the wall behind us where the merch tables usually are, her eyes closed and her head gently swaying back and forth. Trey was still in the main room with Pedro, somewhere near the stage. Other than that, the rest of the venue was entirely empty. Everyone had gone home.

The bartender slid my drink over to me, and I started to smile as I replayed the night again in my mind.

Det. Peters was an impressively efficient machine. Almost immediately after they were led outside, the four copycats were stuffed into two different police cruisers and taken away. And within a few minutes of positively identifying the truck as the likely vehicle that did the damage to that motel in Vegas, he had its front wheels up in the air, hooked to a tow truck and ready to be hauled away.

I don't know what ultimately happened with our impostors, but I can't imagine that they were ever formally charged with anything. I had to assume that at least one of them had an alibi that put them all many miles away from Las Vegas on the night of the accident.

It all ended with a lot of questions that I never got answers to. I don't know how Det. Peters first found out about us and what made him realize that the Twitter account was tied to the same group of guys who damaged that wall. That fucking inconsequential wall. Booker and I joked that maybe he was in the room that we crashed into, doing something illegal himself. That seemed about as likely as him randomly coming across a page dedicated to us on a website that most of the world had never even heard of. But, I don't know. And I don't care.

All I cared about was washing our hands clean of it all, and those guys achieved that by being the unoriginal pricks that they were. When they took the fall for us, and when the truck was then taken away, any lasting implication that could have tied us to the band or the accident or the theft of the truck itself, it all vanished. We were just some regular guys again.

As for the truck, my guess is that Det. Peters brought it to a local impound and not all the way back to Nevada. But I didn't have anyone to ask, nor did I ever find out. In fact, we never saw the truck again after that night. For all of the time that we spent with it and all of the romanticized thoughts that I've had about it since, it was – in the end – just a means of transportation.

Yes, it also happened to be where we slept for the better part of a month. And it was pretty much the catalyst for everything positive that happened to us during the spring of that year. But in the end, all of that was achieved by us, not the truck. The truck was just the vessel that kept us driving toward our fate. We were the ones with our hands on the steering wheel. Or at least I was. The other guys hardly ever drove. And that was alright too.

Booker, Pedro, and I stared at its dimmed taillights as it was towed around the corner and out of sight. I put my arms around both of their shoulders, and I sighed.

"That's it, huh?"

"Not exactly!" Trey shouted.

He came out of nowhere like he was Doc Brown at the end of *Back to the Future* and we were about to have ourselves a sequel.

"We still have a show to put on."

"What? No way," I said.

I put up some air quotes for the next two words that I spoke, even though my arms were still around the guys' shoulders.

"Tuba City just got arrested. Show's over, man."

"Yeah. Copper said so," Booker added.

"So? Start a new band. We have the venue booked, and it's ours to use. Come on!"

He turned around and walked in toward the venue with all of the confidence of a guy who just assumed that we were following behind him. We all looked at each other. Both of the guys shrugged, and I did too.

"Fuck it," Pedro said. "I'm in, I guess."

Trey started yelling some things at the crowd gathered on the sidewalk. Something about a new band taking the stage in a few minutes. He didn't apologize at all for what had happened. In fact, he was acting like nothing had happened at all and that the people milling around in the street were idiots for not going inside. People started to look at each other and question themselves. Not too long after, most of the crowd started to move indoors. Maria looked at me, confused.

"So…we're going on stage," I said.

"Of course," she replied.

Inside, I stopped back at the bar for some refills on our drinks. There was no way that I was going up on stage without at least a little more rum in me. As we walked into the main room, people in the crowd started to turn and look at us. Some started pointing. A few people started to cheer and clap.

"What's going on?" Pedro asked.

"I think they still recognize us," Booker replied.

"They all kept quiet while Det. Peters was here?" I asked, somewhat rhetorically.

"Guess so?"

"Fuck, man."

We all climbed up on stage and the crowd began to cheer. Loudly. Trey was standing near the front of the stage, smiling as wide as his face would permit. Pedro found a pair of drumsticks on the floor and then sat behind the drums. Booker picked up a guitar. I picked one up too. The cheering kept on going as we plugged in our instruments. We had become pretty good at setting up. We hardly ever got past that part, of course, but we had nearly become experts on that one thing. It was going to be different this time.

"Check, check," I said into the mic. "Check, one, two. Check, check."

People in the crowd started to move around and clap and cheer even louder.

"Yeah!" Pedro yelled from the back of the stage.

"Check book," I shouted. "Checks and balances! Check your coat at the door!"

"Yeah!" Booker screamed.

He started to lightly strum the guitar. The crowd ate it up, so he kept doing it a little louder and louder. It almost sounded like he knew what he was doing.

"Check both ways! Check the sky! Check the floor!"

People were screaming, cheering, and clapping like we were the goddamned kings of sound checks.

"Check, check, check! Are you ready?!"

Trey and Maria were on the side of the stage. I looked over at them before I continued, and Trey was nodding. I think that's why I liked him. I nodded a lot too.

"Los Angeles, are you ready to rock your faces off?!"

The crowd surged forward, and the lights started to strobe. Someone in the crowd yelled loud enough for me to hear.

"What happened to Tuba City?"

I had forgotten until right before I was about to say our band's name that we didn't actually have one anymore. Tuba City was gone.

"Oh, right. They had to go. Tuba City had to go. But we're here, and we're going to play for you instead!"

"Who are *you*?" someone else yelled.

I paused and looked over at Booker. He raised his eyebrows and smiled. I had a backup name in mind that I had told him about earlier in the day.

"I'm glad you asked!"

I grabbed the microphone with both hands and brought it up close to my mouth.

"We are Tuba Determined. That's who we are. And we're from right here in Los Angeles!"

The crowd exploded with noise and started to chant.

"T-B-D! T-B-D! T-B-D! T-B-D!"

I looked back at the guys and shrugged. Booker was staring at the floor shaking his head.

"Are you ready, Pedro Bay?"

"Hell yeah!"

"Are you ready, Booker?"

"Fuck yeah!"

I looked out at the crowd and took a deep breath.

"Alright…then let's go!"

Pedro did the drum stick count off.

"One! Two! Three! Four!"

And noise. And then more noise. And then shouting. And then booing.

I don't know what the crowd was expecting to happen, but it didn't happen. Barely twenty seconds had passed, and they had already turned on us. I looked out at all of the angry-looking faces. It was time for us to go.

"Thank you, everyone!" I shouted. "You've been great!"

Somebody threw a bottle toward the stage, hitting Booker on the arm. He looked over at me and laughed, and it made me start to laugh too.

www.ingramcontent.com/pod-product-compliance
Lightning Source LLC
Chambersburg PA
CBHW030549310726
48979CB00010B/2093/J

* 9 7 8 1 7 3 4 5 4 9 7 1 3 *